Wel

Burnt B

One Texas Cowboy Too Many

"A delightful story with a charming, laid-back cowboy and...genuinely sweet, sizzling chemistry. This is one entertaining read."

—*RT Book Reviews*, 4½ Stars, TOP PICK!

"As usual, Carolyn Brown's writing was superb...lovely romance, funny hijinks, and vivid characters... I can't wait for the next book in the series!"

—*Night Owl Reviews*, Reviewer Top Pick!

"Quirky characters and a healthy dose of humor...sweet and sensual romance."

—*Publishers Weekly*

The Trouble with Texas Cowboys

"Touching and heartwarming, and completely believable... [The] characters are hilarious, colorful, and eccentric as ever; what a treat to be back in Burnt Boot!"

—*Fresh Fiction*

"Ruggedly handsome cowboys...a plucky heroine... humorous, heartwarming storytelling...infectious banter...a solid, well-crafted plot...and the chemistry sizzles."

—*RT Book Reviews*, 4 stars

"Carolyn Brown nailed it again! It's Western romance with humor, realism, and captivating characters. I loved every minute of it!"

—*The Romance Reviews*

"Something for everyone: slow-burning romance, steamy sex, humor galore, unique family dynamics, and a hero and heroine who will find their way into your heart. I laughed a lot."

—*Reading Between the Wines*

Also by Carolyn Brown

Lucky in Love

One Lucky Cowboy

Getting Lucky

I Love This Bar

Hell, Yeah

My Give a Damn's Busted

Honky Tonk Christmas

Love Drunk Cowboy

Red's Hot Cowboy

Darn Good Cowboy Christmas

One Hot Cowboy Wedding

Mistletoe Cowboy

Just a Cowboy and His Baby

Billion Dollar Cowboy

Cowboy Seeks Bride

The Cowboy's Christmas Baby

The Cowboy's Mail Order Bride

How to Marry a Cowboy

Cowboy Boots for Christmas

The Trouble with Texas Cowboys

One Texas Cowboy Too Many

What Happens in Texas

A Cowboy Christmas Miracle

CAROLYN BROWN

Cover art by John Kicksee
Cover images © Mary Chronis/VJ Dunraven Productions & PeriodImages.com, Michael A. Keller/Corbis

Published by Sourcebooks Casablanca, an imprint of Sourcebooks, Inc.
P.O. Box 4410, Naperville, Illinois 60567-4410
(630) 961-3900
Fax: (630) 961-2168
www.sourcebooks.com

Printed and bound in Canada.
MBP 10 9 8 7 6 5 4 3 2 1

This book is for my two tomcats, Boots Randolph Terminator Outlaw and Chester Fat Boy, my faithful muses, who protect the house from wicked varmints like mice and crickets so I can write without fear.

Chapter 1

SWOLLEN ANKLES. PUFFY FACE. AND NOW MOOD SWINGS.

Even with all that, Betsy was so jealous of Angela that she could feel her soul turning neon green. It's a wonder she didn't glow with envy like an alien life force.

Angela wiped tears away with a soggy tissue. "It's a boy, and I'm naming him Christian because he's arriving during the Christmas season, and he'll be too old to be baby Jesus next year, and I wanted him to grow up to be a preacher like my daddy and my brother, John, and now he'll grow up to be a… Oh no…"

"What?" Betsy tensed. "Is it labor? Do I need to call Jody?"

Angela grabbed for more tissues. "No, it's worse. Burnt Boot isn't going to have Christmas. It's an omen. Christian will grow up to be an outlaw and put shame on the Gallagher name."

Betsy patted her on the arm and wished she had a shot of whiskey, but there wasn't a drop of liquor in Jody and Angela's house. Angela abstained from anything that had a drop of liquor in it—she didn't even have a slice of butter rum cake at the family holiday parties.

"It'll be okay," Betsy said. "It's a season of miracles. Something could happen so that we'll have Christmas."

Angela's blond hair covered her tear-streaked face when she bent forward, head in hands, and wept. "That would take more than a miracle. It would take magic the way the Brennans and the Gallaghers have both set their heels and refuse to give anything to the church for new Christmas decorations."

"What about the other folks in town?" Betsy asked. "Those who aren't part of this feud?"

"If they help out with the program, then the feudin' folks won't do business with them, so they're between a rock and a hard place." Angela lifted her head and threw a handful of soggy tissues in the trash. "I want a Christmas program at the church, and I want my son to be baby Jesus, and I know you can make it happen, Betsy Gallagher."

Betsy's emerald-green eyes widened. "I'm not a magician."

Angela inhaled deeply, straightened her back, and crossed her hands over an enormous baby bump. "I'm depending on you, Betsy. If anyone in the whole state of Texas can put my Christian in that manger for the Christmas program, you can do it."

"Come on, Angela, you know that Granny would disown me if I lifted a finger to make Christmas happen. You'll have to be content with the Christmas tree lighting on Main Street," Betsy said.

Angela held up a finger and sniffled. "No! I won't be satisfied with that. I want my Christian to be wrapped in swaddling blankets in a manger, and I want the wise men and the shepherds to come and see him." The finger shifted to point straight at Betsy. "And you are going to talk those two old women into letting it happen."

Betsy flinched. "Granny will go up in flames if she hears you call her old."

"I'm sick of this feud. It's time to bury the hatchet or sign a treaty in blood or spit in their hands and shake like a couple of kids—whatever it takes to end this shit," Angela said.

"You said a bad word," Betsy whispered.

Tears started in earnest again. "That should"—*hiccup*—"tell you"—*hiccup*—"how much Christmas means to me?" A final hiccup.

Betsy patted her shoulder and handed her the box of tissues from the coffee table. "I'll do what I can—I promise."

Angela blew her nose loudly and hauled herself off the sofa. "Time to go to the bathroom again. All I do is cry and pee. It's a wonder Jody stays with me."

Betsy quickly pushed up out of the recliner and said, "I should be going anyway. It's getting late."

"I hear Jody driving up in the yard. He'll be excited that you are going to fix it so that we have a Christmas program." Angela smiled brightly. "Why don't you stick around and have a glass of tea with us?"

Betsy needed something a hell of a lot stronger than sweet tea at that moment. She really, really needed a strong shot of good old Irish whiskey, preferably Jameson, or at least a beer. "No thanks. I really do have to go, but you hang in there, girl. It's only another week until that baby boy will be here. Then, according to what I hear, you won't get any sleep for a few months."

Jody pushed through the door, letting a blast of cold November air into the small house. Angela gave him a kiss. "Hello, darlin'. I want to hear about the meeting with Granny Naomi right after I get out of the bathroom. Bundle up, Betsy."

Jody held Betsy's coat for her and whispered, "Whatever you did, thank you. She seems happy."

Betsy raised a shoulder. "I'm supposed to work miracles in the middle of the worst feud war we've ever had. She wants me to talk Granny into having a Christmas program at the church. Might as well try to talk a donkey into changing into Cinderella."

"If anyone can do it, you can." Jody grinned.

Betsy took those words out the door and into the cold night air, wishing she was as mean and tough as everyone thought. Tanner, her favorite cousin, said she was ninety percent bluff and ten percent mean.

"But you don't want to test that mean part." He'd laughed when she'd given him the old stink eye.

Light shined out from the living room window, giving the brown grass a yellow glow, like the star that used to hang from the ceiling at the Christmas program. What Angela wanted was totally impossible, but Betsy would try to think of something. Maybe they could have a Gallagher program at the Christmas dinner, complete with a nativity scene.

She sat in her hot-pink pickup truck for several minutes. Through the window, she saw Jody hug Angela. Their body language said they were in love, and the way Jody's hands went to Angela's rounded tummy left no doubt that they couldn't wait for their son to be born.

Betsy blinked the tears back, refusing to let them fall. She wouldn't cry for what she couldn't have. She finally started the engine but sat for several more minutes, staring at the house. It was one of a dozen small log cabin homes scattered about Wild Horse Ranch. They'd been built one by one as first homes for the newly wedded Gallagher couples. When the couple got on their feet and had enough money to buy their own land, they then moved to another section of the ever-growing ranch. She wanted a house like they had. She didn't care if she never had a big spread of her own. She'd be content to work for her granny and live in a little log cabin the rest of her life if she could have a husband who loved her as much as Jody loved Angela.

Declan Brennan hated playing poker when none of the O'Donnells showed up. There was always tension, but it was worse when only the Gallaghers and Brennans were at the table. When the O'Donnells or even strangers sat in on the game, the tension of the hundred-year-old feud between the Gallaghers and Brennans wasn't the very core of the whole evening.

"Where's Sawyer, Finn, and Rhett O'Donnell? They are usually here." Tanner Gallagher wore a double shot of confidence like a well-worn old work hat. Blue eyes scanned his cards and flashed nothing but disgust every time he looked at Declan or Quaid Brennan.

Declan combed his sandy-brown hair back with his fingers and tilted his chin up a notch as he glared at Tanner. "I expect they're home with their wives—something you'll never have, the way you hop from one woman to the other."

"Me?" Tanner raised his voice, pushed back his black felt Resistol cowboy hat, and looked down his nose at Declan. "You are the one with a womanizer reputation. If you weren't a Brennan, I'd ask you to give me lessons."

Quaid Brennan, Declan's cousin, straightened up in his chair, squaring his broad shoulders defensively and tucking his square-cut chin into his chest as he glared across the table at Tanner. "He could teach you a lot," he said through clenched teeth.

"Bullshit! Tanner could talk the first woman to walk through the barroom doors into bed within an hour. It would take Declan a month to do the same job," Eli Gallagher argued loudly. Eli, a younger Gallagher cousin, had been cut from the same bolt of tough denim as Tanner, with his blond hair and icy blue eyes, but he was a short man with the attitude that went with it. As usual, like a little banty rooster, he was ready to not only start a fight, but also finish it.

Declan added two fives to the ante. "Let's drop the subject of women and play poker. That's what we're here for anyway."

Quaid studied his cards seriously, green eyes narrowing into slits. He threw his hand down on the table. Cowboy boots and chair legs scraped against the rough, wooden floor as he scooted his chair back and crossed his legs. "I'm out. Don't let Tanner rile you into something, Declan. He's got a decent hand over there, and he's trying to throw you off your game."

"How do you know that?" Eli asked.

"I know his tells," Quaid answered. "That's why I threw in the towel."

Eli pitched his cards on the table and leaned back in the chair until it was propped against the wall. "Don't fool yourself, Quaid. Ain't no Brennan alive who could stand up to a Gallagher for poker or women."

Tanner's lips curled upward in more of a grimace than a smile. "Just me and you, Brennan. Want to make this more interesting? Instead of putting money into the pot, I'll bet you a thousand dollars that your reputation with women is as fake as your poker reputation. I bet you the reason you can't keep a woman is that you can't satisfy them and they leave you."

"And what do I have to do to take that money away from you?" Declan asked.

"The next woman who walks through the door, no matter how old, young, rich, or poor she is—you have to make her fall in love with you in one month. That means taking her to bed, dating her for more than one night, the whole nine yards," Tanner said.

"Don't do it," Quaid whispered. "He's baiting you."

Eli whistled through his teeth. "Whoa! Wait a minute. That bet doesn't have a thing to do with poker, but I like it."

Two blue-eyed cowboys from feuding families locked gazes, every muscle in their bodies tensed. Smoke from four cigars spiraled up toward a ceiling fan that tried to push it back toward the poker table. Other than the squeaking noise as the blades turned slowly, there wasn't another sound in the bar for a full thirty seconds.

"I'll take that bet, but only if you win this hand. If I win, then it's a reverse deal, and you have to do all those things you just said," Declan said.

Quaid laid a hand on his cousin's shoulder. "Declan, don't do this. I'm begging you. It will only add fuel to the feud."

"Why a month? Why not a week, or two weeks? What does thirty days have to do with it?" Declan asked.

Tanner's clenched jaw pulsated. "To give you time to take a course in sweet talking. I'm being fair because I don't think you can do it, and I want the whole world to know when it's over that you're not nearly as good with the women as your reputation says."

"In other words," Declan said gruffly, "you want to hold the title for being the biggest player in all of Burnt Boot?"

"Don't listen to him." Quaid's tone was tense. "We shouldn't be playing poker with them, especially without some other folks at the table. They're Gallaghers, and you can't trust them."

Declan stretched his hand over the table and, for the first time in his life, shook with a Gallagher. "Loser has thirty days to make the next woman who walks through the door fall in love with him."

Declan wouldn't have taken the bet if he hadn't trusted in the hand he was holding. A part of him felt sorry for Tanner because he'd just made a fool of himself, but then, he was a Gallagher, and it would be a feather in Declan's hat to best him. Declan would have the money, and the Gallaghers would lose face. Two beautiful birds shot with one bullet.

"Do we have any other rules?" Declan asked before he showed his hand.

"I'll make the rules, since my cousin here has to concentrate on his cards with that much riding on this game," Eli said.

"Wait a minute!" Quaid yelled loudly enough that Rosalie came out from behind the counter.

"You cowboys are free to play poker here, but you'd best remember my rules. This is neutral territory, and by damn, I can—and will—drag that shotgun out from under the counter to enforce them. So keep it civil. Understand?" Rosalie shook her finger at the lot of them.

She hadn't owned the bar very long, but she didn't take crap off anyone. The wrinkles around her eyes testified that she was somewhere in her fifties. The strawberry-blond hair worn in a ponytail sticking out the back of her Dallas Cowboys ball cap didn't have a single gray strand shining in it. Neither Brennans nor Gallaghers wanted to face off with those cold, gray eyes when she was angry.

"Yes, ma'am," Quaid said respectfully.

"Then play cards or gather up your poker chips and get on out of here." Rosalie turned back toward the poker table. "Where's your O'Donnell buddies? I thought this crappy feud might be on its way out when Leah Brennan married Rhett O'Donnell a few weeks ago."

"Never!" Eli said. "As long as a Gallagher is alive, we'll keep the feud alive to show these Brennans who's boss."

"That's crazy. Why do you play poker with them?" Rosalie headed toward the jukebox. "It's all insane anyway. Y'all go to the same church, and nowadays, your kids go to the same school. You're all ranchers, and both families have a granny who runs things. Sounds to me like you are more alike than different."

"It's so sweet to beat them." Quaid laughed. "They whine like little girls when they lose to us Brennans."

"Y'all need to end the feud. A hundred years is long enough for folks to carry a grudge." Rosie plugged the money into the jukebox and chose a few country tunes.

Eli chuckled. "Like that's gonna happen in my lifetime."

Declan glanced over at Eli. "Lay out the rules if there are any. If not, let's finish this game and wait for some old gal to come through the door so Tanner can get on with the business of falling in love with her."

Eli nodded. "Rule number one: you have a month to make her fall in love with you and get her into bed. It can't be a one-night stand. I'll even give you a few extra days, since Thanksgiving is next week and you'll be busy on the ranch."

Declan held up a palm. "Whoa, hoss! You're already talking like I've lost this game. The rules are supposed to be for both of us."

Eli flashed a go-to-hell look across the table. "You have until the week before Christmas. Tanner will want to take his winnings and do some shopping with them. And I'm the one making the rules, so don't be yelling at me. Rule number two: it has to be a woman you've never dated before. Rule number three: just to make it interesting, it really does have to be the next woman who walks into this bar, so that all four of us know who it is, and you can't lie to us about having never dated her."

"So." Declan checked the calendar on his phone. "Friday, December 18, one of us has to be dating, have slept with, and made the next woman who comes through the doors fall in love with him. And how does Tanner prove to you that he did all that? He could just lie and take my money. After all, that's what a Gallagher would do."

"She has to tell it all over town," Tanner said.

"What if *she* doesn't kiss and tell?" Declan asked.

"If you are that irresistible, she'll be bragging all over town that she's snagged you," Tanner said through clenched teeth.

"Okay, you're on. If you win this hand, I'll take that bet. And not a one of us around this table can tell anyone about the bet. It has to be a secret, and if it gets out, then all bets are off."

Quaid threw up his palms. "You're all crazy. What if the woman who comes through those doors is fifty years old and chews tobacco?"

Tanner shrugged. "A bet is a bet. Hope you like older women, Declan. Thursday night's pickin's are pretty slim here."

There was no way a Gallagher was going to beat a Brennan in poker. "I'll be glad to take your money tonight and at Christmas. I heard the crunch of wheels out there in the parking lot, so get ready to meet your woman, Gallagher."

Tanner fanned out a royal flush. "I reckon at Christmas you'll have to shell out more, but this pot is right fine for now. And I just heard that truck door slam out there in the parking lot, so get ready to meet your date, Declan Brennan. Remember, it's a secret, Eli and Quaid. Anyone tells, and this town will see the feud fire up hotter than it's been since your family started it."

"We didn't start anything. Y'all did." Declan said a prayer as he glanced toward the door.

Tanner's cocky little grin faded, and his face looked like someone had smeared ashes all over it when the door opened. Eli's eyes came close to popping out of his head and rolling across the floor, and Quaid sucked all the oxygen out of the air in one big gulp. Declan felt as if he'd just been struck by lightning straight from God's hand.

"You are a dead man, Tanner," Eli whispered.

Quaid exhaled so hard that it whistled through his teeth. "And so are you, Declan. Granny Mavis will kill you if you go after her."

"A bet is a bet. And a Brennan does not run from a fight," Declan said.

Sweet Jesus in heaven. Declan had been in love with Betsy since they were kids in the same Sunday school class. He might have lost the poker match, but here was his chance, and the Gallaghers couldn't do jack shit about it. Poor old Tanner had just set the whole thing up on a silver platter and handed him the rights to the whole thing. Talk about luck—Declan had lost the money on the table, but he'd been given the rights to Betsy Gallagher.

"Let's call it off," Eli said. "Just pretend it never happened and walk out of here."

All eyes went to Tanner.

"Gallaghers don't run either," he murmured.

Betsy Gallagher, Tanner's wild cowgirl cousin who would fight a Texas tornado with nothing but a sling shot, propped a hip on a bar stool. "How's the poker game going tonight, Rosalie?"

She whipped off a black felt cowboy hat, laid it on the end of the bar, and let a heavy work coat slip off her shoulders to drape over the curved chair back. Her bright-red hair fell in waves past her shoulders, and her emerald-green eyes scanned the back side of the bar, trying to decide whether she wanted a shot of whiskey or a cold beer.

"They got a little rowdy a little while ago, but I nipped it in the bud. What will it be tonight?"

"I'll have a single shot of Jack Daniel's and a longneck Coors," Betsy answered. "Whiskey to warm the soul. Beer to sip on all evening. Looks pretty quiet back there right now."

Rosalie poured the whiskey and then dried off a bottle of cold beer and set it in front of Betsy. "I got to admit, it does go better when at least one of the O'Donnell cowboys joins the game. It's like church then. Gallaghers on one side. Brennans on the other. The rest of the folks in the middle. That middle section keeps things balanced."

Betsy nodded and glanced back through the bar to where the poker game was breaking up. Poor old Tanner's face was the same color as the swirling smoke, so he must have lost that night. He'd be like an old grizzly bear with a sore tooth for a week. He didn't like to lose, but it had gotten worse in the past couple of months when he and Eli started letting the O'Donnells and the Brennans into the game.

"Because of those damn Brennans," she mumbled.

"Did you say something?" Rosalie asked.

"Talkin' to myself," Betsy answered. "They're breakin' up the game early."

Rosalie talked as she unloaded the dishwasher. "Looks like it. It's not quite closing time, and I usually have to run them out."

Betsy sipped at her beer and listened to the Bellamy Brothers on the jukebox. "If you want to close early, I'll take my beer with me."

"Naw," Rosalie drawled. "Enjoy your beer and the music. Never know who might drop in even yet. But it's good to have a slow night once in a while. Friday and Saturday nights are ball breakers," Rosalie said.

Betsy liked Rosalie, but she missed the previous owner, Polly. It was amazing how one year could make such a difference in a town the size of Burnt Boot. Just a few months ago, Polly sold the bar to Rosalie and her ranch to Rhett O'Donnell.

"It was those O'Donnells moving to town that started all this," Betsy whispered before she finished off her whiskey and took a long gulp from her bottle.

"What was that?" Rosalie asked.

"I figure it was the O'Donnells coming to town that started all this crap," Betsy said.

"I hear it was the fact that the Brennans had a hellfire-and-damnation preacher runnin' their family back in Prohibition days and you Gallaghers were runnin' moonshine to get by and got caught. Your family blamed the Brennans for rattin' you out, and that started a feud," Rosalie said.

"But"—Betsy tipped up the beer again—"it was the O'Donnells coming to town that set this last round of battles into action."

"Betsy." Declan nodded to her on his way out the door.

"Declan," she muttered and barely looked his way. Lord have mercy! If he weren't a Brennan, she'd have chased him right out the door. She'd had a crush on him years ago, but her granny would see her hanging from the tree in the church parking lot if she even caught her glancing toward a Brennan.

"Well?" Tanner asked.

"I needed a drink in the worst kind of way. How much did you lose?"

Tanner caught Rosalie's eye, pointed at Betsy's beer, and held up his forefinger. Rosalie dried off a bottle and set it before him.

Tanner propped a hip on a stool next to Betsy. "Hey, girl, what brings you to town on a Thursday night?"

"Bad night, was it?" Betsy turned toward him.

"No, I won a bundle," Tanner answered.

"Then why do you look like you just saw a ghost?"

"Don't look to me like he *saw* a ghost. Looks more like he turned into one," Rosalie said.

"I ain't feelin' too good right now. Might be comin' down with something," Tanner answered.

"Well, damn, Tanner. Thanksgiving is a week from today, and you're supposed to fry the turkey. If you've got something, you'd best get over it before then," Betsy said. "And don't give it to me. Thanksgiving is my favorite holiday. I'll never forgive you if you ruin it for me."

"I thought Christmas was your favorite holiday," Tanner said.

"It is, but my favorite part of that was the Christmas programs at the church, and since we aren't having them this year, then Thanksgiving will have to do." She tipped up the bottle of beer and gulped twice.

One side of Rosalie's thin mouth turned up in a slight smile. "I wouldn't mess with a redhead who's got a temper like hers, not when her favorite holiday has been spoiled. If I was you, I'd take them winnings and go buy her a real nice Christmas present."

Betsy pointed to the jukebox. "Listen to that song, and take a lesson from it."

"The Bellamy Brothers at their best." Rosalie

wiped down the bar. "And what they're singing is the gospel truth."

"Jalapeños" was the name of the song, and the lyrics said that life wasn't nothing like a bowl of cherries. It was more like a jar of jalapeños because whatever you do today could come back and burn your ass tomorrow.

Betsy grinned at Tanner. "Remember that. You don't want what you do today to come back and burn your ass at Christmas if you give me the duck."

Tanner gulped. "I don't even have the duck. I think Tyrell got it last year from Randy so he could pass it on to you, but I promise, I don't have it."

"The duck?" Rosalie asked.

Betsy motioned for another beer. "It's the white elephant gift at the Gallagher Christmas party. It all started sometime before Tanner and I were born. Someone gave another member of the family a duck decoy for Christmas as a joke. The next year, the lady who got it painted eyelashes on the thing and gave it to someone else. It's been around for maybe forty years, and every year, it gets more bizarre. Now, it's so decorated, it doesn't look like a decoy, but more like a yard sale reject. I do not want the duck, Tanner, and you'd best be sure Tyrell doesn't give it to me or it'll be worse than a jar of jalapeños coming back to burn your ass."

"I'm not responsible for what Tyrell does." Tanner slid off the stool, settled his black cowboy hat on his head, and started for the door. "See you later."

"He's actin' strange," Rosalie said.

"Yep, he sure is. He's got that ugly duck and is probably planning to give it to me. The Gallagher family has gotten so big that we draw names for the big all-family party, and I know he has my name. If I get it, I swear I'll finagle a way to get his name next year, and he will be sorry," Betsy said. "I'm on my way to the river."

"What's on your mind, kiddo?" Rosalie asked.

"Nothing. Just dissatisfaction at where I am right now, and I think things through better on the banks of the river," Betsy said.

Rosalie turned off the outside lights, locked the door, and sat down on a stool beside Betsy. "I'm a damn good listener. Have two daughters and raised them all by myself after my sorry excuse for a husband left us."

"I'm just antsy," Betsy said.

Sorting out feelings had never been Betsy's strong virtue. She'd always plowed into any situation like a bull in a china shop and tried to lasso it to the ground. She hadn't known Rosalie but a couple of months so she sure wasn't about to tell her all her intimate fears.

Rosalie turned up the beer and took a long gulp. "How old are you, Betsy? Twenty-five?"

Betsy smiled. "Add five to that."

"Lord, girl, you don't look thirty. Why aren't you settled down with one of these cowboys around here? I've seen plenty of good-lookin' ones, and you might be a spitfire, but you're a damn beautiful one."

"Thank you. Problem is that I'm kin to half the cowboys and the other half are my enemies. Haven't found a neutral one that took my eye. No, that's a lie. I found three, but I lost them, and that's probably what's eating at me. That and this damn Christmas season with none of our traditions." Betsy clamped a hand over her mouth. She hadn't meant to say anything, and yet she'd blurted out her problems.

"Who were those three?" Rosalie asked.

She dropped her hand and sighed. "Finn, Sawyer, and Rhett O'Donnell."

"What do you think was the problem?"

It felt good to talk to someone about things, and Rosalie wouldn't charge her megabucks like a shrink.

"I came on too strong, and they fell in love with someone else," Betsy said.

"What do you intend to do different next time?"

"I have no idea, Rosalie. I'm ready to settle down, ready to have a family, and that proverbial old biological clock folks talk about is starting to sound pretty loud," Betsy answered.

"Stop chasing it. Sit down and be still, and it will come to you. Those other three weren't right for you or it would have happened. Now, what's this about Christmas traditions?"

"We lost the Christmas decorations when our private schools were burned down and blown up, so there won't be Christmas at the church this year."

"And you liked that program?" Rosalie asked.

"It was my favorite part of the season. But the most aggravating thing is that the Brennans don't have any babies due between now and Christmas, but my cousin Jody and his wife, Angela, have a new baby coming in just days. It's a boy, and she's going to name him Christian in hopes that his name marks him and he grows up to be a preacher like her daddy and her brother."

Rosalie slid off the bar stool and started cleaning up. Betsy followed her, setting the chairs on the tables after Rosalie wiped them down.

"Your cousin's wife is sad because of this?" Rosalie asked.

"More than sad. It's what she's focusing on, and she thinks if her baby doesn't get to be baby Jesus that he'll grow up to be an outlaw. I really like her, so it makes me sad, and I could strangle those Brennans for burning our school and starting all this."

"But the Gallaghers retaliated by blowing up their school," Rosalie reminded her.

Betsy sighed. "Do you realize how much I'd give to end this feud, so we could live normal lives around this place?"

"It would take a hell of a lot to end a hundred-year-old feud, especially when Naomi and Mavis hate each other so much." Rosalie finished the last table. "Ready to grab that extra beer for the river and call it a night?"

"We're all tired of it, but Granny Naomi and Mavis Brennan." She sighed a second time. "It'd take a damn nuclear explosion for them to ever bury the hatchet."

"Well, miracles do happen during the Christmas season, so keep the shovels right handy. Them two old women just might need them to dig a hole for the feudin' hatchet by the time the holidays are over." Rosalie drank the rest of her beer and tossed the bottle in the trash can, turned off the lights in the bar area, and nodded toward the clock.

Betsy's boots hit the floor with a thud when she hopped off the bar stool. "My therapy session appears to be over."

A smile lit up Rosalie's eyes. "I'll send you a bill next week. Just listen to me, girl. Sit down and let love come find you. That way, it'll work."

Betsy picked up her extra beer and headed for the door. "Pretty hard to do when your name is Betsy Gallagher, but I'll try. Same time next Thursday?"

"I'm open anytime for you, kiddo."

Chapter 2

Aggravated and angry, not to mention cold and downright frustrated, Declan sat down under the limp, bare limbs of the weeping willow tree and tossed a smooth rock out into the Red River. The moonlight lit up the peaks of the swirls that started small and grew outward to the bank. He picked up another rock and threw it the opposite direction, but a big fish flopped up out of the water and spoiled the circles before they reached the red-dirt sandbar.

He wanted—no, he needed desperately to talk to his sister, Leah, about this mess he'd backed into. But she'd probably tell him the same thing Quaid had, which was to give Tanner a thousand dollars and forget the whole thing. Declan shook his head slowly. He could not let a Gallagher win that easy.

But holy hell! Betsy?

He'd admired her since they were kids sitting on the opposite sides of the church. Her red hair, hanging in braids those days, had intrigued him. Those gorgeous emerald-green eyes mesmerized him, especially when they were teenagers. But she was a Gallagher, and that just didn't mean *no, you cannot date her*; it meant *hell no, you will not even think such thoughts*.

"Declan?"

He looked up to see her silhouetted by the moonlight.

Curves in all the right places, red hair flowing down her back, and yet he couldn't believe his eyes.

"Betsy?" he muttered.

"What the hell are you doing here this time of night?"

It was Betsy, all right. With that gravelly, sexy voice, there was no denying it.

"I might ask you the same thing," he answered.

She pushed the branches aside and sat down, leaving a foot between them. "This is my thinkin' place, and you have no right to be here."

"It's also my thinkin' place," Declan said.

"I've never seen you here before, so you are lying to me."

"Cross my heart"—he made the sign over his chest—"and hope to die, I am not lying. I come here all the time. I guess Brennans and Gallaghers don't usually think at the same time or our paths would have crossed before now."

Talk about fate landing luck right in his lap.

This was Betsy Gallagher, not just someone who walked in the bar from off the street, and the very night that the bet had been made, she appeared at his favorite spot. It had to be an omen that he should proceed with the bet, didn't it? A chilly north wind swept the sweet scent of perfume and beer mixed together toward him. He inhaled deeply and studied her with side-glances.

She hadn't changed since they were in Sunday school together. But those curves and that sass were enough to drive a man to unholy thoughts.

Tomorrow, when Tanner thought about what he'd created, it would all change. He'd come crawling to

Declan and hand him a thousand dollars, which would be twice what Declan had lost in the poker game that night. The bet would be off and the Brennans would save face, even though no one would ever know.

Declan was tempted to tell Betsy right then and there what had happened at the poker game. She already hated him because he was a Brennan, but he had made a promise that until the bet was settled, he wouldn't tell. However, when Betsy found out that her favorite cousin had let it go on for even twenty-four hours, she'd shoot first and take names later. And she would find out because nothing ever stayed a secret very long in Burnt Boot.

Betsy scanned the banks of the river. If anyone saw her sitting beside Declan, she really would be in more trouble than she could dig herself out of in a lifetime. Tanner would find a way to have her committed to a convent, and her grandmother, Naomi, would disown her.

"So what brings you to the thinking tree tonight, Declan Brennan?" she asked.

"Life, mistakes, and poker games," he answered.

"What?" Betsy frowned.

"You asked me what I was thinkin' about. That's what I'm thinking about—life, mistakes, and poker games. You shouldn't be here. You know the trees and rocks have eyes, and they can tattle. By morning, your family will be makin' you tie your own noose to hang you with," he said.

"And some trees are Gallagher trees, like this one. I laid claim to it years ago. I will, however, give you all the rocks that you want to carry down the river bank, and you can let me think in peace."

"This is definitely a Brennan tree. I believe my grandfather planted it and held his first church services right here under it, so you can have the rocks. Have a nice evening, Betsy. See you around."

She tugged her jacket across her chest and crossed her arms. "I'm stayin'. And your grandpa didn't plant this tree. Mine did. He needed a place to make his moonshine, and the tree limbs provided a cover for the smoke."

"Well, tonight, I was here first so I'm claiming squatter's rights," Declan said.

"Then you can leave first."

He didn't move a muscle.

"So?" she asked.

He settled against the bark of the tree and stretched out his legs. "I'm not going anywhere."

If the rumors were only half true, and if Declan Brennan notched his bedpost for every woman he'd had sex with, like the cowboys in old westerns notched their guns for every kill, all four of his bedposts would be a knotty mess. Against that smile, those eyes, and the vision of his ripped abdomen under a snug, dark-blue knit shirt—which she saw before he put on his coat in the bar—no woman had a snowball's chance in hell of not being attracted to him. She glanced his way and his sapphire-blue eyes caught hers. She quickly blinked and looked out across the river.

"So since neither of us can admit defeat and leave, tell me, Betsy, what are you thinkin' about tonight?" he asked.

"Life, lost loves, and Christmas," she answered honestly.

"No one can understand life, so you might as well not fry your pretty little brain cells with that topic. Lost loves is way out of my league. As a matter of fact, love is out of my league." He smiled.

"Oh, really? I thought you'd loved many times in your life," she said.

"Dated. Had a good time. Not loved. Never loved," he said. "So that leaves Christmas. What about it?"

"We aren't having it this year."

"Yes, we are. Granny Mavis has been talking about putting up the tree in front of the store all week. It's still going on like every year," he argued.

"I'm talking about the programs at the church. Y'all burned down our school, and that's where part of the decorations were stored."

"Well, y'all blew up our school when you put dynamite in the septic tank. If I remember right, you were right there in the middle of the shit storm and almost got hit with a toilet," he reminded her.

"Doesn't matter who did what. There won't be any of our church programs, and that isn't right. We should have at least one with the nativity the Sunday before Christmas."

"Hard as it is to believe, I agree with you, even though you are a Gallagher, but it isn't about to happen, so you're wastin' your time thinkin' about it."

She shrugged. "I talked to my granny and begged her to donate the money for new props, but she said that it's the Brennans' fault, and they should put up the money."

Why was she talking to Declan about this anyway?

She knew for a fact that his granny had issued the same ultimatum about not donating a dime to the Christmas cause. Angela would have to be content with Christmas music that morning and a sermon about the birth of the Christ child.

Declan pulled a bottle of whiskey from his pocket and took a long swig. He looked at it for several seconds before he held it out to Betsy. She checked the sky for dark clouds and possible lightning bolts before she took it from him and let the warmth of a shot of Jack Daniels slide down her throat.

She handed the bottle back to him and realized that her lips had touched the same bottle that a Brennan's had. Tanner would make her eat soap if he found out she'd been sharing a drink with Declan. Worse yet, he'd blackmail her for the rest of her life.

"Merry Christmas, Betsy." He smiled as he tipped up the bottle for another swig and then put the lid back on before he tucked it away in his pocket.

No wonder women fell at his feet—or, rather, into his bed. One little grin along with a shot of whiskey and Betsy had the desire to push him backward right there on the cold, red sand. If he really turned on the charm, there would be nothing left to do but shuck out of her jeans and boots.

"I'm still cold," he said as he pulled the bottle back out, took another gulp, and handed it back to her. That time, he almost dropped it and they had to do some fancy scrambling to get it passed from one to the other.

"Be a shame to waste a drop of good Tennessee whiskey," he said.

His drawl was more intoxicating than the whiskey

and heated her insides, but what brought on more fire was his touch. Declan Brennan was forbidden fruit. No, he was a whole forbidden tree. He was even worse than that tree that Eve partook of in the Good Book, and the results would be worse than having to wear fig-leaf clothing in the middle of a Texas winter.

"What if…" he started and stopped.

"If what?" she asked.

"Well, what if we kind of did something in secret?"

"Declan Brennan, I'm not ever going to be a notch on your bedpost," she said. "It would take more than half a bottle of Jack Daniels to get me softened up enough for that."

"You're not my type," he said bluntly.

"Well, that damn sure breaks my heart. I just knew you were trying to get me drunk and take advantage of my innocence."

"You probably have more notches on your bedpost than I have on mine if the gossip is true, so don't be calling the kettle black."

She had to fight the heat rising in her neck. No way was he seeing Betsy Gallagher blush. "So you're the kettle and I'm the pot here? What if I want to be the kettle?"

He might be off-limits, but that didn't mean she couldn't flirt a little bit. After all, no one was looking. Just to be sure, she scanned the area again and didn't even see a stray dog or a fish that might rise up to tell on her.

"Gallaghers blow up schools. They have to be the pot. Do you get the pun?" His eyes sparkled in the moonlight.

"Yes, and it's a stupid pun. But if you weren't talking about secret sex, what kind of secret was on your mind?" she asked.

"What the church needs is stuff, right?" he asked.

She nodded.

"Well, Granny Mavis has banned any member of the family from giving a single dime to the church for the Christmas program. So we'll have to get around that," he said.

"So did my granny. She's threatened to throw us off Wild Horse if we set up a fund or donate a penny to buy new things for the programs."

"Okay, then, we cannot ask for money or give money. But that doesn't mean we can't donate or ask for stuff, does it? I bet I can get some Brennans to give me some stuff, like a Christmas tree from a shed that no one is using and maybe some spare ornaments. If I go about it right, Granny wouldn't know," he said.

"And I could do the same with the Gallaghers—like a manger for baby Jesus and maybe some lights. We could both work on the folks who aren't family, like Polly and Gladys and Verdie and the O'Donnells."

"We could talk to the preacher on Sunday after church. I'll ask him if we might come in and visit with him before choir practice that evening. If he'll help us out, we could leave our donations at the church on a particular night of the week and no one would ever know where the stuff came from, not even Preacher Kyle. Then, there could be a Christmas program," Declan said.

Betsy had nodded as he spoke. "You ever wish this feud was over?"

"You don't know how many times," he whispered. "But we might as well wish in one hand and spit in the other. You can guess which one would fill up fastest."

She nodded seriously. "No question about that, but if

I said it out loud, Granny Naomi would probably hang me from the nearest pecan tree with a length of rusty barbed wire."

"When do we start our job of begging, borrowing, or stealing the Christmas stuff?" he asked.

"How about the day after Thanksgiving? That work for you?"

"That will give us three weeks to get it all gathered up in time. We'll keep it secret until, say, December 18. That will give the folks time to get all the stuff we collect set up and put the program together. It's pretty much the same every year anyway. Who's going to be in charge of the play this year?"

"The Gallaghers have a baby boy due right after Thanksgiving," she said.

"We'll have to do some meeting in secret to discuss who we're getting things from, so people won't put two and two together and realize that we're working together."

Betsy wasn't afraid of rattlesnakes. Mice and spiders didn't scare her. If the devil himself rose up out of the Red River, she'd kick him right in his little forked tail and drown his sorry ass right there in the cold water. But the idea of working with a Brennan and the repercussions it could cause came close to making her jump up and run like the wind back to Wild Horse Ranch. Naomi Gallagher scared the bejesus out of her, and meeting in secret with Declan Brennan would cause a stir worse than old Lucifer rising up out of the river.

He shoved his hand out toward her. "Deal? After we talk to the preacher Sunday evening, we'll make plans and a list."

She told herself that the vibes she'd felt were the result

of too much whiskey, but her heart warned her that she was playing with pure fire. She put her hand in his and attributed the fiery jolt that rippled through her body to the fact that she was in cahoots with a Brennan.

The hall clock chimed twelve times as Declan started up the stairs. The house seemed bigger and emptier since his sister, Leah, had moved out and gotten married last August. It felt as if it was waiting on him to do the same, as if he no longer belonged there, even though he'd been born there and had the same room since he was a baby.

He tossed his black felt hat on the bed, threw his coat on the back of a wooden rocking chair in his bedroom, and kicked off his boots. Then the pacing began—from one end of the room, around the foot of the queen-size poster bed, to the other side of the room and back again.

"I hate this," he mumbled. "But I hate to let a Gallagher win even more, and Betsy is a Gallagher. She wouldn't blink an eye at doing the same thing if she were in my place."

He tugged his shirt over his head, unfastened his belt, and quickly finished undressing before heading to the bathroom. One nice thing about not having a female on the second floor meant he didn't have to be careful about running naked from bedroom to bathroom.

Standing under the shower, he kept telling himself that he was a Brennan and all was fair in love, war, and feuds. He'd grown up knowing that it was okay to cheat, lie, or steal from a Gallagher but never from anyone else. And it was never, not even in the wildest stretch of the imagination, okay to date, go to bed with, or even kiss a Gallagher woman.

When he made it back to his room, he slipped beneath the covers and shut his eyes, but all he could see were Betsy's pretty, emerald-green eyes filled with tears when she found out that she'd been nothing more than a pawn in a bet.

His eyelids snapped open, and he chuckled. "Hell, she won't cry when she finds out. She'll come after me with a loaded shotgun and a tongue lashing that will cut me to shreds."

Light from all the windows made a yellow streak across the yard at the Wild Horse ranch house. Betsy inhaled deeply and let it out slowly as she parked her truck in front of the house and got out. A blast of cold air hit her face and brought with it the first snowflakes of the season.

She wiped at the flakes stinging her face and opened the front door. A rush of warm air greeted her along with her grandmother's voice yelling from the well-lit kitchen.

"Betsy, come on in here. I'm having hot chocolate. I couldn't sleep for thinking about the Thanksgiving dinner, so I got up and started making a list," Naomi said.

Betsy stopped at the door and leaned against the doorjamb. "It's getting close to midnight."

Her grandmother had a deal with a very good hairdresser that kept her red hair beautifully styled and dyed so that not a single root or gray hair ever showed. Her green eyes, the same color as Betsy's, were set in a bed of wrinkles, and her round face had begun to resemble a bulldog's, with its drooping jaws.

Betsy studied her grandmother carefully. *She should look like a bulldog because her nature was exactly like one—grab hold of a bone and hang on for eternity, no matter if something better, like a rib eye, came along.*

It took an attitude like that to run this ranch, young lady, the voice inside Betsy's head said loudly.

Naomi pointed at the clock on the wall. "It is past midnight. Where have you been? Down at that bar trying to pick up a man?"

"No, ma'am, to the last. Yes, ma'am, to the first. I had two beers and..." She stopped before she blurted out that she'd gone to the river and talked to Declan.

"And a shot of whiskey. I can smell it on your breath all the way over here. You're not drunk are you?" Naomi leaned closer to Betsy.

Betsy shook her head. "I had a couple of beers and shots of whiskey. I barely got a buzz and I'm not drunk."

"Could you pass a Breathalyzer test?" Naomi asked.

"I wouldn't blow a zero, but I don't think it's enough to haul me into jail," Betsy said. "Why are you being so nosy about how much I drank?"

"You are going to take over Wild Horse when I'm ready to step down. You know that, and it's time for you to start acting responsibly. You are thirty, Betsy. I want to see you settled in marriage within the next year, and that means less drinking and a lot less visiting the bar," Naomi said.

Betsy did a half chuckle, part of it escaping her mouth and the other part hanging in her throat. Yeah right! She'd sure take that message to heart and get right on making it happen.

"You think that's funny?" Naomi asked.

"Little bit."

"Mavis is now grooming Honey to take over River Bend, since Leah screwed up her life by marryin' that hippie cowboy. And I want you to be ready to take over Wild Horse when I step down."

Betsy crossed the room, opened the refrigerator, and took out a jar of salsa. "It would be real nice if this wasn't a competition between you and Mavis. What if I don't want to run Wild Horse, or what if I want to run it different than you do?" She carried the sauce to the table and went to the pantry, returning with a bag of chips.

"You"—Naomi's glared across the table at Betsy—"will take care of this the way I've taught you. You can be displaced just like Leah if you get any fancy ideas."

"You mean like hookin' up with a Brennan?" Betsy dipped the first chip deeply into the red salsa.

"That's blasphemy in this house, young lady. I'd just as soon shoot you as let that happen," Naomi said.

"How 'bout if I promise not to hook up with a Brennan, and you donate enough money to the church so we can have a proper Christmas program? Angela is fretting because she's having a boy and there will be no program for him to play the role of the baby Jesus," Betsy said.

Naomi shook her finger so hard that it was barely a blur. "That is not going to happen if it means letting the Brennans enjoy it. They shouldn't have burned down our school. Then, we could have had a program. They have to pay."

"Be reasonable. Not only are they paying, but so are we, and Angela is upset and the townsfolk who aren't part of this eternal feud are paying too. Come on, Granny, be the bigger person and show the Brennans that we aren't—"

Naomi threw up both palms. "Enough! This conversation is over. I'm not giving the church a penny, and any Gallagher who does will be in big trouble."

"Don't you ever get tired of this feud?" Betsy pushed harder.

"Hell no! It's what I live for. I only hope Mavis Brennan dies before I do so I can spit on her grave," Naomi answered. "They are so high-and-mighty and holier-than-thou because their ancestor was a preacher and ours made moonshine. I'm expecting you to pick up the reins and keep ahead of them, and if you can't, then I'll choose another granddaughter to be the queen of Wild Horse. I'm going to bed now and you'd best think about what I said."

"Yes, ma'am. Married in a year. Runnin' Wild Horse and keepin' up the feud like a good Gallagher. Slow down on my drinking. Can I have one beer a week and a shot of whiskey, or do I have to choose between them?" Betsy cocked her head to one side. "Did I forget anything?"

"Don't you get sassy with me. I won't tolerate it. Good night, Betsy."

"'Night, Granny," Betsy muttered.

"And no pouting either," Naomi said.

"You ever known me to pout?" Betsy said loud and clear.

"No, you're like me. You go after what you want. You stand your ground, and you take out anyone who gets in your way however you have to. That's why you will run this ranch and you will be settled before I turn over the job to you. That means a husband and hopefully a child or two. You aren't getting any younger. If you got married in a year..."

When Naomi inhaled, Betsy butted in, "And a baby the next year. Tell me, Granny, when will I have time to run a ranch with a husband and a bunch of kids?"

"I managed it and did a good job after your grandfather died. Wild Horse needs a strong woman. You think about that, and don't disappoint me."

Betsy crammed chips in her mouth to keep from saying another word. She was tired of the whole conversation, tired of the feud that had been going on over a hundred years, and, most of all, tired of listening to her grandmother issue orders.

Married in a year? It wasn't damn likely.

Chapter 3

Betsy tried to keep her eyes front and center, focused right on the pulpit where the new preacher, Kyle Jones, was sermonizing about things we should be thankful for. But she kept casting side-glances toward the Brennan side of the church.

She'd dreamed about Declan the night before, but that was because of the conversation she'd had with her granny. In the dream, she and Declan had a new baby boy, and they were playing the roles of Mary and Joseph in the church program.

As if that would ever come to pass. The apocalypse would happen first, or the world would implode from the inside out, sending us all flying off this chunk of dirt like rag dolls in a tornado.

If she ever wanted to step into Naomi Gallagher's boots, she should banish the visions in her mind that morning. It would take more than a miracle and magic of the holiday season for her to ever go out on a simple date with Declan, much less for them to play Mary and Joseph. It was all the talk of Christmas that brought on the dream and the insane thoughts. Reality was that no matter how well he filled out those creased jeans, he truly was forbidden fruit.

She might be sick of the feud, but she did like living on Wild Horse, where she was welcome at the main house and had a room at her parents' place as well.

Right now, she could stay at any one of a dozen places over on Wild Horse, but the doors would be shut and locked at all of them if word got out she was sneaking around with Declan Brennan.

It had to be simply business. No fantasies welcome. Lock the door on them and throw away the key. They would talk to the preacher, arrange things so there could be a Christmas program, and Angela would be happy. Betsy would shake hands with Declan when it was all done, and they'd go right on back to the feud, where she'd devise ways to torment his family and he'd figure out ways to get even.

Tanner nudged her shoulder and whispered, "What are you thinkin' about? You look like you just ate sour grapes."

"Not sour grapes, forbidden fruit," she said softly.

Tanner's heart was a chunk of stone in his chest. Betsy was his favorite cousin, and everything in him said to fess up and be honest about what he'd done. He shivered thinking about what would happen if he did. The past had shown him that Betsy could carry a grudge longer than any of the cousins, and nobody wanted to find themselves on the top of her shit list. All he had to do was give Declan the money to call off the bet and maybe she'd never find out.

It wouldn't take anything but a word in passing to stop the whole business before it even got started. He'd have to take a lot of flak, but it would be the right thing to do. So after Sunday dinner, he'd tell her because the fallout would be worse if she heard it through the

Burnt Boot gossip line. After church services, he'd catch Declan out on the church parking lot and end the whole thing.

The preacher took an extra five minutes to wind down and be sure that everyone knew they'd best be thankful for their places in life. Then he called on Declan Brennan to give the benediction while he tiptoed to the back of the church. That way, he'd be in the doorway to greet everyone as they left.

Declan made it a short prayer, which Tanner did appreciate. If Preacher Kyle had called upon Quaid, they would have been there an additional five minutes because Quaid did love to thank God for everything from the green grass to the cows that ate it.

Everything fell perfectly into place as Tanner moved from his seat toward the doors and found himself in line right behind Declan. When Declan turned around and grinned at him, Tanner couldn't do it. He simply could not let a Brennan win the battle, not even if it meant suffering the wrath of Betsy later on down the road.

"Tanner?" Declan nodded.

Tanner talked from the corner of his mouth. "I don't like this. Betsy is going to go up in flames."

"Don't worry. She's not my type, so I'm not falling in love with her. That wasn't one of Eli's rules. But still, a bet is a bet, and for me to win this, she has to fall for me, right? She might hate me, but you are the one who is going to be in her shotgun sights when it's all said and done."

Mavis looped her arm in Declan's. "What are you talking about? Are you two fighting over the same woman? Who is she? You might as well step aside, Tanner. My grandson is a Brennan, and he gets what he wants."

"No, we were discussing Christmas," Declan said.

Mavis drew herself up to her full height. She was only an inch over five feet five inches, but when Mavis set her jaw like that, she appeared to be six feet tall and bulletproof. Ice-cold blue eyes set in a round face glared at Tanner. And then, she shook her finger at Declan. "I don't want to hear another word about that."

Tanner slipped ahead of them and made a hasty retreat out the front door. Betsy waved at him from the window of her truck. He couldn't undo what had happened, but Declan was right. Betsy was going to be one pissed off redhead at Christmas, whether Declan talked her into bed or not.

Declan had managed to tuck a note in Betsy's hand after Tanner had breezed past him and Mavis. It only had two words on it: *Sanctuary. 3:00.*

He'd caught the preacher coming out of a Sunday school room before church and told him that he needed a private meeting and asked for a time. Kyle had quickly agreed and hadn't asked any questions.

Now Declan was sitting at the dinner table with Mavis on one side of him and Quaid on the other, wishing that this only had to do with Christmas and not the bet. There was something exciting about the secrecy, but it was dangerous with the feud. Combined, they took away his appetite, and the Sunday dinner roast beef tasted like sawdust.

"Thinkin' about backin' out?" Quaid whispered.

"Yep," Declan answered.

"I told you not to do it, but you wouldn't listen, so now you've got to go through with it. How in the world are you going to approach her?"

Declan shrugged. "Sometimes destiny helps us Brennans out. The ball is already rolling and Tanner better run because it's going to build up speed as it goes."

"Don't joke," Quaid said.

"I'm not, but don't worry. It's all going to come around and bite him square on the ass before this is over." He clapped a hand on Quaid's shoulder. "What if you had to sweet-talk Betsy Gallagher?"

"I'm not sure Jesus could sweet-talk that redhead." Quaid chuckled under his breath.

"I'm very sure Jesus wouldn't want anything to do with her," Declan chuckled.

The solution came to Declan in a flash. He'd work with her on the Christmas project, but that's all he would do. Tanner could sweat it out for the whole month, wondering what was happening and just how much trouble he was going to be in when the news got out. Declan would put his thousand dollars in an envelope and hand it to Tanner on Christmas Day and Declan himself would tell Betsy what her cousin had done.

That would pay his debt. Then Betsy could take care of Tanner. Suddenly, his dinner tasted a hell of a lot better. Yes, sir, the Brennans might have to cough up some money, but the Gallaghers would be holding the short straw when it was all said and done.

The church doors always squeaked when they were opened. Betsy had asked Tanner a long time ago why he or some of the other men in the church didn't at least put some oil on the hinges, and he'd told her that the preacher wanted them to squeak.

"It's like this," he had explained. "Folks all know that they're going to squawk like a dying bird, so they get here on time. If they're late, there's no sneaking in and sitting on the back pew. The noise makes everyone turn around and the gossip flies around all week devisin' tales about why they were late to church. Were they fighting or making out with their girlfriend in the hayloft? Will there be a baby in nine months?"

When she heard the familiar noise that afternoon at a few minutes until three, she laid her romance book to one side and turned to see if it was Preacher Kyle or Declan.

Declan carefully closed the door and started up the aisle. Betsy watched his swagger and thought again of his reputation. A frown drew her eyebrows down into a solid line and he raised one of his slightly.

"What? Are you backing out?" His drawl echoed off the empty church's walls.

It should be a sin for a cowboy that sexy to be born into the Brennan family, and it definitely should be one for him to have a tight little strut that she couldn't keep her eyes from. There was something about the way he stood with shoulders back, broad chest tapering to a vee all the way below that bull rider's belt buckle that any woman on the face of the great green earth would take a second look at.

"I'm not backing out of anything," she answered. "Are you?"

He removed his hat and brushed his hair back, nodded to Betsy, and sat down on the other end of the pew. Crossing his long legs at the ankle, he laid his hat on the gold velvet pew cushion and said, "I am not. I'm in this for the long haul, Betsy Gallagher. Looks like we are on time. Wonder where Preacher Kyle is."

"I saw his truck out front so he's probably in his office praying before he comes in here," she said. "It's not often he'll be talking to a Brennan and a Gallagher in the same room, now is it?"

"He doesn't know why we're here. I just asked for a private meeting. And we are sitting on neutral territory here in the middle pews. Have you ever sat in this section before?"

Betsy shook her head seriously. "I have always sat on the Gallagher side of the church, just like you've sat on the Brennan side."

Kyle crossed the room from the other side of the church where his office was located. "Good afternoon. Oh, I didn't know you were bringing a girlfriend or, better yet, that it would be Betsy."

"Not a girlfriend. Not even a friend," Declan said quickly.

"But yet, here you are." Kyle sat down on the altar, facing them. "And this problem you want to discuss—does it involve both of you?"

"It involves Christmas and neither of us," Betsy blurted out.

"Okay." Kyle dragged the two-syllable word out into four.

"We want to have a Christmas program. My cousin Angela is having a baby boy any day, and she's got her heart set on him being baby Jesus. She and her husband will be Mary and Joseph. I realize we can't have the four weekly programs that we usually do, but we think we've come up with a plan to have at least one," Betsy said.

Declan picked up explaining when she paused for a breath. "Christmas is on Friday. You could announce it on the previous Sunday, and we could have the program on Wednesday night. That's a Bible study night anyway, but it would work out real good that way, having it right before the holiday. And everyone knows what to do at the program. The nativity scene and the story of the birth of Christ are pretty much the same every year, so three days will be plenty of time for folks to get it ready."

"Does this mean the Gallaghers and the Brennans are going to work together on this project of making this happen? You know we need costumes, props, a Christmas tree, decorations, and all that does not come cheap," Kyle said.

"Hell no!" Betsy slapped a hand over her mouth. "Forgive me for cussin' in church, but the families are not working together, and they'd skin us alive if they knew we were. It absolutely has to be a secret."

"Go on," Kyle said.

"We figure if we collect an item here and one there among all the families in Burnt Boot that, pretty soon, we'll have plenty of stuff for the program," Declan explained. "We just need you to give us permission to leave what we gather up here at the church and be our go-between on this mission. We'll be telling everyone that it's a secret but that they're going to love what happens and that they can't let anyone know who or what they donated. Everyone loves a secret like that."

Kyle chuckled. "With the way gossip flies around this town, do you really think you can keep something like that a secret?"

"Oh, they'll talk, but they'll be very careful not to let either one of the grandmothers know anything because no one wants to suffer their wrath," Declan answered.

Kyle had never doubted that God would answer his prayers if he was earnest when he petitioned his heavenly Father. When he took the job at the Burnt Boot church, he'd had second thoughts, but something kept pulling him to the little north Texas town. It came to him in a dream one evening that it was the feud and his mission was to end the thing once and for all, to bring peace to Burnt Boot. And right here was proof that he'd done the right thing.

He nodded and said, "I will be glad to help in any way I can. It will be wonderful to have a program. Truth is, I was hoping someone would come forward with a plan, but I sure didn't expect it to be a member from each of the feuding families."

"It really, really has to be a well-kept secret," Betsy said seriously. "My granny would scalp me. Don't look at me like that, Kyle. I'm thirty, but she still holds the whip over at Wild Horse."

"And so would mine, and you know very well how big my granny's whip is," Declan said.

"Then it will be. Until and if you two want the credit, my lips are sealed," Kyle said. "What can I do?"

"We need a key to the back door of the church to unload our things once a week. Thursday would be good because that's the evening you make your visits to the sick and the folks who can't get out for church services. That way, you can truly say that the stuff just appeared in the church, and you don't really know where it came from," Betsy said.

Kyle nodded. "And what else? I suppose you have already thought of the fact that using your phones might be dangerous. Anyone could pick them up and, with a few keystrokes, know that you were talking to each other. So why don't I put a tin can under the back porch steps and you can put notes in it if you want to talk to each other. Oh, and the church bulletins usually arrive on Thursday. The UPS man leaves them on the back porch, so could you bring those in for me?"

"We'd be glad to take care of it," Declan said.

"I hadn't thought of the phone business. Notes are a smart idea," Betsy said.

"Sometimes the old ways are best." Kyle smiled.

Burnt Boot was a small town—grocery store, bar, church, and school that made up the core of several ranches. If anyone wanted anything more than what they could find in town, they went to Gainesville or Denton.

But like all little Texas towns, the gossip vines were busy twenty-four hours a day, seven days a week with no time off for holidays, not even Christmas. Lord help if anyone saw Betsy's and Declan's trucks both parked at the back of the church on Thursday nights.

Fear was something that had never been in Betsy's

vocabulary, but it was that Sunday afternoon. A thousand what-ifs played through her mind. As if Declan could read her thoughts, he said, "We'll only bring my truck on Thursday nights. Your pink one would stand out like a neon light above a...café."

She held back the giggle. From the blush, it was pretty evident that he'd quickly substituted *café* for something else, and she'd bet dollars to cow patties that it was *whorehouse*. Betsy had no idea a cowboy as broad shouldered and hot as Declan Brennan could blush, and it gave her satisfaction to know that she wasn't the only one who'd had impure thoughts in church.

"I only have one spare key to the back door. Which one of you wants to be responsible for it?" Kyle asked.

"Give it to Betsy. She wanted this program more than me anyway." Declan glanced down the pew at Betsy. "You be responsible for the key. I'll get us here on Thursday night to bring in the stuff."

"Sounds good to me," Kyle said as he stood, stretched, and rolled his neck. "I'll take care of that now. Like I said, y'all let me know if I can help any other way."

"We will, and thanks. What we tell you, it's like confessional, isn't it? It is confidential?" Betsy chewed at her lower lip.

"As solid as attorney-client privilege or, like you said, confessional." Kyle waved as he disappeared behind his office door.

"So we're really going to do this?" Declan drawled.

"Looks like we are. You afraid?"

He shook his head. "Not me. You?"

"Not me. I live for danger. I'm a Gallagher."

"You saying that Brennans are sissies?"

"If the shoe fits," she answered.

"It doesn't, and I'll make a thousand-dollar bet with you that I can bring in more stuff than you can and keep the secret about why I want it. I can sweet-talk these old ladies into anything I want," Declan bragged.

She sat cross-legged on the pew. "You think I can't sweet-talk the old guys into making a manger and a framework for a nativity scene and donating bales of hay?"

"Bet or not?" Declan asked.

"Gambling in the church. What would Preacher Kyle say about that?"

"I thought you lived for danger," Declan said.

Dammit!

Betsy's green eyes flashed both anger and excitement, and if she'd been any other woman in the whole state of Texas, Declan would have started his mission right then and there to get her into bed. But not a Gallagher! No way was he getting tangled up with Betsy. Declan liked his house, his job, and his place on the ranch too well to screw it up.

Betsy unwound her shapely legs, which were encased in tight denim, and slid down closer to him. With green eyes flashing, she shoved out a hand. "It's a bet. Do we judge by the number or the value of the items?"

"It would be hard to judge by the value, since we'd argue until the devil turned blue from cold about that, so we'll go by the number of items." He wrapped his big hand around her small one and shook it firmly. The shock of her touch was unlike anything he'd ever experienced. Chalking it up to the risks they were both taking, he dropped her hand. The tingling sensation was still there when Kyle returned and gave her the key.

Declan was glad that he'd made the offer for her to be in charge of the thing because right then, his hand was so hot that it would have turned the thing into liquid metal.

"Okay, you two. Let's see if you can bring in what we need for a proper program. When I take stock of it all on the Sunday before Christmas, I'll decide if we have enough. If not, it will be a start for next year," he said.

"I'll see to it that we have enough," Betsy said.

"I understand there is a tree lighting at the store and the bar this next weekend," Kyle said. "So those will be celebrations."

"It's usually a war," Declan said. "The Gallaghers do something to destroy or mess up our party, so then we're bound to have to retaliate."

"How are you ever going to work together to make this program happen?" Kyle asked.

"Don't worry, Preacher. We'll get it done in spite of each other," Declan said. "I'm leaving now. Betsy, we'll meet here next Thursday night to discuss the rules?"

She nodded curtly.

"Okay then. No gathering of items until we talk about it, or the bet is off," Declan said.

"What bet?" Kyle asked.

"That I can bring in more than he can." Betsy shoved her arms into her denim duster.

"So this is a competition?"

"Everything between the Gallaghers and Brennans is a competition," Declan said. "Have a happy Thanksgiving,

Preacher. If you don't have a place for dinner that day, you are welcome at River Bend."

"Or at Wild Horse," Betsy said.

"Thank you both, but I'm going home to Waurika, Oklahoma. My fiancée and I are having dinner at my folks' place."

"Then enjoy it," Betsy said.

Declan crawled into his club cab truck and laughed out loud. He'd win this crazy Christmas war, collect his thousand dollars from Betsy, and give it to Tanner. That would make her even madder at her cousin when she found out what had happened at the poker game. He started the engine and had put the truck in reverse when someone tapped on the window.

Betsy made the motion for him to roll down the window.

He hit the button, and it slid down slowly. "What? Do you want to cancel the bet right now?"

"I just want to know what time we're going to meet on Thanksgiving night since the can for notes might not be in place until after that."

"How about ten o'clock? Park your truck at the bar. I'll pick you up there, and we'll park under the shade trees out back of the church and go inside to set up the rules."

She gave a brief nod and walked away, her cute little butt swaying from side to side and making his mouth go dry.

Chapter 4

DECLAN COULD NOT REMEMBER A SINGLE THANKSGIVING without his sister, Leah. He'd just celebrated his second birthday when she was born, and ever since they were kids, Thanksgiving had been their favorite holiday. She hadn't been welcome on River Bend since she'd married a man Mavis didn't like. So this year, he planned to take her up on the offer to have Thanksgiving with her and her new husband, Rhett O'Donnell. The first plan had been to fix a turkey at her new home on Burnt Boot Ranch. Then the O'Donnells decided to get together with Sawyer and Jill at Fiddle Creek Ranch, so the plan changed.

Granny Mavis shot a dirty look his way that morning when he kissed her on the forehead and wished her a happy Thanksgiving. She didn't say anything, but the cross between a disgruntled snort and long, wistful sigh let him know that she was not happy with him.

As near as he could count, there would be about fourteen people at the dinner, which made it a small gathering compared to the one that would be held on River Bend, with almost two hundred people.

And you, Granny darlin', would give me more than evil looks if you knew that I was meeting Betsy Gallagher tonight, he thought as he got into his truck and drove from Wild Creek to Fiddle Creek.

The trip took all of five minutes and would have been

shorter if he could have gotten there as the crow flies, instead of by the road. Leah met him at the door with a hug and led him inside the Fiddle Creek bunkhouse.

Leah had always been the quiet Brennan, the good girl who did exactly what she was told and made no waves—right up until Rhett O'Donnell arrived in Burnt Boot on his motorcycle. Happiness and that little touch of sass she'd found hiding deep in her soul looked every bit as beautiful on her as her sparkling, sage-green eyes that morning.

Declan hugged her tightly to his side. "This is nice, Leah. Real nice. It's warm and homey, and I'm jealous of you for having it."

"You just got to find a soul mate, Brother, and then it doesn't matter where you live or what you have because everything is wonderful," she said softly.

A blaze in the fireplace crackled, sending warmth throughout the bunkhouse. Two cats were tangled up together, sleeping in front of the flames. The wonderful aroma of a variety of cooking food drifted from the kitchen. Three elderly women, Verdie, Gladys, and Polly, giggled like little girls as they worked together in the kitchen.

All three were the same age as his grandmother and Naomi Gallagher, and the feud would have probably completed destroyed Burnt Boot if it hadn't been for Verdie, Gladys, and Polly setting down ground rules years and years ago, like the fact that the church, the bar, and the store were neutral territory.

"Hey, Declan," Verdie yelled across the room. "It's good to see you here." She wore a bright-orange apron over a pair of baggy jeans and a sweatshirt with a turkey done up in sequins on the front. Two bobby pins held her black hair away from her face and her brown eyes glittered when she looked at Callie and Finn's children playing with the cats.

Gladys peeked around the kitchen door and waved and so did Polly, both wearing matching aprons. They were sisters-in-law and lived together these days, since Polly sold the bar to Rosalie.

But they couldn't have been more different. Gladys was a tall, rawboned, older woman with high cheekbones and very little white streaking her jet-black hair. Polly was just as tall, but her hair had more white than black and her face was softer.

"How's things over on River Bend?" Gladys asked.

"Same as ever," Declan answered. "This place smells wonderful. Do I smell homemade bread?"

"Wouldn't be Thanksgiving without it," Gladys said and went back into the kitchen.

Leah took Declan by the hand and pulled him across the room. "Come on over here. We're making a centerpiece out of leaves the kids gathered for us and an old tree branch."

Jill tucked a strand of red hair behind her ear and frowned. "Do we need candles, or would they get in the way of conversation? I don't like leaning around the centerpiece to visit with folks across the table from me."

Declan smiled at the women around the table. "This is what I imagined when we were kids and we talked about the perfect Thanksgiving."

"It is, isn't it?" Leah sighed.

"Hey, Declan," Callie looked up from the extra fall leaves on the table. "Glad you could make it. Sawyer,

Finn, and Rhett are out hunting down mistletoe, because later tonight, everyone is putting up Christmas decorations. They'll be back any minute."

Callie frowned and glanced across the room at her four kids. She laid a hand on her huge baby bump and stuck another leaf in the arrangement. "I have to use all of them, or one of the kids will get their feelings hurt because their special leaves didn't make it into the arrangement. But it's beginning to look like a pile of leaves out in the yard instead of a centerpiece. After this, I should rethink having a dozen kids, or else we should make more table decorations."

Short, with dark hair and dark-green eyes, Callie was a beautiful woman, but more important than her looks was the fact that she had the mothering instinct down to an art. But then, she'd had lots of experience in raising her younger brother, Martin, and then added to that when she'd adopted three homeless children. Although the baby she was carrying was her first baby, it would be her fifth child.

Declan headed toward a rocking chair and Leah caught him by the arm.

"Was Granny okay?" she asked.

"Of course not. Her world is falling apart a stitch at a time and she's mad as hell."

"She's put her world back together before. I'm sure she'll do it again."

A blast of cold air blew in the door, bringing three tall cowboys with it. Sawyer raised a hand. "Hey, Declan, glad you could make it. You missed the fun of climbing a tree to get mistletoe." He held up a burlap feed bag with enough mistletoe to supply most of Burnt Boot that season. "Jill says we're hanging it everywhere, so I brought plenty."

Sawyer, the man of the Fiddle Creek bunkhouse slash home, was Jill's husband. He set the bag on the floor and hung his heavy, mustard-colored work coat on a rack beside the door. All three of the O'Donnell cousins had features that testified that they were kinfolk—dark hair, square-cut jaws, and chiseled faces. But they all had different eye colors: Sawyer, the comedian, had dark brown; Rhett, the rebel cowboy, had light green; and Finn, the quiet cousin, had blue.

Declan waved. "Leah, how much of that stuff are you hanging over at Burnt Boot Ranch?"

Leah blushed. "Lots and lots, so you'd best be careful if you plan on bringing a woman to the ranch for me to meet."

"I'll be sure to have lots of ChapStick." He grinned.

Coats and hats came off and were hung up. Rhett shook his hair out of his short ponytail, letting it hang at chin level. Leah quickly crossed the room and lifted up on tiptoe to brush a quick kiss across his lips.

"Thank you, darlin', for braving the cold wind to get that for us," she said.

He kissed her on the forehead. "I'd fight a war to get you anything in this world."

Declan wanted what they had. Hell, he'd even be willing to leave River Bend to get it. At thirty-two, he was older than Leah by two years, so he should have found his soul mate before she had.

Sawyer crossed the room and pulled a rocking chair up close to Declan's. "Tell us about that poker game last week. I heard that it got heated and that Tanner won."

"Yep, and believe me when I say it was not easy to see him take that money. Must've been close to five hundred dollars in the pot," Declan said.

Sawyer slapped his forehead. "Ain't that just my luck? I knew I'd pay for not playing with y'all, but I didn't want to go out in the cold. I could've bought Jill that little antique side table she's wanting for Christmas with that money."

"What'd it get heated about?" Finn asked.

"Women," Declan said.

Rhett kicked off his boots, stretched out his long legs, and propped his feet on the coffee table. "Well, that ain't no big surprise, is it? Tanner thinks he's God's gift to the female population."

"So does Declan." Leah laughed.

"Hey, now!" Declan protested.

"What'd y'all get into it about? Who had the most notches on the bedpost? Never seen you speechless before, so I must've hit the nail on the head." Leah crossed the room and tousled his hair.

"Granny would shoot me dead if I started carving on the bedpost," he said.

"Granny would do worse than shoot you if she knew about a certain little black book that's hidden inside the back pocket of your Bible case," Leah said.

"Whoa! Now you're getting personal and telling secrets." Declan smiled.

"I think we'd best turn this conversation to the ball game coming on this afternoon," Rhett chuckled. "Are we all rootin' for the same team?"

Betsy usually loved the holidays, but that day, she wanted to be anywhere else in the world other than sitting beside her grandmother at the head table for the annual Gallagher Thanksgiving dinner. Naomi waited until everyone was served and eating the first course—crisp salad with the ranch cook's special dressing—to tap her glass with the edge of her knife and stand up. She picked up a microphone and flipped the switch.

"Welcome to the Gallagher Thanksgiving dinner. I'm glad you are all here. Please know that each and every one of you is very important to Wild Horse Ranch. It's been my privilege to run this ranch for fifty years, and for that, I'm thankful today. Find something in your hearts to be thankful for and you'll always be happy." She raised her glass high and everyone followed suit. "To Wild Horse."

"To Wild Horse," everyone shouted.

Naomi sat down and clinked her glass with Betsy's. "What are you thankful for today?"

That no one found out about me and Declan on the riverbank, she thought.

"Wild Horse," she said.

"Good girl." Naomi beamed.

Angela caught Betsy's eye and smiled shyly. Betsy winked and Angela's smile widened. She couldn't tell Angela yet, but everything was going to be all right. Baby Christian could kick and scream in his swaddling clothes and Angela would be his mother in the nativity program. Tyrell and Tanner could be shepherds, and Eli could play one of the three wise men.

"Where is your mind? I've asked you the same question twice," Naomi barked.

"I'm sorry. I was thinking about how uncomfortable Angela looks." Like a child, Betsy crossed her fingers and tucked her hand under her thigh.

"I wouldn't mind seeing you in that shape next year at this time," Naomi said.

"What if I don't want children?"

"Of course you want children. That's the future of Wild Horse and the feud."

"What if I don't want to mess with the feud?"

Naomi looked as if she could shoot blue blazes from her eyes. "One more word like that, and I'll kick you off my ranch right now. It's not a joking matter, and you've been raised better than to even let such thoughts enter your mind. What has gotten into you this past week?"

"Nothing. Just restlessness, I guess. I love Christmas, and my favorite part is the weekly programs at church, and we don't have them this year. It's made me cranky," Betsy said.

"Well, snap out of it. The Brennans have to be taught a lesson."

Betsy's eyes went to each person in the room, assessing each for whatever item or donations she might convince them to give to the Christmas secret. She made a mental list, but since it was all Gallaghers, there wouldn't be an argument from Declan over them. He could work his spell on the Brennans; she'd work hers on her family. The fighting would come about over the folks who were neutral, like the O'Donnells, Polly, Verdie, Gladys, and Rosalie. Betsy's eyes narrowed as she thought of Rosalie, and she clamped her jaw so tight that it ached. She wanted Rosalie on her list, even if she had to give Declan both Polly and Gladys.

"She's my therapist," Betsy muttered, then clapped her hand over her mouth.

"What was that?" Naomi asked.

"I was thinking out loud. This is really good pumpkin pie, Granny. Do all of your famous recipes come with your job?" Betsy asked.

"Of course." Naomi beamed and brushed her bright-red hair sprinkled with white away from her face. "And you will add to the recipe box and pass it on to your granddaughter some day."

"Why not my daughter?" Betsy asked.

The smile faded quickly. "You will have sons to work the ranch. They can have daughters and sons, and you can choose your strongest granddaughter to run the place. That's the way it's done."

"Not with you. You married into it and inherited because Grandpa was the oldest son. By rights, my dad should be the next ruler of Wild Horse," Betsy said.

"He will have his place in the business, but you will run the ranch as a whole."

A picture of the little house where Angela and Jody lived flashed through Betsy's mind. That's what she wanted. Not a house with a ballroom big enough to seat two hundred people or a ranch that took hours to drive around on a four-wheeler.

Darkness comes early at the end of November in Texas, but the moon was bright, and it would light up her truck no matter where she parked it, so that evening, she took the old ranch work truck into town. She nosed it into the gravel lot behind the bar, where the beer and liquor vendors parked to bring their wares through the back door.

She had barely turned off the engine when Declan's big, black truck slid in beside her and he slung the passenger door open. She picked up her purse, which had her phone and her list of folks she'd fight to keep, and crawled in beside him.

"We still going to do this, or have you chickened out?" he asked.

"We are doing it," she said.

He wiggled his eyebrows. "Oh, really?"

"Get your mind out of the gutter, Declan. Is that all you think about?"

"Sometimes I do think about food, but that could be simply because I need it as fuel so I can chase women," he said.

"You and Tanner are probably related somewhere in the pre-feud days."

"Hey, now, them are fightin' words, and we've called a truce until we get this Christmas crap done."

"Have we?" She shot a long look toward him.

He parked behind the church and turned to meet her gaze. "If we're going to work together, we should agree not to insult each other."

"Why? What we're doing is business, not personal."

"And it can end right here before it ever starts," he said.

Betsy flashed her sweetest smile. "Little touchy tonight, are we?"

"Not a little—a whole lot, so all kidding aside, let's get into the church where it's warm and decide our next step. I want Gladys and Polly, and since they won't be able to keep their mouths shut to Sawyer and Jill, I'll take them too."

She opened the truck door and dashed across the narrow distance to the porch and fished the key from her purse. "Then I get Rosalie and Verdie and the family at Salt Draw."

He followed her into the church. She flipped on a hallway light and entered the first available room. He sat down in a rocking chair in the nursery and remembered the warm and fuzzy feeling at Fiddle Creek earlier in the day, when he'd dragged a rocker up to the fire. "And since Leah is my sister, I get her and Rhett."

She pulled her list from her purse and sat down in the other rocking chair. "Where's your list?"

He tapped his forehead. "Right here. I've got the Brennans and the ones I just mentioned and the man at the feed store in Gainesville."

Dammit! Why hadn't she thought of him?

"Then I'm taking the staff at the western wear store." She wrote the store name on her paper.

"I get Billy Bob's Barbecue and anyone who comes into the bar."

"Oh, no, not in a million years. You can have Billy Bob's, but we're sharing the bar. I get three nights a week and you can have three."

"Then I want Thursday, Friday, and Saturday."

"In your dreams, cowboy. You can have Thursday and Friday and your choice of the other days. I get Saturday and the other two days you don't want. That's fair since Fridays and Saturdays are the busiest nights."

He grinned. "You drive a hard bargain, Gallagher."

"I drive a fair bargain, Brennan," she said, smarting off.

"We can start in the morning, then, and bring our goods here on Thursday nights, right?"

"That would be the plan. Is the meeting adjourned?"

"I do believe it is. Nice doin' business with you." He stood up and waited beside the door to the hallway for her to go out first.

"You don't have to act like a gentleman. This is business, not personal. I'm not your date," she said.

"Heaven forbid." He grinned.

The next morning at breakfast, Declan had poured a cup of coffee and was in the process of loading his plate from the sideboard in the dining room when his grandmother breezed into the room. Her jet-black hair accentuated every single wrinkle in her eighty-plus-year-old round face.

"I hear that wild hussy Betsy Gallagher drove the ranch work truck into town last night and parked behind the bar. She got into another truck, but no one knows who she was with or where they went. And someone was in the church last night. Kyle has gone home to Oklahoma to be with his fiancée for the holidays, so it wasn't him. I'm wondering if Betsy is having a fling with one of the deacons," Mavis said. "If I find out that it's true, I swear I'll have him thrown out of the church."

"Granny, the deacons, all except Quaid, are sixty years old and married. You think she's having an affair with Quaid?"

Mavis laid a palm over her heart and gasped. "He'd

best not be flittin' around that woman. I'll have him neutered. I swear to God I will. Why'd you have to put that picture in my mind? Leah has brought down enough shame on this family, marryin' that hippie cowboy like she did."

Declan set his food on the table and started to eat. "If it is Quaid, can Leah come back home? After all, she didn't get hooked up with a Gallagher."

Mavis's hand left her chest and waved in the air like a frayed flag on a windy day. "She's made her bed and now she can lie in it. You might do well to remember that, Declan. Which reminds me, it's high time you started thinking about settling down. Honey can't run this ranch by herself. She'll need a strong male presence."

"Then tell her to get married. I'm not interested," Declan said.

Suddenly, he wasn't hungry. He carried his plate to the sink, scraped it off, and turned on the garbage disposal.

"You are wasting good food!" Mavis shouted above the noise.

"Yep. See you later today."

He grabbed a notepad with the ranch logo on the top on the way to his truck and wrote the first message to put into the can:

> *Have to figure out some other way to get this done. Someone saw you last night. Meet me in Gainesville tonight. Movie theater. Back row at the show that starts at seven thirty.*

Chapter 5

Betsy could feel her grandmother's glare the minute she walked into the country kitchen that morning. Since only four or five people had breakfast at the big house on Wild Horse, each person made their own and sat around the old oak table that had been in the family since before the feud started. Tension was so thick that a sharp machete couldn't have cut through it, but Betsy wasn't saying a word until she figured out who had already pissed in Naomi's coffee that morning.

"I hear that Quaid Brennan picked you up behind the bar last night. Y'all went to the church, back into the nursery, and spent about fifteen minutes there and then you went back to your truck," Naomi said in an ice-cold voice.

Betsy poured a cup of coffee and carried it to the table. "You heard wrong. I was at the church, but not with Quaid."

"With who, then?"

"My college friend Iris. I left the old work truck at the bar and she picked me up." She was thankful for her imaginary college friend, Iris. If the poor girl had been real, Betsy would have owed her too many favors to count.

"The mail doesn't run on Thanksgiving," Naomi said.

"The mail doesn't bring the programs. The UPS man delivers them and puts them on the back porch, but he didn't bring them yesterday after all, since it was a holiday. I left a note for Kyle and I'll pick them up today and put them in the church. I'm hungry so I'm going to make my morning smoothie. You want one?" That wasn't a lie; anxiety always made Betsy hungry.

"You should be eating eggs and bacon, not those glorified shakes." A little of the ice had thawed in Naomi's tone.

"I put protein into the shake, and it doesn't have all those fat grams."

"Promise me that you weren't at that church with Quaid Brennan."

Betsy dumped two tablespoons of protein powder into the blender, added yogurt and a banana, and looked right into Naomi's eyes. "Do we need the Bible for me to put my right hand on?" she asked.

Naomi slapped the table so hard that the salt and pepper shakers rattled. "Stop stalling and give me your word."

In a few strides, Betsy was standing in front of Naomi, right hand raised and eyes locked solidly with her grandmother's. "I solemnly swear, right here before God and you—and please know that I'm far more afraid to lie to you than him—that I was not at the church with Quaid last night, and I have no intentions of ever being there with him other than Sunday mornings, when he sits on one side and I'm on the other and never the twain shall meet in the middle. I did not get into his truck or go anywhere with him, and I would never, ever do that anyway. Is that good enough? Can I make my smoothie now and go help Eli and Tanner with the chores?"

Naomi gave her a curt nod. "That's good enough. I swear the gossiping tongues in Burnt Boot are flapping at both ends most of the time. That's a good thing you're doing for the preacher. Next time, park your pink truck right there beside the back door and I'll make sure everyone knows that you are doing something religious. It'll be a good thing, like you slowing down on the drinking."

"Yes, ma'am. You sure you don't want a smoothie?"

"I had fried eggs and ham fifteen minutes ago. And I want you back here to go over books with me at ten o'clock. If the chores aren't done by then, Eli and Tanner can finish them."

Betsy hated the office and being inside the house all day, but that's what Granny would have her doing the rest of the day. Naomi had never entered the modern technology world and still kept a set of books in longhand, but before she gave up her golden scepter and crown, she intended for all the information to be put into the computer. That way, she'd declared, Betsy would be familiar with the past and the present way things were done on Wild Horse.

"Did you hear me?" Naomi asked.

"Yes, ma'am. Ten o'clock in the office. Want me to clean the shit off my boots?"

Naomi's forefinger shot up faster than a speeding bullet and pointed right at Betsy's heart. "You take a shower before you come to work with me in the office. And I want the cussin' to tone down right along with the drinking. Wild Horse needs a heavy hand but also a decent lady to run it."

"Then ten thirty, since I have to take a shower, or do

I work until ten, drive from the back forty to here, take a shower and clean up, and be in there at eleven?"

"Okay, okay," Naomi said. "Come in at noon—have lunch and take a shower. We'll work all afternoon getting things put into that computer. It doesn't like me. It crashes every time I touch it. But I guess everything should be brought up to date before I step down."

"Time to enter the modern world, Granny." Betsy poured her shake into a travel mug, screwed on the top, and dropped a kiss on Naomi's forehead as she headed for the door. She set the shake on the foyer table, put on her work jacket and cowboy hat, and hurried out the door before Naomi changed her mind about the time.

It took five minutes to go from Wild Horse to the church at the right speed. She made it in three, scribbled a note to put into the can telling Declan that they could not meet at the church on Thursday.

The can had held apple pie filling at one time—apples, a symbol for the fruit from the forbidden tree.

Very fitting.

She found Declan's note, tucked it into her pocket, and rewrote hers to say that she'd be there. Then she picked up the manila envelope with the programs inside and took them to Kyle's office. The door was locked, so she propped them against it and sat down in the front pew.

The hands of the clock, hanging to one side of the squeaky door, moved in slow motion, and the five minutes she was determined to sit there seemed like eternity. But the early morning gossips in Burnt Boot would see that she was at the church, alone, in her truck, and that she was supposed to be there.

Exactly four minutes and thirty seconds after she'd sat down, her phone rang. She let it go to the fourth ring before she picked it up.

"Want my recipe for a smoothie, Granny?" she asked.

"What are you doing at the church?"

"I came to put the programs in Kyle's office. I was just leaving to go help Tanner. Do you have a tracker on my truck?"

"I don't need one. There is a whole town full of folks watching your hot-pink truck. Honey, you can't sneeze without someone calling me. There are no secrets in Burnt Boot and you can't get away with anything."

"I believe it. I'm on my way out. Programs delivered. No need to come back to church until Sunday morning now."

"I will see you later," Naomi said, and the call ended.

Declan arrived at the theater first and paid for a ticket. The movie was one of the chick flicks that he'd never have chosen to watch, but it started at seven thirty and there weren't many folks lining up to see it.

He bought the popcorn-and-drink deal of the night and hung back until he caught sight of Betsy's flaming-red ponytail bouncing along with every step she took. He nodded toward the movie when he caught her eye and held up the huge container of popcorn.

The older people were joined by two more couples about their age, and they didn't waste any time getting past the usher when he pulled back the velvet ropes. Declan gave them an extra few minutes to get seated before he went inside and sat in the back row. He'd barely gotten settled when Betsy joined him and stuck her hand into the popcorn box.

"Hungry?" he asked.

"Starving. FYI, I eat when I'm stressed."

"What's got your blood pressure up?" he teased.

"Every bit of this. My granny thought I was sinnin' with Quaid last night in the church nursery."

"Mine knew by breakfast this morning." He passed the drink to her. "Don't look at it like that. We've already shared a whiskey bottle and I got two straws. The short one is yours."

"Is that supposed to mean something?" she asked.

"Just that you aren't as tall as me."

The movie started, and she pulled her legs up and sat cross-legged so she could face him. He leaned toward her so they could talk without disturbing the people who'd actually come to see the show rather than to have a dark, quiet place to plan a Christmas program.

"So I've got a plan," he said.

She grabbed another fistful of popcorn. "What is your plan? I got nothing, other than my truck can go to the church on Thursdays only, so I can put the programs inside. Other than that, I can't even drive the old work truck to town and hide it behind the bar without someone seeing and, worse yet, telling, so if you can find a way to get inside without being seen, we could still meet at the church."

"I think we should rent a storage unit here in Gainesville to unload our things once a week," he said.

"And I could slip a note in the preacher's program envelope telling him what we're doing, so he wouldn't be disappointed that there's nothing piling up in one of the Sunday school rooms. Then, on the last Thursday that we have donations, I could give him the key to the storage unit," she said. "I like it. That way it would be totally anonymous."

"Did you get anything yet?" he asked.

Betsy shook her head. "Granny had me in the office all afternoon so I didn't have time. You?"

He grinned. "I'm ahead by five items, then. And I'm only counting a box of twelve ornaments as one since they're in a box."

"What did you get?" she asked.

"The ornaments. A box of green garland stuff that likely doesn't go on the tree but probably around the ceiling in the church; it looks like fake holly. And a package of gold tinsel, a bale of hay, and a little drummer boy costume. You need to write it down?"

"What size is the costume?"

"I don't know. One of my cousin's kids used it a couple of years ago when the Brennans did that part of the program and he was about this tall." Declan measured three feet from the floor with an open hand.

One second, Betsy was looking at a big rancher's hand showing her how big a little drummer boy was, and the next, Declan had wrapped both arms around her and his lips were on hers.

Her first instinct was to pull back and slap him, but then his tongue traced the outline of her lips. From that moment, all she could think about was Declan. All she could see were sparks dancing behind her closed eyes. And all she wanted was for the kiss to never end.

She opened her mouth enough to allow entrance, and their tongues did a mating dance that sent shivers down her spine. The sensible side of her brain kept shouting something about him being a Brennan, but the part that controls sensation and sexual desire hushed it up right quick.

When he ended the kiss and pulled back, she was speechless for the first time in her life. Her knees had gone weak. Her brain was total mush. Her body wanted to haul him off to the nearest motel, or the back of her truck, and finish what they'd started.

"Your cousin Eli walked in with a girl and I didn't know what to do," he said.

She glanced around the furry edge of the parka hood of her coat, and sure enough, about midway down the theater's aisle, Eli was sitting there with a woman.

"I'd best leave," she said.

"I'll give you time to clear the parking lot and then I'll go," he said. "You want the drink?"

"No, I'm good."

"I'll rent the storage unit and meet you there on Thursday night."

"Leave me a note about where to go."

He nodded. "Will do."

She made it to the truck before she flipped the hood back on her jacket. Then she slid down in the driver's seat and took several deep breaths. It's a wonder the earth was still rotating around the sun after a kiss between a Gallagher and a Brennan.

"And I liked it. I did more than like it. I wanted more. A first kiss has never affected me like that before. It has to be the danger involved. I'm not a teenager. I'm almost thirty years old, and I know my way around the bedroom," she mumbled.

She adjusted the rearview mirror and turned on the light above it, so she could see if her lips looked as hot as they felt. Other than two spots of high color in her cheeks, the woman staring back at her was Betsy Gallagher—red hair, green eyes, and a slightly oval face.

She turned the key in the ignition and had started the engine when her phone rang. Hoping that the Burnt Boot gossip vine didn't extend all the way to Gainesville, she answered it cautiously.

"Hello, Granny."

"Where are you?"

"I came to town to see a movie, but the one I chose was a dud so I'm on my way home," she said. "Do you need something?"

"Angela is on her way to the hospital and I wanted to be there when the baby comes. I thought you could drive me."

"Call Tanner to take you, and I'll go on to the hospital. If he doesn't want to stay, you can ride home with me," Betsy said.

"That sounds good. I'll see you there."

Declan could feel his heart thumping around in his chest as if it wanted to fly out right there in the theater and do a dance down the aisle. He'd kissed Betsy Gallagher and it had been wonderful. It could have been because he was working undercover, or maybe it was the danger of her cousin showing up when he had, but he'd never kissed another woman who'd made him forget where and who he was.

He ate a couple of handfuls of popcorn and washed it down with the soda pop, but he could still taste Betsy's kiss, still feel her arms as they snaked up around his neck and clutched his hair as she pulled him in closer. She'd liked the kiss as much as he did, even though later she might swear that she went home and gargled with Jack Daniels to get the taste of it out of her mouth.

If he was labeled a womanizer, then Betsy was his match. Her temper was only exceeded by her ability to pick up men. He was on his way out of the theater when he got a text message from Leah asking him to come to the hospital.

Fear replaced all thoughts of Betsy as he nervously hit the button to call Leah. She didn't answer until the third ring. He didn't realize he was holding his breath until he heard her voice and his breath escaped in a whoosh.

"Are you okay? Why are you at the hospital?" he asked.

"I'm fine. I was visiting with Callie when she slipped on a throw rug and fell. Verdie made me drive, and Finn sat in the backseat with her in case the fall caused problems with her pregnancy. That means I'm here without a ride and I wanted you to come get me," she explained.

"Is she okay?" Declan asked.

"They're keeping her a few hours for observation, but everything looks fine. I'd call Rhett, but he's over at Fiddle Creek with Sawyer, helping fix a tractor."

"I'm also in town. I'll swing by and pick you up," he said.

"I'm in the maternity waiting room."

"I'll find it," he said.

He asked for directions at the front desk and only got lost once on his way, but when he stepped inside, the first thing he saw was a flamboyant red ponytail and gorgeous green eyes looking up at him.

"What are you doing here?" Naomi Gallagher asked. "One of your girlfriends having a baby? I might have known you'd have little bastards all over the north part of Texas."

He shot a sly wink toward Betsy and then turned to look Naomi right in the eye. "Two of them actually. Nice of them to go into labor the same night, wasn't it?"

"Don't you be smart with me," Naomi said. "Why are you really here?"

Leah stepped out of the ladies' room on the far side of the waiting area and smiled. "That was quick. I'll go check on Callie one more time before we leave, if you don't mind."

"Not at all. I'll be right here. Tell her and Finn that if they need anything at all to give me a call," Declan said.

The only empty seat was next to Betsy, so he eased into it. The chairs were locked together, leaving no space between them, so no matter how much he crunched his wide shoulder, it still touched Betsy's. Naomi glared at him, but if she'd had horns and a pitchfork, he couldn't make his shoulders smaller.

"So who are you here to see?" he asked.

"Angela is having a baby boy." Betsy's voice sounded thin and strained.

"Well, you will probably be here all night. I'm just

here to give Leah a ride home, since Verdie made her drive."

"Why didn't Finn drive?" Naomi asked.

"Callie slipped and fell. Verdie was afraid it would hurt the baby, so she made Leah drive her to the hospital with Finn in the backseat with Callie," he explained.

Naomi continued to stare at him as if he were a cockroach under a microscope.

"Callie's tough. She'll be all right," she said.

"I hope so. She and Finn are pretty excited about another baby, and their other children are counting the days," Declan said. "I see Leah on her way, so you ladies have a good evening, and I do hope everything goes well for Angela."

He escaped before Naomi could say another word. Leah looped her arm through his, and together they headed out of the hospital.

Leah kept glancing over her shoulder all the way to the hospital parking lot. "I keep expecting to see a Gallagher behind us. In my mind, they've got sawed-off shotguns shoved down the legs of their pants."

"Hey, they're interested in the new baby, not us. Callie okay?"

"Doctor says that she's fine, but as a precaution, they'll keep her hooked up to the baby monitor thing for another few hours. She should get home by midnight, and the doc's saying she should have bed rest for a couple of days—at least through the weekend. Verdie will see to it that she obeys," Betsy said.

Declan opened the door for her. "They're good for each other out there on Salt Draw."

"Funny how things work out, isn't it?"

Declan drove out of the parking lot and onto the highway, made a few turns, and was on the way back to Burnt Boot in a few minutes. "Do you believe in fate, Leah?"

"Yes, I do," Leah said.

"Really?"

"If I didn't before, I would now. Sorry to leave you in that rattlesnake den back there. Confession time: I didn't need to be in the bathroom, but I couldn't stand all those Gallaghers giving me dirty looks, so I hid out until I heard your voice." She giggled nervously.

"All those Gallaghers? I only saw Betsy and the grand matriarch, Naomi."

"Did you have on blinders? There were at least a dozen in there."

"Guess I did," he chuckled.

On the way home, he worried about Betsy and then scolded himself silently for feeling that way. She was a bet, for God's sake, not a date. He'd win the money from her by gathering more Christmas stuff and give it to Tanner to pay off his debt, since he had no intentions of sleeping with her. Heaven help Texas if that happened. One kiss came close to sending the movie theater up in blazes. Sex would burn down the state.

Two wild folks like Declan Brennan and Betsy Gallagher did not belong together. Besides, she wasn't his type. He liked short, blond-haired women with big, blue eyes and sweet dispositions. Someone who made him feel like he was macho and who needed him to protect her. He sure didn't need a woman who could scare the horns off Lucifer.

"What are you thinking about? It looks like you are arguing with yourself." Leah laid a hand on his arm.

"You know me too well, Sis. I've got a little deal going but it has to be a secret. You can tell Rhett because I wouldn't want you to keep things from him but..."

Leah sighed. "You've fallen in love."

"Oh, no!" he said too quickly.

"Methinks the man is protesting too loudly," she said.

"No, it's the truth. Why settle with one piece of sea foam fudge when there's a whole candy shop at your disposal? I can't tell you why, but I'm gathering up used or new or anywhere-in-between things that have to do with Christmas. You want to donate something?"

"Sure." She nodded.

"That was quick. You didn't even make me beg."

"Well, I am a schoolteacher, and we always have tons of stuff that we store from year to year. I was going through my school things the other day and ran across three plastic door covers. Anyway, I only need one door cover, and I'm using the life-size Santa Claus this year, so you can have the two others. One is a nativity and the other is a skyline view of Bethlehem with the Star of David in the sky. And you will tell me later why you want this, right?"

"You'll know before Christmas," he said.

"I'll bring them to you on Monday or you can pick them up at the school. Want me to ask the other teachers if they've got anything?"

He grinned. "That would be wonderful."

The baby was born at one minute after midnight, and the first person Angela asked for was Betsy. Jody brought the red-haired baby boy out to show the family and then the nurse whisked him away for skin-on-skin bonding time with Angela.

Betsy peeked inside the window of the labor-and-delivery room before she stepped over the threshold. Jody was sitting beside Angela, and the baby was cuddled up next to his mama's bare skin, both of them wrapped snugly in a blue blanket. Betsy's eyes misted as she waited in envy for one of them to motion her inside.

Angela saw her first and her smile was probably every bit as beautiful as Mary's was the day that Jesus was born. "Come in and meet Christian. He has your red hair, and he's going to be a perfect baby Jesus at the program this year."

"Now, darlin'—" Jody started.

"Yes, he will," Betsy said as she crossed the room. "He's beautiful. Looks like Jody, doesn't he? Only with red hair."

"I thought so," Angela said.

"And how are you?" Betsy asked.

"Fine. I took the drugs and it was a breeze. I may have another one next year," Angela said.

"It might not be the time to bring it up, but I'm working on something that could help the cause in the long run. It's a secret so you can't tell a single soul that you donated anything, but would you be willing to give something with a Christmas theme to my secret cause?"

Angela nodded seriously. "I want to give a tree topper. My granny crocheted an angel for my mama's tree years ago. We were going through what we had for decorations when I went into labor and I saw it there. They'll probably let me go home tomorrow, so come on by the house and pick it up anytime. And neither one of us will tell. I want this program to happen so badly, so my Christian can be baby Jesus, I'd keep a secret from God if I had to."

The Gallaghers waited an extra hour for the baby to go to the nursery, where they could see him through the glass and exclaim about his red hair. According to Naomi, he was the first red-haired child to be born into the family since Betsy, and that made him very special.

"And now I'm ready to go have breakfast at the all-night waffle house and go home," Naomi said. "I'm not good at waiting. You won't make me sit in an uncomfortable chair when you have your babies. You'll have them like I did. One hour in the hospital and the baby will be here."

"You sure about that?"

"Positive."

Betsy shook her head slowly. "Why didn't you make that decree for Angela?"

"She's not a Gallagher. She only married into the family," Naomi said.

"Granny!"

"I'm hungry and I'm tired and I'm cranky. Let's go," Naomi said crossly.

"Aren't you going to stop in and see Angela and Jody?" Betsy asked as they headed down the hallway.

"Already did. I slipped in after you left. Never heard of them putting the baby up on the mama like that. They sure do things different nowadays. When you was born, they took you straight to the nursery and your mama didn't see you until you had a diaper and a little shirt on your scrawny body. You only weighed five pounds, so you looked more like a red-haired monkey than a baby."

"Well, thank you so much for that. If I'd known you were going to insult me, I would have let you ride home with someone else," Betsy said.

"Don't threaten me, young lady. And while we're arguing, I saw the way you looked at that Declan Brennan. Don't think your glances his way got past me."

"I'm going to call him to come over to Wild Horse for a booty call soon as I get you home."

Naomi slapped her on the arm. "That's not a joking matter. Go get the truck and pick me up at the door. I don't feel like walking all that way."

When Betsy drove up, Naomi crawled inside the passenger side. When her grandmother was mad, she puffed up and always reminded Betsy more of a bullfrog than a bulldog, but both had the word *bull* in them, and that part was right because Naomi was definitely *bullheaded*! Her chin tucked down into the layers that made up her neck. Her shoulders hunched forward, and air seemed to inflate her whole body into a round ball, with skinny arms and legs protruding at strange angles.

"Declan has always been a good-looking cowboy, and that's why women flock to him like flies on honey," Naomi finally said.

Traffic was almost nonexistent at that time of night, so Betsy pulled out onto the highway and headed toward the waffle house. "No argument here."

"I don't like it when you give him that once-over that says you like what you see."

Betsy's shoulder raised an inch. "I love to look at all the Christmas ornaments in the stores this time of year. It doesn't mean I'm going to buy them all."

Naomi sighed, and the bullfrog disappeared. "But you might buy one, right? And when you get it home, it might be the wrong one."

"Or it might be the one that I'll put on my tree for the next fifty years. Stop worrying, Granny. Just because Leah Brennan moved away from River Bend doesn't mean you're going to lose me." Betsy reached across the console and patted Naomi's hand.

"I feel a change in the air, and I hate change," Naomi said.

"Everything changes, and the more they change, the more they stay the same."

"That sounds like a load of philosophical bull. Forget the waffle house. I want to go home and have a shot of Jameson and go straight to bed."

"Sounds good to me." Betsy took the next exit, made a loop, and caught the highway north toward Burnt Boot.

Chapter 6

THE HEART MIGHT WANT WHAT THE HEART WANTS, BUT sometimes it has to be trained to want something else. Betsy's heart was about to get its first lesson in cross-training and learn to forget that steamy kiss she'd shared with Declan. For the past forty-eight hours, she'd pined for him, but now she realized it was nothing more than a game. Even the Christmas decorations were a competition, and everything else most likely had something to do with the feud. The Brennans were trying to stir up trouble in the Gallagher court so Mavis could one-up Naomi at Christmas.

The Brennans, including Declan, were not to be trusted.

It was time to suck it up and stop letting her heart lead her around by her hormones. And there wasn't a better night to get the job done than a Saturday night at the Burnt Boot bar. One single shot of Jameson was all she would have, so her grandmother wouldn't fuss. The place would be hopping with cowboys, so her plan was simple: dance with a dozen or more good-lookin' guys and take the one that made her forget all about Declan home for the night. Sneaking a one-night stand in and out of the big house right under her grandmother's nose held enough danger and excitement, even for Betsy.

She turned around slowly in front of the floor-length mirror. Rhinestones created the outline of a cowboy hat and boots on the back of her shirt. She'd tucked it in to show off the blinged-out pockets on her designer jeans as well as the belt that sparkled even more than the shirt and jeans. Makeup was perfect, hair down and curled, and expensive perfume settled on her like a fine mist.

She repeated her mother's words. "Spray it in the air and walk through it."

And you should be going to dinner with her and your dad, rather than trying to find a one-night stand—the voice in her head belonged to Tanner.

"If you knew what was really going on, you'd be out there hunting down a stranger for me, Tanner Gallagher," she mumbled. "I'm going to Sunday dinner at home tomorrow, and I promise not to have a hangover, so hush. Mama and Daddy would both be willing to kill their firstborn to keep them from hooking up with a Brennan, and since I'm the firstborn, I need to get him out of my mind."

She grabbed a fancy denim duster, picked up her hat, and made it out of the big house without Naomi catching her in the foyer. Tanner's voice in her head had gone silent. Those were both good signs, weren't they?

The two-foot layer of smoke hugging the ceiling of the bar was so heavy that the ceiling fan didn't do anything but stir it a bit. Blake Shelton was belting out "Goodbye Time" from the jukebox. All of the lyrics didn't relate to Betsy's situation, but the one where he sang that it was good-bye time sounded loud and clear in her heart.

She slid into the only empty bar stool, pointed to the Jameson, and held up one finger. Rosalie set a red plastic cup in front of her and generously poured more than two fingers, wiped the moisture from a longneck bottle of beer, and put it on the bar.

"You know me too well, but no beer tonight. Just a shot of Mr. Jameson to warm me up." Betsy smiled.

"I know when you're all dressed up like that you are on the prowl, and I haven't seen a cowboy in here tonight that will take your eye without twice that much whiskey and two or three beers in your gut. Pickin's are slim, darlin', unless you want to take a peek at the Brennan table. That Declan would give a holy woman a case of hot flashes." Rosalie smiled.

Betsy sipped the whiskey, letting the warmth slide down her throat. It didn't create the fire that Declan's kiss had, but the night was young.

"I came to dance," she said.

"Vertically or horizontally?"

"Depends on who wins."

"Who's in the fight?" Rosalie asked.

"Heart and mind."

"You might want to rethink that one-shot idea. That's a tough fight. You know what they say about the heart, right?"

A blast of cold air brought four cowboys into the bar and let a little of the smoke escape at the same time. A tall, dark one with brown eyes, scuffed boots, and a sexy swagger took her eye. He hung his hat and denim jacket on an empty hook and slung a bar towel over his shoulder.

"Looks like you really do need some help, Miz Rosalie," he said.

"Betsy, I'd like to introduce my son-in-law, Bart.

Married to my oldest daughter. He's going to run the bar tonight and let me do the cookin'." Rosalie grinned.

"Just my luck," Betsy said.

"What was that?" Bart asked.

"Pleased to meet you," she said over the top of the fast song on the jukebox.

She slid a couple of bills toward him. "I'm paying for a double shot of Jameson."

"Thanks," Bart said.

She hopped down from the bar stool, picked up her red cup, and headed back to where several Gallaghers had claimed a table. Tanner pointed to an empty chair, but a cowboy caught her on the way, wrapped his hands around her waist, and started swaying to an old song called "Country Bumpkin."

"I'll be your country bumpkin, darlin', for tonight or forever. God, you're the prettiest thing I've ever laid my eyes on. My name is Jimmy Ray, and I hail from over the river up in Grandfield, Oklahoma. Go home with me and I'll be the luckiest man on the earth."

She nodded toward Tanner and her cousins. "Nice to meet you, Jimmy Ray from Grandfield. My family is waiting for me."

"You are Betsy Gallagher? I heard you was the prettiest thing this side of the Red River, but they was lyin'. You are the most gorgeous woman in the whole state," Jimmy Ray stuttered.

"Thanks for the compliments."

"Here, let me carry your drink to the table and, Miz Betsy, may I have this dance? They're playin' our song."

Left standing in the middle of the crowded dance floor, she scanned the room for the Brennan table. Sure enough, there was Declan, sitting with his back to the wall. Her chest tightened. Declan was dressed in all black that night: black jeans that hugged his thighs, shined black boots, and a black shirt with white pearl snaps glowing in the semidarkness. His sandy hair was feathered back, but one sexy, little strand had fallen down on his forehead. Her mouth went dry when he winked slyly. Her heart fluttered, letting her know that it hadn't thrown in the towel just yet and that the battle with it and common sense was not over by any means.

Time stood still and even though it was seconds before Jimmy Ray returned, it felt like she and Declan had lived a whole lifetime in those moments. Then suddenly, Jimmy Ray, with his dark-brown hair worn a little too long, green eyes, and cute little goatee, had her in his arms, and they were swing dancing to "Honky Tonk Christmas."

"How did this get to be our song?" She smiled up at him.

"I came here to get over a woman who left me last spring, just like this song says, and you're going to put her out of my mind. We're in a honky-tonk and it's talkin' about playin' Christmas records on the jukebox in an old honky-tonk. You are my lucky charm," he said.

"But what if you aren't my charm?" she asked.

"That's up to you to decide, but if you give me a chance, darlin', I can charm you seven ways to Sunday," Jimmy Ray said.

"I'll think about it," she said.

"One more dance, then. This could be our song too."

"How do you know that?"

"I'm the one who loaded the jukebox, and this is the

last song I plugged in, so it's my lucky song." George Strait's voice came through loud and clear as he sang "When It's Christmas Time in Texas."

Jimmy Ray swung her out, lost grip of her hand, and suddenly, another cowboy grabbed it and brought her to his chest.

"Hello, Miz Betsy," Declan said.

Her hand tingled, her pulse raced, jitters danced around in her stomach, and she couldn't take her eyes off his lips.

"You are gorgeous tonight. See you later."

He twirled her out, and she landed back in Jimmy Ray's arms. The flutters stopped as suddenly as they'd begun.

"One for the heart. Zero for the mind," she said.

"What was that?" Jimmy Ray asked.

"I'm thirsty. After this one, I'm sitting out a couple."

"Then I'll work on making you jealous by dancing with a few more women, but, honey, I swear you've got the winning ticket. You just tap me on the shoulder and I'll follow you anywhere."

"How long you been practicing that line?"

"Five years. Since my first date, when I was a sophomore in high school."

Sweet Jesus! The kid was barely old enough to drink.

She laughed. "Well, you keep practicin' a few more years, honey, and I bet it works for you someday but not this one. You have yourself a good night and good luck."

His hand went over his heart and he shut his eyes. "And I didn't even get a kiss. Couldn't I just have one kiss for all the leather I've danced off my boots?"

Betsy shook her head. "No, sir. Not even one kiss."

He leaned forward. "But when you walked in the door, I bet all my friends over there at that table I could get a dance with you and a kiss before I left the dance floor."

"Pay 'em up, sweetheart. And don't ever make a bet that relies on anything from a redheaded woman. We're meaner than a den of hungry rattlesnakes." She pinched his cheek and tousled his hair. "You are cute, but you were still playing in a sandbox when I went off to college."

"Age is just numbers on paper," he argued.

"Nice try, Jimmy Ray. Enjoy your Saturday night." She turned around, took two steps, and sat down in the chair beside Tanner.

Eli handed him five dollars.

"What's that all about?"

"Kid told us he had a bet going with his friends. Crazy fools thought you'd feel sorry for him and kiss him. I know you better." Tanner chuckled.

She whipped the bill from his hand and tucked it into her pocket. "Don't ever use me to make money on a bet, Cousin, or it will come back and bite you square on the butt."

A drummer without a sense of rhythm was beating out a rock tune in Declan's head when he awoke on Sunday morning. The mother of all hangovers reminded him of why he should not chase every shot of Jack Daniels with a bottle of beer. He inched his hand across the sheets before he even opened his eyes. He didn't remember leaving Burnt Boot Bar and Grill with a woman, but it could have happened.

The coast was clear, so he opened one eye, expecting to be in a motel either in Gainesville or across the Red River at the casino hotel if he'd really been wiped out.

He sat up so quick that the room did a triple spin right along with his stomach. "Thank God!" he mumbled when he realized he was in his own bed, right there on Wild Horse.

"I'm a lucky man," he said as he reached for his jeans and checked his wallet to make sure all the credit cards and money were still there.

"Yes, you are." His father, Russell, poked his head in the door. "I heard you staggering up the steps last night. Let you sleep until the chores were done, but now it's time to get ready for church or explain to your grandmother why you aren't going."

"Tell her I have a headache. It's not a lie."

"There're bananas on the buffet, and eggs. Don't forget to take three aspirin with you." Russell leaned against the doorjamb. "What's her name?"

"Who?"

"Whatever woman has you this messed up."

"No one. I'm fine. I'll be down soon as I get a shower and brush my teeth."

Russell chuckled. "A woman is the only thing that would make you stagger and come home singing something about the more you drink."

Declan held his head in his hands. "Blake Shelton. It's all his fault."

"The country singer? Was he at the bar last night?"

"Only on the jukebox. I didn't intend to drink a drop. I just went for a good time. And then...well, then I got frustrated and started doing shots with beer backs."

Russell shook his head. "I'm just glad there's not a big brunette in your bed."

"So you've heard the song?"

"Yep, but Blake does a better job of it than you do. Who brought you home?"

"I drove myself. Real slow, with Quaid driving right behind me. He offered to help me in the house, but I didn't think I was that drunk," Declan said.

"Well, Son, it's time to get downstairs to breakfast, or else your grandmother will be up here fussin' at you for the way your eyes look," Russell said as he closed the door.

"Banana and then eggs and three aspirin," Declan recited his father's remedy for a hangover. Just thinking about eating a banana turned his stomach, but it had worked in the past, and he had confidence that by the time the preacher got wound up in the Sunday morning service, his headache would be gone. Maybe when the headache was gone, it would take the heartache with it.

Dream on, big brother, Leah's voice said loud and clearly in his head.

"This bet is going to kill me," he said as he stood under the shower. "I should have listened to Quaid—both at the poker game and last night when he told me it was time to stop drinking."

Betsy was wedged between Tanner and her grandmother that morning in church. She'd picked out a cowboy old enough to take home when the bar shut down, but when they got to the parking lot and he laughed at her pink truck, it was like ice water had been poured on the whole thing. She'd sent him packing without even kiss.

Now she was cranky and wished she had someone to talk to about this whole mess. Tanner had always been her person, the cousin who was more like a brother that she'd talked everything out with, from boyfriends to which bull to buy for her own private herd. But she couldn't say a word to him or he'd find a way to kill Declan Brennan. The choir sang a song about putting your problems in a basket and taking them to Jesus. Betsy didn't have a basket, and besides, she'd learned from past experiences that it took too long for answers to come back from heaven.

She stole a glance across the middle section, where the O'Donnell families were all lined up on three different pews. Betsy's eyes kept wandering until she spotted Declan on the far side of the church. Every time Honey Brennan hit a high note in the choir, Declan shivered. So he had a hangover. Well, praise the Lord and let Honey sing louder. He was suffering too, even if his was physical and her pain was down deep in her heart.

Preacher Kyle took the podium and in a loud, booming voice, said, "Good morning."

Declan slapped a hand over one ear.

"This morning, I'm going to talk to you about how a person's life can do a complete one-hundred-and-eighty-degree turn in a matter of seconds. Just look at Adam. All it took was a moment to partake of the fruit of the forbidden tree. All it took was a few seconds for the serpent to talk Eve into taking the first bite," Preacher Kyle said softly as he leaned over the podium.

Tanner whispered, "Is he talking about that kid you

were dancing with last night or the one you let walk you to your car?"

"I went home alone. Did you?" she asked.

"Shhh." Naomi shot a dirty look their way.

Yes, she knew how things could turn in a second, and it usually involved forbidden fruit of some kind or shape. She gave up trying to listen to the preacher when he went into the story of Ruth and Naomi, and how, if Naomi hadn't left her country with her husband, then Ruth would have never married Naomi's son. Because she made a spur-of-the-moment decision to go back to Naomi's country with her, Ruth had a place in the lineage of Jesus.

Three times, he said "Naomi" in the span of a minute. That must mean that Betsy was supposed to consider her grandmother and put all this desire behind her. She should be concentrating on the ranch and her duties. Even if most men didn't make her insides go to mush, there were lots out there who'd be fine mates and fathers, who'd help her take care of Wild Horse.

Services ended with Rhett O'Donnell delivering the benediction, and afterward, as luck would have it, everyone was slow in standing up, so Betsy and her grandmother were among the first out of the church that morning.

"Fine sermon, Kyle," Naomi said as she pumped his hand up and down. "I hope the young people were listening and think before they bite into that forbidden fruit."

"So do I, Miz Naomi," he said.

"A word in private," Betsy whispered.

"Wait for me in my office. You can come in the

back door and go through the hallway if you like," he said softly.

"Hey, Tanner, can you give Granny a ride home? I've got dinner plans with my college friend, Iris," Betsy asked.

"Sure thing," Tanner said. "You should bring Iris to dinner sometime. You've talked about her for years and we've never met her."

"She's shy, and I sure don't want her around you," Betsy said.

"Come on, now. I'll be nice."

"That is exactly why I haven't brought her home to meet all y'all."

Betsy waited until most of the Gallaghers had gone before she made her way around to the back of the church, let herself inside, and tiptoed through the hallway to Kyle's office door.

She eased it open and sat down in a chair across from his. Crossing one leg over the other, she thought about what she was going to say. Would she be honest, or would she tell him that her friend Iris had this terrible problem? She was so thankful for her imaginary college friend.

The north wind whipped a tree branch against the window at the same time the door opened. She turned slightly, expecting to see the round, ever-smiling face of Preacher Kyle. But she looked up at Declan Brennan instead.

"What are you doing here?" he asked.

"I might ask you the same thing," she said coolly, but her heart raced.

Chapter 7

"Well, I see you are both here." The preacher breezed into the room. He loosened his tie and hung his jacket over the back of his chair before he sat down. "Ahh, it's always good to sit after delivering a sermon. I've been invited to Fiddle Creek for dinner with Sawyer, Jill, Polly, and Gladys. They said it will be thirty minutes, but I can call them if you need more time. Your problems are more important than my growling stomach."

"She's a Gallagher." Declan slumped into the other chair.

"He's a Brennan."

"Well, now that we've established the lineage and DNA, what else has you in here?"

Declan set his jaw so hard that it ached. "I wanted to talk to you in private."

"So did I," Betsy said.

"But it's the same problem. I could see the looks you were giving each other across the church. Do you want to stop this idea of the Christmas program?"

"No," Declan said. He'd wanted to talk to the preacher about his feelings, not put an end to the program.

Betsy shook her head and smoothed the wrinkles from her long, denim skirt.

"I kissed her in the movie theater. We can't meet at the church to put our Christmas stuff in the back room because someone saw us, so we met at the movies and her cousins came in, so I kissed her and pulled up the hood of her jacket to cover her hair so that he wouldn't know we were together." Declan kept his eyes straight ahead and didn't look at Betsy.

"I kissed him back," Betsy said.

"This is not a confessional. I'm not going to make you do penance for kissing each other. You are both consenting adults, and kissing does not make babies. It can lead to what does make them, but again, you are consenting adults, so what's the problem?"

Declan had wanted to bare his soul about the bet and ask Kyle's advice on what to do about that before it went another day further, but he sure couldn't mention it in front of Betsy. She might be a member of the family that was his family's archrival, but no woman deserved to find out she'd been the object of a bet.

"We've decided to rent a storage space to put the donated items in, rather than bringing them to the church. Since we can't sneeze without everyone in town bringing us chicken soup, we thought it would be best to do it that way," Declan said.

Kyle smiled. "Excellent idea."

"But I'll still bring the programs into the church for you on Thursday. I kind of like sitting in the quiet sanctuary alone and thinking," Betsy said.

"Thank you. Is the therapy session over, then?"

"Can I talk to you later? Alone?" Declan asked.

"Of course. How about later this afternoon, about three?"

"And me?"

"Four?"

She nodded.

"Okay, then. Let's go get some Sunday dinner and catch a nap before our chats. Remember, we don't have services tonight because both of your families will be lighting up their trees down on Main Street." Kyle stood up and reached for his jacket. "Next week, I'm leaving on Friday morning to go see my fiancée. We've got some wedding plans to work out. A friend of mine will be preaching. That's the sixth of December, but I'll be back by the thirteenth, and we'll take stock of what you've got gathered up that Sunday afternoon. At that time, you'll only have one more week to get it all done, so we can announce it on the Sunday before Christmas. How's it coming so far?"

"Pretty good. I've got twenty items," Declan answered.

"I've got fifteen," Betsy said.

"It's amazing what a little bit of work can accomplish." Kyle ushered them out the door, following them, and locked it. "See you later. And I don't need to know the location of the storage locker until it's time to get the things and bring them to the church. You might want to leave separately, or the whole town will have you married by morning."

"So what are you doing for Sunday dinner?" Declan asked Betsy.

"I'm meeting my friend Iris. You?"

"I don't want to go home, so I'm going to grab a burger in Gainesville and hang out at the kiddy zoo until time to talk to Kyle."

"I'll meet you at the zoo," she said.

"What about Iris?"

"She'll understand. I want to talk about this thing between us before I talk to Kyle," she said.

Declan reached out and ran his knuckles down her cheekbone. "Me too. I'll wait for you at the entrance."

~

Betsy ordered a double bacon burger with extra bacon, sweet potato fries, and a chocolate shake, then drove straight to the children's zoo. She parked her truck in the nearly empty parking lot. Not a lot of people would brave the north wind and gray skies to take their kids to pet goats on a Sunday afternoon—especially not on the Sunday when ninety percent of the population was busy decorating their Christmas trees.

Declan parked across the lot from her and carried his paper bag of food over to her truck. She appreciated his self-confidence and courage. Most men wouldn't be caught dead even touching her hot-pink truck, but he climbed right in and made himself at home in the passenger's seat.

"What'd you get?" he asked.

She pulled the ticket from the bag and handed it to him.

"I'll be damned. We ordered the same thing except I got a strawberry shake. I love sweet potato fries." He took a thick burger from the sack, removed the paper wrapper, and took his first bite.

She did the same. "Pretty good Sunday dinner. I get tired of steaks or ham or big meals sometimes."

"Me too," he said. "Now, about that kiss."

"It knocked my socks off. I liked it, but no more, Declan. We aren't love struck teenagers with big ideas of changing the world. This thing in Burnt Boot hasn't changed in a hundred years, and it won't in another hundred."

"I agree. Whew! Those fries are hot."

"Blow on them," she said.

"If I blow on the fire between us, you reckon that would put it out?" he asked.

When she looked up, his blue eyes went all soft and dreamy. "It's the danger, the secret, and the fact that we are both forbidden fruit, like the preacher talked about. If we were normal people, as in not Gallaghers or Brennans, we probably wouldn't even feel like this. It was one kiss, and it's over now. We'll get this business of Christmas finished and go our separate ways."

"Who are you trying to convince—me or you?"

"Both of us. Now eat your sweet potatoes. They get soggy when they get cold, and it'll happen fast in this weather. Look!"

Betsy pointed, and Declan jerked his head up, expecting to see either Mavis or Naomi or both coming at them with shotguns locked and loaded. But no one was there, not even a parking lot pigeon begging bread crumbs.

"It's snowing, Declan."

"Yes, it is. It's early for the first snow, but that's sure enough what it is. Turn on the radio and see if we can catch a weather report."

She punched a button and "Let It Snow" blared loudly. She quickly adjusted the volume and said, "It's an omen. We're going to have a white Christmas, and Angela is going to have her nativity scene at the church. It's all going to work out."

"I always thought you were a spitfire, but there's a soft heart hiding inside all that bluster," he said softly.

"Kind of like the wind out there, but the snowflakes are soft and delicate right in the midst of it."

She laughed. "Why, Declan Brennan, you are a hopeless romantic, not a womanizer at all."

"Shhh. Don't tattle on me. I rather like the reputation I have. Don't you?"

"Like your reputation or mine?"

"Either or both."

"I won't tell if you don't."

"So we're agreed, then. This is business and that's all?" he asked.

"Looks like that's the best."

"Shake on it?" He extended a hand.

She wiped hers on a napkin and was not one bit surprised at the reaction she had when his hand touched hers.

Declan pulled his hand free. "So we'll light up our community tree first this year. What are the Gallaghers going to do to ruin it?"

"I have no idea. I'm sick to death of this feud so I'm steering clear of the whole thing. I have to go because I'm the elf who takes the kids' pictures on Santa's knee, but I'm not getting in the middle of the crap. What are the Brennans going to do to retaliate? You'll have to do a lot to outdo last year, when your bull ruined our Santa Claus suit."

"So will y'all," Declan said. "I do remember a little red-haired kid from your side of the tracks who turned two mice loose on the table at our party."

"Granny was wrong!"

"About mice?"

"No, about Christian being the next red-haired

Gallagher after me. My cousin's demon child has red hair. I could strangle that kid on a good day. We won't talk about a bad day. He drives Granny crazy, so she probably doesn't want to claim him either."

"Hey, now, you are talking about a relative." Declan grinned.

"I don't claim him. I'd give him to the Brennans if they'd take him—or sell him to Wallace down in Salt Holler."

Declan shivered. "Don't say that about any kid. Granny used to threaten to give me to Wallace when I was a kid. Believe me, it straightened me up every time. I never did see that man when he didn't have on that bloody apron."

"Well, he does slaughter hogs for a living," Betsy said.

"He might be scary, but there's no feud in Salt Holler, so that's a good thing, right?"

Betsy stole one of his fries, because hers were all gone. "I might be putting in my application to move there real soon."

"I'll believe that when I see the moving van hauling your stuff away from Wild Horse. That would be a reverse Cinderella story for sure."

"What do you know about Cinderella?"

The door clicked and a few snowflakes landed on the seat as he crawled out of her truck. "I've got a sister, remember? Now that we've decided what we're going to do in the future about the past, I've got an errand to run, and then it'll be time for my visit with Kyle."

Betsy couldn't keep her eyes off him as he crossed the short distance from her truck to his. That cowboy swagger was so damned sexy, it sent shivers down her backbone, but then she imagined he affected most women that way. With those dreamy eyes, plus those muscular arms and sandy-brown hair—she shook her head and made herself stop listing all the reasons why women were attracted to him. All it did was create more problems, and Betsy damn sure didn't need any more trouble on her plate.

She wished that a genie would pop out of the trash. If that happened, she wouldn't even have to think twice about what she'd ask for—it would be that Declan was not a Brennan.

Chapter 8

A SNOWFLAKE TO THE ACRE RODE THE NORTH WIND down from gray skies while Declan hunched his shoulders against the cold and waited. He was about to give up and go home when the preacher rounded the corner of the church and held up a key.

"I'm so sorry. I thought I'd just take a little power nap and it turned into an hour-long siesta. That turkey pot pie set heavy on my stomach and put me into a sound sleep."

Declan followed him into the church. "Very understandable. Leftover-turkey pie is one of my favorite dishes. I like it even better than the Thanksgiving turkey."

"After Christmas, my fiancée, Lindsey, will be joining me in the parsonage, and she's a good cook. You'll have to come to our place for dinner sometime. Come on in the office. It's warmer than the church. I turn down the thermostat to save on electricity after services are over, but I keep the office warm with a little space heater." Kyle talked as he made his way through the sanctuary.

Both cowboy and preacher removed heavy coats and hung them on a rack with four hooks. Declan's black cowboy hat went on another hook, and Kyle tucked his stocking hat inside his coat pocket.

"Now have a seat and tell me all about this problem between you and Betsy. I'm sensing it goes even deeper than the feud." Kyle pushed his glasses up his nose, ran a hand down one side of his round face, sat down, and got right to the heart of the matter.

Declan fidgeted in his chair, picked at a piece of sawdust that had stuck to his boots, and cleared his throat. Would it be a breach of his promise to tell what happened at the poker game?

"When you're ready," Kyle said.

"It happened like this," Declan started, and the words spilled out as he described the game, the way the feelings were running strong, and the bet.

"Wow!" Kyle said when Declan finished.

"And that was only a week ago, and I like Betsy. I know I should tell her what happened and be honest, but if I do, the Christmas thing will be finished. She'll either shoot me or rake me over hot coals, but she won't work with me. I didn't even care if there was a program at the church, but it means so much to her that I want her to have it. I'm rambling and not making a bit of sense." Declan ran his fingers through his hair and bit his lower lip, two telltale signs that he was nervous. He quickly dropped his hand to his thigh and clamped his teeth tightly together.

"You're making far more sense than you realize. Did you just want to talk, or do you want my advice?" Kyle asked.

"I'd like your opinion," Declan answered slowly.

"First answer a question. Is this totally business?"

"She says it is."

"Then let it ride itself out until the weekend before Christmas. I'll borrow a flatbed and truck from Sawyer and go get all the stuff you both have collected on

Saturday, and you can tell her then. That way, she'll have her Christmas, and you need to be miserable for making a bet like that, so you'll have your penance. This feud needs to stop," Kyle said.

Declan nodded. "I'd like nothing better, but I sure don't see it happening."

Kyle glanced toward the clock. "Looks like it's Betsy's turn, and then we'll go to the tree lighting. I'm glad you felt like you could talk to me, Declan. I'm here for more than preaching on Sunday morning."

They heard the church doors squeaking. Declan pushed out of the chair, picked up his hat, draped his coat over his arm, and said, "Thank you, Kyle. Reckon I could book another session next Sunday."

"I won't be here then, remember? But I'll make a note that you're coming to see me on the thirteenth at three. I'll even try not to oversleep."

Kyle turned around at the door. "What day are you getting married?"

"The last day of the year. It's a Friday, and we're planning a short, little honeymoon on a warm island. I'll be absent from church on the first Sunday in January, but we'll be settled in the parsonage by the next weekend."

"Why the last day of the year?" Kyle asked.

"We wanted to start the New Year out as a couple." He smiled brightly.

Declan's heart threw in an extra beat when he saw Betsy sitting in the front pew, waiting her turn. She'd pulled her hair back into its normal ponytail and wore an old mustard-colored work coat over her cute little denim skirt.

"Your turn," he said.

"What did you tell him?"

He propped a hip on the corner of the pew. "What goes on behind closed doors is private."

"Maybe that's a good thing," she said.

"I think it is. I'm finding a storage unit tomorrow. Remember to look for the address in the can."

When she looked up at him with those green eyes, he came close to spitting out the truth right there and not waiting until they'd gotten the things gathered for the Christmas program.

"I'd rather you called me. I'm careful with my phone," she said.

"And if by chance Naomi grabbed it before you could get to it and saw my name? You think you'd live to see your new little cousin in the role of baby Jesus?"

She inhaled deeply and let it all out in a whoosh. "It's just so crazy, but then, so is what we are doing. I should be going. Kyle is waiting."

"I'll probably see you tonight. Wouldn't it be something if everything went all smooth and folks forgot about the feud in the spirit of the holiday?"

"The sun would stand still in the sky or all the pigs from Salt Holler would sprout wings and fly if that happened."

He chuckled and headed toward the door but stopped long enough for one backward glance at her. Did she even realize how much her sexy hip sway made a man's mouth go as dry as if he'd eaten an alum sandwich?

Kyle motioned her into the office with a wave of his hand. "Take off your coat and hang it on the rack. Getting colder by the minute isn't it?"

Betsy nodded. "It's spitting snow out there, but that's a nice touch to the Christmas tree lighting tonight. It's always nice when it's cold. There's been some years when it was so warm that everyone showed up without jackets, and we had to turn on the air-conditioning to keep Santa from sweltering in that heavy suit."

"Tell me about this Christmas tree thing. I've lived in towns where they put a tree in the center of town and put up all kinds and sort of decorations, but this is something new," he said.

She removed her coat and hung it over the back of a chair before she sat down. "You've never lived in a feuding town, have you?"

He shook his head.

"The Gallaghers and the Brennans can't agree on anything. Years before I was born, the folks wanted to put a tree right in the middle of town, like you just said, but the feuding families wouldn't compromise about who got to put it up, who got to decorate it. They even argued about who got to plug in the lights." She sighed.

She paused and took in the office. An old wooden desk that had probably seen better days back when the feud first started, a chair that had duct tape on the arms to cover the holes, and carpet so worn she could see the webbing holding it together in places. It should have had a decent desk, maybe even a credenza over against the wall behind her, to hold his wedding pictures. This place was a disgrace to the whole town of Burnt Boot.

Kyle wasn't the first preacher she'd heard preach from the pulpit, but he might be the sweetest, with his baby face and thinning, light-brown hair. He had a way about him that made a person either want to bare their souls or take him home for dinner. Burnt Boot was lucky to get him and she hoped that he and his new wife would be happy in the parsonage for years and years.

"I'm sorry. I was woolgathering," she said. "Back to the story. So the Brennans declared they'd put up their own personal tree and the Gallaghers did the same. The Brennans always have had the space in front of the store, and the Gallaghers put theirs up at the bar. Since the Brennans come from pious people who did not drink in those days, they have a whole array of finger foods, punch, coffee, hot chocolate, Christmas cookies, and other good things to eat at their party, which is set up inside the store."

"And the Gallaghers?" he asked when she paused.

"We provide Santa Claus and pictures of the kids sitting on his knee. Plus, we give out bags of fruit and nuts and maybe a little toy of some kind. And Santa Claus plugs in the tree. We play Christmas carols from the back of a flatbed, and it's not a bit unusual for folks to be dancing in the parking lot."

"And the feud?"

"The bar and the store are neutral territory, so everyone is invited to both."

"But there're usually problems?"

She nodded. "I absolutely hate this feud. Something always happens at the Christmas tree party. I think folks come from miles away to see the feud show, rather than enjoying what Christmas means."

Kyle slipped off his shoes and set them beside his desk. "Maybe the surprise will be that everything will go well this year."

"I wouldn't hold my breath if I were you."

He propped his feet on the desk and leaned back. "Pardon my socks, but my shoes are new, and they aren't broken in yet. You wanted to talk about something other than lighting up Christmas trees?"

Betsy didn't know where to begin. She opened her mouth, but words didn't come out, so she shut it and scanned the office again. It was a shame that their preacher had such a terrible place to work—especially when she compared it to the office that she sat in at Wild Horse. Maybe she and Declan should work on taking up donations for decent things for his office after they finished the Christmas project.

"Okay, I'm ready," she said.

"No hurry."

"Declan is that forbidden fruit that you talked about in church this morning."

"Forbidden by God or by the Gallaghers? They both start with the same letter, but there's a big difference," Kyle said.

She finally smiled. "Maybe in your eyes, but don't you let my granny hear you say it, or you might be looking for a new job."

"I was looking when I found this one. God takes care of his children. I understand why you think Declan is forbidden fruit, but tell me: Why do you care since this is only a business deal?"

She hated it when she fidgeted, but she had a hard time controlling it. "Because I've had this crush on him for years and because I liked that kiss. I liked it a lot and I wanted more. There's something between us that goes beyond danger and secrecy. I'd like to get to know him even better, but there's a line drawn in the dirt, and I can't cross it."

"Why can't you cross the line?" Kyle asked.

"To take one step over it would mean I'd have to give up my place on Wild Horse and my future. So this has to be totally business and no one can ever know we did it together," she answered.

"What you have to pray about is the fork in the road, Betsy. There are two paths in front of you. One will bring you happiness; the other will bring you security. It's your choice and only you can make the decision."

"Tell me which one to take," she begged.

"It's not for me to do. You can ponder it for a few weeks. You don't have to make the decision now or even next week or this year. But someday, you'll have to get off the log and start walking."

"Do you think I'll take the right path?"

Kyle's shoulders raised a couple of inches. "I hope so, but whichever one you decide to follow, don't ever look back with regrets. That would ruin your future for sure."

"Thank you. I've got to get home and put on my costume. I'm the elf who takes the pictures tonight," she said.

"I'm glad to listen anytime, Betsy, and I'll be praying that your choice is the right one and that you enjoy the journey your path takes you on."

"Thanks again," she said.

She picked up her coat and headed back through the church, not sure if she'd gotten help or if she was more confused than before she talked to the preacher.

Chapter 9

Decorated with blinking Christmas lights all around the windows and the porch posts, the general store looked festive that evening. Garland had been strung around the two gas pumps, and the parking lot was already full when Declan arrived. He found a spot at the back of the store and nosed his truck into it. Weaving his way through the vehicles and people to the porch, where a dozen men huddled together, he was glad that it was cold that night because it brought out the Christmas spirit.

The bits and pieces of comments that he heard didn't do much for his holiday cheer though. Everyone seemed to be less concerned about lighting trees than they were about what the Gallaghers might do that evening to keep the feud going. If anything was going to happen it would come from them, since the Brennans always got the honor of lighting their tree first. Declan ignored them and made his way into the busy store, where Sawyer and Jill were sitting behind the checkout counter.

A space in the front of the store where the grocery carts were usually parked had been cleared for an eight-foot table. Covered in a festive, red-plaid cloth, every inch was covered with Christmas cookies, finger sandwiches, and all kinds of Christmas candy. Red punch filled a crystal bowl at one end and two tall coffeemakers sat on the other, one with hot chocolate and one with spiced tea. A big pot of coffee sat in the display window along with extra supplies for the party. The store was packed with people, but Declan quickly spotted Rhett and Leah leaning against the counter talking to Sawyer and Jill.

He wound through the crowd and then leaned back, arms on the counter beside Leah. "No shenanigans yet?"

"I've been watching for that little hellion that turned the mice loose last year. I can spot that red hair real easy," Leah said. "But so far, so good. Maybe the grannies have decided to let sleeping dogs lie."

"I doubt that, but I'm real glad that the food isn't getting thrown all over the store," Declan said.

"Me too. I don't want to clean it up," Sawyer chuckled. "Another twenty minutes and then we'll lock the doors and go outside to light up the tree. Did you see the nativity scene they've got out there on a flatbed?"

"Granny sprung for a big show this year, since she's being so stubborn about giving anything to the church. She says when the party is over, she's taking the nativity scene back to the ranch and leaving it on display until after the holidays," Leah said.

Declan peered out the window and wondered how in the world he'd walked right past that thing and never even noticed it. True, there was always a flatbed trailer, so whoever was announcing the lighting could stand up there and talk over the noise with a microphone.

The figures were life-size and looked as if they could have been hand-painted. Mary, Joseph, baby Jesus in his manger, three shepherds, three wise men, a drummer boy, and even a star had been suspended from a tree branch to shine above the shed. His grandmother hadn't said a word about a buying a nativity to him, but then she wouldn't. She'd have known that he'd have argued that she should give the money to the church, so the whole town could enjoy their traditional program.

"Beautiful, isn't it, Declan?" Mavis said at his elbow.

"Expensive is more like it," Declan said tightly.

"Yes, it was, and I'm going to enjoy it for many years, both here and at the ranch. I plan to put it out by the road, so when you drive into the lane, there are lots of pretty lights. That way, folks can drive past it and enjoy it during the whole season." Mavis smiled.

"It is lovely," Leah said.

Mavis didn't even acknowledge that her granddaughter had spoken.

"Granny, Leah made a comment," Declan said.

"I heard her," Mavis said before she went straight to the refreshment table, picked up a cookie, and smiled at her new favorite granddaughter, Honey.

Honey was a vision in a white velvet dress that hugged every curve on her tall, thin body. Her dark hair made a halo around a delicate face with bright-red lips and lovely blue eyes. She laid a hand on Mavis's shoulder and whispered a few words to her. Mavis nodded sorrowfully and kissed Honey on the cheek.

Declan pushed away from the counter and hugged Leah. "It's okay. She'll come around someday, and when she does, she's going to be sorry she treated you like this."

"Maybe. Maybe not. I have to do what I know is right to live with myself. The rest is up to her. Did you get a cookie?" Leah smiled up at him.

Declan hugged her tighter. "Don't want one. I can get better cookies at your house."

"That's the truth," Rhett agreed. "And she's already started making them, so come by anytime."

How on earth his grandmother could set her heels so hard against someone as good-natured as Rhett O'Donnell was a total mystery to Declan. The man had a little two-inch ponytail, a tat on his forearm, and rode a motorcycle, but that wasn't a solid reason to hate him, especially when he made Leah so happy. And Leah, bless her sweet heart, had never been unkind to anyone in her life. She deserved to be happy, and Declan had had just about enough of their grandmother treating her like dirt.

Everyone talked at once, and the sheer noise of the conversation echoed around the store until Declan was sure it would bulge the walls and blow out the windows. Then suddenly, everything got quiet, and folks started to file out of the store to watch the lighting of the Brennans' tree.

"Good evening, everyone," Quaid said into the microphone. "Isn't this nativity scene the most gorgeous thing you've ever seen? And my grandmother has told me to announce that it will be sitting close enough to the road as you turn up our lane to River Bend that everyone in Burnt Boot can drive past and enjoy it the whole holiday season."

Declan headed toward the door. "Looks like Quaid has started talking, so they'll light up the tree pretty soon. We might as well go on out there and join them."

Leah and Rhett got up slowly and followed him out of the store, with Sawyer and Jill following.

"Feels like we might get a big snow. Wouldn't it be something if we had two white Christmases in a row?" Leah asked.

"I ordered one special for you because I know how happy it would make you," Declan said.

Leah flashed him her most brilliant smile and looped her arm through his. "You are the best big brother ever."

"I smell gasoline. Someone must have spilled a few drops on the ground out at the pumps," Rhett said.

"It happens sometimes," Jill said.

Leah pointed at the ten-foot tree, laden with oversize ornaments and garland. "Think those ornaments will withstand the weather for a whole month?"

"They're tied on, rather than just hung, so maybe that'll give them a better chance," Declan answered. "But it always looks pretty bad on New Year's Day when we come to haul it away."

Quaid stood beside the tree with a microphone in one hand and an extension cord in the other. "If my cousin Honey will join me, we are going to ask her to do the honors tonight."

"Is that whiskey I smell?" Leah asked.

"You're imagining… No, I got a whiff of it too. Raw, cheap whiskey, not the good stuff. It almost smells like moonshine," Declan said. "Somebody has been celebratin' early."

Honey had donned a matching white velvet cape lined with snow-white, shimmering satin with a hood she covered her hair with. She looked every bit the part of an innocent angel up there on the flatbed trailer. "The Brennans would like to welcome you to Burnt Boot and wish you all a very Merry Christmas." She took the cords from Quaid and snapped them together, and hundreds of sparkling lights lit up the tree.

The crowd applauded.

Leah sighed.

Declan thought maybe a miracle had really happened because nothing had gone awry. Then *poof*. In an instant, the whole flatbed went up in flames. The poor shepherd's faces melted into scary monsters instead of smiling men dressed in brown. Applause turned to gasps and several children started to wail that someone had killed baby Jesus, so there wouldn't be Christmas.

Quaid quickly jumped off the trailer and held out his arms to help Honey. She jumped to the ground and hurried inside the store to get away from the smoke, while Quaid ran for the water hose beside the gas pumps. He turned on the faucet and began to spray, but it did little good.

"Alcohol and gasoline. It'll burn quick. Thank God for this wind. It will blow the stink on down south. And that's what Granny gets for being mean to you," Declan said.

"Don't say that, or she'll think I caused this," Leah whispered.

Jill sighed. "And I had a moment when I thought everything was going to go off smoothly."

"All that will be left is clumps of plastic." Leah grabbed her nose and ran back into the store as the crowd headed toward the bar, to the Gallaghers' tree lighting and party. The energy level was higher than ever as everyone now wondered what the Brennans would do in retaliation and would it happen that night or later?

"So what will y'all do to retaliate for this?" Rhett asked.

"I'm not doing a thing. Cookies are all gone, and there's very little punch left, but I do see a whole platter of ham and cheese sandwiches and lots of hot chocolate. The fire will be burned out by the time the fire department could get here from Gainesville, so let's lock the door and have a picnic of our own. I'm starved," Declan said.

"Sounds like a plan to me," Rhett said.

Declan's phone rang, but he ignored it. He was honest when he said he wanted nothing to do with the payback.

"Welcome, folks. Come right on into the bar, where we're serving coffee and doughnuts while we wait on Santa Claus to get here. He'll be arriving any minute, wearing his cowboy hat and riding a big, white horse this year. He said to tell all you little cowboys and cowgirls that Rudolph is on vacation right now, but he'll be home by Christmas Eve, and he'll be in his sleigh that night," Tanner announced from the back of a pickup truck. "Y'all enjoy the music and the refreshments while we wait. Mercy, what is that smell coming from up the street? Smells like the Brennan party got a little hot."

Laughter, catcalls, and whistles filled the air. The public had come for a show, and they'd have it, but there was no way the Brennans could top what the Gallaghers had just done. Tanner had even taken precautions in case the Brennans had another cattle stampede lined up. There was no flatbed at the Gallagher tree lighting that night. Tanner had moved his microphone and equipment to the bed of his pickup truck. No way would a bunch of cattle run over Santa Claus while he was lighting the tree if he was safe in the back of Tanner's big, club-cab truck.

Betsy scanned the crowd for Declan but couldn't find him. The news of the fire had made her angry and then teary. There were no holiday miracles, and if Mavis didn't have time to plan something that evening, she would make sure that Naomi got the full brunt of her anger in the next few days. Lord help them, she might even attempt to burn down the main house on Wild Horse.

Christmas music came through the speakers, and Tanner laid the microphone down. He hopped over the side and did some fancy swing dance steps with Betsy. It wasn't easy to match him step for step in her elf shoes, but she did her best and got a round of applause for her efforts.

"Ten minutes, folks," Tanner yelled without the help of the microphone. "I heard that Santa will be here in ten minutes. So you kids get your lists all memorized."

There was more applause as he threw an arm around Betsy's shoulders. "What do you think the Brennans will do? Have we covered all the bases? I heard through the gossip vine that Mavis spent more than ten thousand dollars on that nativity scene."

"Were you in on it?" Betsy asked as they made their way back inside the bar. She went to work checking the camera and making sure the computer was ready to print pictures.

"You know Granny. If we're chosen for a project, we aren't allowed to kiss and tell." He laughed. "Did you see Mavis's face? It melted as bad as those big old statues. One minute she was smiling at Honey, and the next she looked like an alien."

"Ten thousand plus dollars up in smoke," Betsy groaned. "Ten thousand dollars given to the church would have let us have all four of our regular programs.

And all the little kids were howling because baby Jesus was burning."

"Well, we'll make them happy that they have Santa Claus. And that'll teach those Brennans to run cattle through our party and ruin our Santa suit. We had to burn the costume and buy a new one this year," Tanner said and changed the subject. "You have a good time with Iris?"

"I always enjoy the time I spend with her," Betsy said. It wasn't a lie. When she was with her imaginary friend, there was no feud and no tension.

"Santa! We want Santa!" the chant outside grew louder and louder by the minute.

Tanner fished his phone from his hip pocket and hit the number to call Tyrell. It went straight to voice mail, so he said, "Hey, Santa Claus, your adoring public awaits. Call me and tell me how close you are. I'm going out there to let them know you're on the way."

Betsy should have gone out and worked the crowd, handing out candy canes and telling them that Santa would be riding in at any time. But her elf costume wasn't warm, and the wind was bitter cold. Besides, the soles of her elf shoes were nothing more than felt, and she could feel every rock in the gravel parking lot. She took her phone from the pocket of her tunic and dialed Tyrell's number, left a message, and looked at the clock. Surely he had the phone somewhere on him, and she had no doubt he could hear the thing ringing.

She waited one minute and dialed him again, then waited another minute and dialed again. Nothing. Nada. Where was he? The crowd was getting restless. Tanner could only appease them so long with promises, and they'd already gotten tired of Christmas music. They needed Santa Claus to wipe the vision of a burning baby Jesus from their minds.

She checked everything again. Camera ready. Printer full of photographic paper. Candy sacks all lined up to give away. All they needed was Santa. The Brennans couldn't get even until Santa arrived. Unless... She inhaled sharply. That's the way they were retaliating. They had stolen Santa Claus.

Naomi breezed out from behind the bar, where she'd been talking on her phone for the past half hour. Her eyes were barely slits and her face looked worse than Tanner had described Mavis's when the fire started. "I've called Tyrell a dozen times, and there isn't an answer. So I sent Eli, Randy, and Hart to see where he was. He's not at the ranch or on his way here. Those rotten Brennans have stolen our Santa Claus. I intend to kick Mavis's sorry butt all the way to the cemetery and make her dig her own grave."

"Granny, maybe he was running a little late. You know Tyrell is never on time. And maybe he took a different route that took longer."

"Nope, the Brennans have kidnapped him to retaliate for that fire. Now what are we going to do?" Naomi wrung her hands.

"I'll do the best I can," Betsy said.

She took a deep breath and wove her way through the thick crowd to the truck. Someone stepped forward and helped her up inside the bed with Tanner, and she took the microphone from his hands. "There's been an accident, folks. Seems Santa was thrown when a big, mean rattlesnake spooked the horse. He's been taken to the hospital to get his arm stitched up, so he can continue to work on toys until Christmas Eve. Don't worry. He just now talked to me on the phone and said that other than some mud in his pretty white beard and that cut on his arm, he's fine. But he wants me to sit in his chair and listen to what you want for Christmas. I've got a good memory, so I can tell him every single thing, and Tanner here is going to take the pictures. So line up and let's get this show on the road."

Tanner took the microphone from her hands. "Hey, kids, let's give a big shout up to the sky to Santa Claus for doing his best and remember to watch out for snakes."

The kids yelled so loud that if Tyrell really had been in a Gainesville hospital, he could have heard it.

"Where is he really?" Tanner whispered as he helped her over the side of the truck and followed her back into the bar.

"The Brennans have probably kidnapped him because of the fire. Hope it was worth it," Betsy said.

"We'll get even," Tanner said through gritted teeth.

At daybreak, Betsy got a phone call from Tyrell. The kidnappers had taken his beard and his Santa boots. He'd ridden to a motel on the north side of Dallas and rented a room. His horse was tied to a tree, and he was going to sleep until someone came to rescue them. He gave her the number on the phone beside his bed. "Call me after you talk to Granny, please."

Betsy sighed. "You could ride the horse home.

Granny might be cooled down enough to put away the shotgun by the time you got here."

"Quit teasing me and go tell Granny."

"Who says I'm joking? Why didn't you call her to begin with?"

"I know you can smooth it over with her. Come on, Betsy. I'll owe you one."

"And I will collect," she said as she hit the End button on the phone.

She stretched and knuckled her eyes before she went downstairs to talk to her grandmother. "Tyrell called," she said and gave Naomi the story and the motel's number.

Naomi reached for her phone as she spoke. "I'm going to murder Mavis one of these days."

On the way back up the stairs, her phone rang and a picture of Tyrell's smiling face appeared on the screen.

"Yes, Tyrell?" she said.

"Is she mad? Is she coming after me?"

"Yes, she's mad and if you beg, she might bring you home with that horse. She's more worried about him than you right now. What happened?"

"One minute, I was riding along humming 'Jingle Bells,' and the next, I was jerked off my horse and something stung my neck. I woke up in a barn with no boots. It's cold riding a horse ten miles with nothing but socks on your feet."

"At least you had your Santa suit to keep you warm. Were you aware of the fire?"

"It was my idea." He laughed.

"Paybacks are a bitch." She turned her phone off and went back to sleep.

Chapter 10

Betsy was glad there was turmoil in the house because no one even knew when she snuck out that evening or noticed that the backseat and passenger seats in her truck were filled with boxes. After a trip by a flooring store and an office supply place, she was on her way to the address written on the paper in her pocket.

The storage place turned out to be closer to Lindsey than Gainesville, and the units were behind a white, six-foot-high privacy fence with a coded entrance. Betsy took out the paper, rolled down the window, and punched in the numbers at the bottom. The gates swung to the inside, and there was Declan, down at the very end, with a couple of teenagers who were helping him take things from the back of his truck. He waved and propped an elbow on the front fender.

Was he crazy or stupid? Or did he have an acute case of both? For this to work, it had to be wrapped tightly in secrecy, and he'd brought help to unload? By the time she backed her truck in beside his, she was ready to strangle the cowboy.

"What are you thinking?" she fumed as she got out of her truck.

"Evidently the same thing as you. That's not Christmas in the back of your truck. I see carpet, a credenza thing, and a brand-new oak file cabinet, right?"

Her hands went to her hips and she would have gone nose to nose with him, but he was too damned tall. "I'm not talking about donations. Why did you bring those guys to help unload? This is a secret, remember?"

"I paid for the rental space and since I got the biggest one in the place, it comes with help as needed. Those two guys are the sons of the man who owns the place, and I doubt very much if they're interested in Burnt Boot. And has anyone ever told you that you are cute when you're mad?"

Desire replaced anger immediately when he grinned. "So what have you got to contribute to the cause?"

She playfully slapped his arm and brought back a tingling hand in a blast of brightly colored sparks. He grabbed her hand and pulled her against him so tightly that she could feel his racing heartbeat.

"Don't start something you can't finish," he said.

"Hey, Mr. Wiseman, does your wife need help with that big old cabinet before we leave?"

"Yes, she does," Declan said.

"Wiseman? Wife?" she whispered.

"Mr. and Mrs. Joseph Wiseman. It's the best I could do on the spur of the moment. And you are Mrs. Wiseman, don't forget it."

She pushed away from him and rounded the back of her truck, where she could see inside the storage place. There was a gorgeous new desk and two nice wingback chairs along with a black leather desk chair. "I guess you noticed the condition of Kyle's office too."

"I did and figured we could make it a two-for-one collection."

She peeked inside the storage unit and gasped. "Good

grief, Dec…I mean Joe. You could park a couple of semis in this thing."

"It was the last one we had." The guys brought in the file cabinet and started to put it among the things they'd already unloaded.

"Oh, no, that goes on this side." Betsy pointed.

The guys looked at Declan, who shrugged and chuckled. "The wife and I are having a competition."

"What does the winner get?"

Declan wiggled his eyebrows, and they both laughed.

They brought in the rolled carpet next and laid it on Betsy's side.

"I'd work real hard if I were you, man," the tallest one said.

"I really want to win, so I am working hard." Declan nodded and handed them each a ten-dollar bill. "Just a little something for all the work."

"But we come with the territory. Our daddy pays us well, but we thank you," the shorter one said.

"We can get the rest of it. You guys go on," Betsy said.

"Yes, ma'am, and good luck on the competition."

She waited until they were gone to look around. The whole thing was the size of four normal storage units, half the size of a small warehouse. Even with the new desk taking up space on his side, it still looked empty. Her thirty items weren't going to fill up much more space.

It was as if he'd read her mind when he said, "We still got time to bring in more stuff, and we don't have to wait until Thursday if we have a truckload. And I promise, it was the last unit available at a place with a privacy fence. That pink truck of yours could be spotted a mile away."

She paced off the distance from one wall to the other and stared back. "This is the halfway mark, right here at that stud. I'll mark it so we'll know which side belongs to the Brennans and which to the Gallaghers."

Declan's nostrils flared in anger. "I thought this was a joint effort. I didn't realize it was part of the feud that you keep saying you hate so much."

She whipped around to face him, her green eyes flashing. "It is a joint effort, but how else do we mark our territory? You are a Brennan, and I am a Gallagher."

He stormed outside, gulped in lots of cold air, grabbed the duct tape from the back of his truck, and met her coming out as he started back inside. "You wouldn't happen to have some paper in your truck, would you?"

"I thought you'd left," she said.

"Not without settling this. You want a division, we'll have it, but it's got nothing to do with the feud. Understand?"

Betsy nodded, but her expression said she could still chew up his belt like beef jerky. "What do you want paper for?"

"We need two sheets. Size does not matter. I'll show you rather than tell you," Declan said coldly.

The stud she'd used to mark the center of the space had a green streak on it, probably where someone had scraped it with a piece of painted furniture. Declan had seen it when she was stepping off the distance, so he used that as his reference. When she returned, he was laying out a line of duct tape from one side to the other.

"I guess that's good enough. Here's the paper you asked for," she said.

"Hold on to it until I get finished," he said and then added, "Please."

She sat down in one of the office chairs and waited. When he finished, he held out his hand, and she put the paper in it. He whipped a pen from his pocket and wrote "Wife" on one piece and "Husband" on the other and taped them down firmly at the corners right under the steel beam with the green smudge.

When she gasped, all the anger left his body and he chuckled. "You wanted a division. Now you've got it. No feuding in this place."

"Just writing that could bring the wrath of two families down on your head, Mr. Wiseman." She smiled.

He sat down in the other office chair and said, "Yes, it could, Mrs. Wiseman, but this is a secret, remember? And a wife can never testify against her husband, or him against her, so this will keep us safe."

Declan could hardly keep his eyes off the way her jacket fell to the sides, bookending breasts encased in a tight, dark-green knit shirt. It was the same color as her eyes and enhanced her thick, red hair.

"You ever think about being a wife?" Declan asked.

"Granny thinks about it enough for both of us," she answered. "What about you?"

"Those kind of thoughts scare the devil out of me." He grinned.

Betsy laughed—not a giggle, not a chuckle, but one of those bursts that come from the gut and soul. Declan liked the sound of it as it bounced around the cavernous space surrounding them.

"But now a husband," he went on, "is something I hear about daily, especially now that Leah is married. I should be settling down and having a family. The ranch depends on me, and I need a wife to help me do that. I told Granny that she was training Honey to run the ranch and no house was big enough for two women. Know what she said?"

Betsy nodded emphatically. "To build your own house and fill up a yard with little Brennans to carry on the feud when she was gone."

"They're an awful lot alike to be such enemies, aren't they?"

"That statement could bring down the wrath as much as the two words on that paper." She laughed again. "But yes, they are alike. And so are all their offspring. We're all ranchers, all go to church, and the kids in our families go to the same school."

Who would have thought that a storage unit with boxes of Christmas decorations and office furniture could be so peaceful? Or that sitting in it with Betsy Gallagher could make him happier than he'd ever been in his life? Maybe it was because they'd left the feud outside and they were just a man and a woman, Mr. and Mrs. Wiseman, enjoying a quiet Monday evening.

"I hear you loud and clear," Declan said.

"I don't think the rest of my stuff is going to unload itself," she finally said.

"Or mine. I only had the guys help with what was in the back of the truck. Want to get some ice cream after this and take it to the parking lot at the kid's zoo?"

"It's too cold for ice cream," she said as she pushed up out of the chair.

"Then how about hot sweet potato fries?"

Her eyes glittered in the dimly lit room. "And a latte from Starbucks to chase it?"

He followed her out of the building. "Or a bottle of Jack to share. That would warm us up real good."

She opened the back door of her truck and took out the first box. "After last night, I don't think Granny would get a single one of us out of jail if we got caught drunk driving. That was some stunt, stealing Santa Claus like y'all did. And besides, she's made me promise to drink less."

"Holy smoke, Betsy. I didn't think anyone had that kind of power over you."

"It was to shut her up more than anything else. Don't stand there and tell me that you haven't done things to shut your granny up," she said.

He threw up both palms defensively. "More than once, and for the record, I didn't even know about Santa getting kidnapped until this morning. And, I might add, that was some stunt y'all did, burning baby Jesus down to nothing but a big clump of stinky plastic. But we leave all that at the door, Mrs. Wiseman. In our new home, we are not Brennans or Gallaghers, but the Wiseman couple who are collecting things for our church."

What would it be like if that were really true, if they were two normal people, say with names like Jones and Smith? Could Declan, or any other man, live with the fiery Betsy Gallagher?

"What an idea," he mumbled, not knowing she was right behind him.

"Idea?" she asked.

"Just thinking out loud."

"Be careful. That could get you in a whole mess of

trouble. So what all did you collect? Did you make a list?"

He set down the boxes on his side of the tape and shook his head. "Way I figure it is if we get too much, then Kyle can donate it to another church. I counted each person that gave, not what they gave. Some only handed me a box of ornaments they didn't need anymore, but some gave two or three items. Their names are right here, not so much to prove anything to you but to keep me straight, so I don't go back to them again."

"I did the same. Seems the fair way to go, doesn't it? I've got thirty names and the promise of a shed built from old barn wood next week. We'll have to open up those garage doors at the end of this thing to get it inside," she said.

"I've got a manger coming and six hay bales." He started back out to his truck for more boxes.

She followed behind him. "Have you seen the inside of the parsonage in the past few years?"

He shook his head. "I hope it looks better than the church office, or his poor little wife is going to cut and run right back over the border to Oklahoma."

"She might anyway when she realizes that she's walking into this feud and that the two grannies of the town are the she-coons in the whole thing," Betsy said.

He held up a finger. "Do we need to get a jar and put a ten-dollar bill in it every time we mention what isn't supposed to be talked about in this room?"

She clamped a hand over her mouth. "Oops! Won't happen again. That's all of my stuff, and now I'm ready for sweet potato fries. I'll make a deal with you. You go get a couple of large orders of those, and I'll go by Starbucks for lattes, and we'll meet at the park."

"You got it. Only this time, we eat at my apartment," he said.

A puzzled expression crossed her face. "Where? Do you have an apartment in town?"

"If this is our home, then our trucks are our apartments," he said. "It's the Wisemans' inside joke. And I'd rather have hot chocolate, please, ma'am."

"You got it," she said. "Do we have two keys or just one?"

"One to keep us honest," he answered. "You've got the one to the church. I've got this one. If you need to unload something, leave me a message in a can on Thursday when you take in the programs."

He snapped the padlock shut, walked beside her, and opened the truck door so she could get in. "See you at the zoo."

"This is not a date, Declan. You don't have to open doors for me."

He leaned into the truck, cupped her face in his hands, and watched her eyes flutter shut as he leaned in for a kiss. Yes, sir, it was every bit as fiery as the one in the movie theater had been, so that hadn't simply been a fluke. There was red-hot, steamy chemistry between him and Betsy.

Her mouth opened enough to invite him inside, and he teased her tongue with his, tasting a mixture of cinnamon and coffee. The kiss went from sweet to passionate and sent him into instant arousal. He wanted Betsy, and with that rotten bet in place, plus everything else, it was an impossible situation.

He broke away and brushed a quick kiss on her forehead. "You drive careful now, Mrs. Wiseman, and don't spill the fancy latte and my hot chocolate. See you in a few minutes."

Cowboys like Declan should come complete with a blister pack attached to their belt buckles that held some of those little anti-hot-flash pills. No wonder the women flocked around him like flies on sugar. Any man that could make a woman's hormones start whining like Betsy's were right then could probably turn her whole body into nothing but a mass of quivering desire with a bout of hot sex.

"I wouldn't need to marry him. Taking him to bed would be plenty good enough for me," Betsy muttered as she drove through the security gates and turned right toward the Starbucks.

There was a line six cars long, and the first five must've ordered a dozen drinks each because it took forever for her to get to the window. If she hadn't been blocked in so tight, she would have parked and gone inside, but there was nothing to do but wait, and Betsy was impatient, jittery from that kiss, and the adrenaline rush wouldn't die down no matter how many Christmas songs on the radio she sang along to.

"Okay, woman, settle it down and get ahold of yourself. That is an order," she said loudly.

Finally, it was her turn, and to speed matters up, she ordered two hot chocolates. A cute little blond with long, dangly earrings shoved the cups out to her, and she carefully set them in the cup holders, paid the girl, and had to wait another five minutes before she could pull out onto the main road that led to the zoo.

Declan's truck was still moving toward a spot at the back of the lot when she pulled in. She parked right beside him, opened the door, got the hot chocolate, and slammed the door with her boot heel. No way was she spilling a drop after the wait she'd had. She might even lick the inside of the cup when she finished drinking it.

The passenger door of Declan's truck flew open, and she caught a whiff of hot sweet potato fries. Her stomach growled, and she remembered that she hadn't had supper. "They smell wonderful," she said.

He took one cup from her, their hands brushing and sparks flying in the transfer.

"So we are Mr. and Mrs. Wiseman in the storage building. Who are we in our apartments?" she asked breathlessly as she slid into the passenger seat and slammed the door shut.

"You are Betsy, and I am Declan. The plates on our apartment doors have no last names or numbers. Just first names. Yours is in hot pink and silver, and mine is in gold and black. And, Betsy, I was hungry when I got to Sonic, so I ordered us each one of those double bacon burgers we had last night. If you don't want yours..."

She cut him off with a wave of the hand. "Oh, no, Declan with No Last Name, I'm eating every bite of that. I didn't have supper, and I'm starving. Now, about that kiss?"

He reached inside the sack and handed her a thick burger, took his out, and then flatted the sack on the console and poured all the sweet potato fries on it. "Which one?"

She removed the paper wrapper from the burger and inhaled the aroma of bacon and hot cheese. "God, I love this kind of food. I could eat one of these every day. We already talked about the first one, and this is supposed to be business. I could sue you for sexual harassment."

"Not if the kiss was in the Mr. and Mrs. Wiseman storage house."

"But it was in my apartment, not in the storage place," she reminded him.

"And you kissed me back, so it's not harassment, and the business agreement is between a Brennan and a Gallagher, and in our apartments, we have no last names, remember?"

She bit into the burger, held up a finger, and chewed fast, so she could talk without having food in her mouth. "You'd make a very good lawyer."

"I enjoyed the kissing very much, and I would like to ask you out on a date. Dinner and a movie, maybe in Oklahoma City, away from prying eyes, or dinner and a ride down the river walk at Bricktown and maybe listen to some country music at the Wormy Dog Saloon. It's a sweet little bar," he said.

She stopped breathing. Her chest hurt and her palms went all sweaty.

"But I don't suppose you'd be that brave, would you?" he asked.

"Bravery," she finally whispered as she sucked in a lungful of air, "has nothing whatsoever to do with it."

"I'm not your type?"

It was tempting—too damned tempting—but she really wasn't crazy, and she did like her red hair intact upon her head and not on the end of a bloody knife. "Come on, Declan, it's not like taking a cat off to the country."

His eyebrows drew together in a solid line. "What? What do cats got to do with us going on a date in Oklahoma City?"

"You know, if a cat needs to find a new home, you put it in the car and take it to someone's barn, but if you don't cross water with it, you know it will find its way back. Just because we cross the Red River into Oklahoma doesn't mean Burnt Boot wouldn't have eyes on us."

He picked up a fry and held it out to her. She held his hand steady and took a bite off the end. Then he popped it into his mouth.

"This is a date right here, Betsy. We have shared food, eaten from the same potato stick, so we are on a date."

"Does that mean I get another kiss at the end of the date?" she teased.

His blue eyes danced with mischief. "If I'm lucky."

"Well, I do like your apartment here. Love the decor." Flirting with him was so much fun that she completely forgot that she did have a last name. "The table here"—she tapped the console—"looks like it came from a high-dollar furniture store. And I do love these seats. Do they recline?"

"Yes, ma'am, and I special ordered the bench backseat so it can be used as a bed."

She turned around and glanced over her shoulder. "And how many women have been in that bed?"

"I'm waiting for the right woman to sleep with in that particular bed, so the answer is that I have never been with a woman in that bed. FYI, darlin', I've never even made out in the backseat of this truck. Would you like to be first?"

"Oh!" She faked shyness and fanned herself dramatically with her hand. "I simply could not. I'm saving myself for marriage."

She thought for a few seconds that he was going to choke plumb to death before he swallowed and burst into laughter so loud that it probably woke up every goat in the kiddy zoo. "It wasn't that funny."

"Yes, it was. You should be onstage, darlin'."

"As a comedian?" She cocked her head to one side and laughed with him. "Now, wouldn't that go over like a cow patty in the punch bowl at a church social."

He laughed harder.

"Turnip greens," she said.

The laughter stopped and his nose twitched.

"See? My two lines are used up. Everything I say is not funny," she said.

"But why turnip greens?" he asked.

"Because I hate them. I don't care how much bacon the cook puts in them, I still hate them, and when I was a little girl, I had to eat at least one bite of everything on the table."

"Me too, and you are so right; turnip greens are not funny, no matter how you say the words."

She blew on a hot fry and said, "There went my clown hat, and it wasn't even warm yet."

He reached across the seat and traced the outline of her lips. "I like you, Betsy. We could be good together in another world."

"Yes, we could," she said. "But we're living in this

world. Now, it's time for Cinderella to finish this burger and go home."

She gulped down her burger past the lump in her throat and leaned across the console to plant a kiss on his cheek. "Thanks for this evening, Declan. It was fun and I loved every minute of it, but right now, I really am taking my chocolate and going home."

"Don't forget to hook your bra," he said.

Her hands automatically went to her back. "You rat. My bra isn't undone. That kiss didn't knock me off my balance that much."

"But it made you doubt for just a minute, didn't it?"

Betsy was humming when she walked into the ranch house but stopped when she heard Naomi fussing in the kitchen. She was back in the Gallagher world, and all she wanted to do was get in her truck and go back to the storage unit where she was Mrs. Wiseman. Or even Betsy with No Last Name in Declan's apartment-slash-truck.

"Betsy, is that you? Where have you been? I swear that Tyrell has stepped on my last good nerve. My favorite horse has a cut on its leg from having to carry that man for ten miles through mesquite and brush. He's one of my best stud horses, and I didn't even want him to be used to take Santa to the party, but I gave in and let Tanner talk me into it. This is all Mavis Brennan's fault. I want you to come up with something that will pay her back for this. I can't trust your male cousins to do a job right." Naomi talked all the way from kitchen, through the dining room, and into the foyer.

"No, thank you. I had to let every kid in north Texas

sit on my lap and tell me what they wanted for Christmas. That is enough of a contribution to the feud," she said.

Naomi sniffed the air. "Have you been drinking?"

She started up the stairs. "No, ma'am, unless you call a cup of hot chocolate from Starbucks drinking. Last I heard, they did not put women in jail for that."

"Don't you walk away from me when I'm talking to you," Naomi said.

Betsy took off her coat and sat down on a step. "I thought we were through. What do you want to talk about?"

"What were you doing in Gainesville for starters?"

She almost said, "It's a secret, and if I tell you, I'll have to kill you," but caught herself in time. "Granny, I'm almost thirty years old. I think that's plenty old to go when I want and come in when I want and not have to answer to you about my whereabouts. If you want to control me that much, I'll move back home with Mama and Daddy, or I can always move into one of the newlywed cabins."

"You will not! Not unless you are married."

"Anything else?"

"Your truck has been seen pretty often in Gainesville. It's not hard to keep up with you when you insist on driving that ugly pink truck. Are you seeing someone?"

"Is that how you're keeping up with me? Tomorrow morning, I'm taking that truck to the dealership and trading it in for a black one, or maybe a white one. There are lots of those on the road."

"Answer me, Betsy Gallagher." Naomi's voice got louder and shriller with every word.

"Okay, Granny, I can honestly say that I'm not seeing anyone."

"That's all I wanted to hear. You could have said so in the first place. I hear that the preacher's wife has a brother who is a good veterinarian. I think we should invite him to dinner sometime." Naomi's tone had done a complete turnaround.

"Why, are you going to get married again?"

Naomi threw up her hands. "You are impossible."

"It's the Gallagher in me." Betsy picked up her coat and hurried up to her room, where she threw herself on her bed, stared at the dark ceiling, and played out every nuance of the whole evening.

Chapter 11

Declan parked far enough out in the store parking lot that he wouldn't block anyone trying to drive up to the two gas pumps. Fuel was always at least ten cents per gallon more expensive in Burnt Boot than down in Gainesville, but it was nice to have it when a rancher needed it.

He pulled his work coat tighter across his broad chest and made sure to close the door as quickly as he could, so he didn't let too much cold in or too much warmth out.

"Hey, Declan," Jill O'Donnell called out from the back of the store. "Think we're going to get a white Christmas two years in a row?"

Declan shivered. "That would be a miracle, but I'd sure like to see another one for Leah's sake. She loves the holidays, and this year is going to be tough on her. I hadn't seen a white Christmas since I was little boy until last year. Two in a row might go beyond a miracle and take some pure old magic. Granny asked me to come by and pick up ten thick-cut pork chops. She's got some hogs about ready to butcher, but we're waiting on the weather to get a few degrees colder."

"I'll get them cut and wrapped. There's hot coffee in the pot up there on the counter if you want a cup. I figured with this cold snap, folks might like something warm to wrap their hands around while they shop."

"Thank you. That does sound good." He followed the aroma of hot coffee to the counter and poured a cup. The store window became a Technicolor screen for pictures of Betsy, both past, when she was a little girl with red braids, and up through the years to the present, when she'd worn those tight-fitting, fancy jeans to the bar last weekend.

Someone touched him on the arm and startled him so that if he hadn't finished off the coffee, he would have spilled it all over his coat.

Jill laid two packages wrapped in white butcher paper on the counter. "I didn't mean to startle you. Your mind must've been a million miles away."

He tossed the empty cup in the trash can. "Not quite that far."

"So I hear that the Brennans kidnapped Santa Claus. What do you think they'll name this battle? We've had the pig war and the shit war this past year."

"I wish they'd name it the final battle," he said.

Jill wrote up the bill for his pork chops and flipped it around for him to sign. "I don't see that happening in our lifetime. Besides, Burnt Boot would probably shrivel up and die without the feud."

Declan initialed the bottom of the ticket. Jill pulled it off to file in the box under the cabinet and tucked the yellow copy in the sack with his order.

"There you go," she said.

A movement outside caught his eye, and he glanced outside to see Betsy slide out of the truck. Staring at her wasn't wise, but he couldn't look away. She was beautiful even in her scuffed-up boots and old, mustard-colored work jacket.

"If that wind don't blow something across the river, I'll be surprised, Jill," she said as she pushed into the store. "Oh, hello, Declan. I didn't see your truck."

"Betsy." He tried to keep his voice cool. "I parked on the side instead of out front."

"Remember, folks, this is neutral territory," Jill reminded them. "I understand that feelings are running high between your families right now, but no arguing or fighting in here."

Betsy turned away from him. "Granny sent me to get two pounds of bologna and a pound of white American cheese."

"I was about to leave anyway. See you around, Jill. Betsy?" Declan tipped his cowboy hat at the two ladies and pulled a piece of paper from his pocket on his way from the store to his truck. Making sure no one was looking as he passed Betsy's truck, he quickly opened the door, tossed the note on the seat, and eased the door shut, making as little noise as possible.

"So where did y'all find Santa Claus? I heard he was all the way down in Houston and that you had to get him and the horse out of an animal rescue place. They're saying he was stripped of everything but his long johns and socks," Jill said as she sliced bologna.

"Truth is he called us from a motel in Dallas. Those Brennans took him to a barn out in the middle of nowhere and stole his boots and beard. I wouldn't put it past Mavis to put them in a frame and hang them above the mantel, like Granny did Mavis's hairpiece after they got into that fight last year," Betsy said.

"Y'all did burn up baby Jesus," Jill said.

"And the next chapter begins. Wonder what they'll call this one," Betsy said.

"Declan and I were just wondering the same thing."

"And what did he say?"

Jill wrapped the meat and laid it on top of the meat counter. "The final war is what he'd like it to be called, but I don't see that happening. I bet it's something like the Santa war."

"It would be nice if that's where it landed and not on something worse."

Betsy signed the ticket and carried a brown paper bag with her meat and cheese to the car. She threw it over into the passenger's seat and was about to get inside when she noticed the folded paper. She picked it up and laid it on the dash, slammed the door, and drove out to the road before she opened it.

"What in the hell were you thinkin'? The can is for notes. What if someone saw you?" Betsy fussed, but the corners of her mouth turned up as she read the note.

> *Mrs. Wiseman, please bring your offering to the Wiseman estate on Wednesday evening at eight o'clock. We should be safer than usual, as a lot of the town's concerned citizens will be in church at that time. See you there.*

If he'd put it in the can, she wouldn't have found it until Thursday, and taking stuff to the storage unit on Wednesday was a great idea. Most of the gossipmongers would indeed be in church at that time, not holding a phone in one hand as they pulled back the draperies with the other one.

"This secret business gets more complicated by the hour. Rumor would have it that I was having an affair with Kyle." She tucked the note into the glove compartment and made sure it was locked before she continued on toward Wild Horse.

Her mind whirled around in circles worse than the dead leaves in the middle of the road that afternoon. She and Declan would definitely have to figure out ways to get notes back and forth. It wasn't like it would be a forever thing; it was just a few weeks until Christmas, and then there would be no more Wisemans, or Betsy and Declan with No Last Names.

She was cranky when she got home, and seeing a moving van there didn't help matters one bit. Her grandmother hadn't mentioned buying new furniture, and yet some of the cousins were moving in beds, and was that a baby bed?

"Hey, you better get into the house with that sandwich stuff because Granny is fussing about it," Tyrell yelled. "On second thought, don't rush and you can be on top of the shit list instead of me."

She picked up the sack and took the porch steps two at a time. "What's going on?" she asked Tanner.

He shrugged. "You'd better ask Granny. I'm not sayin' a word."

Betsy carried the sack to the kitchen and plopped it down on the countertop. "Why did you buy a baby bed?"

"I didn't buy any of that stuff that's coming into the house," she said. "I wish I would have told you to buy an extra pound of cheese. We'll be feeding a lot of folks for lunch."

"Why?"

Naomi pointed toward the pantry door. "Get out two loaves of bread and start making sandwiches while we talk."

Betsy brought out a loaf of wheat and one of white bread, took mustard and mayonnaise from the refrigerator. She had removed the twist tie from one loaf while Naomi added more noodles to the simmering pot of chicken broth on the stove.

"It's like this. You don't llke the office. Angela needs something to keep her busy, but she also needs to be close to her baby. I should have realized that one woman can't run this ranch the way I have. It'll take two, so you and Angela are going to do it together. She'll take care of the business end, and you can continue to work outside. I've given them the old nanny's suite right across the landing from your bedroom."

Betsy kept slathering bread with mustard.

"Well?" Naomi said impatiently.

"What's the real reason? You know I can do the work even if I'd rather be outside as opposed to cooped up in an office. So be honest with me and stop all this nonsense, Granny."

Naomi stirred the chicken soup and pursed her mouth into a tight, little pucker. "Something's not right with you. It started right before Thanksgiving. I think you are seeing someone on the sly."

The mayonnaise jar slipped and Betsy had to do some fancy juggling to catch it before it hit the floor. "Why do you keep badgering me about that? You might have babies and marriage on the brain when it comes to my life, but believe me, you are the only one."

"Angela's brother, John, will be here Thursday

and staying through Monday. He's coming to preach for Kyle and he'll be staying here at Wild Horse," Naomi said.

"I thought he was a vet."

"He is, but he's also a lay preacher. So he's a good man who knows his way around a ranch," Naomi said.

"Well, ain't that nice. I'll take him to the bar and introduce him around on Friday night," Betsy said in a sugary-sweet tone.

Naomi's head jerked around so fast that Betsy heard the neck bones pop. "You will not do any such crazy thing. He's a fine young man, and you are going to a youth revival meeting with him on Friday night over in Saint Jo."

"Not me. I've got plans Friday. Make Tyrell go with him. He's the one who let himself get caught and messed up Christmas."

"John is not gay!" Naomi snorted.

"I know that. I met him at Angela and Jody's wedding. Didn't impress me then and won't now," Betsy said.

Naomi's beady little eyes narrowed into slits and the wrinkles on her forehead deepened. "You will do what I say."

"Or what? You'll throw me off Wild Horse like Mavis did Leah?"

"No, but you will forfeit your room here in this house and your place. I expect Jody and Angela can run this ranch together and you can go on back to working on your Daddy's place." Naomi's voice was almost a hiss.

"That can be arranged right now. Hey, Tyrell," she yelled.

Heavy boots on hardwood preceded him into the kitchen. "Dinnertime?"

"Not quite, but you got any extra boxes out there? I can put my stuff in my truck, but I'll need a few boxes to pack up some of it. I'll take my sandwich up to my room and pack while I eat. Granny, you reckon I could have the place that Jody and Angela are moving out of?"

"Not unless you do what I tell you," Naomi said.

"Granny?" Tyrell asked.

"If she can't follow orders, then she should get out of my house," Naomi said.

"What's going on? Is dinner ready? I'm starving." Tanner joined them.

"No, dinner is not ready, but you know how to make sandwiches, so here's the mayo knife. The mustard one is over there on a saucer. I'm not the fair-haired child anymore. I'm moving back home to Daddy's place until I can either get a trailer brought in or build my own house." Betsy picked up two sandwiches and carried them with her.

"And she won't get a dime of my money to do either one."

"Didn't ask, Granny. I do have my own herd and my own money," Betsy said.

Tanner's blood ran cold in his veins when he walked into the tense kitchen that day. Someone had found out about the bet, and now there was a war within the family. He'd be the next one exiled from the big house and possibly off the ranch.

He should have called it off the moment that Betsy

had walked through the door, but he hadn't thought for a minute that she'd give Declan Brennan a chance—not when she was in the direct lineage to run the whole shit and caboodle called Wild Horse.

"Why?" he asked cautiously.

"I've got to go to a rotten old revival with Angela's brother, John, or else. Granny's ultimatum," she said.

"She will obey me," Naomi said.

Tanner nervously raked his fingers through his blond hair. "Why won't you go, Betsy? It's just one evening, and I like him. He can talk ranchin' for hours."

Betsy turned around at the kitchen door and asked Naomi, "Am I still welcome at Sunday dinner?"

Naomi slapped the cabinet so hard that the mustard and mayonnaise jars rattled against each other. "When you apologize for your insolence, then we'll talk about it."

"How about church? Do I still get to sit with the Gallaghers, or are you throwing me over into the Brennan camp?"

"One more smart word, and I'll put you off Wild Horse quicker than Mavis got rid of Leah. And I mean permanently, not just until you come to your senses and listen to reason. I mean the whole ranch, smarty-pants." Naomi's hand shook as it snapped up to point toward the door. "Think about that while you pack."

Betsy gave Tanner a look that sent cold chills down his back. This all started after the poker game. That's when his cousin started acting weird and that look she gave him said that she knew something. He was still standing upright and breathing, so she hadn't found out about the bet. Still, something wasn't right with Betsy, and Tanner didn't need a compass pointing him in the direction of River Bend to know that Declan figured into it. What if Declan had talked her into a date or two and she really was falling in love with him?

Tanner threw an arm around Naomi's shoulders. "Granny, cut her some slack. The whole reason you're moving Jody and his family in here is to make her see how great it'd be to have a husband and a baby. She's not going to do that if she's not living here."

Tyrell joined him in the kitchen. "And you know how wild she is. She's liable to do something crazy if you don't have her close by. That's why you moved her into the big house after that happened with Leah over on River Bend anyway, wasn't it?"

Naomi shrugged Tanner's arm away. "She needs to learn to follow rules. She's had a taste of the good life. Now she can think about that. I'm reasonable. When she comes back and apologizes, then I'll take her back into my good graces."

Tanner's mouth went dry. Betsy, apologize? World peace would be easier to accomplish.

Betsy sat down on the overstuffed love seat facing the window in her huge bedroom. The one she'd be moving into wasn't half as big, and her daddy was going to be furious with her for upsetting Naomi when she still wasn't over the Santa Claus stunt. Maybe they should combine all the battles of the past year and call this one the Christmas pig shit war.

It was a good thing she didn't know Declan's phone number, or she would have called him. She might as well hang for a sheep as a lamb, and she did want to talk to him. His sister had handled exile with so much grace, but then Leah Brennan had always been a lady, something Betsy had never been in her whole life.

Before she finished eating and began to pack, she decided she was not going to her parent's house, at least not right away. She threw her clothing into a suitcase until it was full and then peered downstairs. There were no boxes at the bottom, so evidently Granny had told her cousins they couldn't even help with that much. She stormed down to the kitchen, gathered up an armful of plastic grocery sacks from the pantry, and stomped back through the dining room and foyer. A few boxes or lack of them would not stop her from plowing full speed ahead with her plan.

It took several trips, but not a single big, strong cowboy relative so much as opened a door for her. That was just fine. Paybacks could be painful. She was on her way to Gainesville when her phone rang.

She answered it on the fourth ring. "Yes, Mama?"

"You've had enough time to get home. Where are you?"

"On my way to the school."

"What for?" her mother, Willa, asked.

"Give me that phone." Betsy heard her father, Henry's, voice.

"In a minute," Willa said. "Why are you going to the school?"

"To talk to Leah O'Donnell about renting their bunkhouse and leasing some of their land to put my cows on," Betsy said.

"I guess you'd best talk to your father." Willa repeated what Betsy had said as she handed off the phone.

"I told you living with your grandmother would never work. You need to come home, not move off Wild Horse. That won't help, and it'll just make things worse," Henry told her.

She braked and came to a stop in the bar parking lot. "Right now, I don't care if it makes things worse. I'm near thirty years old, and this is ridiculous. I don't want to go out with Angela's brother."

"If I were you, I wouldn't either. Mother had no right to do that to you," Henry said.

Betsy's anger began to cool down. "Thanks, Daddy."

"And until you are welcome in the big house, then your mother and I won't be going to Sunday dinner either. Your grandmother has gone too far this time."

"You don't have to do that. This is my fight," Betsy said.

"No, this time it's our fight. I'll help you unload your things. Your mother is putting fresh sheets on your bed. She's missed you being here."

"Granny made me so mad when she told me I had a year to get married and then started pushing John at me," Betsy said.

"Come on home and we'll talk about it."

"Okay, but I think it's time for me to start looking for my own place," she said.

"We'll talk about that too."

Chapter 12

Declan arrived at the storage unit before Betsy, so he unloaded his stuff and wrote down the names of all the people who had donated on the slip of paper on his side of the big room. With its high ceilings and big floor space, the place would most likely still look empty when Kyle came to take everything away.

It was cold as an Alaskan well-digger's belt buckle outside, and inside wasn't a bit warmer. He sat down in one of the office chairs and drew his coat closer to his chest. Where was that global warming when a person needed it? He could remember playing football with his cousins on Christmas day when they were kids, but the past couple of years had been bad winters, and it looked like they were in for another one.

He heard the crunch of gravel and then a door slam. She was carrying two boxes that didn't appear to be heavy, but they were tall enough she could barely see over them.

"Need some help?" he called out.

"Open the door?" she yelled. "I know you're here because I saw your truck."

"Yes, I'm here. I'm holding the door for you so the wind won't whip it shut. You'd best pull around to the end, and we'll open the garage door to get that shed thing inside. Who helped you load it?"

"Daddy did," she said.

"Did you tell him what we're doing?" Declan asked.

"Nope, told him it was a secret for the church that I was undertaking and that Elijah O'Riley had made it for me. Daddy might have an idea what's happening, but I did not let the cat out of the bag," she answered. "And Mama donated those two boxes of cedar garland. She used to string it around the windows, but here lately she's just been using tinsel."

Together they got everything situated on the right side of the duct-tape line, closed both doors, and plopped down into the office chairs.

"Want to talk about what happened at Wild Horse?" he asked.

"I lost my place because I wouldn't go out with Angela's brother, John. It's no big deal."

"And you're back in the house with your folks?"

"Temporarily. I'm looking for a place of my own that is not connected to Wild Horse. There're a couple of small ranches for sale between us and Gainesville that I'm going to take a look at after the holidays. One has a house on it, but it's small. The other is just land, so I'd have to build or move a trailer onto the place."

Declan knew exactly which two places Betsy was talking about. He'd looked at both of them with the same idea. The one without a house butted up next to Finn and Callie's ranch on the south. The other was another three miles down the road, and the white frame house was in need of a paint job and a new roof.

"I thought you Gallaghers were only interested in buying land connected to what you've got," he said.

"Like the Brennans, right?"

He nodded.

"Maybe if a few of us disconnect from the ranch, then..."

"You dream big, don't you?" He smiled. "Let's go to my truck. I've got a surprise for you."

She smiled back at him, their gazes catching in the space separating the two chairs. "I do like surprises, like the note in my seat yesterday morning."

"We have to improvise, since the can is only available on Thursday." He stood up and extended a hand.

She put hers in it.

He pulled her to his chest, wrapping his arms tightly around her. "I'm sorry you've had a rough time. With all the rumors flying around, I didn't know what to believe."

She leaned back and looked up into his eyes. "Thank you, Declan. It is what it is, and really, it wasn't a big deal. Daddy told me when I moved into the big house that Granny and I were too much alike to live together. I should have listened."

The way her green eyes looked right then, kind of sad and yet excited at the same time, seemed a lot more important than a bunch of words. Her tongue flicked out and moistened her lips, and her eyes fluttered shut as he leaned forward. Then, his mouth was on hers, and they were in a vacuum, with no outside world, people, or feud to disturb them.

Her arms went from his chest to around his neck, one hand splayed out in his hair, holding his head steady. His rough hands left her soft cheeks and roamed down her back, clasping her closer and closer until he could feel her racing heart keeping time with his. Good! That meant she was as affected by his touch and kiss as much as he was by hers.

Betsy melted into the kiss, forgetting who she was and who Declan was. At that moment, she didn't care about anything but putting out the fire that he was building with his fiery kisses. Her body wanted more and more. Her brain was screaming at her to take a step back, but she turned down the volume and ignored it.

Finally, Declan pulled away and brushed a soft kiss on her forehead. "My surprise won't keep forever."

Lucifer's nightmare! She wasn't interested in a surprise. She wanted more kisses and a bout of hot sex on the concrete floor.

Holy damnation, woman! What are you thinking? To leave Wild Horse and buy your own place is one thing; to have sex with Declan is taking it a step too far. It was Tanner's deep drawl in her head that jerked her back to reality.

Declan laced his fingers in hers and headed outside, turning out the overhead light and locking the door behind them. "I really was worried about you today."

"The rumors must be horrible." Her voice was still breathless from making out.

"The best one is that you've been seeing another O'Donnell and that he's ten times worse than Rhett. They say you met him at one of those big O'Donnell affairs, like Thanksgiving or their end-of-summer picnic, and it's all been on the sly. Naomi says she won't even be shirttail related to the Brennans."

"What?" Betsy stopped.

"Leah Brennan married Rhett O'Donnell. If you marry his cousin, then you'd be kin to the Brennans, right?"

A grin twitched the corners of her mouth. "If that is the worst rumor in the basket, I could blow them away with the truth. Hey, would you believe that Betsy Gallagher has been kissing Declan Brennan? My grandmother would drop graveyard dead of acute cardiac arrest and so would Mavis Brennan."

Declan settled her into the passenger seat and rounded the back of the truck. "That would be so hot that it would fry the gossip vines, telephone lines, and maybe even give a few more old-timers heart attacks," he said.

"I wonder what Mavis would think of that."

"I saw smoke coming out her ears when she heard the news of you and an O'Donnell. She laughed and said it would be good enough for Naomi, after trying to take Leah from her last year. Remember when she sent Tanner to try to sweet-talk Leah into dating him just to get back at Naomi?" He reached over the seat, brought out a small cooler, and opened it to reveal a quart of ice cream.

"Peanut butter fudge. How did you know it's my favorite?"

"I didn't, but it is Leah's, and she always made me eat it with her after she'd had a tough day."

"So I'm like your sister?" She took a plastic spoon from his hand and dug into the ice cream.

"I don't kiss my sister except on the cheek or the forehead." He dipped as deep as the spoon would allow and brought up enough that he could lick it like an ice cream cone.

Suddenly, he leaned across the console and tipped her chin up, licked a drop of ice cream from the corner of her mouth, and then went back to eating. The sensation was surreal. Cold ice cream in her mouth, a cold tongue licking her lip, and heat chasing through her body like she'd just been hooked up to a moonshine IV.

"I've never done that with my sister either," he said in a matter-of-fact tone.

"Declan, what happens after Christmas?" she asked.

"We celebrate with more ice cream. It can be used for good days as well as bad ones," he answered.

"You know what I mean," she said.

"I reckon things will take care of themselves a day at a time," he said.

Was that a hint of something sad in his voice?

"I guess it will." She definitely recognized sadness in her own voice.

It would be over after the holidays, and all that would remain would be memories of the secret they'd shared. No one would ever know that, for a few weeks, a Gallagher and a Brennan had banded together for the betterment of the town—that they'd been responsible for bringing Christmas to the church. It would be something both of them would take to their graves, but it would definitely be something she would never forget.

"Do you realize that three weeks from tonight, the Christmas program will take place at the church? And the Wisemans will have done it all?"

Betsy smiled up at him. "Not all, Mr. Wiseman. We had lots of folks who donated their leftovers and some who donated precious items—like the angel for the top of the tree. Angela's grandma made that. I realize we can't give everyone credit for what they gave, but lots of folks will recognize the items and know that everyone in town came together for the program."

"Gives you a warm and fuzzy feeling, huh?" Declan said.

As quick as lightning, she smeared ice cream across his cheek, mouth, and all the way to his ear on the other side. "Don't make fun of me," she said.

"Now you have to lick it off," he said.

"I do not," she protested.

"Afraid to?" he asked.

She shoved her spoon back into the ice cream container, picked it up, and set it on the dashboard, threw the console back, and straddled his lap. "I'm not afraid of the devil. I'm not even afraid of his mother, who happens to be my grandmother. And I believe your grandmother is a cousin of his."

She leaned forward and slurped up the ice cream on one side of his face and then the other. She felt him harden through his jeans, against her thighs, but didn't stop. He groaned when she started on his mouth, teasing his lips by slowly tracing the outline with her tongue. When he tried to kiss her, she put a finger over his lips.

"You are killing me, woman," he groaned again.

"I feel the evidence," she said as she leaned back and checked his face by the light of the moon. "I think it's all gone. The ice cream, not the evidence of you being killed."

His hand was nothing more than a blur when he returned the favor. Ice cream suddenly swooped across her cheek and her lips. Instinctively, her hand went to wipe it away, but he pinned them to her sides.

"My turn," he said as his tongue started on one side and followed the same pattern she had, landing on her lips last.

Her toes curled up inside her cowboy boots and her breath caught in her chest. Her insides tightened against the hot lava burning inside her body, and every nerve in her body ached. She couldn't imagine sex with him if just touching turned her on this much.

"All done," he finally said. "That was fun. Let's do it again."

She quickly moved to her side of the truck and popped the console back down. "I don't think so, cowboy."

"Why? It was just getting good."

"And what happens when the truck catches on fire?" she asked.

He chuckled. "So you felt it too."

"Yes, I did, and now I'm going to get in my truck and go home."

"Good night, Betsy." He ran his knuckles down her cheekbone. "Do we have a date for next Wednesday, right here?"

"We do," she said as she crawled out of the truck and made her weak knees carry her to her vehicle.

Chapter 13

Betsy flipped on the light in the back hallway, but the church was still cold and dark that Thursday night. The emptiness was eerie, and every time the old frame building groaned against the wind, a shiver tiptoed down her spine. Who would have thought a church could be scarier than a horror movie?

She found the door to the office swung wide open, which added to the weirdness of the evening. Kyle never left it unlocked, and she stood outside for a full minute trying to decide whether to prop the envelope on the doorjamb and run or to go inside and put it on his desk.

Kyle probably only has one key and left the door open for John. It's a church, for God's sake. Nothing can happen in a church, a strange inner voice said. That the voice didn't have her grandmother's demanding tone or Tanner's warning drawl was even more eerie than the dimly lit building.

She took a deep breath and stepped across the threshold into the room, laid the envelope on the desk, and noticed that several papers were fluttering. Her first thought was that someone had turned on the ceiling fan, but when she looked up, it was barely moving. A hard north wind swept through an open window and cut right through her coat. She took a step in that direction and stumbled over a chair leg, tried to right herself, but couldn't get a grip on anything but icy air. Then two strong arms caught her from behind, and before she could blink, she was sitting in Declan's lap in the swivel chair behind Kyle's desk.

"Good thing the chair was here, or we might have both ended up on the floor," he drawled.

"You scared me," she said breathlessly.

Declan shifted her weight so she was facing him. "I wanted to surprise you, not scare you. I didn't want to set off the gossip alarm by turning on a light, so I waited in the dark. I noticed the window wasn't locked the last time I was in here so I came in through there."

"What would you have done if it had been John coming into the church?" she asked.

"Never thought of that. Guess I'm a lucky man that it wasn't." He grinned.

Half his face was in dark shadows; the other half lit by a full moon that hung outside the window like a big, translucent beach ball. A five-o'clock shadow darkened his strong chin, and although she couldn't see the glimmer in his eyes, she could feel it as he looked down into her face.

"Guess I didn't think things through very well," he said huskily.

"Why..." she started.

He put a finger over her lips. "I wanted to see you, so I parked at the bar and walked to the church, staying away from the road as much as possible."

"Are you..."

He cupped her chin in his hand and brushed a sweet kiss across her lips. "I'm sure no one saw me. Didn't pass a single car or truck on the way."

Her arms had a mind of their own as they snaked their way around his neck. Conversation stopped when her mouth found his, and suddenly, the north wind wasn't even cold anymore.

Declan's hands found their way past her coat and slipped up under her snug knit shirt to clasp her ribs. The sensation was surreal—warm skin, cold hands, a melting quiver down deep in her insides that shot desire through her veins. For the first time in her life, Betsy was powerless, and she didn't even give a damn. She wanted satisfaction and Declan was the only person who could deliver it.

Not in the church! She could visualize her inner voice shaking its finger at her, but she ignored it. She'd gladly have sex with Declan right there on the desk, or under it, either one, with the freezing wind blowing over her naked body, if it would put out the aching fire inside her body.

His fingertips massaged her ribs ever so gently as his hands moved from waist level upward, his thumbs finding their way under the band of her bra. When they inched up to gently tease her nipples into hardened peaks, she groaned, and without her lips leaving his, she shed the coat. She'd been sitting on the tail of it, so now it hung from her butt to the floor as Declan pulled the knit shirt up and over her head, tossing it on the preacher's desk. With a couple of deft movements, her bra joined it, and then he pulled her coat back up and helped her slip her arms into it.

"You'll freeze without it," he whispered as he found her lips again and his hands played up and down her back, across her breasts, and around to her belly button.

Lord love a duck! When did a belly button become such a sexually stimulating zone?

Her hands itched to touch him in the same way, so she pulled his shirt free from his belt and went exploring. His belly was ripped with muscles and his chest covered in soft, fine hair. He gasped when her fingertips brushed against his nipples and groaned when she dug her fingertips into the area between his shoulders.

"Please go home with me and stay forever. I will hide you in my closet and take you out at night, and I promise to be gentle," he said between kisses.

She smiled and pushed back from him a little, the chill of the room settling on her naked torso and sending a chill down her back. She quickly leaned forward to draw from his warmth again. "Declan, this is all wrong. We can't do this."

"You mean in a church? I know where there's a fine motel," he said.

"We've both forgotten who we really are," she said.

"You are Betsy. I am Declan. Unless it's Sunday morning, we don't have last names." His hands laced with hers, and he lowered his head to claim her mouth again.

She arched against him, feeling his hardness against her thigh. She reached for his belt and started undoing it. She'd barely gotten the buckle undone and had her fingers on the top button of his jeans when she heard whistling. Thinking it was more bells and whistles joining the steamy-hot sparks dancing around in the pastor's study like a band of colorful gypsies doing a dance around a bonfire, she ignored it. She tugged the button free and felt around until she had the zipper tab in her hand.

Then, a deep voice floated through the darkness, saying something about it being cold. “Someone is in here,” she whispered.

She and Declan were on their feet in a split second, her coat gaping open, the tail of his belt hanging down like a frayed flag, and the cold wind howling through the window in chastisement.

“I hope the pipes haven’t frozen. If they do, we won’t have bathrooms for Sunday.” The voice penetrated the darkness.

“Hide behind the door,” Betsy said as she quickly zipped her coat and threw her bra and shirt at Declan.

He caught them and disappeared just as John flipped on the light.

“Who are you?” John asked.

She turned away from the front of the desk and held up the envelope of programs. “I don’t imagine you’d remember me from Angela’s wedding. I’m Betsy, Jody’s cousin. I deliver the programs on Thursdays for Kyle, since that’s his normal night to visit the sick folks and the elderly.”

“Why would you open a window?” He started across the room to close it.

“I was about to ask you the same question.”

Declan needed that window to stay open, so he could make his escape. There was no way he could get from behind the door and down the hall without being discovered, and he was holding Betsy’s bra and shirt in his hands. She needed a diversion, and it had to be quick, so she quickly took a step in front of John and purposely stumbled right into his arms.

When he caught her, she spun him around in the

fracas, so his back was to the window and the door. "I'm so sorry. I must've tripped on the leg of a chair."

She looked up with as pitiful of an expression as she could fake and was surprised to see John's eyes fluttering shut as his lips came down on hers. Hers eyes stayed wide open as she watched Declan cross the small room in a couple of long strides and crawl out the window. Her bra strap hung on the ledge, and her breath caught in her chest. He couldn't leave it there, but then it popped and must've hurt like hell when those hooks hit, because she heard him swear under his breath.

She pushed away from John and took a step backward. "What was that all about?"

"I should apologize, but I'm not sorry." He removed a black felt cowboy hat, laid it on the desk, and hiked a hip on the edge. "I do remember you, Betsy, very well. I wanted to kiss you from the moment I laid eyes on you. Do you remember the first time we met?"

"The night that Jody and Angela married," she answered.

"That's right and now here it is, two years later, and my prayers have been answered, all because you fell into my arms in church. I'd say that's an omen."

"I'd say it was a moment and that I should leave. Folks will talk if they see a light in here and my truck outside. I'm sure yours is there also," she answered.

"Can we have dinner or go out while I'm here?" he asked.

"Not this time. I've got lots of things going on this week."

"Betsy, I might be a preacher, but I'm also a man, and I felt chemistry between us when I kissed you," he said.

"Good night, John," she said and left the room. Halfway down the hall, she heard the window pop shut and the whistling start up again. She'd started the engine of her truck when her shirt and bra sailed over the seat, the shirt landing on the passenger seat and the bra on the dash.

"You might need to put those back on," a deep drawl said from the backseat. "I thought we were caught for sure when that damn bra got caught on a splinter in the window frame."

"How—"

"Your truck wasn't locked, so I waited. Seems like I've been here forever. Did the preacher's kiss lead to something more?" Declan asked.

She backed the truck up under a big shade tree, removed her coat, and hurriedly put the bra and shirt back on. "I thought lightning had come to strike us both dead when he flipped the switch."

"Did you really fall into his arms?" Declan asked, but she couldn't even see anything by peeking into the rearview mirror.

"I faked it so you'd have time to get out." She shivered as she slipped her arms back into the sleeves of her coat. "Thank God this thing zips and doesn't button."

"So did you fake it with me too?"

"I'm not having this conversation with you. Just lie there and be quiet. I'm going to the bar for a shot of Jameson to get this taste out of my mouth. I deserve it after that business. You said your truck is parked there, right?"

"Which taste out of your mouth? Mine or his?" Declan asked.

"You are not being quiet."

Declan chuckled. "He isn't a Brennan."

And he isn't you, she thought.

"But he is a preacher. Can't you just see me in the role of a preacher's wife?" she said.

The chuckling quickly developed into a guffaw that bounced around the cab of the truck. "Maybe I'll change my heathen ways and become a preacher. Would you be interested in marrying a preacher then?" he said when he could catch his breath.

"Are you proposing to me, Declan Brennan?"

"I'm not the marryin' type any more than you are," he answered. "I just had a vision of the two of us hellions being a preacher and a wife."

"So we're just in this for a little instant gratification, are we?"

"You tell me what we're in this for, or better yet, Miz Betsy, you tell me, what is it possible for us to be in this for? Are you ready to step inside the bar with me, sit at a table with me, and go tell your mama and daddy that we are dating?"

She slammed on the brakes, left black marks for a good fifty feet, and made a loud squeal that probably brought out the gossipmongers in at least half of Burnt Boot. "Get out," she said.

"Are we at the bar?"

"We are not. We're about a block away, but you can walk the rest of the way."

"Got a little too close to the truth, did I?" The door slammed, making as much noise as the squealing tires, and he quickly blended in with the shadows of the naked trees. She had no illusions that she and Declan would ever fall in love and get married. It would take a miracle for that to happen, but the truth bit into her heart deeply when she realized that, somewhere, she'd been entertaining that very notion. In that moment, she realized how stupid she'd been in letting things go as far as they had.

~

"Hey, Betsy, where have you been keeping yourself? Haven't seen you in days," Rosalie called out from behind the bar when Betsy parked on an empty stool at the far end. "What can I get for you? Beer?"

"A shot of Jameson. No beer."

"Where have you been? You look all flustered." Tanner claimed the stool on her left. "Your mama said you'd gone to take the programs into the church when I stopped by your place a while ago. Something happen there?"

"John spooked me by turning on a light when I wasn't expecting it, but other than that, everything is fine."

"You don't usually order a Jameson unless—"

"Hello, Tanner," Declan said as he slid onto the stool on Betsy's right. "Cold enough for you? How are you, Betsy?"

"What happened to your face?" Tanner asked.

Declan glanced up at their reflections in the mirror above the bar and chuckled at the scratch across his cheek where the bra hooks had hit him. "Rest assured, she was pulling me on rather than fighting me off."

Betsy sipped the Jameson, but neither the grin on Declan's face nor the ashen expression on Tanner's got past her. She thought about spilling her beer in either her cousin's lap or Declan's, maybe both, to get rid of them.

Tanner glanced around her back and glared at Declan. "Want to elaborate on exactly how you did get that scratch across your cheek?"

"A Brennan does not kiss and tell."

Betsy's senses kicked into overtime. "What's going on between you two? Y'all fightin' over the same woman?"

"I wouldn't have anything he would want," Tanner said curtly. "If you need a ride home after all that"—Tanner nodded at her drink—"just let me know, and I'll drive you back to the ranch."

"Come on, Cousin, I'm only having a single shot." She unzipped her coat part of the way and realized she had her shirt on backward and inside out and quickly zipped it back up.

"Just sayin'." Tanner nodded toward a table where Eli waited. "Join us. We've got extra chairs."

"I'll be there soon," she said.

Declan picked up a cardboard coaster and flipped it over, took a pen from his shirt pocket, and drew a frowny face. He wrote "I'm sorry" underneath and slipped it into her coat pocket. Then he yelled at Rosalie to bring a pitcher of beer to the Brennan table and slid off the stool.

In her peripheral vision, Betsy could see Honey Brennan touch Declan's face and ask a question. He laughed it off and told her the same thing he'd told Tanner. What was it about that egotistical statement that had made all the blood leave Tanner's face? Betsy would bet dollars to earthworms that Declan was trying to steal one of Tanner's girlfriends on the sly. Kissing her one night and someone else the next. Yes, sir, that was Declan Brennan's reputation for sure.

A spurt of jealousy shot through, leaving a really bad taste in her mouth that even the Jameson had trouble erasing. She tossed back the last dregs in the plastic cup.

Do you reckon Declan felt the same when he got a glimpse of you kissing John?

"Oh, hush, he's..." She caught herself talking aloud and stopped before someone overheard her arguing with herself.

Rosalie wiped down the counter where Declan had been sitting. "What's got your underbritches in a twist tonight?"

"Men."

"That's the story every time. You can't live with 'em, and it's against the law to shoot them. Need something to get your mind off them?"

Betsy nodded.

"Go over there in the storeroom and get out the Christmas decorations. You can make the crowd help you put them up or do it yourself and tell them all to go to hell if they get in your way," Rosalie said.

Betsy hopped down off the stool and laid a bill on the bar. "Yes, ma'am. That sounds like fun."

Rosalie slid the money back toward her. "Your drinks are on the house if you'll put up my tree and decorations."

"Poor time to be cuttin' back on my drinkin', isn't it?"

"Why would you do that?" Rosalie asked.

"Need a clear head all the time these days. Have big decisions to make," Betsy said.

When Betsy threw back the last of that expensive whiskey, Declan expected her to leave. But then she went to the storage closet, fumbled with the string to turn on the light, and shut the door behind her. When it opened again, her coat was gone, her shirt on right, and her sleeves pushed up. She'd whipped her red hair up into a ponytail, and she pushed a box out of the room with a faded picture of a Christmas tree on it.

"Looks like Betsy is going to put up the tree for Rosalie," Honey said.

"Looks like it," Declan said.

"I can't wait to run the ranch, so I can take her down a notch."

"Oh, so you're going to keep the feud alive and kickin', are you?"

"Damn straight! Granny will be proud of me. I heard that she got kicked off Wild Horse because she wouldn't go to a revival with the preacher who's standing in for Kyle on Sunday. I could imagine an angel dancing with the devil easier than I could that." Honey laughed.

"And if the preacher were a woman, could you see me going to a revival meeting with her?" Declan asked.

"Oh, honey, if she was good lookin', it wouldn't matter to you what she did for a living; you'd still try to seduce her," Honey said.

"And that's all right for me but not for Betsy?"

"What mean bug crawled up your ass tonight?" Honey's tone changed to ice.

"Nothing. Just seems to me like some of us on both

sides of the feuding fence get the raw end of the deal sometimes." His voice was every bit as chilly.

Quaid kicked him under the table. "I can't believe you are taking up for a Gallagher, and Betsy at that."

"I'm just stating facts. Hey, Tanner, you going to help your cousin, or do you want me to lend her a hand? That's a big tree she's trying to manhandle," Declan yelled across the room.

"You wouldn't dare," Honey growled.

Tanner shot him a mean look and went back to talking to his cousins. Declan pushed back his chair and stretched all six feet two inches of his height to an upright position. He ambled over to the jukebox, plugged in several quarters, pushed buttons, and went to the bar, where he ordered two longneck bottles of beer.

Rosalie eyed him through narrow slits and said, "Remember, this is neutral territory."

"Yes, ma'am, but I sure wouldn't want the Gallaghers braggin' around town that they had the sole job of decoratin' your bar. Next thing you know, they'd be sayin' that they've got you in their pocket and us Brennan folk best watch our ways in your bar because you'll take the Gallaghers' side against us. So if it's all right with you, I think I'll help Betsy with the decoratin' tonight," he said.

"Long as there's no fightin' and she don't mind, it's fine by me. But remember, she is the boss. I gave her the job and if anyone says I'm in anyone's pocket they'd best be thinkin' again," Rosalie said.

"Yes, ma'am."

He glanced over his shoulder to see Tanner set his jaw so hard it's a wonder the cowboy's teeth were still intact.

Declan handed Betsy a beer just as Tim McGraw

started singing "Dear Santa." "I'll get the tree out and put the limbs on the pole if you'll fluff it, as Granny calls it."

The lyrics fit him to a tee when it said that he hadn't been good all year and he wasn't askin' for anything for himself, but he wanted her to have a miracle to get them back to where they were before.

"You tryin' to say something with that song?" Betsy asked softly.

"Maybe I am," he said. "You know how to fluff a tree?"

"I reckon I can," she said.

In short order, he had the tree put together and carried over to set it beside the jukebox. "I'll bring out the lights while you make it look presentable. Right now, it's uglier than Charlie Brown's tree."

"Hey, what can we do?" Quaid asked at Betsy's elbow when she started working with each limb to make the tree presentable.

When Declan returned, Eli took the box from him and Quaid followed Declan back to the storage room to get the tinsel.

"What are we doing?" Quaid barked.

"Decoratin' a tree so that the Gallaghers won't think they've got Rosalie in their pocket. It won't kill us to work with them," Declan said.

"No, but Granny might," Quaid said. "This has to do with that bet, doesn't it? Have you already made a play for her?"

"You'll know at Christmas," Declan said. "Here, you might as well carry out this box of ornaments and put a smile on your face. It's the holidays."

"Yeah, right. You're doing this to piss Tanner off."

Declan clamped a hand on Quaid's shoulder. "Two birds with one stone."

"Just don't get shot through the heart with an arrow while you're throwing rocks at the birds," Quaid warned him.

"Ain't about to happen," Declan told him.

He carried the lights out to the tree, which looked fantastic now that Betsy had worked on it. Rascal Flatts was taking their turn with a Christmas song on the jukebox and Betsy was humming along with them. "I'll wrap this around my arms and follow you as you circle the tree and fasten the lights on the tree, Miz Betsy."

"Looks to me like you've done this job before," she said.

"Many times." He slipped the wires onto his arms from the cardboard they'd been wound on.

"Hey, let's get out that stuff that Polly put up every year," Honey said. "You know that red and green tinsel that she draped up to the ceiling and then hung a ball of mistletoe in the middle of it."

She and a couple of other Brennans headed to the storage closet, and before long, folks were working together, forgetting all about a feud. Christmas music played loudly. Decorations went up on the walls and around the jukebox. The tree was coming along, with Declan and Betsy bumping into each other with every move.

"So, you going to kiss me if I stand under the mistletoe?" Declan whispered.

"Hush!" She gasped and several people from both sides of the feud stopped to look her way. She grinned impishly and said, "I was thinking that Honey ought to kiss Tanner under the mistletoe."

"Hell ain't froze over yet," Tanner said quickly.

"You are crazy as a cross-eyed mule for even sayin' that, Betsy. Naomi would string you up if she heard such a thing," Honey said. "I thought you could hold your liquor better than that."

"I'm sober as a judge."

"Then you'd better get drunk because you are crazy when you're sober," Honey said. "Tanner, I bet those things that go on the tables are still in that storage room. Polly never threw anything away."

Tanner sat down and sipped at his beer. "I'm not taking orders from a Brennan. I don't care if it is Christmas."

"Then take the order from me, since Rosalie said I'm the boss, and go get those table decorations," Betsy said. "We want to get this done before closing time tonight."

"And," Rosalie yelled from behind the bar, "there's a free beer for everyone who stays until it's done. It's my first Christmas as owner of the bar, so this will be my new tradition. Whoever follows Betsy's orders gets a free beer."

George Strait started singing "Christmas Cookies," and Declan sang along with him. The words said that he sure liked the Christmas cookies and sugar, and when he sang about them being impossible to resist, Declan wiggled his eyebrows seductively.

"You covered that pretty good by saying that about Tanner and Honey." He grinned.

"You are horrible, even for a Brennan," she whispered.

"Did you ever think we'd be working together right out in public like this, and we've got the whole bunch of them working with us?" he asked.

"It's either magic or the free beer. Never knew a Gallagher or a Brennan to turn down a free drink, even if y'all did come from a Bible-thumpin' preacher," she said.

"Meet me Sunday at the storage unit. I have to pick up a couple of things after church that I can't hide," he said.

"I've got some stuff that I need to bring too."

"So our fight is over?"

"We'll talk about that Sunday."

"How about meeting me at the river on Saturday night? Up under the willow tree? I'll bring the beer if you'll bring the food."

Betsy's heart yelled yes. Her mind tried to override the noise by reminding her that only a couple of hours before, she'd been determined to take a step back and put the whole thing back into business mode. She listened to her heart and nodded.

"I might even bring some brisket and potato salad," he said.

"With or without arsenic?"

"We are just Betsy and Declan at the river," he said.

Another quick nod, and then Quaid and Tanner joined them to put icicles on the tree. By the time Rosalie was ready to shut the place down, it had taken on a festive holiday look, and everyone who wanted one left with a beer in their hands.

Thirty minutes later, Betsy found the note in her pocket when she tossed her coat over the rocking chair in her room. His actions had spoken far more than the note had that night, when he'd stepped up and helped her with the decorating job, but still, she read the words a dozen times.

A soft knock on the door made her hustle to get the note hidden in a nightstand drawer. Later, she'd put it away in a boot box with the others, but right then, she had to think as fast as she had in the pastor's study that evening. Without thinking, she reached up and wiped John's kiss from her lips.

Her mother, Willa, crossed the floor and sat down on the edge of the bed. Willa was one of those women who stayed in the background but whom few people had the desire or will to cross. She could hold her own with a simple look or a few softly spoken words. Her dark hair was pulled back with a knit headband, and her face had been scrubbed clean of all makeup. She wore green pajamas that matched her eyes. Willa was not a small woman, and Betsy barely came up to her shoulder.

"I just heard that you and the preacher who's standing in for Kyle this week were at the church together tonight. There's talk that he's asked you to go to a revival with him on Saturday night."

"Yes, we were very briefly. Yes, he did, and yes, I turned him down. There's no use starting something that isn't going anywhere. I don't feel a thing for him," Betsy said.

"And I also heard that the Gallaghers and the Brennans worked together to help Rosalie decorate the bar tonight. You and Declan Brennan started it, right?"

"I started it, and he was afraid that everyone would think the Gallaghers had Rosalie in their pocket, so he insisted on helping, then everyone pitched in. It's amazing what folks will do for a free beer. It was nice, Mama. It reminded me of the church programs at Christmas when the kids and old folks, Gallaghers and Brennans alike, worked together to produce something festive and sweet," she said.

"Is that the whole thing? You and Declan weren't flirting, were you? You know that sure can't go anywhere, don't you?"

"I'm a Gallagher, Mama," she said.

"And he's a Brennan. Both of your grandmothers would see y'all in the grave before they'd allow such a thing."

"I reckon someone had best get out the smelling salts for when Granny hears that I even decorated a Christmas tree with him."

"And hide the shotguns." Willa kissed Betsy on the forehead. "See you tomorrow. Your dad wants you to drive over to Ringgold to look at a horse he's had his eye on for a year."

"I'll be ready bright and early. Think he'll take us to dinner at that little café over there? It's got the best chicken fried steak in the whole state."

"For you, he'd do about anything…except be happy about you dating a Brennan."

A twinge of guilt shot through Betsy as her mother blew her a kiss at the door. She hadn't fallen in love with Declan so the whole thing could end Saturday night. There was enough stuff in the storage unit to outfit a program, and if she gathered up anymore, she could figure out a way to give it to him. She didn't even care if she lost the bet. She just wanted peace in her soul.

Yeah right!

"Stop it. I don't want to argue with you," she mumbled.

I'm not going away tonight. You have fallen for a Brennan, and now you have to make a choice or you will never, ever have peace. You'll never be satisfied with anyone else, and it's not going to be easy, but you are tough.

"Not that tough." She sighed.

Come on, girl. Even mild-tempered Leah Brennan fought for what she wanted. What's the matter with you?

"She knew that Rhett loved her, wanted to marry her. That makes a big difference." She wiped a tear from her eye. "God, why does this have to be so hard?"

You can only sit on the fence so long before your butt goes numb and you fall off. Choose what you want, Betsy, and go after it. You didn't need me to tell you what to do when you were chasing after those three O'Donnell cowboys.

"They weren't Brennans, and I'm not listening to you anymore tonight," she said loudly.

Chapter 14

THE SKIES TURNED GRAY ON FRIDAY EVENING, AND THE snow started in earnest, putting down an inch-thick layer on everything. When it stopped, the sky dropped an inch of icy sleet on top of that. On Saturday morning, Betsy awoke to two more inches of snow and the sound of small tree limbs breaking with the weight of the ice that had accumulated on them. She sat up in bed and looked out the window, hoping that she'd been dreaming. But reality was right there on the other side of the glass—snow and ice mixed, which was far worse than just plain old snow.

She threw herself backward, pulled the covers over her head, and groaned. She'd be chipping ice from the watering tanks and feeding cows out there in the cold all day. *AND*—every letter was capitalized in her head in the single-syllable word—tonight, she had promised to meet Declan at the river. Heart and mind had argued all day Friday starting the moment she'd opened her eyes that morning about what she had to say to him. Why did life have to be so complicated?

The smell of bacon and coffee found its way under the quilt and comforter to her nose. She stuck her nose out, inhaled deeply when her feet hit the cold hardwood floor, and tiptoed to the bathroom. She sucked air even more when she sat down on the cold potty and her bladder shriveled up to the size of a marble.

While she was dressing as quickly as possible, but remembering to put on long underwear and an extra pair of socks, she listened to the morning weather report on the radio—more freezing rain in the forecast and there was a possibility that some schools would be closed on Monday. Roads were slippery. Travel was discouraged.

She headed for the coffeepot the minute she reached the kitchen.

"Looks like you bundled up," her mother said.

Her father pushed his empty breakfast plate back. "Ready to get some work done?"

Henry wasn't much taller than her mother and had been blessed with the Gallagher good looks. Pictures of him in his younger days showed him about forty pounds lighter than he was now, but then, Willa was a fine cook. And in those days, his sandy-colored hair had been twice as thick. But his smile was the same, full of love and life.

"Soon as I get a cup of coffee and a biscuit filled with bacon and grape jelly," she answered. "It's not supposed to do this two years in a row in north Texas. We hadn't had snow since I was a little girl until last year."

Henry patted the chair beside him. "Your grandmother says the O'Donnells caused it. They came up here and upset normality. Speaking of them, I expect that you and I'd better get real serious about that property after Christmas, or else some more of their cousins might come visiting and want to stay and buy up one or both of the places that are for sale right now."

Betsy opened up a biscuit and stuffed eight pieces of bacon inside it, added a tablespoon of grape jelly, and then poured a cup of coffee. She carried both to the table and sat down beside her father. "Maybe one of them will have a thing for redheads."

Willa pulled out a chair and joined them. "Your grandmother hates them almost as much as the Brennans. She blames them for the whole past year, so I'd steer clear of them if they do buy up some property in this area."

"Can't date an O'Donnell. Stay away from the Brennans. Who's on the list of those I can see?"

"Preacher John comes to mind," Henry said with a wide grin.

"I'd rather stay single the rest of my life," Betsy said. "Let's go do chores and forget all about this. It's enough to drive a woman plumb crazy."

Declan bailed out of bed, got dressed, and met his father on the landing. "Looks like we're in for another winter like last year," he said.

"Looks like it. The weatherman says it's not going to melt over the weekend and schools are already looking at closing part of next week. They're calling for another two inches of freezing rain throughout today." Russell led the way down the stairs to the kitchen.

"Good morning." Mavis was as cheerful as a bird in springtime. "Can you believe this weather, and guess what I heard? That Betsy Gallagher is trying to seduce the preacher who's here to preach for Kyle on Sunday. He's a brother to her cousin's wife, the one who just had a baby boy. Well, anyway, they were together in the church on Thursday night, and I bet they weren't just talking."

"You're getting slow in your old age, Mama," Russell

chuckled. "I heard that yesterday at the feed store in Gainesville."

"Well, did you hear that your son helped that hussy decorate the bar for Rosalie and that he talked Quaid and Honey into participating? Cavorting with the Gallaghers all evening like there wasn't a feud and like they didn't set fire to my baby Jesus." Her voice got higher with each word.

"I do believe that we stole Santa Claus in retaliation," Declan reminded her seriously.

"They deserved it," Mavis said. "Eat your breakfast and go think about who you are as you help your dad with the feeding this morning."

"I'm a thirty-two-year-old man. That's enough of who I am," he said.

"And it's time you settled too." Mavis glared at him.

"Too? Who else in the family is planning a wedding?" Declan asked.

"Honey is looking for a husband?" Mavis said. "Honey has been man hunting since she was sixteen but settling on one person to spend the rest of her life with isn't easy."

Declan said. "Don't push us."

Mavis scowled. "Don't you sass me. I can replace you as quick as Naomi did Betsy."

"Oh, now this is a competition between you two about who will kick their grandchildren out, is it?" Russell asked. "This is Declan's home. He was born here, and if you make him leave, I'll be right behind him."

"You didn't act like that when Leah moved out for that hippie cowboy she married," Mavis said.

"Leah moved out because she wanted to, and I

support her in her decision. She wasn't kicked out, even though you won't let her come back. But I can take my cattle and my share of this place and move out tomorrow if you're going to start issuing threats," Russell said.

"Who's issuing threats?" Honey yawned as she headed toward the coffeepot.

"Granny is," Declan said.

"Well, I hope it's not concerning our preacher this week because I have a date with him tonight to go to a revival meeting. I hope this damned rotten weather doesn't keep it from happening."

Declan's chuckle grew into one of those guffaws that filled the room. Three people stared at him as if he was crazy but he didn't care. He'd never felt so alive than he had since the bet had gone down in the Burnt Boot Bar and Grill.

The laughter stopped as soon as it started, the quiet in the room becoming more awkward by the moment.

The bet!

In his excitement over Honey having a date with John, he'd forgotten about it.

Betsy parked the four-wheeler at the edge of the Wild Horse property line, crawled over the barbed-wire fence, and made her way to the church, slipping and sliding on the frozen ground the whole way. She was almost giddy when John's vehicle was not parked in the lot or beside the back door, but she got nervous when she pulled the can out from under the porch and found a note in it. It wasn't Thursday and she had no legitimate business at the church, but someone had said they'd seen Declan's truck parked there last night. Rumor had it that he was telling John to steer clear of his cousin Honey, but she wanted to be sure there wasn't a note in the can. After this week, she and Declan had to figure out another way to communicate.

If you get this note, please meet me in Gainesville in the parking lot in front of the Cracker Barrel. Eight o'clock?

She tucked the note into her pocket and shoved the can back under the porch. She had taken two steps back toward the ranch when she heard a door slam behind her and John's voice calling out.

"Hey, Betsy, did you need something? I swear if I had been driving anything lighter weight than this big truck, I would have been in a ditch the way I slipped and slid all the way from Wild Horse to here this morning," he said.

"I was looking for one of my house cats. She ran out the door ahead of me this morning and I trailed her as far as the fence. Thought maybe she was hiding up under the porch. If you see a big, black cat with green eyes, just call Wild Horse, and they'll patch you over to my house," she lied.

Did God take vengeance on a lie or kissing in the pastor's study faster? She quickly glanced at the sky, but it was still gray and peppering down sleet that stung her face when it hit.

"I'll keep an eye out for her. Is she friendly?"

"Oh, yes. She'll come right in the church if you open the door," Betsy said. "My friend Iris gave her to me a couple of years ago."

"What's her name?"

"Angel. Thanks, John. See you around. Hope this weather doesn't keep you from your revival tonight," she said.

"So does Honey Brennan. I invited her to go with me," John said.

Betsy stopped in her tracks. "Does Granny know that?"

"I have no idea."

"I wouldn't be standing on the rooftops telling the world about it if I were you."

"Oh, yes. The 'famous feud.'" He bookended the last word with air quotes. "That doesn't affect me, Betsy. I don't care about a feud that should have ended years ago."

"Talk to Angela about that when you get back to Wild Horse."

"I will, and if I see your Angel cat, I'll call."

"Thanks." She waved and made her way back to her four-wheeler, crawled on, and headed for home, making plans the whole way. She found a note on the kitchen table saying that her parents were at the barn babysitting a heifer that was having trouble delivering a calf.

Betsy wrote on the bottom of the same paper telling them that Iris was in Gainesville at a meeting, stuck there for the weekend, and she was going down to join her. She threw a few things in an overnight bag and made plans to meet Declan at the Cracker Barrel, tell him what she had to say, and then check into the Hampton Inn right there in the same parking lot—alone. No way was she driving down there on slippery roads and back the same night. Besides, she and her imaginary friend had lots to talk about and neither of them wanted to be in church the next morning.

What usually took twenty minutes, driving from Burnt Boot to Gainesville, took an hour and ten minutes. She'd planned on getting there early enough to eat a plate of dumplings before Declan arrived, but it didn't happen. He was sitting in his big, black truck, waiting for her in a nearly empty parking lot.

She pulled in next to him and rolled down the window. "Been waiting long?"

"Just got here. Those roads are horrible. Wouldn't surprise me a bit if the transportation department doesn't shut them completely down. Your truck or mine?"

"Mine," she answered.

"Then yours it is." He only slipped once as he walked from his vehicle to hers. "I packed a suitcase in case they shut down the roads before I can get back to Burnt Boot. I hope the hotel over there isn't booked solid."

"Doesn't look like it," she said. "I only see about six cars in the lot. Folks have hunkered down and aren't getting out in this. Only crazy people who keep a feud alive for a hundred years drive in this kind of weather," she said.

"I could go in there"—he nodded toward the restaurant—"and get some food and then take it over to the hotel. It'd be warmer than a picnic on the river tonight."

"No strings?"

"None whatsoever," he said.

"I am starving," she said. "And, Declan, I've already got a room booked. I called it in on the way down here."

His wide grin heated the whole truck even more. "I'm impressed. No way would I have tried to talk on a cell phone and drive in this at the same time. I kept both hands on the wheel."

"I used the speakerphone. I'll have chicken and dumplings, steak fries, a baked potato, and hash brown casserole. Need to write that down?"

Declan shook his head. "I got it. Wait for me in the lobby?"

"I'll be the one with the red hair and growling stomach."

His grin lit up the whole parking lot. "And the sexy, tight-fittin' jeans and the gorgeous green eyes and a swing to the hips that makes men's eyes pop right out of their heads."

Chapter 15

Betsy fidgeted as she waited in the lobby, key card to a room on the third floor in her hand. It wasn't too late to cut her losses and get back into her truck, drive another half a mile, and get a room at a different hotel. But they were grown adults, and she'd rented a suite that came with a sofa, a small dining area, and a microwave and fridge.

She took a deep breath and stiffened her backbone as well as her resolve as she made plans. They would have supper in her room, not even look at that big, king-size bed, and talk about Christmas stuff. Then he would call down to the lobby and get his own room, probably on a different floor, and tomorrow they'd go home. And then she saw him carrying in two big sacks from the restaurant and a duffel bag, and her determination flew out the door when it slid open.

He was sexy as hell with snowflakes shining on his black cowboy hat. A few had made their way up under the brim to stick to his sandy-brown hair that covered half his ears. His blue eyes caught hers staring at him, and he winked.

That gesture plus his distinct swagger made her mouth go dry. Maybe, she decided right then, they should eat before she said anything. It would be a shame to get into an argument and spoil the dinner. He'd clearly spent a lot of money on those two bags of food, and she really was hungry.

You are hiding from what you know is the right thing to do, her conscience fussed.

I know, but I want one real dinner with him, and he's gone to the trouble to bring it, and I'm not going to put myself in a position to even kiss him. It's just dinner, for God's sake. Go away and leave me alone, she argued.

"Ready?" he asked.

She held up the key card and pointed toward the hall leading to the elevators. "Third floor."

"Weatherman on the radio just now said that we're in for a real blizzard tonight. I called Leah, and the roads are now officially closed into and out of Burnt Boot. Guess we're here for the night. After we eat, I'll call the desk and book a room."

The elevator opened immediately when she pushed the button. She carried her bag inside and held the door while he maneuvered the food and his duffel in, and then she hit the button for the third floor.

"I don't ever remember the roads being completely closed. Do you?" he asked.

She shook her head. "Not even last year when the snow got so deep. I guess it's got to do with that layer of ice under the snow."

"Poor Honey," Declan chuckled. Lord help, but the man even had a southern drawl when he laughed.

"Why poor Honey?"

"She was going to a revival meeting tonight with the preacher that you kissed. Guess maybe he'll have to be satisfied with coming to the house for dinner instead. Granny will be so proud to have a preacher there, and believe me, if Honey doesn't get him branded, Granny will be disappointed. We haven't had a preacher in the family since back when the feud started."

The elevator came to a stop and the doors slid open. "You go on first. Room 312. I'd like to be a fly on the wall at Wild Horse when John announces that he's going to River Bend to have dinner with Honey. This may start a brand-new battle in the feuding wars. They may call it the love war."

When they got into the room, he set the food on the table and tossed his duffel bag toward the closet. "Sounds much better than the pig war and the shit war, doesn't it?"

She started unloading the sacks. "Good grief, Declan! Did you buy enough for a week?"

He kicked off his boots and began arranging food on the coffee table. "We can sit on the floor, can't we? Kind of like those fancy Asian places? But you got to take your boots off."

She removed hers and tossed them over next to his and helped him put take-out containers down the center of the coffee table. Dumplings, three kinds of potatoes, pinto beans, greens, corn bread muffins, biscuits, and two big chicken fried steaks.

He brought out two paper plates, plastic cutlery, and paper napkins. "I thought we'd share. If it hadn't turned out so cold, we'd be having potato salad and ribs and brisket by the river with a blazing fire going up under that willow tree. This isn't as romantic, but it's hot, and we don't even have to worry about anyone catching us. They're all stuck in Burnt Boot. We can't get in, and they can't get out. Pretty nice, isn't it?"

She dipped into the dumplings and then put a chicken fried steak on her plate. "So who are we tonight?"

He set two cups of sweet tea on the table and sat down beside her, instead of across the table. "I think we should be the Wisemans, don't you?"

"Did you bring the duct tape?"

He popped his palm against his head. "Forgot it. How about you are Betsy, and I'm Declan."

"I'd like that," she said.

Declan had never been so nervous in his life. He was a player, and he could seduce a woman in two hours tops, but he wanted more than sex that night. Betsy deserved to be treated like a lady, like the person he'd come to know and appreciate the past couple of weeks. She was worthy of so much more than a quick romp in the sheets over a damned bet.

He wanted to tell her about the poker game. It was on the tip of his tongue to come clean about it, but he couldn't. He could not hurt her, not today, and for damn sure not when they were in a small hotel room where she could throw him out the window. When it was all said and done at Christmas, he intended to tell Tanner that Tanner had won the bet. Declan would shell out the money, and no one would ever know how the Christmas program or the lovely new office and parsonage furniture came about.

"What are you thinking about? You look like you're fighting with yourself," she asked.

"Do you ever do that? Fight with yourself?"

"Daily." She smiled.

"About this thing with us?"

"Hourly," she admitted.

He glanced toward her and their eyes locked, sparks flittering about the room like the snowflakes swirling around outside the window. His fingertips grazed her cheekbone and pushed a strand of red hair behind her ear. The skin on her neck was soft as satin sheets and her hair as fine as silk. He could sit there for hours merely touching her face and hair. She raised her head, and her eyes fluttered shut, but he wasn't ready to kiss her lips. The desire to taste the hollow of her neck and work his way from there to her lips was too strong to be denied.

She moaned when his mouth caressed that sensitive part and slowly went from there to underneath her chin and from there to claim her lips in a fiery kiss that sent him into instant arousal. His hand left her neck and unfastened the top button of her shirt, showing the top half of her breasts, sitting so sweetly there in a bra that only covered three-fourths of them.

A shiver down her spine let him know what effect he had on her. He put enough distance between them that he could look deeply into her eyes while he unbuttoned the rest of her shirt and pushed it over her shoulders.

"You, Miz Betsy, are beautiful," he said hoarsely.

She reached out and, with one flip of the hand, opened every snap on his western shirt. "You, Declan, are sexy as hell."

He leaned in and kissed the top of her breasts. "And how sexy is that?"

"Think of the heat down there in hell. You are seven times hotter than that."

"Wow!"

Her lips parted when he kissed her again, this time allowing his tongue entrance, and together they teased, flirted, and made wild, passionate love with nothing but steamy, hot kisses.

~

That little voice inside her head screamed, ranted, raved, and tried to talk sense to her, but she mentally hit the mute button and ignored it altogether.

Her insides were quickly turning into a melting pot of oozing hormones, begging for release. Every kiss fueled the fire beneath the pot, and every touch of his hands made it bubble even more.

Rough palms gently moving from shoulder to wrist and then his fingers lacing with hers were as sensual as the kisses. When he removed her bra and peeled her jeans and socks off, she changed positions so she was sitting astride his lap, naked breasts against the soft hair on his chest.

"My turn," she whispered as she undid his belt and unzipped his jeans, releasing the throbbing erection into her cold hands.

His sudden intake of breath put a smile on her face. "Lord, that feels good."

She jerked his jeans down and removed them without leaving his lap or his lips for more than thirty seconds at a time. That niggling voice in her head tried to talk her out of going down the path she was headed for, but she listened to her heart instead as she stood up and led him to the king-size bed, flipped the covers back, and invited him in with a tug of the hand.

"Are you sure about this?" he asked. "We can stop right now and not go another step."

"More than anything in a long time."

He drew her close, his arm around her shoulders, the kisses resuming as his hands massaged her back. "I feel like a little kid on Christmas morning."

"Presents are unwrapped," she said. "It's time to play with the toys." She rolled over on top of him, and in one swift movement, he was inside her.

He put both hands on her waist, and in another roll, he was on top, and together they started a rhythm that went from slow to fast, until they were both panting so hard they could scarcely breathe. Then, he slowed the pace until she groaned and dug her nails into his back.

She'd always been in control when it came to sex, but that night she lost it all, letting him take the lead, letting him decide when they'd fall off the ledge of the mountain they'd been climbing for the past hour or more. It was a new experience, one that created a heady feeling that she couldn't get enough of.

"Now?" he whispered.

She was speechless and could barely nod. The tempo picked up, and the buzz in her ears was so loud, she thought they would explode. This was more than a romp in the sheets. It was more than sex. Declan had made love to her, and already she could feel the afterglow setting in when he growled her name and collapsed on top of her.

"My God," he groaned as he moved to one side, pulling her into his embrace.

She rested her head on his shoulder and tried desperately to get enough air in her lungs to utter even a simple sentence. She'd just had amazing, mind-boggling sex with Declan Brennan, and the hotel was still standing. Snow still fell outside, and the world had not come to a complete end. Hell, the moon wasn't even dripping blood, and somewhere out there, the sun was shining on some part of the world.

"Intense." She finally got out one word.

"It was bound to be."

He didn't need to explain. She understood. A hundred years of desire between two feuding families had been satisfied that night. She could feel those ancestors who hated the feud applauding her even though the sensible side—called her conscience—reminded her of what Naomi Gallagher would do if she had an inkling of what had just happened.

"I'm hungry," she said.

He propped up on an elbow. "You are amazing."

"Because I'm hungry?"

He kissed her on the tip of her nose. "No, because you are you. Now tell me, sweet darlin', what are you hungry for?"

"Food first and then another round of whatever we just did to see if it was a fluke or if it was really that good."

"Will you starve if we take another five minutes to enjoy this nice fuzzy feeling? This is something new to me."

"Never had afterglow before?" she asked.

"Is that what this is? It's wonderful. Have you had it before?"

She shook her head, being honest. "I thought it was something that romance writers cooked up to make everyone think they'd found the gold at the end of the rainbow."

He toyed with her hair, his touch already starting another fire. Or was it the embers of the afterglow that made it so easy to get heated up again?

"I feel like I slid down the rainbow and landed in the pot of gold," he whispered.

"That's a pretty good line, Declan."

"It's not a line, darlin'. It's the pure gospel truth."

"Speaking of that, I don't guess either of us will be in church tomorrow. I wonder if anyone will put two and two together."

Declan shook his head. "Not in a million years. I'm snowed in because I came down here to pick up a tractor part for my dad and the tractor place was closed due to weather. What are you doing here?"

"I'm visiting my college friend Iris."

"Is she in this hotel?"

Betsy giggled. "She's in this room with us."

Declan's eyes widened. "Tell me you are kidding and she's not in the bathroom."

"She is my imaginary friend. She gets me out of dinners I don't want to attend, family arguments, and, this morning, the imaginary cat she gave me got me out of a tight spot at the church when I went looking for a note." She went on to explain what had happened.

"God bless Iris. I don't even mind that she's sitting on the sofa watching television while we tear up the bed." He laughed and then whispered seductively as he kissed the soft spot under her earlobe, "But you are so much prettier and sexier than Iris. She's just not my type at all."

Chapter 16

Declan opened one eye and could see that it was still snowing. He pulled the covers over his head and wished he were in Florida or somewhere warm and sunny instead of north Texas, getting ready to feed cows in deep snow. The aroma of bacon, coffee, and maple syrup blended together to make his stomach growl, and suddenly, he remembered that he was not on River Bend but in a hotel room with Betsy.

"Good mornin', sleepyhead." Her hand started at his neck, skimmed its way down his back, and squeezed his butt cheek. "Wake up. I've been down to the dining room and brought breakfast up to share with you. Pancakes and bacon with an omelet on the side and lots of coffee."

He reached behind his back and laced her fingers in his, rolled over, and brought them to his lips to kiss each one individually. "And you for dessert?"

She bent forward and kissed him on the forehead. "If you eat all your breakfast, you can have whatever dessert you want. After last night, you need strength."

The jeans she must've worn down to the dining room had been thrown at the sofa and missed. His shirt from the night before was all she wore as she sat there beside him, cross-legged, with a food tray on the foot of the bed. With no makeup, sleep still in her gorgeous green eyes, and her body a row of pearl snaps away, she absolutely rendered him speechless.

"I can't have dessert first?" he asked.

"Not after I got dressed and went out for breakfast. Sit up, cowboy, and let's eat." She untangled her hand from his, scooted back far enough to put the tray between them, and poured syrup on the warm pancakes.

He sat up, picked up her hand, dipped her fingertips in the syrup, and then proceeded to lick every drop from each one. Her eyes had gone all soft and dreamy by the time he finished the last fingertip. He leaned across the tray and kissed her, soft at first, then deepening into something lingering and more demanding.

"Mmmm!" she mumbled when he straightened up and picked up the plastic fork.

"The pancakes won't taste nearly as good as your fingers," he said.

She dipped her fingertip in syrup and applied it to his full mouth like lipstick, then began to lick it off one micro section at a time. His pulse quickened. His heart raced. He had to hold his hands tightly on top of the folded-back covers to keep from throwing her on the bed, kicking the breakfast onto the floor, and having wild, hot sex with her right there, right then.

"You are killing me," he said.

"What's good for the goose…as they say." She smiled. "Let's eat before it gets so cold we have to heat it in the microwave."

He shoveled a forkful of omelet into his mouth and nodded. "Good," he mumbled.

"Not as good as the ones I make, but it'll give us energy. I can't believe we slept this late. They were starting to put things away when I got to the dining room," she said between bites.

He glanced at the clock on the nightstand. "Is that clock right? I haven't slept this late in years. Is it really nine thirty?"

"It is. I woke at nine, jerked on the first clothes I found on the floor, and went down to get us some food so we didn't have to go out. I wish they had room service here, but about all we can get delivered is pizza, and that's if the pizza place is open on a day like this," she said.

"How many times did you wish for enough snow to build a snowman when you were a kid?" he asked.

"Every single winter, but I only remember getting to do that one time. I was about ten," she said.

"I was twelve, and the snowman wasn't even as big as me. We got about two inches, and by the time Quaid, Leah, Honey, and I got our snowman finished, the yard was completely cleaned of every single flake."

An instant visual of Declan at twelve popped into Betsy's head. He had been all legs back then. Sandy-blond hair and big, blue eyes, skinny as a newborn colt, and it took a couple more years for him to grow into his long legs. It was strange to think of the Brennan kids over there on River Bend doing and feeling the same things that the Gallagher children did on Wild Horse.

"Have I told you this morning that you are gorgeous?" he asked.

"No, but I believe you covered that topic quite well last night. Iris was very impressed with you," Betsy said.

He looked around the room. "Where is she this morning?"

"She had to go back to Dallas. They've got Interstate 35 cleared to the south. The bridge is closed to get across the Red River into Oklahoma because of the ice, but they're hoping to have it scraped and ready for travel by noon. But the weatherman is still issuing a severe weather alert and telling folks to stay off the roads."

One of his sexy eyelids slid down in a slow wink. "Isn't that too bad? Any idea when they might have the country road up to Burnt Boot open for traffic?"

"They're saying tomorrow. I went ahead and booked this room for tonight. I'm so sorry we are missing church this beautiful Sunday morning."

"It is a total shame. I'd looked forward to hearing John preach."

A soft, little-girl giggle escaped from around a bite of pancakes. "You are telling lies right here on Sunday."

"So are you. We're both sinners. But on a different note, I doubt that they have church this morning. No one will be able to get out to services."

"And that makes me wonder if Preacher John will be having dinner at Wild Horse with his sister or River Bend with Honey. Maybe I should call home and get the lowdown on what is happening with the love war."

The words had barely left her mouth when her phone rang. She leaned over the bed, not caring that Declan got a flash of her naked butt, and grabbed it from the nightstand.

"Where are you?" her mother asked.

"Holed up in the Hampton Inn waiting for the spring thaw," she teased.

"Well, don't try to come home today. The roads are a mess and there're road blocks up. We didn't even have church. I can't believe we're getting hit like this two years in a row. Maybe Naomi is right. Those O'Donnell cousins brought bad luck to Burnt Boot." Willa laughed. "Is Iris there with you?"

"She went back to Dallas. Roads south of here have been cleared for travel," Betsy answered. "I heard that Preacher John had a date with Honey Brennan last night." She looked across the bed to see Declan grinning like a possum eating grapes through a barbed-wire fence.

"Whole town is talking about it. They're calling it the love war. Your grandmother threatened to throw him out in the snow when he went over to River Bend last night for supper. She's livid because if Honey gets serious about him, then there would be a hairline connection between the two feuding families, what with him being kin to a Gallagher. Mavis is delighted that she's getting under Naomi's skin and possibly dragging a preacher back into the Brennan family. All over a preacher, mind you. And the love war? It doesn't carry the pizzazz that the pig war and the shit war did, does it?"

Betsy gave Declan a thumbs-up and mouthed, *Love war, it is*.

He put up his palm, and they did a silent high five.

"Are you still there?" Willa asked.

"I'm here. So what's your opinion of this whole love-war thing between Honey and Angela's brother?"

"I figure Naomi will rethink Angela and Jody living in the big house if Angela's brother gets mixed up with Honey Brennan—and that Mavis will put more than one feather in her hat if she can make trouble on Wild Horse. What are you doing all day?"

The question caught Betsy off guard so much that she stammered, "Ummm, well, it's snowing, and I guess...I suppose I'll watch some reruns on TV and maybe go outside and make a snowman."

"Sounds like a boring day. Call if you want to pass the time."

"Thanks, Mama. Maybe they'll have things cleared off so"—she caught herself before she said *we*, cleared her throat, and went on—"so I can get home tomorrow."

"I hope so, but drive safely. Talk to you later."

Betsy pushed a button and the face of her phone went dark. "They're calling it the love war already."

One side of Declan's mouth turned up in half a grin that was even sexier than a brilliant smile. "The love war. Granny is going to hate that as much as she did the pig war, but she'll be rootin' for Honey. She's always wanted a preacher, and if it can make Naomi Gallagher mad, then she'll be one happy old gal." Declan held a piece of crisp bacon near her lips.

She bit off the end. "And Angela might find herself living back in the little house before long if Honey takes a shine to John. I think the 'love war' fits this feudin' battle very well, but right now, I'm thinkin' it's time for dessert."

Declan set the tray on the floor beside the bed. His hand was a blur as it grabbed the tail of the shirt she wore and every snap came undone with a popping noise. "I do like pearl snaps, and I really like what's under them."

She wrapped her arms around his neck and slid under the covers with him, both of them stretching out so she was pressed against his side, his arm around her, their noses just inches apart.

"I also love your kisses," he said as his lips found hers and his tongue traced the outline of her lips. That gesture started the hormones to boiling immediately.

"I like your whole body and what it does to mine." Her hand followed his hair from his chest all the way down to find that he was definitely ready for dessert.

He rolled her over onto her back and kissed her until they were both breathless. "Ready?"

"Been ready since I woke you up." She wrapped her legs firmly around him and tangled her fingers in his thick hair.

With a firm thrust, he started a gentle motion that made her moan for more and more, which he gave her right up until she whispered his name hoarsely and together they satisfied the fire inside their bodies.

"If it keeps getting better every time, we're going to burn ourselves into nothing but ashes," he muttered between gasps.

"But what a way to go." She wiggled out from under him.

He rolled to his back, and she settled in next to his side, sated and yet wanting more. She'd never felt like this before, but then she'd never spent the entire night with a man before, never had breakfast in bed with him, and for damn sure never looked forward to another bout of hot sex after having it three—no, four times since they started they night before. Usually once or twice and she was ready to go home and forget the guy, no matter how handsome he was. She had managed one six-month relationship back when she was twenty-one and still in college. And another one that lasted three months when she was about twenty-five.

And this one won't last a day past Christmas, no

matter how good you are in bed with him or how much chemistry there is between you.

"Shhh," she said.

"I didn't say anything," Declan said.

"I know."

"Voices in your head? I'm doing the same thing. They're telling me that we're going down a fool's path and that this can never develop into a relationship. Is that what you're hearing?"

She nodded and bit back the tears threatening to escape from behind her thick lashes.

"Are you going to listen to them?"

"Not today," she said.

"Good. Let's go take a shower, get dressed, and go outside in that big, empty parking lot behind the outlet mall and make a snowman. This may be the only opportunity we ever have to make one together."

She rose up on an elbow, her breasts brushing against his side. "So you don't think we have a chance at anything more than an occasional secret rendezvous?"

"No, I don't think that we'll ever see this much snow again in our area of the world. We'll have to see if the other thing is strong enough to withstand the big rocks that will be thrown at it," he said.

He crawled out of bed, scooped her up in his arms, and carried her to the bathroom. He sat her on the edge of the tub, went back into the room, and touched a few buttons on his phone.

Mark Chesnutt started singing "Ol' Country," and Declan came back and extended his hand. Together, they swayed to the music, doing a two-step around the bathroom floor wearing nothing but smiles.

The lyrics said that the city sun went down at night and the country boy was lookin' at the moon. It talked about a city girl and a country boy, but she got the gist of the story. The girl and the boy in the story were as mismatched as she and Declan. When Mark sang about the fact that she'd never been loved at all until ol' country came to town, Betsy leaned back and looked up into his blue eyes and read his mind.

"It's our story," he said.

"Yes, it is. You promise to have the hotel ready with ice and drinks and have everything perfect?"

"Anytime, darlin'. Anytime you can get away to have a night with ol' country here and you'll promise to kiss me and hold me tight," he answered.

"Why does it have to be so complicated?"

"To make us enjoy it when ol' country does come to town. Now for a shower and then snowman building, and by then, we'll be hungry and this cowboy would like to take you to lunch at the Cracker Barrel. What do you say?"

She stood on tiptoe and pulled his lips to hers. "Yes, darlin'."

Chapter 17

Five inches of snow lay like a big, white, fluffy blanket on the enormous empty lot on the huge mall parking lot behind the hotel. Not a footprint or tire track anywhere in it—not even a few little rabbit tracks like Betsy would see in the country up around Burnt Boot.

She'd dressed warmly in long underwear under her jeans, which were tucked inside her cowboy boots, a flannel shirt, and her mustard-colored work coat over it all. She'd pulled a ski mask over her red hair and face, leaving only her eyes showing. Declan had dressed pretty much the same way except that he'd forgotten to pack long underwear, but he did have a pair of work coveralls in his truck. So he'd zipped them up over his clothing, tucked the legs down into his cowboy boots, and pulled a ski mask over his face.

Betsy was glad that the mask didn't cover those pretty blue eyes because she loved seeing the laughter and excitement in them. Right now, he was looking at the snow like he was that little, long-legged twelve-year-old boy again. She couldn't help but wonder if the same happiness showed in her own eyes.

Declan took her gloved hand in his "Well, darlin', I do believe we have enough here to build a snowman or maybe two. The only question is where do we want him to stand when we get done?"

"Over there by that lonesome tree. We might even borrow a few twigs from it to make his arms," she said.

"Then we'll begin rolling right here." He dropped her hand and made a snowball about the size of a baseball.

She did the same. "I'll make the middle while you do the bottom."

"How big do we want him?" Declan asked.

"Tall as you," she answered.

"And how do we plan to pick up his fat, little middle section? We don't have a crane," Declan said.

"I'll make it about half the size it should be, and we'll put it on the first part and then pack snow around it until it's big enough. This is wet snow. It's going to pack really well," she said.

"Go on and start rolling then," he said.

"Why?"

"Because I want to be behind you, so I can see that cute little butt of yours." His eyes said he was grinning even though she couldn't see his mouth.

"Maybe I had the same idea about your tight, little cowboy butt," she said, smarting off right back at him.

"Oh, so you think I've got a cute rear end?" he asked.

"No, I think you've got a sexy ass, Declan Br—"

He shook his finger. "No last names. We're out here playing in the snow like a couple of kids who only know each other's first names."

"Okay, then let's make this snowman one that will still be standing here in this parking lot when Christmas morning comes around," she said.

"Yes, ma'am, and on that day, we'll come back here and take pictures of him or what's left of him, okay?" Declan asked.

"It's a date."

Two hours later, they stood back to look at their creation. They were tired, covered in wet snow, and half-frozen, but a six-foot snowman stood before them. Declan had taken several pictures of it with his camera to prove that they had indeed built the huge thing and hadn't even begun to use up all the snow on the parking lot. But alas, although he had stick arms, he didn't have a carrot for a nose or any other facial features.

"We could use rocks, but they're all covered up," she said.

"We could go into the Cracker Barrel and buy a carrot and some black candies for his eyes and mouth and maybe even get him a hat," Declan said.

"Yes, yes, yes!" She clapped her gloved hands together and snow flew everywhere.

It only took a few minutes to talk the salesclerk out of a carrot from the kitchen and to find a bag of big licorice gumdrops. Betsy found an old straw hat that was on sale for half price and bought their snowman a bright-green-and-red-plaid scarf to tie around his neck. But by the time they paid for their purchases, the snow that had accumulated on their boots and clothing had begun to melt, and they left a puddle of water in front of the cash register.

"I'm so sorry about this mess," Betsy said.

"Go on and finish your job," the saleslady said. "We'll clean this up. What a honeymoon you're having. Be sure to take pictures of all this."

"Honeymoon!" Betsy said when they were out of the store and trudging back to their poor faceless snowman. "Why would she think that?"

Declan laughed. "Only stupid kids, silly teenagers, or

crazy newlyweds would be out in this weather making a snowman."

"Well, since we are past the kid and the teenager stage, that only leaves one category, and she chose it," Betsy agreed.

"So now we have to be Mr. and Mrs. Wiseman the rest of this trip because only married people go on honeymoons," he said.

They rounded the north end of the mall and saw that tire tracks had plowed through the snow all the way from the hotel to the snowman. A woman was standing outside a bright-red Jeep, taking pictures of every angle of the snowman. When she saw them, she waved and motioned them forward.

"I believe it's time to pull our ski masks down, Mrs. Wiseman," Declan said.

"Why? Are you getting cold?"

"No, but if you will read what's written on the side of that Jeep, you'll see that woman is from the Gainesville newspaper. This big snow is front-page news, and several folks in Burnt Boot get the newspaper."

"Oh no! What are we going to do?" she asked.

"Well, the one thing we are not going to do is let her see our faces." He quickly pulled his mask back on.

She followed his lead and jerked her ski mask from her coat pocket and made sure every bright-red strand of hair was tucked up under it.

"Check me out," she said.

"I have many times, and I've liked every angle. There's a bit still showing in the back. Here, I'll put it under your collar and adjust the back of the mask so it covers it. There we go," he said.

"Hey, are you the newlywed couple who built this big, old boy?" the lady yelled when they got closer.

"We are," Declan said.

"Come stand beside it and let me take your pictures. It's the best one I've found and I've been out scouting the town all afternoon. What're your names?" She snapped dozens of pictures as they gave the snowman a face, wrapped the scarf around his neck, and settled the straw hat on his head.

"We are the Wisemans. Maria and Joe," Declan said.

"Well, Maria and Joe, will you please remove your ski masks for the camera? I want to put you on the front page of tomorrow's paper with your snowman."

"Can't do that," Declan said. "And we'd appreciate it if you didn't use our names. We kind of eloped, and our families don't know. They think we're on business trips, so we'd better not let our faces show."

"Why don't you take a picture of us from behind, putting on his hat?" Betsy asked.

"Would you mind if I put it in the cutline that you are newlyweds who have to tell your folks before your names can be released and then maybe tell everyone you're Maria and Joe Wiseman in a later edition? And maybe you could take my card and send me a picture of you together to put in that edition?"

"Sure thing," Declan said.

"Okay, pretend you are putting on his hat, and let me get a picture of that. He's a gorgeous snowman. Looks like he should be on a Christmas music album," she said. "Oh, by the way, I'm Lacy, and here's my card."

Declan took it and shoved it into his pocket.

"Don't forget to send me the picture," she said.

"We won't," he said and then picked Betsy up by the waist and held her high enough so she could pretend to put the hat on the snowman.

"That's fantastic." Lacy snapped at least a dozen shots in the thirty seconds Declan had Betsy in his arms. "Let's go have a cup of coffee. I'll treat since you've been such good sports."

Declan set Betsy on the ground but kept her hand in his. "We've got plans and..." He had to think fast and fake a sneeze before he said *Betsy*. "Maria is getting really cold, so I think we'll go on in for a while. We'll look for the picture in the paper tomorrow. Remember, darlin', we'll have to cut it out and put it in our wedding album."

"Yes, we will," Betsy said. "Thanks for the offer of coffee, Lacy."

She managed to keep the laughter inside the ski mask until she reached the elevator in the hotel. The mask was a blur as it came off her head, red hair with static electricity sticking up like she'd stuck her finger in an electrical socket, and laughter echoing off the walls of the elevator.

Declan removed his mask, grabbed her around the waist, twirled her around a couple of times, and kissed her so hard and passionately that she went limp in his arms. "That was more fun than anything I've done in years."

"What?" she asked breathlessly when he finally set her down. "The lies or the snowman?"

"All of it," he said. "I'm hungry. How about you?"

"Starving. That aroma of cooking food in the Cracker Barrel almost made me stay there, rather than going back to finish up Mr. Snowman."

The elevator doors opened, and they were just closing

the door to their room when they heard a voice calling out, "Joe and Maria. Hey, Joe! You lost something."

"Dammit!" Betsy swore even though she'd been doing so good at not cussing. "She caught that other elevator. Put your mask on or do something. I'm hiding out in the bathroom."

"Hell's bells!" Declan muttered. He opened the door just enough to stick out a hand. "What did I drop?" he asked.

"My business card." She smiled and snapped a picture of one eye, his hand, and the door. "Here it is." She put it in his hand and turned back toward the elevator.

"So much for going to the restaurant for something to eat. We'd better order some pizza," she said.

"Pizza sounds good. I'll order while you get out of those wet clothes. Hang them over the shower rod and they might be dry by morning," he said.

"And to look on the bright side"—she rose on tiptoe to kiss him—"if we order pizza, we can get a six-pack of beer with it and some pasta and breadsticks, and we can always hit the vending machine for snacks, so we'll be good for the whole day."

He ran a forefinger from her temple to her lips. "I like cold kisses."

"I like hot dessert," she grinned.

"It'll take at least forty-five minutes for them to get our order ready and drive all the way out here on these roads. How about we combine the kisses and the dessert while we wait?" he asked.

She started stripping out of her clothes while he picked up the menu card beside the phone and dialed the number.

"You need what?" she heard him say and then put his hand over the receiver. "He has to have a name and a room number to call back to the hotel and verify that this is legitimate. What if that nosy newspaper lady is in the lobby?"

"Give me that phone." She held out her hand.

"This is Betsy Gallagher. I'm in room 312, and you can call this number"—she rattled off the number on the phone—"to verify it. But there's a stalker in the lobby. A woman with a big camera, and if she asks you any questions, you are to say that you are delivering the order to Maria Wiseman. Write that down because it will mean a twenty-dollar tip if you do what I tell you. If you don't, I'll make you wish you had. Do you understand me?"

"Yes, ma'am. I do this kind of business all the time." The young man laughed. "Maria Wiseman, what would you like to order?"

"A meat lover's pizza with hand-tossed crust." She looked up at Declan to see him holding up two fingers and said, "Make that two large ones of the same. A tray of chicken Alfredo and one of spaghetti and meatballs, a medium order of breadsticks with sauce, and two large bottles of Pepsi. And a six-pack of beer, preferably Coors."

"That's sixty-nine dollars and seventy-five cents total with tax," he said. "We take cash, credit cards, or checks if they are local."

"It will be cash," she said.

"I'll be there in forty-five minutes or I'll cut the bill in half."

"Thank you." Betsy ended the call and laid her phone on the desk.

"You're pretty good at that. This isn't your first rodeo, is it?" Declan asked.

She smiled. "Not really. I'm pretty open with everything I do, but I do have a few secrets."

"Me either," he said. "Always been right out in the open."

"No secrets about anything?" she asked.

"Well, I don't kiss and tell." He grinned.

She unbuttoned her flannel shirt and carried it to the bathroom. When she turned around, Declan was right behind her. He put the lid down on the toilet and sat down, reached out, and drew her to him, burying his face in her midsection.

"I wish we could go public, but if we did, it would turn Burnt Boot upside down, and we'd never get the stuff we need for the Christmas program," he said.

She kissed the top of his head. "We're like the song. Even though I'm not a city girl, it's the same thing. We come from two different worlds that are really just alike but they can't be mixed. So we'll enjoy what we have a day at a time, Declan, and when it's over, we'll have our memories."

He pulled her tighter into his embrace. "What if that's not enough?"

"Then we'll cross that bridge when we get to it. Forty minutes now until the pizza gets here, so let's go curl up under the covers and get warm," she teased.

He tugged her long underwear down to the floor and slung it up over the shower rod with her other wet clothes and then stripped out of his own, leaving all of it in a pile on the bathroom floor.

"Nice outfit there," she said.

"I like yours much better." He picked her up and carried her out of the bathroom, flipped back the covers on the bed with one hand, and tossed her into the middle. She squealed when she bounced, but he landed beside her and his lips found hers in a searing kiss that erased every sane thought from her mind.

When the pizza guy arrived thirty-nine minutes later, Declan met him at the door, handed him a fistful of bills, and brought the food to the bed. "The woman is still in the lobby, and she took a picture of him delivering pizza to the newlyweds. She offered him ten bucks to take a picture of either or both of us with the camera on his phone."

"That hussy! Why would she do that?" Betsy fumed.

"I think she smells the lie and is curious," Declan said. "She'll leave pretty soon. The desk clerk isn't allowed to give out information about guests."

"Too bad it's against the law to shoot people like that. We were nice to her."

Declan chuckled. "You can't shoot her. You don't have a gun."

Betsy inhaled deeply and let it out in a whoosh. "I never leave home without a gun. Dammit! I hope to hell she doesn't go pokin' around our vehicles. That pink truck stands out like a sore thumb out there."

"You are a legitimate guest here, and, honey, I never leave home with the tags on my truck that really go with it. Right now, I'm running Oklahoma tags from a 2001 truck that is sitting in a junkyard." Declan flashed another of his heart-stopping grins.

Betsy eyed him. "Why?"

"Protection. Oh no!" He gasped.

"What?" she asked.

"Speaking of protection…"

"I'm on the pill."

He swiped a hand across his forehead in a dramatic gesture. "I should have asked, but when I'm with you, I'm worse than a teenager. And, Betsy, the thing about protection with the truck is not against jealous husbands. I don't date or go to bed with married women. It's just that I've been caught speeding so often that I can't afford to get caught again and lose my license. So I've got a couple of fake ID's and a bunch of truck tags just to keep me out of jail. If I can stay out of trouble for six months, then I'll be fine."

"I didn't ask," she said.

"I know, darlin', but I want you to know that."

"Thank you. I swear I'm trading in that pink truck for a black one, or a maybe a white one. You see a lot of those on the roads, so no one would recognize it. Do you reckon you could get me one of those junked plates sometime?" she asked.

"Got a few extra in the barn. I'll bring you one next time we go to the storage unit."

Chapter 18

Betsy listened to the radio all the way home on the slippery roads Monday afternoon. Because of the bad weather, the hotel had generously offered all its guests a late checkout at two o'clock that day. Declan had left first, and she had made one more sweep through the room to be sure nothing had been left behind—especially anything that would identify either of them if that nosy lady from the newspaper came snooping around.

Bless his heart, Declan had parked a mile down the road from the hotel and waited for her. Every so often, she'd check the rearview to make sure that Declan was still back there behind her, seeing to it that she got home with no problems. She tapped the steering wheel to Miranda Lambert's singing and then to an old classic from Dolly Parton. She wondered if he was listening to the same station she was or if he had a CD in.

She'd just pulled into town when her phone rang. She touched the face and put it on speaker. "I'm about to turn in to the ranch lane, Mama," she said.

"I thought you might be getting close to town. Go on down to the store. Gladys has it open today. I called in my supply list, and she'll have it ready for you. And pick up a package of those chocolate cookies your daddy likes so well. I don't have time to bake, since it's taking all hands to keep the chores done in this weather. I'm glad you're home. We need you here," Willa said.

She kept going until she reached the store, came to a long, slippery slide in the parking lot and almost lost her footing when she stepped out. When Declan's truck went past, she came within a split second of throwing her hand up to wave at him. Giving herself a solid talking-to about being cautious, she kicked the snow off her boots before she entered the store and wiped them again on the rug right inside the door.

"Hey, we been lookin' for you for an hour," Gladys said in a gruff, gravelly voice.

"Might as well get a cup of coffee and tell us how things look between here and Gainesville," Polly said from behind the counter.

"Looks like the whole gang is here." Betsy smiled.

"Yep," Verdie said, "we all got a case of cabin fever, and Jill was needed on the ranch today to help Sawyer take care of things, so we decided to run the store together and catch up on all our visitin'."

"I didn't realize it until right now, but y'all are now officially shirttail kin since you are all three affiliated in some way with the O'Donnells," Betsy said.

Gladys poured a cup of coffee, handed it to Betsy, and pointed at a chair. "That's right, but we been closer than blood kin for years. You might as well sit a minute."

The store hadn't changed in Betsy's lifetime. A white frame building, it had a porch across the front, big windows that looked out onto the gravel parking lot and two gas pumps. A meat counter stretched across the back of the store. A freezer took up one side, and down the middle, there were two rows of canned and bottled merchandise and a row of produce. One of the end cases toward the front had a candy display that had caught Betsy's eye when she was a little girl and did the same that afternoon.

"Put one of those chocolate bars on the ticket." She set her coffee down and picked out one with nuts and caramel.

"It's on the house," Gladys said. "Did you stay at the Hampton in Gainesville?"

Betsy removed the paper from the candy bar and nodded. "That's where Iris and I usually stay when she's in town. The mall is all but a ghost town, but the hotel is right by the Cracker Barrel, so we don't have to go far to eat."

Polly pushed the morning paper across the counter. "Did you see these people?"

"We didn't think we'd even get the paper today, but I guess the roads were cleared up enough that the carrier could get through. It came late, but it got here," Gladys said.

"The paper is calling them the mystery couple and is offering a free year's subscription to anyone who can identify them and tell where they live. It's a contest that's going to run until Christmas," Verdie said.

Betsy swallowed hard and fast to keep from choking on the candy in her mouth. "So that's who built that big snowman in the parking lot. It was really something. Iris and I saw it from the window of our room."

"Are you gay?" Verdie asked bluntly.

Betsy had just taken a sip of coffee, and she spewed it all over her coat and the floor. "Why would you ask that?"

"You go see this Iris pretty often, and no one has met her. Lord God Almighty, Naomi would probably pass little green apples if she found out you were gay, so I just thought maybe you were keeping it a secret," Verdie said.

"Well, I am definitely not gay. Iris is my friend, but I don't want her all up in this feud stuff. What if she came to Burnt Boot and fell for a Brennan? Then Granny would pitch a fit every time I mentioned her name," Betsy said.

"Well, that settles that," Polly said.

"And Naomi would pitch if Iris fell in love with a Brennan." Verdie nodded. "You're a smart woman, Betsy."

Gladys shoved the paper across the counter. "Look real careful at the pictures. I'd like to win that contest."

Polly chuckled. "You've got a two-year subscription to that paper, old woman. You're just nosy."

Betsy studied the picture on the front page. There she and Declan were, backs to the camera, putting the hat on the snowman. Thank God her hair was covered, because the picture was in living color. The cutline identified them as Joe and Maria Wiseman, and the short article said that more pictures could be found inside on page five.

Betsy flipped the pages, and there was a half-page spread of pictures. One of her and Declan holding hands as they walked back to the hotel, and one of them coming toward the photographer right after they'd put their ski masks back on. Thank goodness they were taken far enough away that his brilliant-blue eyes didn't show up, or someone could have recognized him.

"Are Joe and Maria Wiseman really their names? Are

they really newlyweds? The mystery of the folks who left a snowman behind will be solved," the cutline said.

"So did you see them?" Gladys asked.

"No, but whoever took this picture right here has got things all wrong." Betsy pointed to the one with nothing but fingertips coming out of the door to take a business card. "I can't believe this."

"What?" All three women leaned forward in their metal folding chairs.

"That says room 312 on the door. That's the room I was in. This is all a big hoax. I bet that newlywed couple didn't even stay in that hotel. They probably live right there in Gainesville and were shooting that reporter a line of horse crap."

"Who was in there with you? That hand is too big to be yours," Gladys said.

"Iris is six feet tall and gripes that she has hands like a man. She said that a woman said she was looking for the Wisemans and handed her a card. We laughed about it and then she got a call saying that the roads were clear, so she left. I ordered pizza and watched movies all evening after that. I wonder who they are and what their story is."

"I was so sure that we'd figure out who those people were." Verdie huffed. "Hey, did y'all hear that Lottie Miller is having an estate auction this week? Sorry time to have it, with all this weather, but take a look on the back page, Betsy. She's selling off her house, her furniture, and all her Christmas stuff. Auction is Wednesday, and if things don't thaw, there won't be many folks there."

Betsy turned to the back page of the paper and ate her candy bar while the ladies talked about how long

Lottie had been in Burnt Boot, what all she used to do for the church, and how wonderfully her crocheted items always sold at the bazaar.

"That's back when we had a bazaar." Polly sighed. "I always liked that, but then the feud got in the way, and we had to stop having it."

"Hey, don't look at me. It's not my fault that I was born a Gallagher," Betsy said. "I see that she's selling her acreage too, but not at the auction. It doesn't say how much she has."

"Five hundred," Gladys said. "A good start, and it could raise a family if folks worked hard at it. It's been cleared and is good grassland so it would support a good herd."

"Sounds like a nice place." Betsy folded the paper. "Now, what can you tell me about the love war? Mama says that Granny and Mavis are at it again over Angela's brother, John, and Honey Brennan."

"Latest news is that Angela and Jody are moving back into one of the cabins out there on Wild Horse because Naomi pitched a fit about John going to River Bend for supper on Saturday night," Polly said.

Gladys shrugged. "I heard he had quite the sermon prepared for church on Sunday about folks who don't forgive and who keep a stupid feud alive when it should have been buried years ago. When Naomi heard what he was going to talk about, she told him to leave Wild Horse, and that made Angela mad, so she insisted Jody move her back into her own place."

Verdie picked up the story when Gladys paused for a sip of coffee. "Mavis is tickled to death with the whole thing. She told John he could stay on River Bend indefinitely. Only trouble is that he likes Honey a lot, but I hear that he's way too wild for her."

Betsy's eyes popped open so wide that a pain shot through her temples. "Too wild for Honey? He's a preacher."

"That's what I heard," Verdie said. "He's looking for a wife, and he wants her to move up around Waurika, Oklahoma, which is where he and Angela and our preacher, Kyle, are all from."

"But they only met a couple of days ago. Wife?" Betsy said.

"That's the rumor."

"Wow! A lot can happen in a short time around here."

"Yes, it can, and since the weather is bad and John didn't get to preach Sunday, he's staying the week at the parsonage, so Kyle can have a few more days to help his sweetheart plan their wedding," Polly said.

"I thought Mavis said he could stay at River Bend," Betsy said.

"She did, but he said he'd rather stay at the parsonage, on neutral ground." Verdie smiled, softening the wrinkles in her face. "Do you think he and Honey will have some hanky-panky out there in the parsonage?"

Betsy felt the blush rising, and there wasn't a thing she could do about it. "If they do, they'd better be careful. Burnt Boot has eyes everywhere."

The bell above the door rang, and all four women turned to see Declan pushing his way into the store. "Mornin', ladies. Granny needs a couple of whole chickens. She's making dumplin's for supper. Where's Jill?"

"Helpin' Sawyer with the cattle today. We're runnin' the store. Heard you got stuck in Gainesville for a couple of nights. Have you seen today's paper?" Polly asked.

Declan nodded. "Yes, I did. Y'all talking about that mystery couple?"

Betsy handed it up to him without meeting his eyes. "There's a contest going on, but they goofed. I was in room 312 with my friend Iris. The mystery couple must have been somewhere else."

"Great-lookin' snowman. I wonder what all the excitement is about this couple. Looks to me like they didn't want anyone to know who they were, so folks ought to leave them alone. Honey showed me the paper the minute I got in the house and wanted to know if I'd seen the snowman," he said.

Gladys ambled back toward the meat counter. "I betcha they're both married to someone else."

"Well, if that's the case, they'd better hope no one finds out their identities," Polly said. "Changing the subject here. Is River Bend going to buy Lottie's property?"

"Not that I know about. It's across the road from us."

"I might buy it," Betsy said.

The store went silent. She had their full attention. Even Gladys stopped in her tracks and turned around.

"Oh really, and why would a Gallagher want Lottie's place when it's not connected in any way to Wild Horse?" Declan asked.

"I've wanted my own place for a while. It would be a good starter ranch, and I like that small house of hers," Betsy said. "I should be going. Mama is waiting on the groceries. Thanks for the coffee. Y'all all have a good afternoon with your visiting, and if you figure out who those folks are in the paper, let me know."

She found the note in her seat when she got into the truck but waited until she was on Wild Horse property before she stopped her truck and read it. Declan had seen the paper and warned her about it, told her that the weekend was amazing and he'd never had so much fun, in and out of the hotel, and he said he intended to drop by the bar that evening.

The first thing her mother did when she was in the house was ask her about the couple in the paper; the next was to tell her that her grandmother had forgiven her, what with the new development between Angela and Naomi, and that she was free to go back to the big house anytime she wanted.

"Amazing," Betsy said as she set the brown paper bag of groceries on the counter. "I forgot to get Daddy's cookies. Gladys, Verdie, and Polly were all minding the store today, and they got to talking about that paper thing and I forgot."

"Don't worry. There's still half a pecan pie in the fridge." Willa pulled her dark hair down from a ponytail and fluffed it out. "He won't starve. So you saw the snowman but not the couple?"

"That's right, but the room number is wrong." Betsy went on to give her mother the same explanation that she'd given the ladies in the store. She had to come clean about that much, in case some amateur sleuth started digging into the story for their fifteen minutes of fame and found out it was registered to Betsy Gallagher. "Maybe the mystery couple was staying in 212 and whoever took the picture got mixed up."

"Maybe so. Guess the ladies told you about Angela's brother staying at the parsonage." Willa rolled her eyes toward the ceiling.

A blast of cold air shot through the kitchen when Henry pushed the door open. "Well, well! Look who finally came home. I thought we were going to have to come get you in a one horse open sleigh." He hung his coat on a hook and kicked off his wet boots. "You see the paper?"

"I did see the paper, Daddy, but what interests me most is Lottie Miller's place."

"I thought you might like that sweet little acreage, so I called her this morning."

Betsy inhaled and held it. "And?"

"Price is reasonable, and with this weather, she's not going to do a bit of good at an auction. You want to go over there and take a look at it tomorrow morning? She says she might call the auction off and sell as is, lock, stock, and barrel, if someone is willing to buy it as such," Henry said.

"How about the cattle?"

"She sold them last week, but you've got a good starter herd that could be moved over there without a problem," Henry said.

"Naomi?" Willa asked.

Henry shrugged. "She will pitch a fit. She still wants Betsy to do her job someday. She's over her snit since things didn't work out with Angela and Jody. She told me this morning that it was all for the best because she is too damned old to have a crying baby in the house." Henry opened the refrigerator and brought out the pecan pie. "But Betsy needs to make up her own mind about her life and do whatever her heart leads her to do."

Declan scanned the bar that evening when he arrived. No Betsy but Eli and Tanner were playing cards at a back table with a couple of cowboys he'd never seen before. He hung his hat on the rack inside the door with his coat right beside it.

"What can I get you?" Rosalie asked.

"Not very busy tonight, are you?"

"Real slow with this weather, but folks get cabin fever, and I got a cot in the back room, so I can stay here if I want. Beer?" she asked.

Declan nodded. "But not a bottle. A pitcher and two cups."

"Got a date?"

"No, just in case someone comes in who'd like to drink with me," he said.

"Come to think of it, I haven't seen you with a woman in several weeks. You sick or dyin'?" Rosalie filled a pitcher and set two red plastic cups on the bar beside it.

"Folks are more interested in Christmas right now than dating." He smiled.

"Hey, that reminds me. Did you hear that Lottie Miller is selling her place? If I had the money, I'd buy it since it butts up next to this property on the south side. I asked your sister if she and Rhett were going to make a bid on it, but she said that they had all they could handle right now."

Declan poured half a cup of beer and sipped it. "How'd you go from talking about me dating to you buying a ranch so fast?"

"It was what you said about Christmas. She has an amazing collection of antique Christmas bulbs. They were featured in the Gainesville newspaper last year as their human interest holiday story," Rosalie said. "Which reminds me of something else. Have you seen the paper today? There's this big mystery couple in it." She reached under the counter and put it on the bar. "That could be you. Right height. Right build and the eyes look right in that one, even though I can't see any other part of the guy's face. Fess up, now. You had some woman in that hotel, didn't you?" Rosalie winked.

"Good grief! That could be anyone. He's wearing coveralls and a ski mask. But it is a fine-lookin' snowman, isn't it?"

"Is she married?" Rosalie asked.

"The article says that she is Maria Wiseman."

"And Joe Wise…man. Come on, Declan! They pulled those names out of a red Christmas stocking. I'm surprised they didn't tell the reporter her name was Mary. You sure that's not you?"

"Come on, Rosalie!" he fired back at her. "If I wanted to come up with fake names, don't you think I could do better than that? But speaking of Christmas, this bar looks mighty festive."

"Thanks to you and Betsy. Let me see that paper." She jerked it out of his hands and studied it. "No, that's not Betsy. That woman is too heavy to be Betsy."

Declan had to swallow fast to keep from spewing beer across the bar. "Betsy Gallagher? You think that could be me and Betsy."

"For a minute I did. Y'all seemed to have some chemistry when you were decorating here the other night, but it's not y'all. The girl is too fat, and the man's head is too pointy."

"I agree," Declan said.

"Hello, Rosalie," Betsy said as she shut the door behind her.

"Well, speak of the devil and he shall appear. We were just decidin' that this picture in the paper can't be you and Declan because the girl is too fat."

Betsy fought the urge to look down at her body to see if it did indeed look fat, but she hopped up on the bar stool at the opposite end of the bar from Declan and said, "Why would you think I'd be making a snowman with Declan? He is a Brennan, and I am a Gallagher, and never the twain shall mix."

"Kind of like Romeo and Juliet?" Rosalie said. "Jameson?"

"No, beer. Tap, not bottle, and just a cup, not a pitcher. And Romeo and Juliet both died in the end. I'm not ready to drink poison, just beer once in a while and an occasional shot of good whiskey."

Rosalie filled a cup and set it before Betsy. "Not buyin' for the boys playin' poker?"

"They can buy their own beer," she said.

"You got something against poker?" Declan asked.

"Nope, I got something against buying them beer tonight."

"Whew! I was wrong about that chemistry between you two the other night," Rosalie said. "Y'all are colder with each other than the weather. From the sounds of all those slamming doors out there in the parking lot, I'd say that I was right about folks gettin' cabin fever."

Declan carried his pitcher to the table on the side of the bar away from Tanner and Eli and waited. Finally,

Tanner made eye contact with him, and Declan nodded toward the jukebox. In a few seconds, Tanner said something about it being too quiet and pushed his chair back.

"You're not picking out all the songs. You'll be playing nothing but Christmas," Declan declared.

"Remember, this is neutral territory, boys," Rosalie yelled from the bar, which was now full, and people kept coming in by the droves.

"Yes, ma'am," Declan hollered back.

"You ready to throw in the towel?" Declan asked as he plugged coins into the jukebox and picked songs out at random.

"Hell no!"

"She's going to make buzzard bait out of you if she finds out."

Tanner shook his head. "A Gallagher never backs down."

"Okay, then, I'm tired of all this. I've got a woman I want to see, and this bet is getting in the way." Declan pulled a roll of hundred dollar bills from his pocket. "They're all there. Ten of them under the rubber band. I'm calling it quits right now. You win, Tanner."

"That's the best news I've had since this thing started," Tanner put his coins into the machine and deliberately picked out all Christmas music.

"Crazy thing is that you can't tell anyone other than Eli because Betsy'd shoot you for using her like that," Declan said.

"Probably, but it is sweet to know that I beat you. See you on poker night?"

"Wouldn't miss it," Declan said and went to his table.

The bet was done, over and finished. Now maybe the guilt that kept him awake at night would disappear, and he and Betsy could beat the odds. Romeo and Juliet did.

And like Betsy said, they died, his conscience said bluntly.

One of Tanner's sappy Christmas songs started playing, and Tanner raised a can of beer toward him. Declan ignored him, but it wasn't easy. His cousins, Quaid and Honey, joined him at the table before he could talk himself into starting a fight with Tanner. Honey picked up the pitcher, poured the extra cup all the way to the brim, and sucked down half of it before she came up for air.

"I'm in love," she said.

"That's your hormones, not your common sense, talking to you." Quaid picked up the pitcher and drank from it.

Declan was glad for anything that took his mind off Tanner's smug grin. "With the preacher?"

Honey nodded.

"Then what in the devil are you doing here in a bar?"

"I can't go to the parsonage. Everyone in town would see me there, and it would ruin his reputation, maybe even keep him from getting the church he's wanting up in Marlow, Oklahoma."

"You've known him all of two days, and you're in love? Think about this, Honey. For God's sake, use your head. You aren't cut out to be a preacher's wife even if the relationship did go that far. And Granny will have a fit," Quaid said.

"It's not Granny's life. It's mine, and when love hits,

you just know it's the right person. I guarantee, when you two find the right woman, you will know it from the beginning," Honey protested.

Declan listened to them argue, but what Honey said stuck in his mind. He glanced toward the bar where Betsy was nursing her beer and talking to Rosalie. With very little imagination, he could see her naked in the shower with him; he could feel her naked body against his as they danced in the bathroom. Was that feeling of contentment in the hotel, that simple excitement of building the snowman together—could that be love and not pure old lust?

Betsy caught him staring, and her lips curved up into a slight smile. His pulse went into double time and sparks flew around the bar, dimming the glitter and shine of all the Christmas decorations.

"What are you thinking about, Declan?" Honey poked him on the arm.

"What you said about love—describe that to me," he said.

"It can't be described. It is what it is. It's either there or it's not, and you can't make it happen or keep it from happening. I felt it when I first laid eyes on John, and when I think of him, my heart does this fluttery thing in my chest."

"You sure it's not the beer?" Declan asked.

"Darlin' Cousin, I'm very sure that beer doesn't cause this. I intend to marry that preacher and leave River Bend. It might not be until next summer, but y'all can get ready for a wedding because my heart will have what it wants," she said.

Declan believed her. "Granny wants a preacher in

the family so bad that she might forgive you, especially if it means she's put one over on Naomi."

"They're calling this the love war, you know," she said.

"I heard." Declan nodded. "I'm going to the bar for another pitcher."

Chapter 19

A TINY BIT OF SUN PEEKED THROUGH THE GRAY SKIES that Tuesday morning as Betsy drove from Wild Horse to Lottie Miller's place. She'd always heard it called "Lottie's place" and was mildly surprised when she drove onto the ranch and saw the old, weathered sign above the cattle guard welcoming her to the Double L Ranch.

The house looked solid and sturdy, with natural rock siding, a chimney on one end, and a wide front porch, open at the south and north ends to catch the breeze. The house facing the west meant that she could see the sunrise from the back porch and watch it set from the front.

Inhaling the cold morning air as she crossed the yard, she felt peace surrounding her, as if the ranch were already her home. Two rocking chairs with chipping, bright-yellow paint peeking through a blanket of snow on the seats and arms beckoned to her. A couple of feisty, yellow pups bounded around the house and jumped up on her legs, leaving big, wet paw prints on her jeans.

"Get down from there," Lottie yelled from the door. "Come on in out of the cold. Two winters in a row like this is why I'm heading for warmer climates. Them pups go with the ranch, so I hope you like dogs if you decide to buy the place. My old mama cow dog had four puppies on Halloween."

"Ranch ain't a ranch without a couple of good cow dogs," Betsy said.

"Well, them boys will take some training to ever be good cow dogs. I made Christmas cookies yesterday after you called. Come on in the kitchen, and we'll talk around the table." Lottie held the door for her.

Betsy had been in the house back when she was a little girl and Lottie had been her Sunday school teacher, but looking at it through the eyes of an adult who might be living there for the rest of her life was a very different experience. The living room was small and cozy, with a blaze going in the fireplace, hardwood floors with bright-colored throw rugs tossed about, and a big window that overlooked the front of the property. A big, well-worn, brown leather sofa that looked as inviting as the rocking chairs on the front porch took up a big chunk of the room.

Lottie's rubber-soled shoes squeaked as she crossed the floor. Her slacks ended an inch above her ankles, and red-and-green-striped socks filled in the space between slacks and black lace-up shoes. Santa Claus was checking his list on her red sweatshirt, and a charm bracelet with holiday trinkets jangled with every step. Her white hair was pulled up in a tight little bun on top of her head.

"You look festive today," Betsy said.

"Dressed up for y'all." Lottie led the way through a small dining room. Betsy stopped at the huge picture window to admire a small herd of deer close to the tree line.

"I don't allow no huntin' on my property and the deer know it." Lottie motioned for her to follow her through an archway into the kitchen. "You can hang your coat on the back of your chair while I pour you a cup of coffee. Sugar or cream?"

"No, ma'am, just black," Betsy said.

She was mighty glad that she'd answered before she noticed Declan Brennan sitting at the table with a cookie in one hand, a cup of coffee in the other, and a big smile on his face, because at that moment, she couldn't have uttered a word. So Lottie meant "y'all" as a plural.

"Help yourself to the cookies. I made plenty, so don't be shy," Lottie said.

Declan held one up. "They are really good, just like I remember from Sunday school."

Betsy removed her coat, hung it over the back of a chair, and sat down with a thud. Her knee touched Declan's under the table and she quickly pulled it back.

"What are you doing here?" she whispered.

"I imagine the same thing you are," he answered.

"And you'll both do well to remember that the feud ain't got no place here on my ranch. I don't care about your last names or why Wild Horse or River Bend wants this place, but I do care about who is going to live here. I've given sixty years of my life to this land, and I want to know it's took care of proper." Lottie carried a cup of coffee to the table and set it before Betsy.

"I want to buy this, not for Wild Horse but for me. It will never be a part of Wild Horse," Betsy said.

"And I want to buy it for myself also. It will never be a part of River Bend," Declan said.

"Why? You go first, Declan," Lottie said.

"Bigger is not always better. I want to start my own business separate from River Bend," he answered.

"Why?" Lottie asked a second time.

"I like the life Leah has," he said honestly.

"Your turn, Betsy." Lottie turned her attention from Declan to her.

"The same reasons. I want out of Wild Horse, but ranchin' is in my blood. I want to live in Burnt Boot. It's home, and I want my own place that's away from the feud. I'm so sick of it, I could scream."

"Both good, solid reasons. I was hoping one of you would give me something that I didn't like, but you didn't, so if you're serious about this place, then this is what we're going to do. You are going to help me finish getting it ready for sale, and if one of you is still standing when Christmas comes, I'll give that one first chance at buying it."

"What if we're both still standing?" Betsy asked.

Lottie wiggled her finger. "Now that would be a miracle, since you are a Gallagher and Declan here is a Brennan."

"Together. You want us to work together?" Declan asked.

"If you want out of the feud, this is a good way to do it," Lottie said.

"Granny will have a fit," Betsy said.

"Naomi Gallagher has been throwin' hissies long as I can remember. I don't reckon one more will kill her, or Mavis Brennan either. That's my terms, kids."

"I'm really not a kid," Betsy said.

Lottie's thin mouth turned up at the corners. "What are you, twenty-five?"

"Thirty next spring."

Her brown eyes sparkled when she turned to Declan. "And you are the same age?"

"Thirty-two last summer," he said.

"I expect it's past time my Sunday school lessons took root and y'all figured out you should get away from all that fussin' and fightin'. This last year has been the worst I've seen in my lifetime."

"And what would you like me to do first?" Declan asked.

"Not 'me,' 'us.' You are going to work together," Lottie said.

"Sweet Jesus," Betsy mumbled.

Lottie pointed a finger at Betsy. "No blasphemy in this house. Today, you can clean out the hay barn. I want the whole thing swept until there ain't a single bit of straw on the floor and the tack room put to rights. Mice have been in there because I kept horse feed in the closet, so it smells like urine. That should take all day tomorrow and the next day. On Friday morning, we'll meet back here at eight o'clock and talk about what the next job is."

"Starting now?" Declan asked.

"Did you bring your work gloves?" Lottie asked.

He nodded.

"Finish your cookies and coffee and then you can get to it. Dinner will be served at noon, and you can leave at six. If your people throw you out, I've got one spare bedroom that Betsy can have and the bunkhouse sleeps four, so I expect Declan could stay down there, but there will be no hanky-panky on my ranch," she said.

"I'm a Gallagher," Betsy said.

"And he's a Brennan, but you're also a man and woman," Lottie said. "You can leave your good trucks parked in the yard and take my old work truck anywhere on the ranch you need to go, but it ain't been tagged in twenty years, so don't be drivin' it off the ranch."

"Speaking of that, where is your truck?" Betsy asked Declan.

"In the backyard. I came in through the kitchen door," he answered. "Are you ready to do some serious work?"

"Are you?" Betsy shot back.

"Yes, ma'am," he answered.

"Y'all come on back in here at noon, and we'll have a bowl of good, hot soup together. It'll give you energy to finish up the day," Lottie said. "I go to bed at nine o'clock, so if you want a bedroom or the key to the bunkhouse, you'd best be back here before that."

Lottie sat down on the corner of the sofa and called Gladys on an old black phone that had sat on the end table for at least thirty years. "They both showed up and I did what we talked about."

"I still think that's who is in the picture in the paper," Gladys said. "She would have had on long under britches, and you know what they say about the camera adding ten pounds."

"You ready to see what happens next?"

"Me and Polly's been sittin' here waitin' on your call. You want to let Verdie know, or should we?"

"I'll do it. I'm making them clean the hay barn and tack room today and tomorrow and the day after that. When they get that done, I'm going to make them put up all my Christmas decorations, inside and out. I called off the auction. With this weather, it would have been a bust anyway."

Gladys giggled. "Keep us posted about what's happening. Mavis and Naomi are going to have fits."

"It's got to end, or the next stunt they pull could end Burnt Boot altogether," Lottie said.

Betsy kept her gloved hands tucked deep in the pockets of her coat and bent her head against the hard north wind whistling down across the river, bringing spitting sleet with it again. She should turn around right then and walk away. Neither of them had said a word from the house to the barn. She'd bailed out of the passenger side of the truck without waiting for Declan to play the gentleman and open the door.

She could see the house from the barn doors, and her heart yearned to live there, to curl up on that sofa in the evenings after a long day's work with those two pups on the rug in front of the fireplace. There were two more small ranches for sale, and either one of them would work just fine, but Betsy wanted this one, no matter what it took.

Her phone rang, and she fished it out of her hip pocket, saw that it was her mother, and answered, "I want this place so bad I can taste it, Mama, but there's a hitch in the deal."

"Your daddy and Naomi say that you are to come home right now. Naomi says you can move back into the house and she'll retire right after Christmas. Your daddy says that you are not spending a day with a Brennan," Willa said.

"How did you know all of this so fast?"

"The gossips must've seen your truck and his both

out there at Lottie's place, and Gladys talked to Lottie a few minutes ago, and, girl, this is nothing but trouble. I'll buy you either one of those other ranches. Let Declan Brennan have that one."

"I will not be bested by a Brennan," Betsy said. "I've got a beep, and it's Granny."

"I wouldn't want to be you right now," Willa said.

"Bye, Mama."

Betsy took a deep breath and answered the phone, but before she could say a word, Naomi started in. "What is going on? Wild Horse doesn't want Lottie's place. It's not attached to our land. Get in that ugly truck of yours and get your ass back here where you belong."

"And let Mavis Brennan win again this week?" Betsy said slyly.

"What?"

"She's done took your preacher away from you and caused Angela and Jody to move back into their little house. You're going to let her win again. She'll be struttin' all over Burnt Boot by the end of the day, tellin' everyone that she's whippin' your butt."

A long silence made Betsy look at the phone to see if Naomi had hung up on her. When she put it back to her ear, her grandmother said, "You sit tight on that place. I heard that Lottie offered you a bedroom. Take her up on it so you can get in better with her. We'll whip them Brennans on this deal and Mavis can lick her wounds when Wild Horse buys the ranch."

"Granny, I don't want this to be a part of Wild Horse. I want it to be mine and not affiliated in any way with Wild Horse," Betsy said.

"Of course it will be Wild Horse property. You're going to take care of the whole business."

Betsy took another deep breath. "No, ma'am. I am not. If Lottie sells me this ranch, I'm going out on my own, independent of Wild Horse."

"I won't have it," Naomi hissed.

"It's either this way, or I can walk away from it and Mavis wins. But know this, Granny: if I don't buy this one, I'm buying one of the other two listed in Burnt Boot right now."

"If it and you are not a part of Wild Horse, then you are on your own. Decide right now," Naomi said.

"I'm on my own. I'll tell Lottie at noon that I'll be staying in that bedroom. If you change your mind, you know my number." Betsy ended the call and turned to see Declan just inside the barn talking on his phone too.

He was tucking it back inside his shirt pocket when she came through the wide-open expanse created when he'd swung open the overhead door. "Did you get an ultimatum?"

"I did. This is crazy, Declan."

"It's just another facet of the love war, isn't it? I love this ranch. You love this ranch. We both would love to get away from all the crap of the feud. I'm not going anywhere. My grandmother ordered me to stay, so she could beat yours, and then got mad at me when I told her that when I bought the place, it would not be a part of River Bend."

"Sounds like we had the same conversation." She sighed.

He laid a hand on her shoulder and pulled her back into the shadows. "You're right. It's crazy, but it does give us an opportunity to spend time together. Only trouble is, I don't think I can fake being your enemy."

She laid her head on his chest and listened to the steady heartbeat of the man she could so easily fall in love with. "Especially when there's to be no hanky-panky on this ranch."

Declan chuckled and kissed her on the forehead. "We'll save the hanky-panky for other places, like the church on Thursday nights."

She pushed away from him. "Enough. You're not going to sidetrack me with hanky-panky talk. On Christmas Day, I plan to own this ranch."

He picked up a shovel and handed her a wide push broom. "Not if I can sweet-talk Lottie out of it before then."

Quaid met Declan on the porch of the main house at River Bend as Declan carried his first load of things out to his truck. Quaid threw up his hands, set his jaw, inhaled deeply, and spoke.

"Are you out of you mind, Declan? A thousand-dollar bet isn't worth losing your whole lifestyle over. Give Tanner the money. It's no big deal, and besides, he can't tell anyone. Betsy would tear him apart limb by limb." He dropped his hands and crossed his arms over his chest. "Come stay with me until Granny gets over her snit."

"I'm buying that ranch, and the bet is called off. I gave Tanner the money and warned him about bragging," Declan said.

Quaid removed his cowboy hat and combed his thick, blond hair with his fingertips before he resettled it. "I know y'all were doing some sneaking around. How far did it go?"

Declan pushed past him and carried the two suitcases to the truck.

Quaid followed him and opened the back door to the club-cab truck. "What did Uncle Russell say?"

"That I had to follow my heart and that he wished to hell he'd followed his own advice years ago. And that he can't wait to retire and move away from River Bend himself."

Quaid followed Declan back into the house when he returned. "Talk will have it that you left River Bend for a Gallagher."

"I'm leaving River Bend because I want my own place, not because of Betsy," he declared. "I've got some boxes of books. Want to help me carry them down?"

"Sure. Granny won't even mind if I help you since she's mad at you. There is a weird feeling in the air. She's mad at you, and yet she's lording it over Naomi, telling everyone that her Brennan grandson is going to win the battle against Naomi Gallagher's granddaughter."

Quaid stacked one box on top of the other and said, "I thought you said there were books in here. This feels like lead or concrete."

"Just books," Declan said.

"Does it seem strange at all to be leaving?"

"Little bit, but it's not much different than when I went to college."

"But that time, you came home every weekend."

Declan grabbed the last duffel bag and followed Quaid down the steps. "When I buy this ranch, maybe you'll decide to defect and join me."

"Not me. I've got a place of my own even if it is affiliated with Wild Horse. I like where I am just fine," Quaid said. "And I would not work with Betsy Gallagher for two weeks for a chance to buy a front seat in heaven. That woman is evil. I'm glad you gave Tanner the money and called off the bet."

"Oh, so you think I couldn't get her into bed or couldn't sweet-talk her into falling in love with me? Thanks for the vote of confidence there." Declan swung the duffel bag into the back of the truck and took the top box of books from the stack.

"Not that you couldn't. I'm just glad you didn't. See you Thursday night at the bar for poker?" Quaid asked.

"Wouldn't miss it. Tanner's got some money I need to win back." Declan grinned. "Come on over to the bunkhouse and visit if you get bored in the evenings."

"Thanks for the invite, but until Betsy is off that ranch, I'm not settin' foot on it," Quaid said.

Declan was surprised when he found the bunkhouse in decent shape. The two yellow pups raced in ahead of him, sniffed out every corner, chased a small mouse out of the kitchen, and played with it until it was dead. Declan turned around slowly, taking in the whole place a section at a time.

Two sets of bunk beds were shoved up against one side of the room. A zippered plastic bag holding bedding and a pillow was placed in the middle of each bed. The brown-and-orange-plaid sofa facing the fireplace was probably forty years old, but it was still in good shape and comfortable. Wood was to the left of the stone fireplace, and Declan hoped the whole time he started the fire that the chimney wasn't clogged up with bird nests or other debris.

"Well, how about that?" he said as the pups flopped down in front of the fire and the smoke spiraled up like it was supposed to do.

One puppy put his paw on Declan's thigh and whined, so he rolled back on his butt and took time to pet both dogs. "Y'all going to be bunkhouse boys? Will you let me know when you want to go outside?"

The other puppy yipped and Declan took that as a yes. He fished his phone out of his hip pocket and took a picture of them to send to Betsy, then realized he didn't have her number. Well, he'd sure remedy that tomorrow, because now that they were on the same ranch, they could text and call whenever they wanted.

It was well past midnight when he stretched out on a bed in a strange place where every noise got his attention. It didn't matter if it was a scrub oak branch brushing against the window of the bunkhouse or a coyote singing a lonesome song off in the distance or even one of the pups whining in his sleep beside the fire—Declan couldn't sleep.

The moon, with glimmering stars all around it, hanging out there in the distance, captured his attention. He'd seen Betsy's pink truck parked in front of the house when he drove back onto the property, so evidently she'd moved into the spare bedroom. Was she looking at the same moon? Was she wondering what she'd done? Or was there a big weight lifted off her shoulders?

Betsy's new room was about half the size of the one she had in her parents' house, which was smaller than the one at the big house. She did not have her own bathroom but would be sharing one with Lottie, and it was even smaller than her private bath at home.

Her things were unpacked, and she had played a game of cards with Lottie before the woman said it was time for the nighttime snack she always had before bedtime. By nine o'clock, Betsy could hear her new roommate snoring loudly in the room across the hall.

She picked up a book and tried to read, but not even the hot, steamy castle romance could keep her attention. At a few minutes until ten, she finally put her earbuds in and listened to Christmas music by country artists. Some of them made her giggle, a few put a tear in her eye, and all of them reminded her in some way of Declan.

At midnight, she sat up in the bed and stared out the window at the moon and stars. It was the first clear night in a long time, and they looked so beautiful hanging there like ornaments on a tree. Lottie had said they would be decorating the house and trimming the Christmas tree tomorrow. That meant when Betsy bought the house, it would already be beautiful for Christmas morning.

She could see the bunkhouse down there, backed up into a small copse of naked scrub oak trees. The moonlight put a sparkle in the snow and the roof. She wondered if Declan was sleeping or if he was as antsy as she was in a new place. Was he sitting up in bed, looking out the window at the same moon? He really was a romantic soul in spite of his rough cowboy exterior. Underneath all that was a sweet, gentle man who had stolen her heart.

"Whoa," she whispered. "Stop right there. My heart is still mine, and no one is stealing it, not when this ranch is riding on me keeping a steady head and a firm purpose."

Chapter 20

"FORGET HANKY-PANKY RULES," DECLAN DECLARED ON Wednesday evening as he and Betsy finished cleaning the tack room. "We weren't following Gallagher and Brennan rules, and we're out of sight of anyone."

Betsy dropped the broom and wrapped her arms around his neck. She rolled up on her toes and her eyes fluttered shut. "I've wanted to kiss you all day."

"Oh, honey, every time you moved today, I imagined what we could be doing instead of cleaning up this tack room."

Her fingers whipped off his stocking cap and tangled up in his hair. One of his hands rested gently on her cheekbone, the heel of his palm tilting her chin up to his lips; the other cupped her butt and pressed her closer to him.

"It's been a month since Sunday," she said between kisses.

"Six months," he drawled. "Bunkhouse is warmer than this place, and Lottie is at the store."

"She's been gone fifteen minutes already, and if she catches us together in the bunkhouse, believe me, she won't think we were in there reading the Bible."

He shifted an errant strand of red hair back behind her ear and kissed the lobe, moving down to the soft, sensitive spot on her neck. "We are adults, Betsy. We should be able to go to bed with each other if we want."

She traced his lips with her forefinger. "How bad do you want this ranch? Enough to forget about the bunkhouse and lock the tack room door?"

"It's already locked." He backed her up against the rough wooden table.

She quickly undid his belt buckle and smiled when she saw that he was "going cowboy," as they called it in Texas. Things would have been much easier if she'd been wearing a skirt that would simply flip up, but it was a different story with jeans.

However, he quickly moved them and her underpants down to her boots, and she was naked except for socks from the waist down. Then, with a wiggle and a hop, she wrapped her legs around him.

"Much better than that cold table against my butt," she whispered.

Without losing his grip on her, he whipped a horse blanket from a nail, flipped it out onto the floor, and laid her down on it. With her legs still wrapped firmly around his waist, it just took one firm thrust, and they were rocking together and neither of them felt one bit cold.

"I feel like a teenager," she murmured against his neck.

"I'm addicted to you, Betsy Gallagher."

"Just Betsy. On this ranch I'm just Betsy." She pulled his lips to hers.

It was fast, furious, and intense, and she thought she heard him say her name, but the way her ears were ringing, he could have been calling the cows in for feeding time. She went limp, dropping her legs and panting for her next breath.

"Who needs words?" he asked.

"Right," she managed to get out before she inhaled deeply.

"You do have a window in your bedroom. You could sneak out and come down to the bunkhouse to see me after Lottie is asleep," he said as he rolled over and sucked air when his bare butt hit the cold floor.

"Or you could come see me." She twisted away from him and grabbed for her clothes.

"We make too much noise to do this in the house."

They both froze when they heard Lottie yelling at the puppies. "Only a couple of nights and Declan has spoiled you. You'll never make good cow dogs the way he's letting you sleep in the bunkhouse. All you'll ever be is a couple of big, old, overgrown pets."

Declan was a blur as he jerked his jeans up, got things put to rights, and unlocked the door. Betsy made sure all her hair was stuffed under the stocking hat, checked to make sure her boots were on the right feet, and grabbed the broom. When Lottie pushed the door open, two puppies ran in ahead of her, and she continued to fuss at them.

"You are ruining these mongrels, Declan Brennan. But I guess that's your problem if you buy this place or Betsy's if she does. I got to admit, I ain't seen this barn look like this since the day it was built. Next owner is going to appreciate it being all clean and ready for next year's hay crop. Tell me, now, will either of you put up small bales, or are you both into them big, round ones?"

Betsy leaned on the broom. "I like both small and round. Round ones are nice for winter feed, so you don't have to go to the pasture twice a day. But the small ones are good for feeding inside the barn."

"Declan?" Lottie asked.

"Same as what Betsy said. Is this a test?"

Lottie propped her hands on her hips. "It was, but y'all didn't help a bit. It's a tie goin' into tomorrow's business. But right now, supper is ready to put on the table. I made a pot roast and hot rolls. Folks work hard, they need sustenance. So put the broom away and come on to the house. And don't let those pups in the back door. They ain't comin' in my house. If you want dogs in your house when you buy it, if you buy it, then that's your business, but long as I'm the owner, they are stayin' outside."

She rattled on and on as she walked away.

When they couldn't hear her voice anymore, their eyes caught across the room and high color filled Betsy's cheeks. "Five minutes earlier, and we'd have been caught."

"I didn't know women still knew how to blush." He grinned as she crossed the room, picked her up, and swung her around.

She giggled. "Well, we near got caught quite literally with our britches down around our ankles."

"Promise you'll come to the bunkhouse?"

"Maybe tomorrow night, after we decorate for Christmas. My heart isn't going to stop thumping until midnight," she said.

"Because we almost got caught or the sex was that good?" He planted a kiss on her forehead.

"Both," she said honestly.

Chapter 21

THURSDAY MORNING, BETSY AWOKE WITH A SMILE ON her face after a beautiful dream about Declan. Along with the aroma of sausage and coffee, the dull sound of a conversation going on in the kitchen wafted through the door into her bedroom. She sat up, pushed the covers back, and dressed quickly. One glance out the window made her glad that she was working inside the house for most of the day.

Big snowflakes floated silently from the gray skies that morning. A couple of inches had covered what had been left from the weekend blast, and Burnt Boot was a winter wonderland again.

Declan was setting the table, and Lottie was talking nonstop as usual when Betsy padded to the kitchen in her socks. Her hair was pulled into a ponytail at the nape of her neck, and she didn't have a bit of makeup on her face, so the light sprinkling of freckles across her nose shined like bits of coal out there in the snow-covered ground.

"Good morning, beautiful," Declan whispered as she passed him.

She slid a wink his way and made a beeline for the coffeepot. "Do I smell biscuits and sausage gravy?"

"You got a good nose. Break those eggs into the bowl right there and whip them up. Gravy is about thickened up, and it's time to get the eggs scrambled. And there's a little pan of cinnamon rolls in the oven for breakfast dessert. Me and my Leland always liked to have dessert at every meal. I've missed having him to talk to this last year, so I'm glad you kids are staying with me these next two weeks. It won't be so lonely leaving the ranch in good hands, and it gives me someone to talk to. Put just a dab of milk in those eggs so they'll be fluffy. Nobody likes old, flat eggs." Lottie always used fifty words where five would do fine.

The doctor said that Leland Miller died from a heart attack, but Betsy wondered if Lottie hadn't talked him to death. Suddenly, the job of decorating the house for Christmas with Lottie underfoot didn't seem nearly as exciting as it had when she first awoke that morning.

"Okay, butter is warmed just right. Pour them eggs in this skillet and I'll put the rest of breakfast on the table. Time we get that done, the eggs will be ready and you can just set them in the skillet to keep them warm. Cast iron cools down right slow, so it will keep them from going cold. Leland loved his eggs for breakfast, but he hated to eat them after they'd got cold."

Betsy followed orders and hoped that she was passing more tests than Declan because, every day, she wanted the ranch more and more. Lottie sat at the head of the table on one end and Declan had a place at the other end. That put Betsy on the side, where Declan could reach under the table and squeeze her knee or run the toe of his foot up her leg. She could imagine his touch on her skin as surely as if they were back in the hotel room—or the tack room.

"The decorations are all stored down in the bunkhouse," Lottie was saying when Betsy finally turned off the vision of Declan in all his naked splendor with her body next to his and started listening again, "so I suppose I can trust you two to go together down there and load them in the truck and bring them up to the house. I store them in the closet, and that's all there is in it, so it won't be hard to locate. And you know the rules. Any hanky-panky goes on, and I'll sell this place to one of the O'Donnell cousins. I hear that there's another one coming up here to spend Christmas with Sawyer and Jill and maybe get hired on over at Fiddle Creek. I swear to God on the Good Book that them O'Donnells are going to take Burnt Boot plumb over. I bet you could kick any mesquite bush between here and Galveston and a dozen O'Donnells would come runnin' out."

"Yes, ma'am." Declan smiled.

His foot made its way from her ankle up the outside of her thigh, and she shivered.

"Is it too cold in here, Betsy? Leland liked it cool. Said that breathing hot air wasn't good for a body, and I was in the kitchen with the oven on half the time, so I was plenty warm, but if it's too cold, I could throw another log on the fire or jack up the central heat a little. Don't like to use it no more than I have to since it is more expensive than burning logs."

Betsy reached over and patted Lottie's veined hand. "I'm just fine. A goose walked over my grave and made me shiver."

Lottie's eyes sparkled. "Leland used to say that. Declan, you'd best have another helping of biscuits and gravy."

"It's a fine breakfast, Miz Lottie, but I couldn't hold another bite. I have to save room for breakfast dessert."

"Well, fizzle! I nearly forgot that the cinnamon rolls were in the oven." Lottie jumped up and grabbed a hot pad on her way to the stove.

"Lottie said an *F* word," Declan whispered.

"She did not," Betsy argued.

"She said fizzle and that is creative cussin'. Are you going to tell her?"

Betsy shook her head. "No, sir. It might be a test, and I'm not sayin' a word if she yells the *F* bomb in the middle of church on Sunday morning. I'm not losing a single point."

"And here they are, fresh from the oven. If we don't eat them all right now, we'll take a break about ten o'clock and have a snack with a cup of coffee. Betsy, you can serve us up one each while I refill coffee cups. My Leland's favorite breakfast dessert was cinnamon rolls, and we always had them the day we decorated the house for Christmas. So, sweetheart"—she looked up at the ceiling—"I'm thinkin' of you today. Don't walk up to them pearly gates too fast. I'll be along to join you before long, and we'll talk to Saint Peter together."

Betsy's eyes misted, but she kept the tears at bay. That's what she wanted, after she bought the ranch—a love that endured on past this life and into eternity.

"These are delicious," Declan said.

"Leland thought so. I usually make up a little pan full and put them in the fridge when I make hot rolls for supper. That way they're ready to pop in the oven the next morning while we're having breakfast and we can eat them hot. We was married fifty-four years, and even after a year of being without him, I really miss my Leland," she said wistfully. "But like I said, it's good that y'all are here the last two weeks of my time in Burnt Boot."

"I want what you and your Leland had—a love that lasts years with a woman I can work with on this ranch," Declan said.

"Well, honey, it takes two to make what we had. I hope you find it," she said.

The windshield wipers couldn't keep up with the fast-falling snow, so Declan drove the old truck slowly down to the bunkhouse. A patchwork quilt covered the bench seat, because the original fabric was worn and had holes in it. The heater worked half speed at best, and not at all on such a short distance. The headliner had long since been ripped away, leaving bare metal showing, and the radio hadn't worked in years. But the engine purred away like a kitten.

"Reckon we could call in both families and they'd come help us like they did at the bar when we decorated?" he asked Betsy.

"I doubt it very much. Anyone who sets foot on the Double L would have a hell of a time explaining it to our grandmothers," she answered. "Speaking of that, if you get the ranch, are you renaming it?"

"I haven't decided. How about you?"

She shook her head slowly. "I don't think so. It's been the Double L for more than fifty years. Be a shame to change it."

He backed the truck up as close to the bunkhouse porch as he could get it, and they both bailed out at the same time. By the time she reached the door, he had opened it and was standing to one side.

"Welcome, darlin', to my humble abode. It's not the mansion at River Bend, but there's no one in here that will shoot you on the spot."

She stopped right inside the door and stomped the snow off her boots, onto the inside doormat. He came in behind her, wrapping his arms around her waist and burying his cold face in her hair.

"You smell like warm coconut and cold snow," he whispered.

She whipped around and pressed her body close to his. "Kiss me, cowboy."

He kicked the door shut with his boot heel right after two puppies raced inside, shook the snow from their fur, and headed straight for the rug in front of the fireplace. He didn't notice or care what the dogs did. He'd wanted to kiss her since she'd walked into the kitchen that morning with sleep still in her eyes.

Her lips tasted sweet, like cinnamon with a hint of coffee, and he could have stood there forever kissing her and feeling her body next to his, but she pulled away.

"I do believe that was hanky-panky, and you can bet your sweet, sexy ass that Lottie looked at the clock when we left. I bet if we're not back in twenty minutes, she will blast through that door to see what we're doing," Betsy said.

"I looked that up in the dictionary." He followed her to the closet and groaned.

"What?"

"Hanky-panky. I looked it up in the dictionary."

"And what did it say in there? I believe I have a damn

good idea, but give it to me in technical terms. Holy smoke, Declan, there is a pickup load of decorations here. She must have the house like that one in the movie I saw when I was a kid."

"The Griswolds' house?"

"That's the one, and tell me the definition."

"According to the dictionary it is"—he pulled a piece of paper from his shirt pocket and read—"hanky-panky is 'frivolous and slightly indecent sexual activity.' Kissing is not a sexual activity so we haven't broken a rule."

"Today." She giggled. "Can't testify about yesterday, but so far today, we've not indulged in hanky-panky."

"And by the time we get all this up in the house and on the house, we'll be too tired," he said.

"Speak for yourself," she said. "But wait, you have a poker game tonight, after we do all this."

"I'd forgotten. I'll try to get out of the game before midnight if you'll be waiting on me right there on that bed." He pointed through a door into his bedroom.

"At which time rules, like piecrust, will be broken?" She picked up the top box and headed outside.

"I certainly hope so," Declan said.

The boxes were unloaded in the kitchen, and Lottie danced around giving orders. The first thing they were going to do was put up the tree, and from the weather report Lottie'd gotten on the radio while they were gone, the snow was supposed to let up right at noon. So the inside of the house would be first, and then Betsy and Declan could take care of the outside decorations.

"Oh, it's going to be lovely for our last year here, Leland. I hope you are looking down from heaven and liking everything we're doing. Oh, we need Christmas music," she said.

She opened the top of an old stereo system with a turntable and removed a stack of vinyl records from behind a door on one side. "We'll each choose one. These were mine and Leland's favorites."

It was no surprise that they were all country music, all older artists, and that most of them had several artists on one record. When they'd all picked one, Lottie put them on the turntable and music filled the small house. More than a little bit scratchy and a lot of twangy guitar and whining fiddles, it made Betsy think of the old holiday movies she liked to watch every year.

Declan removed the artificial tree from the box held together with both masking and duct tape. "Looks like this has been around for a while."

"Forty years. Them first years we went out in the woods and cut a tree, and every year my Leland would take sick during the holidays. Took me a while to figure out it wasn't the weather but that damned cedar tree, so I saved up my egg money all year and bought that one, and he didn't get sick no more. Y'all might do well to remember this, whichever one of you gets the place, that there is a little part of the land in the back forty corner that I have to fight the cedar on. I keep them brush hogged off every spring, but if you don't take care of them, they'll take over the place."

"I'll remember. We had to fight those damned things at Wild Horse more than the mesquite," Betsy said.

Lottie shook her finger at Betsy. "One more cuss

word and the contest won't be tied no more. This is your warning."

"Yes, ma'am," Betsy said.

Lottie declared that the tree had to sit in front of the big window overlooking the front lawn. "That way, it can be seen when folks drive down the lane, while they're out lookin' at the lights. Me and my Leland, we got a big kick out of driving around and seein' what everybody else was fixin' up for the holidays."

The house phone rang and she threw up her palms. "Y'all go on and get it all fixed and ready while I answer this. I hope that it's not Verdie. She'll keep me talking for hours. That woman talks more than anyone I ever knew."

Betsy rolled her eyes toward Declan, who stifled a chuckle and handed Betsy an armload of artificial tree limbs to stick into the metal tree trunk he'd set up.

"I think these go in the bottom, since they are longer. I'll do the top ones," he said.

Lottie was in the kitchen on a corded wall phone, out of sight, so when Betsy bent over to put the very bottom limbs on the tree, his hand cupped her bottom and gave it a gentle squeeze. She jumped like she'd been shot and glanced in the direction of Lottie's voice.

Declan's arms went around her, and he kissed her long, hard, and passionately. She forgot where she was, what she was doing, and the stakes if they got caught in Lottie's living room, for God's sake, and clung to him after the kiss ended. Then reality hit, and she took a step back, stumbled over the coffee table, and fell backward onto the sofa.

"Are you crazy?" she whispered.

"Couldn't resist, and besides, she can't see through walls. So are you inviting me to make out with you on that big, old, soft sofa?"

"Hell no! And if you tell on me for cussin', I'll file sexual harassment charges on you with Lottie for touching my butt," she teased. "And we'd best have that tree ready for decorations before she gets back."

He extended a hand and pulled up her to a standing position, tipped up her chin, looked deeply into her eyes, and kissed her on the tip of the nose. "This is the ugliest tree I've ever seen. The only hope it has is if we completely cover it up with decorations."

She giggled. "By what I'm seeing over there in those boxes, that is totally possible."

They had it looking as good as possible when Lottie joined them again. "It was Verdie, and she had to know what all was going on over here. I told her about the barn and the decorating today, and she told me that she's having a hard time keeping Callie on bed rest. Lord, you'd think that was her blood grandbaby the way she goes on about it. And those other kids have flat-out put some new giddyup in her step. Me and Leland wanted kids but the good Lord didn't see fit to bless us, so we just had each other. But Leland said once we taught our Sunday school classes that he was kind of glad that we didn't have to deal with all the problems that people have with their kids."

She stopped for a breath and Betsy pointed at the tree. "What do you think? Is it ready for decorations?"

"Looks beautiful. You did a fine job of pulling out the branches to make it look all full and pretty. Now we're ready for the lights. Declan, you can wrap them around your arm and Betsy can fix them on the tree. I still use the big lights. Them little twinkly things never did appeal to me and Leland. We checked them every year before we stored them, so they should be good to go."

Betsy spoke up before Lottie went off on another tangent. "Checked them for what?"

Lottie's giggle reminded Betsy of a little girl with playground secrets. "If one burns out, then the whole strand won't light, so you have to check each bulb to see which one is out. But we already did that. Let's get them on the tree. I'll sit back here on the sofa and give y'all advice about where they need to be."

Every time Betsy unwound a three-foot strand from the roll on Declan's arms, her hands brushed his. Heat made her think of a hell of a lot more than frivolous sexual activity. It made her yearn for that hotel room again and for pure, old, unadulterated sex with Declan Brennan.

If her grandmother could have read her mind over at Wild Horse, she would've dropped from cardiac arrest right there on the foyer floor. If Mavis Brennan could have read it, Betsy would've been a dead woman within twenty-four hours.

"This ain't y'all's first rodeo, is it?" Lottie asked.

"No, ma'am. We decorated the Burnt Boot Bar and Grill for Rosalie and our job was the tree," Declan said.

"You work real good together. Too bad you come from the feuding families or you might make a nice couple. But I don't suppose you could ever get past that fizzlin' crap and date each other, could you?"

"Creative cussin'," Declan whispered.

Betsy bit back a grin. "Probably wouldn't be a healthy idea if we dated each other, would it, Miz Lottie?"

"And if you did, you'd wind up exiled forever. I was like that when I married Leland. My daddy didn't like him one bit and my mama wasn't too fond of him either. They said he'd been one of them kind that sow wild oats on Saturday night and go to church on Sunday to pray for a crop failure. He usually sat in the back pew, and I fell in love with him when I was only fifteen. We ran off and got married when I was sixteen and he was nineteen. Mama said I'd made my bed and I had to sleep in it." She paused and cocked her head to one side. "You got a saggin' one there, Betsy. Mama was so mad at me that she didn't let me come home for a whole year. Then she wrote me a letter, even though we both lived right here in Burnt Boot. I wrote her back, and we did that for another year, and then we both got a telephone. She called me one day out of the blue and asked me to come to Sunday dinner. I did, and after a couple of weeks, she called me again and asked me and Leland both to come to Sunday dinner."

"Did she ever learn to like Leland?" Betsy asked.

"I don't think so, but me and her made up after about five years. We'd go to Sunday dinner once a month, and my mom and I would talk while we washed the dishes, and I guess she finally figured out how happy I was with him, and those last years, things was good. I loved my Leland, so it was worth it waitin' on her to come around. But a girl needs her mama and a mama needs her daughter, so it was good to be able to talk to her."

"Would you have regretted marryin' Leland if she'd never come around?" Declan asked.

"Lord no! I loved him with my whole heart. I just had to give Mama some time to get her thinkin' all straightened out. You'd be surprised at how much a little patience helps." Lottie smiled.

Betsy finished the lights and Declan plugged them in. Sure enough, every one of those big suckers lit up. Red, blue, green, and yellow, they reminded her of one of those silly Ring Pops that kids buy and suck on all day. Would she be willing to never see her mother again until she was on her deathbed if she could have a life with Declan Brennan?

She mulled that question over as she and Declan wrapped red and green tinsel around the tree, looping it the way Lottie said, in all the right places.

At noon, Lottie served barbecued chicken, fried potatoes, baked beans, and hot biscuits with pecan pie for dessert. The woman was pure magic in the kitchen, cooking a few minutes and coming back to tell them what she wanted done next, disappearing for a bit and returning, and not one thing burned or even scorched.

According to her, they were going to put the lights around the house that afternoon, and then Lottie would tell them where else they could string up the rest of the lights. From the half-dozen boxes still left of nothing but lights, Betsy figured they'd be able to put them on the barbed-wire fence all the way around the whole ranch.

"Now I'm going to stay in the house and y'all kids can do the work. When you get it all finished, I will come out and see it. I'll make a fresh batch of Christmas cookies and some hot chocolate, so you can come in every hour and warm up," Lottie told them. "There is a plug for the ones around the house up under the eaves at the back of the house, so you want to end there. Me and Leland found out that if you start at the south corner, chances are you'll come out at the exact right place. We just left the hooks up from one year to the next, so you don't have to worry with those things."

When they were outside, Betsy shook her head involuntarily.

"Mosquito at this time of year?" Declan asked.

"No bugs. My brain is trying to get rid of so many words. I don't think I've heard so much talking in my life. Even church ends in thirty minutes," she said softly.

Declan had one foot on the ladder, but he came back down, checked the windows, and backed Betsy up against the house, his strong arms trapping her in a cage of masculinity.

"Poor Leland. The writin' on his tombstone should read 'Here lies Leland Miller. Poor old cowboy was talked to death.'" He brushed a soft kiss across her lips and climbed up the ladder. "We can do this without talking, darlin'."

"Thank you," she mumbled.

After supper, Declan declared that it was poker night and disappeared without a backward glance. Betsy said she was going to read a book and escaped to her room. Lottie grabbed the telephone and was busy telling Gladys all about how her house looked when Betsy shut herself into her bedroom, fell back on the bed, and put a pillow over her ears.

"I need a beer so bad," she said. "Or better yet, a whole bottle of Jameson."

Betsy was too restless to sit still after Declan had left that evening, and lying on the bed with a pillow muting the sound of Lottie's chatter wasn't helping. Finally, she threw the pillow on the floor, sat up, and made a decision. She had to get out of the house. Maybe sitting on a bar stool, sipping a single beer would help. She grabbed her purse and coat and waved at Lottie on the way out of the house.

"I'll be back by bedtime," she called out.

She heard Lottie telling Gladys that both her hired hands were gone for the evening so she would be over to her house in thirty minutes for a hand of canasta with Gladys and Polly.

Fearing that Lottie would try to flag her down for a ride into town, Betsy jogged to her truck, fired up the engine, and only slid once when she started too fast.

Shame on you! How are you going to feel if that poor, sweet soul has a wreck and hurts herself on the way to Gladys's house? You should go back there and offer to take her to town.

"Hush! I'm not listening to anything you have to say and I'm really tired of anything that has to do with listening, period," Betsy growled.

She shed her coat inside the front door of the bar, hung it on a rack right beside Declan's, and almost gave thanks that there was a whole row of empty bar stools to choose from. She hopped up on the one at the very end and Rosalie held up the Jameson.

Betsy shook her head. "Just a good, cold beer tonight."

"I've missed you, but I've also heard the gossip about

the Double L," Rosalie said when she pushed the beer across the bar on a coaster. "How's that going?"

"Lottie talks—a lot!" Betsy said.

Rosalie chuckled. "You should've visited with Polly before you agreed to stay out there."

"Didn't have anywhere else to go."

"You could come live in my spare room," Rosalie said.

"I want that ranch and to get it I have to live there and beat Declan."

"Feud again?" Polly set the beer in front of her.

"Not so much the feud as it is..." She paused and sipped the beer slowly. "I don't know what it is, so I can't tell you. He wants the ranch for the same reasons I do. We want out of the feud and we want a small place that is ours and not a part of the empire."

"Maybe you ought to pool your resources and buy it together. That would shake the empire," Rosalie suggested.

Before either of them could say anything else, Honey Brennan pushed her way into the bar and chose a bar stool. Her crystal-clear blue eyes started at Betsy's boots and, inch by inch, traveled up to her red hair.

"Betsy." She nodded.

Betsy held up her beer and nodded. "Honey."

"I don't like my cousin living out there on the ranch with you," Honey said bluntly.

"That is your problem, not mine," Betsy said.

"Why don't you go back to Wild Horse and let him have that place? You can't run it by yourself, and rumor has it that Naomi says she'll shoot anyone who comes to help you. A beer, Rosalie," Honey said.

"There're always O'Donnells. I hear a cousin is

coming to stay with Jill and Sawyer at Christmas. I bet I could get another one to live in my bunkhouse and help me out. You might want to wait and see who shows up before you get too serious about John," Betsy said coldly.

"John and I are just fine, thank you very much," Honey said. "Granny is happy. Naomi is pissed. The world is good. Rosalie, would you please draw up a pitcher? I'm going to treat Declan and Quaid at the poker table."

Betsy really wanted to slap Honey for her smugness but even more because she could take a pitcher of beer back to the table to Declan without a problem. *Damn it to hell in a plastic beer pitcher*, Betsy thought.

Her phone set up a buzz in her hip pocket, and she made sure that she looked at the ID before she answered it. She didn't want Gladys to be calling to ask her to come and get Lottie because she'd killed Polly with her constant chatter. It was Angela, so Betsy answered it.

"Hello, hello, where are you? What is all that noise?" Angela asked.

"I'm at the bar," Betsy said. "Hold on. I'll take it to the ladies' room."

She slid off the stool, carried the phone to the restroom, and locked the door behind her. She put the seat down on the only potty in the room and sat down on it. "Now can you hear me, Angela?"

"Yes, that's much better. Why do you go to that place when it's so noisy?"

"Because I like it and because Lottie doesn't even have beer in her house for medicinal purposes," Betsy said. "Did you get moved back into your house all right?"

"Yes, thank God. That big place intimidated me. I guess you heard about the feud over my brother. Why couldn't you have liked him? It would have made things so much easier, and I really don't want a Brennan for a sister-in-law."

"He's not my type, and if you're calling to get me to step in and break him and Honey up, the answer is no."

Angela took a deep breath, audible even through the filtered noise from the jukebox and loud conversations. "Dear Lord no! John is smitten with Honey, and I wouldn't stand in the way of love, but he liked you and wouldn't have looked at her if you'd been nicer to him. I'm calling to tell you to be very careful out there on the Double L with that weasel Declan Brennan."

"Other than being a Brennan, what makes him a weasel?"

"Well, I overheard Tanner and Eli talking just before the big blow up at the ranch, when John went to the parsonage. And I've prayed and prayed about it, whether I should tell you or not, but it's a burden on my heart. Besides, you're living on a ranch with him, and you need to know what happened," Angela said.

"And that was?" Betsy asked.

"Well, it was the week before Thanksgiving, and they—that would be Tanner and Eli and Quaid and Declan—were in one of those unholy poker games that they play," Angela said.

"That's what they're doing tonight," Betsy said.

"But that night Tanner and Declan got into a big argument about all their past loves or women or whatever they would be called. And they made this bet that whichever one of them lost the hand had to… Oh, this is so hard to tell you because it's going to make you mad and I'm afraid you'll blame the messenger," Angela said.

"Spit it out." A tingle had started on the back of Betsy's neck and already had her hair standing on end.

"Whichever one lost the hand had to make the next woman who walked in the bar fall in love with him. He had to take her to bed and she had to fall for him, or else the loser had to give the winner a thousand dollars. Isn't that horrible? Anyway, Declan lost, and you were the next woman to walk in the bar, and now I'm afraid he'll try to seduce you out there on that ranch so he can win the money," Angela said in a whoosh, as if she was afraid she would lose her courage.

"And why didn't you call me before now?" Betsy's heart landed somewhere down between the wooden floor and hell.

"I had to do some serious praying about it. I'm going to hang up now. Christian is crying, but I do feel better for getting that off my chest. You be careful."

Betsy dropped the phone on the floor, leaned over, put her head between her knees, and made herself breathe. The whole room had done several spins, and she felt as if she might throw up any minute. She should have known from the beginning that Declan was just a Brennan after all.

And you are only a thousand-dollar bet.

Anger quickly replaced the pain shattering her heart, and she picked up her phone, stiffened her spine, and walked out of the bathroom. There all four of them sat, along with a couple of O'Donnells. It was a good thing she didn't have a gun, or Tanner would have gotten a hole right below his left ear. Damn him for making a bet like that anyway, and double damn him for not calling it off when she had been the one who walked into the bar.

"Give me a pitcher of beer, Rosalie?"

"Bad news? You are as pale as a ghost."

"Worse than I wanted to hear tonight," Betsy said. She blinked back the tears and held on to the anger. "I just need a good full pitcher of beer."

"Sure you don't want a shot of Jameson?"

"Hell no! That's too expensive."

Rosalie drew the beer and set it in front of her. Betsy paid her for it and the beer she'd had earlier. "Grandma Got Run Over by a Reindeer" was playing on the jukebox as she carried it ever so gently to the poker table.

"Hey, Betsy, did you bring us a pitcher?" Tanner asked. "These Brennans won't share what Honey gave them."

She caught Declan's sneaky, little wink and wanted to string him up by the toes to the ceiling fan until all the blood in his body dripped out his nose and ears.

"Well?" Tanner asked.

"Yes, I did bring the person who used to be my favorite cousin a pitcher of beer," she said coldly.

"Who pissed in your whiskey? You look like you could eat nails," Eli said.

"You sons of bitches did." She raised the pitcher and dumped it on Tanner's and Eli's heads. "The next time you fools decide to make a bet with a Brennan, you damn sure better call it off if it has anything to do with me."

Declan's face went blank as Tanner and Eli jumped up and brushed the wet beer from their heads and shirts. She looked right at him and pointed. "I will deal with you later, and it will not be as pleasant as a beer bath."

She grabbed her coat on the way out, got into her truck, and drove back to the Double L. Thankful that Lottie was still gone, she went straight to her room, curled up on the bed, and sobbed until there were no more tears. Her heart hurt so bad she thought she'd die from the pain and she sure didn't want to hear any excuses from Declan. Not tonight. Maybe not ever. So she turned off her phone and found another gallon of tears hiding in her soul. They made their way to her eyes and flowed down her cheeks, wetting the pillow, and they didn't stop until finally, from exhaustion, she fell into a restless, dream-ridden asleep.

Chapter 22

Betsy had never dreaded anything as much as she did walking into the kitchen where Declan and Lottie were already making breakfast that Friday morning. She dressed slowly and started to apply makeup but decided against it. Her eyeballs were bloodshot and eye shadow and mascara wouldn't do a damn thing to make them look better.

"Good morning," Lottie said cheerfully.

"Good morning to you," Betsy muttered without even a sideways glance toward Declan.

"We're having waffles and sausage for breakfast this morning, and I made a pan of cranberry orange muffins for dessert. I like to dip my muffins in the leftover maple syrup to give them a little extra kick," Lottie said.

I wouldn't mind having a saucer full of Jameson to dip mine in for a little extra kick this morning, Betsy thought.

"What are we doing today?" Betsy asked.

"Declan is going to walk the fence line and fix whatever needs fixin'. You are taking me into Gainesville in that pink truck of yours so I can do some shoppin'. After all, I'm flying out of here on Christmas Eve. I've already sent a lot of my stuff down to my sister's place in Florida. I need some clothes to wear in a warm climate, and believe me, I'm going to be glad to get away from this cold snow and hard winters. Take them waffles out of the iron and put another batch in. Declan is going to need all the warmth he can get this morning out there in the cold weather."

That familiar antsy feeling that Betsy got when someone was staring at her made her look up, and Declan's blue eyes bored into hers as if he was trying to explain, to tell her something. But that was just a player's charm and she'd never trust him or any Brennan again. If she didn't get the Double L, she might just go back to Wild Horse and mount the biggest feud the century had ever seen.

Tanner and Eli? the voice in her head asked.

They are kin, so I can't kill them, but they'll be sorry the rest of their lives for not calling that bet off when I walked into the bar.

"We need to talk," Declan whispered.

She shook her head. "Not today, cowboy."

The way his jaw worked and his mouth clamped shut in a firm line said that he didn't like her answer. Right then, she didn't care what he liked. The only thing she wanted to know was if the whole thing between them was a seduction or if any of it was real, and that question didn't have to be answered until she was over her mad spell.

Immediately after Lottie said grace, she picked up the platter of waffles, put two on her plate, and said, "Now let's eat. Christmas is two weeks from this day, and we've got a lot to do. My plane ticket is bought and my sister is ready for me to get there. Did I tell you that I'm buying a little house right on the beach next to hers? Cute little place with two bedrooms but not quite as big as this one. Got a deck that overlooks the ocean, and it's painted pink."

"Lottie, am I going to lose points today by shopping rather than ranchin'?" Betsy took one waffle and one sausage from the platter. Swallowing would be a problem, but there was no way she'd let Declan know that she was hurting, and he'd never see her cry a single tear. She was a Gallagher and they produced strong women.

"No, you won't, and Declan won't gain any extra points by fixing the fence. Both need doing and I really don't care who does which. I figured you might be a better judge of what kind of clothes I should buy than Declan. But if he wants to shop with me, then you can stay behind and fix fence," Lottie said. "Me and Leland, we always stuck to the old goose-and-gander law. I wasn't too delicate to go outside and work, and he wasn't too masculine to help me clean house on Saturday or help with the dinner dishes."

Thank God for Lottie's constant prattle—I never thought for a single second I'd live to see the day I'd be grateful for that.

"I'll gladly do the fencing. I'm not much good at shopping." Declan pushed back his chair. "I'll refill coffee cups while I'm doing mine."

"Thank you, Declan," Lottie said.

He took care of Lottie's cup first, then laid his hand on Betsy's shoulder as he reached over her to pour. Her body responded with a shiver up her backbone, jitters in her stomach, and a picture of him sleeping next to her in that big hotel bed. She was mad at him—she should not have a desire to fall into bed with him.

He squeezed ever so gently when he backed away and filled his own cup to the brim. It was cold outside and still spitting snow, so she didn't blame him one bit for putting off going out there for the day to walk a fence line.

"Come on back to the house at noon, Declan," Lottie was saying when she started paying attention again. "There's ham and cheese in the fridge and potato salad and chocolate pie for dessert. And we promise to bring you some take-out food for supper."

"I'm going to have a burger at the bar tonight," he said. "Quald and I are meeting there for a visit."

"Then that settles that. You going out tonight too?" Lottie looked over at Betsy.

A slight shrug was the answer.

"Yes? No?" Lottie asked.

"I have no idea. It depends on when we get back from the shopping trip," she answered. "Hey, while I'm thinking about it, Lottie, I'm working on something for the church. It's a surprise, so I can't give you details, but would you consider donating your Christmas collection of figurines?"

"I wondered if you'd ever ask me about those. Verdie let the cat out of the bag about you taking up donations, and I wanted to give them to a good cause. That's why I put the box in my bedroom when y'all brought the stuff from the bunkhouse. I don't think I could hardly bear to look at them this year and then leave them behind. It's a fancy little nativity scene that would look real good on the altar at the church. My Leland gave me a piece every year for Christmas, and there're more'n fifty of them in the collection. Yes, you can have them, long as you promise me they'll stay in our church. Shame what y'all did to each other's school buildings, burning down all the props and such for the church plays. I swear, this feud has got to end."

"She started it," Declan said.

"I didn't do jack"—she bit back the cuss word—"a thing. My family did, but I didn't. Just like your family did, but you said you didn't; however, who knows? You Brennans, for all your pious backgrounds, do lie and cheat to get your way or a thousand dollars, don't you?"

"Hey now, this is neutral as the church or the store. No fightin' here, kids," Lottie said. "I reckon we've lollygagged over breakfast long enough. Time to get about our day's work."

"I'll get dressed to go to town and be out in ten minutes," Betsy said.

Declan finished his coffee with a gulp and said, "And I'm going to the tack room for supplies."

"I'll have this kitchen in shape by the time you get back out here." Lottie grinned.

"Okay, girl, spill the beans right now," Lottie said when they were settled into Betsy's truck. "I know about the bet and about what went on at the bar last night and that you have a right to be mad at him. But I want to know the whole story."

"How did you find out?"

"Rosalie called Polly soon as the bar closed up. That Polly and Gladys can stay up until midnight and sleep all the way to eight o'clock. Not me. I'm yawning at nine o'clock and can't sleep a wink past four thirty. Five o'clock is sleeping in to me. So anyway, Rosalie called Polly, and Polly got up to go to the bathroom at four thirty, so she called me to see if I knew anything more about it. You should know that you or Declan can't burp without everyone in Burnt Boot talkin' about what y'all had for dinner. Y'all and Honey and that preacher are the talk right now," Lottie answered.

"You want to hear hanky-panky and all?" Betsy asked.

"You think me and Leland didn't enjoy a little of that when we were young? Just because I'm old and wrinkled now don't mean that we didn't like going to bed in the middle of the day for a little fun or that I didn't enjoy it. So talk to me."

Betsy bit her lower lip. "Does what I'm going to say put Declan or me in first position?"

"What you do with your personal life don't have a lot to do with whether you can run a ranch, so no, it's not going to have much to do with my decision about who gets to buy the Double L. But you are about to explode, girl, and if you don't talk, the top of your head is going to blow your brains all over this pretty truck. You know what? I might buy a pink golf cart when I get to Florida. They tell me that's what the old toots ride around in down there. You goin' to talk, or am I goin' to have to slap the fizzles right out of you to get you started?"

"You already know most of it. Tanner and Declan got into it about their womanizing ways during a poker game and made a bet. Whoever lost had to make the next woman who came into the bar fall in love with him by Christmas. Declan lost, and I was the woman," Betsy said.

"And what happened? Did he ask you out?"

"No, he went to the river, and I showed up on that same night because I needed to think about Christmas. Angela was crying because she wants her new baby boy,

Christian, to be baby Jesus in the church program, and I talked to Rosalie and, well, I just wound up on the banks of the river," she said.

"And you got to talking about Christmas and came up with the idea to gather up stuff so Angela wouldn't be disappointed, right?"

Betsy inhaled deeply. "A week from Sunday, Kyle is going to announce it in church, and there will be a program on the Wednesday night before Christmas. You'll still be here, right?"

Lottie's gray bun bounced up and down as she nodded emphatically. "What a wonderful thing you kids have done for the church. I don't fly out until Thursday, and your last job is going to be taking me to the Dallas airport. I have already fixed things so my lawyer can take care of the money deal and put it in my new Florida account."

Betsy thought she'd dodged a bullet by talking about Christmas, but she was dead wrong. Lottie's eyebrows knit together in a solid line and she said, "Now about this hanky-panky? Was that all there was to it, or did you fall in love with Declan? Last time that happened, they took the man out and hung him from what I hear about history. I can't just remember if it was a Gallagher or a Brennan that got hung though."

"I don't know," Betsy said.

"Hard to trust your heart to someone who's used you as a bet and who's a Brennan, right?" Lottie asked. "Before you answer, maybe you ought to know that he paid Tanner the thousand dollars and called off the bet a few days ago."

Betsy frowned. "He did what?"

"Yep, Polly got that news last night when Tanner was leaving in a huff. Said he didn't know why you were in such a huff because he'd won the bet. He was bragging that Declan knew he couldn't ever get you to go out with him so he just paid up even before Christmas so he could go chasin' some other skirt that had caught his eye. You hear of him goin' after another woman? I haven't," Lottie said.

Betsy shook her head. "But that doesn't mean I'm not still mad."

"You got a right to be mad for a time. Take as long as you need to get over it, but don't let the anger ruin your life. Now let's go to that little dress shop down there by the Big Lots store. I like pants with elastic in the waist and shirts that button up. Old woman like me has trouble with them pullover things and gettin' my britches down when it's time to go to the bathroom if I have to unzip and unbutton them."

Declan threw a roll of barbed wire in the back of the old truck along with stretchers, an extra pair of gloves, and half a dozen metal fence posts in case he had to replace one of the wooden ones. Then he drove about five hundred yards through the snow to a place where he could park, got out, and started walking back, checking posts and barbed wire all the way. When that much stood the test, he went back to the truck and had gotten inside when he saw his father pull off the side of the road and stop.

They met at the fence line, Russell on one side, Declan on the other—clones of each other with twenty-five years and a few pounds extra on Russell.

"Heard there was a little dustup at the bar last night. That true that you and Tanner had a bet?"

Declan nodded. "It's true but I lost and paid him several days ago."

"Never did ask Betsy out?"

"It's complicated," he answered.

"She's a Gallagher. You know you can't trust them. Tanner probably had a bet with her that she couldn't get you to fall for her. I bet he made a thousand dollars off her too and that's what made her mad enough to dump beer on his head. Your grandmother is elated that there's trouble in the Gallagher camp. She says for you to drop whatever you're doing and come home to River Bend."

Declan removed his black cowboy hat and cocked his head to one side. "And what do you say, Dad?"

Russell's gloved hand crossed the fence and came to rest on Declan's shoulder. "The same thing that I said when you left. Follow your heart. I wish I'd done that all those years. You in love with Betsy?"

"I could be," Declan said. "But a fat lot of good that will do me now. You really think that Tanner was playing a double game?"

"I wouldn't put nothing past him. Whatever you decide, you keep your guard up with him. So I reckon you are stayin' put for a while longer even though you have to walk the fence line in the middle of snow?" Russell removed his hand.

"I'm not letting her win and get the ranch. I want it too bad, and you always said a fence needed to be checked three times a year," Declan told him.

Russell gave a brief nod. "That's right. Winter, summer, and once more, especially if it's a wet spring.

You did listen to a few things, Son. Holler at me if you need anything other than walking a fencerow in three inches of cold snow. That I'm not willin' for."

"Thanks, Dad, for understanding," Declan said.

"Glad we had such a good talk." Russell waved as he walked back to his truck.

Betsy walked into the bar that evening and went straight to the jukebox and put enough coins in the slot to play six songs. Then she poked the numbers in to play Terri Clark's "I Just Wanna Be Mad." While the first song played, she found a bar stool and pointed at the Jameson.

Rosalie poured two fingers in a red cup and set it on the bar in front of her and made change for the bill that Betsy gave her. "So I guess from the song you just picked out, you want to be mad for a while longer. You sending a message to Tanner, Declan, or the whole Gallagher and Brennan clans? I've heard all kinds of rumors."

"Biggest rumor?" Betsy sipped the whiskey.

"That Tanner was bettin' with both of you and wound up with two thousand dollars. Second biggest is that Declan really won the bet, but he fell in love with you and that's why he paid off Tanner, so he could ask you out on a real date. Either one of them true?"

Betsy shrugged. "First one isn't. I did not have a bet with Tanner. You'd have to ask Declan for answers to the second one, not me."

"Holy smokes! That song is coming on again," Rosalie said.

Betsy held up six fingers. "It's going to play for the next twenty minutes. Six times in all. Some men are dense. Like second grade students, they need lots of repetition to get the message."

"Well, he ought to get the message that you aren't going to drive a stake through his heart but that he'd best give you some space," Rosalie said.

Terri sang that she wasn't ready to make up, that she thought she was right and he was wrong and not to try to make her smile because she wanted to be mad for a while. Betsy tapped her fingers on top of the bar, keeping up with the beat through every song. When the last one finished, the whole crowd applauded.

Declan made his way through the crowd and went to the jukebox, plugged in a fistful of coins, and poked a few buttons, then raised his red cup in a salute toward Betsy.

"I think he got the message." Rosalie smiled. "Another whiskey?"

"No, maybe a club soda," Betsy said. "I want to be sober."

Jamie O'Neal started singing "When I Think about Angels" and Betsy glanced across the room at Declan, who winked. The lyrics said that everything about her was a beautiful distraction and everywhere he went or everything he did made him think about her, and that when he thought about heaven, he thought about angels, and when he thought about angels, he thought about her. A girl was singing, but Betsy heard it as a song from a guy because Declan had played it for her.

The next song came from Sammy Kershaw—"She Don't Know She's Beautiful"—and Rosalie smiled. "I think y'all need to talk, rather than fighting with the jukebox."

"Not yet. I'm not done being mad," Betsy said.

Rosalie went to the other end of the bar and drew a beer for a customer, then made her way back to Betsy. "Got to admit, it would take more than twenty-four hours for me to get over that too. I hear that Mavis is crowing now that John and Honey are an item and this new battle in the feud has been dubbed the love war. Kind of fitting here at Christmas."

"I could care less about the love war," Betsy declared.

"Sounds to me like you might be the biggest star in this war." Rosalie laughed. "A preacher and Honey wouldn't be anything like a Gallagher and a Brennan falling in love."

"You know what love is?" Betsy asked.

"Trust?" Rosalie said.

"It's a four-letter word, and I've been warned many times about those damn things."

Tanner propped a hip on the bar stool beside her and motioned for Rosalie to bring a pitcher of beer. "Betsy," he said softly.

"If you're planning on pouring that on my head, I wouldn't," she said coldly.

"I came to apologize. I should have told you or put an end to the bet when you came in the bar that night, but it would've been letting a Brennan defeat me," he said.

"Did you hear that song I just played six times? Do I need to play it another six? I'm mad, and it's going to take me a long time to get over it," she said.

Tanner put up his palms. "Will you call me when you're over it?"

"It might take fifty years."

He dropped his hands. "That's a long time to carry a grudge."

"That was a nasty thing you did. You caused this, and I hope Granny punishes you."

Eli started across the room, and she gave him an evil look that stopped him in his tracks. He went back to the jukebox and chose half a dozen Christmas songs, but even that didn't sweeten her mood.

"Tell me you didn't really go out with Declan. Please promise me that you didn't..." Tanner stopped. "You didn't really fall for that line of bull he puts out, did you? It's all a lie."

"And you know because you use the same lines, right? All of you are pigs from hell. You wouldn't know love if it bit you square on the ass. Rosalie, I need a burger basket, double meat, double cheese, lots of onions, so I can breathe on these sorry suckers who want to sit close to me and talk," Betsy said.

Tanner started to walk away but stopped when Betsy tapped him on the shoulder.

"One more thing, darlin' Cousin. I'm not promising anything and I'm not telling you just what we did do in that big, king-size hotel bed."

His face went pale. "When Granny hears that, she'll send one of us gunnin' for Declan."

"And if a single one of you lays a hand on a hair on his head, you will answer to my shotgun. I mean it, and you can spread the word. If anyone gets to shoot him, it will be me, and I haven't decided if I want him dead yet. Understood?"

"But Granny—" he said.

"I'm meaner than Naomi Gallagher ever hoped to be and don't you forget it."

Rosalie chuckled. "Sounds like a love war to me. You just took up for a Brennan."

"I didn't take up for him. I'm saving him until I decide what his punishment is going to be. For the record, I'm still deciding what Tanner's and Eli's ultimate fates will be too."

"Maybe we'd better rename this new feud the come-to-Jesus war."

"Or come-to-Betsy war." She finally smiled.

Chapter 23

Betsy found a note in her coat pocket on the way home that evening. It simply said, "You have a right to be mad as long as you want. When you are ready to talk, call me. Until then, know I am sorry for all this." At the end was his phone number written in big letters.

She tried.

She really, really tried to get over it as she drove toward Lottie's place on slippery roads. But the big, gaping cut across her heart still hurt too badly. She'd bluffed very well, but Tanner was her favorite cousin. And Declan? A lump formed in her throat.

She wasn't ready to go home, so she made a loop around town, driving slow and looking at all the Christmas lights. The tree in front of the grocery store was still standing although the wind had tangled the garland and knocked a few of the ornaments off. The angel on the top of the tree beckoned to her with open arms, but what could a plastic angel do to relieve her heartache?

Driving past the bar again, she glanced over at the Gallagher tree. It didn't look a whole lot different than the Brennans'—garland twisted up from the hard north winds and a few busted ornaments, but both were still standing.

The church was dark and that was a crying shame. It was Christmas. The church should be the first building in town to show the spirit, not the bar and the store. If the feud ever ended, Betsy made a vow that there would be no trees in town and that a lovely, life-size nativity scene would be placed on the church lawn.

With all the lights in town shining brightly, a soft glow covered Burnt Boot that Friday evening. It reminded her of a Thomas Kincaid picture on her grandmother's calendar. She'd given it to Naomi for Christmas last year, and looking back, the year had been anything but peaceful and sweet. And it was ending on a note that said she might never be welcome at Wild Horse for the holidays again.

She found herself at the locked gates at the end of the road leading down to the Red River. Not sure how she'd gotten there but knowing that she could think better under her old willow tree than anywhere else, she parked the truck, climbed over the fence, and made her way down to the very tree where she and Declan had started this whole mess. Was it only three weeks ago? Mercy, it seemed like years.

But you've known him your whole life, her conscience argued as she trudged through the snow on the uneven ground.

"Which means I should have known better," she said.

The limbs of the poor weeping willow dragged to the ground with the weight of the ice and snow, but they did provide enough cover that part of the ground under the tree was still bare. Enough that she could sit down and pretend she was in an igloo somewhere far, far away from Burnt Boot. Maybe that's what she needed—a trip out of the forest for a few days.

"Can't do that. I want that ranch too bad to throw in the towel now. And besides, a Gallagher does not run from problems," she whispered.

"Neither does a Wiseman." A branch cracked and ice filtered down on her boots as Declan pushed his way uninvited into her Texas-style igloo.

He sat down and left a foot of space between them, but that didn't stop the sparks from heating up the tiny space. If it had been natural heat, the ice would have melted in seconds, sending a shower of cold rain down on their heads. She didn't look at him, didn't dare, not the way the emotions were rattling around in her body. Anger and peace made strange bedfellows. Or maybe they made impossible bed partners because she couldn't have one when the other was present.

After several minutes of silence, he laid his gloved hand on hers.

She left hers on the sand and didn't jerk it away because his touch brought a measure of comfort to her troubled soul. A herd of deer appeared on the other side of the river and cautiously approached the still, cold water for a drink before bounding back into the wooded area and disappearing in the mesquite and scrub oaks.

The moon tried to throw off a little light, but dark clouds kept covering it, along with the stars. Was this what it was like when baby Jesus was born in that stable more than two thousand years ago? Did the shepherds and wise men have trouble following the bright star?

She looked up through the icy limbs at the sky. Three stars peeked out boldly from behind a cloud. Which one should she follow? The one that pointed her down the sandbar, over the fence, and back to Wild Horse? The one over there that seemed to be sending her back to the Double L to fight for the place her heart wanted so badly? Or that one right smack above them that said to follow Declan wherever he led?

After a while, Declan stood up and walked away. He didn't look back or say a word, and his absence created a big empty hole in her heart. When she looked back up, a bright star was shining right above her head.

On Saturday morning, Lottie announced that she and Betsy would spend the day in the kitchen making cookies. "We'll make a dozen different kinds to wrap up and take to the neighbors on Monday. I have to make them this year since it's my last year here. And, Declan, the ranch books are right there. Today you get to go over them. I put a brand-new spiral notebook and a pencil there beside them so you can take notes. And there's a calculator there too. I set up a card table over there in the corner of the living room for you to work on. One day next week, you get to look over the books, Betsy. This way you'll know exactly how the ranch has produced for more than fifty years and know that I'm giving one of you a really good deal on this place."

"You don't have it on a computer?" Declan asked.

"Why would I? Whole world has gone crazy after all this technology, but not me. House catches on fire, I know to grab those books and the bag of money I got socked away that the bank or the IRS don't know about. It's my egg and butter money, and I figure I paid taxes on the chickens and cows once, so it's fair and square. I'm not big enough to carry one of them big computers out of here," Lottie said.

"They make laptops," Betsy told her.

"What if it went boom, or what is it that you young folks call it when one of those idiot machines quits working?"

"It crashes," Declan said.

"That's it. Think about it. *Crash* is not a good word. No, thank you. I will keep my books on paper. Now if y'all want to put all them figures into a computer after I'm gone, then that's your business, but until then, it's paper and pencil. Not even pens because sometimes I have to erase." She turned from him to Betsy. "We'll start with gingerbread cookies. We make them in a bar pan and cut them into squares. Recipe makes a lot, but then we'll be visiting quite a few houses on Monday, so that's good. Get five pounds of flour from the pantry, Betsy."

"I may come to the little kids Sunday school class tomorrow if you're bringing cookies," Betsy said.

"I always take cookies to Sunday school class."

"I remember," Declan called out from the living room.

By suppertime, Betsy was physically exhausted and Declan was in the same shape mentally. They sat down to a meal of homemade chicken noodle soup and thick chunks of toasted homemade bread with a side dish of cheese, pickled okra, and black olives and a huge platter of cookies for dessert.

Neither Declan nor Betsy had said more than a handful of words to each other all day and that had been at the table when one of them asked for salt and the other one for butter. Lottie had prattled about everything, anything, and nothing, but Betsy had learned to pick out the thread of the conversation and let the rest float away.

"I'm not one to meddle in other folks' business but I've got something to say. Pass the soup down to Declan, Betsy. His bowl is empty and he's trying to figure out a way to ask for it without using words. This cold business between y'all has to stop. I know you are both angry, and rightly so, but you ain't never going to get this resolved by the silent treatment. At meals, you are going to talk to each other and to me, or you can pack up your bags and get off this ranch. I don't like tension," Lottie said.

"Would you like some more soup, Declan?" Betsy said.

"Yes, ma'am. I can pass my bowl but please don't accidentally drop it in my lap," he answered.

"That's better," Lottie muttered and went back to eating.

"Bread?" Declan asked.

"Yes, please," Betsy said.

"The Sunday school class is going to miss you," Declan said.

Lottie's old eyes lit up when she smiled. "I know, and I'll miss them, but it's time to move on. My bones get cold in winters like this, and I can't get out and take care of the cows with snow and ice on the ground. Last year it was tough getting the hay in the barn."

"You hauled hay?" Betsy exclaimed.

"I'm a rancher," Lottie huffed. "Hired me a boy to throw it on the truck after I got it baled, but I helped him stack it when we got to the barn. When it was all gone this winter, I knew it was time to sell the cows and the ranch. I can't do that another summer."

"How long has it been since the bunkhouse was used?" Declan asked.

"Before you moved in, maybe ten years. Me and Leland, we sized down but we took care of the place ourselves with help from one or two hired boys in the summertime."

"And before that?" Betsy asked.

"We had four hired hands all the time. Leland never would make none of them the foreman, but whichever one was the oldest got the bedroom with a door. The others had to make do with the bunk beds."

Betsy kept a close eye on Declan's soup bowl. Words, hard as they were to say, weren't going to keep her from having this ranch. And evidently, he'd found some very nice figures in those books for him to talk to her.

When supper was finished, dishes done, and Declan off to the bunkhouse, Betsy took a long, soaking bath. The bathroom was small and gave testimony to its age. The wall-hung, pea-green sink had a floral curtain hanging around it, hiding the plunger, various cleaners, and a brush to clean the potty, which was the same color as the sink. The tub though—now that was pure luxury, even if Lottie had painted the outside to match the rest of the fixtures. The inside of the deep claw-foot tub was shiny porcelain, and the water came up to Betsy's chin when she laid back.

When the water went lukewarm, she got out and wrapped a big towel around her body, padded softly across the hall to her bedroom even though a SWAT team storming the house wouldn't have awakened Lottie. She'd worn herself out with all the baking and cooking that day and had gone to bed right after eight o'clock.

Betsy dressed in flannel pajama pants and a thermal knit shirt before picking up her latest novel, a thick romance titled *The Traitor* by a favorite author, Grace Burrowes. It seemed fitting after the ordeal with both Tanner and Declan.

She opened the book, but before she read the first sentence, a bit of bright neon-orange caught her eye on the nightstand.

"A sticky note?" She frowned.

It hadn't been there earlier before she'd gone to take a bath. Where had it come from and who put it there? She stared at it a full minute before she reached across the bed to pick it up.

Stuck to an individually wrapped Twinkie, she brought both up at the same time and peeled the note off. She stared at it for several seconds before reading the familiar handwriting:

> *You were in the fifth grade. I was in the seventh. Miz Lottie's Sunday school room about Christmastime. She had to be gone that Sunday, and the substitute brought a basket of individually wrapped treats. There was one Twinkie in the basket and you grabbed it first and said it was your favorite snack in the whole world. Enjoy this one tonight.*

It was signed with Declan's initials inside a heart.

She carefully removed the wrapper from the snack, eased the cake out without leaving a sticky mess, and ate the whole thing before she put the note and the wrapper in a shoebox where she stored all her Declan memories. Someday, she might burn them, or when she was past eighty and making cookies in the kitchen of this very farmhouse, she might remember that Christmas when she and Declan fought over who would own the ranch.

Chapter 24

Kyle was back on Sunday morning, but he still turned the preaching over to John that day. For the first time in his life, Declan sat in the middle section with those folks who were neither Gallaghers nor Brennans. Lottie sat between him and Betsy, and the chill in the room had nothing to do with the freezing temperatures outside.

His attention was more focused on the emerald-green ribbon and note in his shirt pocket than it was on whatever John was preaching about that morning. He only had a few items in the secret boot box, but if they could help Betsy understand the past, maybe she would forgive him and move on toward the future. His dad had asked him if he was in love with Betsy and he'd thought about it a lot over the past two days.

He wasn't sure about love, but he did know that he didn't want to lose her. His life had never been more complete than it was right at that moment. Even though she was angry at him, he still wanted her by his side. That could easily lead to love if she was willing.

"Now we'll ask Declan Brennan to deliver the benediction," John said.

Hearing his name jerked him back to reality and he stood up, bowed his head, and barely said a long enough prayer for John and Kyle to get down the aisle to the door. The whole time he was asking the Lord to bless the people of their community what he really wanted to ask Him to do was make Betsy forgive him.

"I'm having Sunday dinner with Gladys and Polly. There're leftovers from last night in the fridge at home if y'all want that. If not, you are on your own," Lottie said the minute the last amen was said.

"We've got some things to deliver to our cause," Betsy whispered.

"Well, take that box right behind the door in my bedroom with you. It's the only one in there, so you can't miss it. And after services tonight, we are going to watch a movie and have popcorn and hot chocolate. Yes, you are required to be at church and at the movie, and yes, it will be points taken off if you fail to show. You might as well take one truck down to Gainesville. Whole town has seen you sittin' together during church," Lottie said.

"We were sitting with you, not together," Betsy stammered.

"Don't think the Gallaghers or the Brennans saw it that way. And you were in the same pew so sorry, kids, in God's eyes you were sitting together. I was just the chaperone." Lottie laughed. "Give me your keys, Betsy. I'll take your truck to Gladys's place, and we'll meet at home at four thirty. I've got just the movie picked out for us to watch after church services."

"Which is?" Declan could foresee some old black-and-white western with Roy Rogers or maybe even Gene Autry in it. He'd be yawning halfway through the thing and lose points for sure.

Betsy held out her keys, but her expression said she sure didn't want to give them to Lottie. Finally the old gal snatched them from her and said, "Wipe that horrible expression off your face, girl. I can drive anything that's got four wheels on it, from a covered wagon to a hay baler. I won't put a single scratch on your pretty pink truck. But just between me and you, it looks like it's been sprayed down with Pepto-Bismol. What in the great green earth possessed you to buy the thing? I hope it was on sale."

"Right now I wish I'd bought any other color in the world."

"Well, darlin', get the thing painted or trade it in. A ranchin' woman don't drive a pimp wagon," Lottie said.

Declan could feel his eyes almost popping out of his head, and Betsy's blank expression said that she was as shocked as he was.

"Lottie Miller!" Betsy said.

"I did not cuss, and it does. There's Gladys. I'll see y'all at four thirty." She left them totally speechless, standing side by side.

"Well?" Declan said.

"I guess we're going to the storage unit in your truck. I'm in shock that Lottie said that."

"I'm going to pretend that she didn't. I can't imagine my old Sunday school teacher even knowing what a pimp is. Want a burger for lunch?"

"I'd rather have dumplings from Cracker Barrel."

The corners of his mouth tilted upward but only slightly. "You think we're safe that close to the hotel?"

"Probably not. So we'll make a quick stop by the house. Do you have anything at the bunkhouse?" she asked.

"No, we'll get your donation and get something to eat before we go to the storage unit," he answered.

"I'll be ahead of you if you haven't gotten a donation this week," she said.

"I got something, but the furniture stores have to deliver it."

"Stores as in two?" she asked.

"Stores as in four," he said. "They will be there at two thirty."

He opened the door for her, and she crawled into his truck right out there for the whole town to see for the very first time. Her grandmother frowned and glared at her with enough fire that Betsy could practically feel the heat. Mavis Brennan shook her finger at the truck as Declan drove away.

"Guess we're in bigger trouble than we could ever imagine." He smiled.

"Looks like it," she said.

The ride wasn't awkward but more like a comfortable silence with an old friend. She started to mention the note and treat from the night before, but she couldn't find the right words. Betsy Gallagher had always been the I-don't-give-a-damn girl made of gunpowder and lead, the person who didn't take shit off anybody and went after what she wanted with no holds barred. So being tongue-tied was a whole new experience for her, and one that she wasn't sure she liked.

Declan parked in the front yard and said, "I'll get that box for you."

"Thanks," she mumbled.

So he had four people donating, and she had one for the week but she'd exhausted her supply of contacts.

That meant he would win and she'd owe him a thousand dollars, which meant he'd get the money back that he'd given Tanner. She crossed her arms over her chest.

A smile spread across her face and she talked out loud to herself. "Tanner, I have decided on your punishment. You are going to give me the money you made on that bet, and I'm giving it to Declan. It seems only fair, and if you don't give it to me, I will never forgive you," she whispered.

Declan slung the door open and set the box on the backseat. "It is heavy, but I bet them figurines will look real nice on the altar during the program and for church services until after New Year's."

"Maybe so." She smiled.

"Aha! She smiles," he said.

"Don't get all feisty and misread it," she said quickly. "I was thinking about something other than our problem."

"I don't care if you were thinking of murder. It's nice to see you smile."

A few flakes fell on them when they left Burnt Boot. The snow got increasingly heavy with every single mile until the windshield wipers couldn't begin to keep up when they finally slid into a parking spot at the restaurant.

"Do you think we cause all this snow when we come to Gainesville?" he asked.

"It's a possibility. You sure your donors will bring stuff out on a day like this?"

"They've got enclosed trucks, and we've got a big, roll-up door they can back right into. We probably need to tell Kyle to bring lots of help and an enclosed cattle trailer. I bet my dad would let him borrow one from

River Bend," Declan said. "You ready to brave this, or you want to change your mind and go to Sonic so we can eat in the truck?"

"A big, greasy burger does sound good," she said.

"Then Sonic it is."

He backed the truck up slowly, but the wheels had trouble getting traction. Finally, they had managed to get out on the highway, which wasn't quite as slippery as the parking lot, and had pulled under the awning at the Sonic when Betsy's phone rang.

"Hello, Kyle," she said.

"Hey, do you have a couple of minutes for me to shoot an idea past you?"

"Sure, if you'll hold five seconds. I want whatever number is a bacon cheeseburger, a large order of tater tots, and a cup of coffee," she said. "Now, my order for dinner is done. What's on your mind?"

"How close are you to having all your donations done?"

"Hold on just a minute?" She turned to Declan. "Do you have any more folks to talk to after today about donations? Kyle wants to know."

"This is it. When my stuff gets delivered today, then that's all of it," he said.

"Is that Declan?" Kyle asked. "If it is, put it on speaker and I'll talk to both of you at the same time."

She poked a button and laid the phone on the console between them. "You are on speaker and Declan is right here beside me."

"Good. I thought I'd have to call him next. Here's my plan, and by the way, it was good to see you two sitting in the center pew this morning. After services tonight, I'm going to announce that I'm making a special announcement on Wednesday night, but I'm going to refuse to say what it is. Everyone will think I'm resigning and giving John my endorsement for a replacement, so they'll show up. Some will want him to stay and some won't—you know how the feud works—but everyone in town will be here for the announcement."

"Are you resigning?" Declan asked.

"No, I like it here in Burnt Boot. Is making this Christmas program going to be doable?" Kyle asked.

"With a lot of work and a couple of trailers, I think it just might be. But remember we can't beg, buy, or borrow a trailer from either feuding family," Betsy said.

"I've got that covered. The Gallaghers can have the nativity scene, but the Brennans are going to have the choir and lead the singing and do the Bible readings for it."

"That ought to go over like a cow patty in the punch bowl—or maybe a mouse," Betsy said.

Kyle chuckled. "We'll see. That's going to be the rules to even have a program and I think they'll do what I ask. I want you two to be here tonight and on Wednesday night for sure, and of course, I need the key to that storage unit to get the stuff brought in here tomorrow morning bright and early."

"Wouldn't miss it," Declan said. "But you might want to have the National Guard on standby. There could be a riot right there in the church."

Kyle's deep laughter filled the cab of the truck. "Might not be a bad idea but I'm hoping for a miracle. So if either of you have one up your sleeve you might bring it with you."

"We'll get to church a little early and give you the key and the address," Declan said.

"You sure that we'll need two trailers? That sounds like a bit much for one program," Kyle asked.

"There's a surprise or two in the place. We'll see you later," Betsy said.

"Well, thank you in advance for all of it. Weatherman says that the sun is supposed to come out bright enough tomorrow to melt some of this, and we'll have fairly decent weather until Christmas Eve, when they're calling for nothing short of a blizzard. That's another reason I'd like to have this on Friday. I could sneak away before the storm hits to be with my fiancée both Christmas Eve and Christmas, and John will be glad to have the evening service for me—when Christmas is on Sunday, we don't have a morning service, just the evening one and then a potluck afterward. I'll look to see you later this afternoon then."

The phone went quiet, and Betsy picked it up. "I guess this means you win the contest. I owe you a thousand dollars, right?"

He started to say something and she held up a hand.

"Not yet. I've got a phone call to make before we talk about money."

She poked a button and immediately Tanner answered, "I'm so sorry, Betsy. I can say it a million times and it wouldn't begin to cover how sorry I really am. Please forgive me?"

"I might forgive you, but only if the conditions are right."

Tanner groaned. "Name the price. I miss you."

"Your pride meant more to you than I did, so here's

what it's going to take for you to get out of hot water. You have to give me the money that you won from Declan on the bet. It's only fair since you messed around with my life," she said.

"Come on, Betsy. That's pretty steep."

"It's the price. Can I expect it this afternoon? I'm going to the church probably about four o'clock to drop something off. You can bring it to me there," she said.

"Well, dammit!"

"Yes or no?" Betsy asked.

"Yes. Will a check do? I don't have that much cash on hand," he asked.

"A check will do fine but leave the recipient line blank."

"Why?"

"You aren't in any position to ask why after what you did."

"Then I'm forgiven?"

One side of Betsy's mouth turned up in a crooked smile. "Of course, darlin'. You are my favorite cousin, after all."

She ended the call, put the phone in her shirt pocket, and felt Declan's gaze. "What?" she asked as her green eyes locked with his blue ones.

"You are incredible."

"Thank you. You will have your money from Tanner when we get to the church. Both of you had best remember to watch that gambling problem you have from now on."

"Yes, ma'am," he said.

Betsy figured she might have time for a nap, but the trip back to Burnt Boot took longer than she expected, and they got back just in time for services that evening. She was surprised to see Tanner already sitting in a back pew.

"What are you doing here?" he asked Declan.

"We're here to see Kyle," Betsy answered.

Tanner's face turned ashen. "What for?"

"Personal business," Declan said.

"Betsy, we need to talk before you do this," Tanner drawled.

"Do what? I'm just giving him a key. I've been bringing in the programs for him. You know that. What'd you think we were going to see him about?" Betsy asked.

Tanner wiped his brow. "Nothing, just thank God I was wrong! Here is your check. And if you decide to see Kyle for…well, you know… Don't. Just don't."

He made a hasty retreat out the door, leaving Betsy holding a thousand-dollar check and Declan with a smile on his face.

Kyle poked his head down the hall and yelled, "I'm in my office. Y'all got time to visit?"

"Not really," Declan answered. "We're supposed to go home right after services tonight. Lottie says we both have to be there for popcorn and a movie."

He motioned them on back to his office. "Well, I sure wouldn't want to disappoint Lottie."

Declan stood to the side and let Betsy enter before him, then he took the key to the storage unit from his pocket plus the business card of the establishment. "Here you go. I've told the man at the unit you'll drop the key by on your way out. That will save us a trip back down there, and we only had it rented for a month."

"Thank you both for this. I appreciate it, but more so, the church is grateful. Without you two working together, this would have never happened. I understand it was a contest. May I ask who won?"

"Declan did for sure after his last delivery, and I'm handing him this check right now in front of you and God." Betsy laid the check on the preacher's desk.

Declan slid the check across the desk. "And I'm donating it to you, Kyle. Not to the church but to your honeymoon fund. Just fill in your name and do something special on your trip."

"That is very generous, but I see this is a check from Wild Horse."

Betsy eased down into a chair and visualized the office in a couple of weeks with decent furniture. "It's like this," she said and told him the whole story.

"I see, and how are you two with everything now?"

"I'm still a Brennan," Declan said.

Betsy sighed. "And I'm still a Gallagher."

"Just as I thought," Kyle said. "Well, thanks again for all of your help, and I'll look to see you later this evening. Don't expect that many will be out for Sunday night services tonight, with this weather being what it is, but that's okay. The ones who I want to hear about my Wednesday night message will be those who'll spread the news for me."

"And we'd better get going if we're going to make it to Lottie's by four thirty," Betsy said.

"So what is the big news that he's going to deliver on Wednesday?" Lottie asked that evening on the way home.

"You know everything else, so we might as well tell you, but this is something no one can know about before Wednesday, so you can't tell Polly or Gladys or Verdie," Declan said.

"I'm a good secret keeper." Lottie grinned.

Declan looked across the console and nodded at Betsy. "You tell her what's going on here."

Betsy gave the shortest version that she could, and Lottie clapped her hands and squealed. "I knew it. This is perfect. Just perfect. I won't tell a soul, living or dead. I won't even tell Leland until Wednesday and keeping secrets from him is real hard."

"You can tell Leland." Declan smiled.

She clapped her hands again. "He's going to be so happy."

When they reached the house, she bustled around getting her coat off and then went straight for the kitchen. "Movie is in the player, and popcorn just needs to be microwaved. Declan, you can have Leland's recliner, and I'll get one end of the sofa. Betsy you can have the other one. Y'all get comfortable. While the popcorn cooks, I'm going to make the hot chocolate and bring it in, then we'll get it started. Hang your coats on the kitchen chairs and kick off your boots. I been waitin' all day to watch this with y'all. Ain't seen it since Leland died, and it was one of our favorites."

"If you snore, you'll lose points," Betsy whispered.

"So will you," Declan shot back.

"What are we watching?"

In a few minutes, Lottie set the mugs of steaming chocolate on the coffee table and handed one to Declan. "Leland liked my hot chocolate. I use real cream and make it with cocoa. None of that artificial stuff. We're watching *McClintock!* with John Wayne. Y'all ever seen it?"

They both shook their heads.

"It's an old-days western about a couple who are finally getting a second chance. I got to admit, I don't take kindly to him spanking her, but it is kind of funny." Lottie giggled.

She hit a button on the remote and neither Betsy nor Declan snored one time. They laughed with Lottie at the humor and sighed at the end when there was a happily ever after.

Then the day came to an anticlimactic end when Declan folded the throw he'd had over his legs and feet, stretched, and announced that he was going to the bunkhouse for the rest of the evening.

"See you in the morning," he said and was gone.

Just like that, without even a hand on Betsy's shoulder, even though it had been possible several times while he was putting on his boots and she was helping Lottie clean up.

"I think I'll call Verdie and visit for a while. Missed her in church this morning. She wouldn't let Callie get out in the weather, since she's supposed to be on bed rest and all," Lottie said.

"I'm going to read. Thanks for the movie and popcorn, but most of all for the hot chocolate, which is the best I've ever had. Probably has a million calories and fat grams, but it was delicious," Betsy said.

Lottie shook her finger in Betsy's direction. "You don't have to worry none about that, girl. You are built just right and a ranchin' woman don't have to watch what she eats because she'll work it all off. Pretty nice first date wasn't it?"

"Date?"

"Sure. Movie. Popcorn. Y'all can't go out to the real movies without a load of bad stuff fallin' down on your heads, but you had a date tonight and guess what, he can kiss you on the second date." Lottie beamed.

"I'll sure look forward to that," Betsy said on her way to her bedroom.

She turned on the light and sat down in the rocking chair. It was past ten o'clock, which was a late night for Lottie. She could read a couple of chapters of *The Traitor* before bedtime even if she couldn't finish the book.

With book in hand, she noticed a gray thing in the middle of her bed. It had her name on it in Declan's handwriting.

It wasn't heavy or sealed, but she held it for several seconds, staring at it the whole time. He must have put it in there when he ran in for the box of Christmas things that Lottie donated to the church. Her hands shook as she opened it and found a length of green ribbon. She held it between her fingers wondering what it had to do with anything as she unfolded the note.

> *Seventh grade for me. Fifth for you. You dropped this in church one Sunday morning and I've kept it ever since. It was Christmas, and you were wearing a green sweater and a red-and-green-plaid skirt. Your red hair was pulled away from your face and had this ribbon in it. I wanted to touch your hair so badly that I did on the way out of church that morning. You*

never knew. Through the years, I pretended the silk ribbon was your red hair when I touched it.

It was signed with another heart and his name.

She sat down in the rocker with a thud. Declan Brennan had had a crush on her as big as the one she'd had on him. But like she'd told the preacher, she was still a Gallagher.

Not if you changed your name, her conscience said bluntly.

"That would require more than silk ribbons and Twinkies," she said aloud.

Chapter 25

On Monday morning at breakfast, Lottie announced that Declan would fire up the tractor with the blade on front and plow the snow away from the lane and the road from her place to the church, so they wouldn't miss the big announcement on Wednesday night.

"And me?" Betsy asked.

"I've decided since I only own the one tractor with a blade that you can have a day to go over the books. The card table is in the hall closet, and you can take it to your room because I didn't get to talk to Gladys and Verdie and Polly nearly enough about this big announcement. Don't worry, I'm not letting the cat out of the bag, but I do want to hear what everyone is saying about it. I'm glad Kyle isn't going to resign and that John isn't coming to town. It would make the feud worse, what with him and Honey all moon-eyed over each other. So y'all get on about your rat killing."

On Tuesday morning, the puzzle was still the topic of conversation. It had even gone above and beyond the love war, and the phones buzzed all day with information, whether real or not. A big trailer had arrived at the church on Monday night and several men unloaded stuff into the sanctuary and then at the parsonage. Kyle said it was part of the announcement for Wednesday night and the church would be locked until that time.

"Lord only knows that you can't get a man to talk

about anything that goes on," Verdie fussed when Lottie talked to her that morning before breakfast. "You'd think if he was leaving though he wouldn't be moving stuff into the parsonage or the church. I'm still on the purchasing committee, and there ain't been a thing said about any new church pews or choir chairs. I wonder what's in there that he don't want us to see."

"Well, darlin', I guess we will find out tomorrow like everyone else. I'm awful glad I'm not leaving until Saturday. I don't want to miss this before I get on that airplane for the first time." Lottie winked across the room at Betsy. "Betsy is up, and I hear Declan coming down the hallway. I'll talk to you later." Lottie put the phone receiver back in the cradle.

"Your first time to fly?" Betsy poured a cup of coffee and sipped at it.

"Yes, and I'm nervous about it. I don't like the idea of being crammed into a tin can and shot across the skies, but I'm too old to drive, and my old truck wouldn't make it down there anyway. I sold my car when I decided to do this so I wouldn't back down," Lottie answered.

"Are you sure you want to do this? Have you even been to Florida before?"

"Me and Leland drove down there every five years and spent a week in the fall when the ranchin' slowed down enough we could pay someone to do chores for us."

"Good morning, ladies. Coffee smells good and so does the bacon. What are our chores today?" Declan asked.

"Whatever you want to do is fine. Today, I need to do some serious thinking," Lottie said.

"Then I'll spend the day in town with my dad," Declan said.

"And maybe I'll go do some Christmas shopping. I haven't done any at all," Betsy said.

"Sounds good to me. I'll see y'all at suppertime." Lottie nodded. "I'll scramble up some eggs, and breakfast will be ready."

The sun was out brightly on Wednesday morning, but the temperature was well below freezing with no hope of rising. They were finishing breakfast and Lottie was still fussing about the doings at the church when Betsy's phone rang.

"It's Kyle," she said and listened for a minute before she glanced over at Lottie and asked, "He wants to know if me and Declan can come help him today."

"Lord, yes. Ask him if I can do anything."

"I heard her, and tell her thanks, but you two will be good enough," Kyle said.

"He says just us two, and he'll meet us there in fifteen minutes. He also said we'll have dinner and supper at the church so not to cook for us and that he hopes to see you at the meeting tonight. Do you want us to come back and get you, or will Verdie pick you up on her way?"

"Verdie can take me," Lottie said.

The church looked like it could have been featured in an episode of *Hoarders*. From big items, like the three-sided shed for the live nativity scene, down to the tiniest single ornament, stuff was scattered all over the front six pews and the raised stage where the pulpit stood.

Kyle stood there, bewildered. "I am so happy with all the new furniture for the parsonage and spent all day yesterday arranging it and my new office. I promised that today I'd get this all done, but when I looked at it, I knew that I couldn't do it alone."

"We're here," Betsy said.

"But where do we begin?" Kyle scratched his head.

Betsy took charge of organization. "First thing is for y'all to get that shed set right there and then set up the Christmas tree over by the piano. While y'all do that, I'm going to unload boxes and lay out the decorations for the tree on the first three pews. Lights will be on the first pew of the Brennan side. There is going to be too many, so we'll decide where to put the rest when we get done with the tree. Garland on the first row of the neutrals and ornaments on the Gallagher side. We have one big tree and several that are about three feet tall. I guess we could put one in each Sunday school room."

"One is pink," Declan warned.

Kyle chuckled. "Put that one in the teenage girls' room. They'll get a kick out of it. I knew I was right in calling y'all to help me."

Kyle and Declan situated the nativity stable complete with a rustic-looking feed box to be used as a manger with a bed of hay. While they decided how much hay to scatter around it, Betsy found the box with Lottie's donation. She set the pieces on the top of the old upright piano, one by one, and squealed when she found a gorgeous Battenberg lace cloth in the bottom of the box.

She held it up for the guys to see. "I bet she put this on the mantel, and it's about the same size as the altar. Isn't it gorgeous?"

"What is it?" Declan asked.

"A mantel cloth," she answered.

"I'm glad you know that. I wouldn't have," Kyle said.

"Tree next and it's one of those fancy things that you just pull up out of the box, and presto, it's ready except for a bit of 'fluffing,' as Granny says." Declan removed it from the box and sure enough, it sprung right to life.

"I'll make sure none of the limbs are twisted if you'll wrap that first length of lights around your arms," Betsy said.

The phone startled all three of them, and Kyle laughed. "I'm surprised we got this much done. It's been like this since Sunday night when I made the announcement. I have to answer every call in case it's one of the flock in trouble, but most of the time it's just folks wanting to gossip. Carry on, please."

"They say the third is the charm," Declan said as they started circling the tree.

Betsy clipped lights to the tree branches. "What does that mean?"

"This is our third tree to decorate together. The bar, Lottie's, and now the church."

Betsy smiled up at him. "What's it supposed to charm?"

He nudged her shoulder with his. "Betsy, what are we going to do about us?"

"I'd say we have to figure out who we want to be before we can make that decision." His touch, even though his chambray work shirt and her faded plaid flannel shirt, sent waves of heat from her shoulder to her boots.

"What does that mean?"

She snapped a few more lights in place and said, "Do I want to be a Gallagher all my life? And I'm not just talking about my name. And do you want to be a Brennan? Again it's attitude, not name. Because a Gallagher and a Brennan have no future together."

"Just as I thought," Kyle said as he crossed the room. "It was someone asking me not to leave. Got to admit it is nice to be wanted. Now what?"

"You ever done this job?" Betsy asked.

"Couple of times for my grandmother," Kyle answered.

"Then take over for me and I'll unpack more boxes so we can see where we are with all this," she said.

Declan kept an eye on what Kyle was doing with the lights, but he also watched Betsy from the corner of his eye. What she said made sense, and although he'd made the decision to separate himself from his family to some degree, was he ready to take it to the final step for Betsy Gallagher? Then again, would she be willing to do even more for him, because if the relationship went to the big step, she would have to change her name to Brennan? They'd both been indoctrinated since they were in diapers that the other side was even more evil than Lucifer, so how would she feel about her final step in the big picture?

"Thinking about her?" Kyle whispered.

Declan nodded. "Can't seem to stop doing that."

Ten minutes before Kyle unlocked the church doors at exactly seven thirty for Wednesday-night service, they plugged in all of the lights. All three of them stood in complete awe at what they'd created that day.

"It's more beautiful than it's ever been," Betsy said softly.

Declan slipped an arm around her shoulders. "We

still need to open all the doors into the Sunday school rooms and get those rooms lit up. Who would have thought we'd have enough to do the whole church? I've never seen it look like this."

Kyle nodded seriously. "Well, since this is my first Christmas here, I can't compare, but it's the prettiest I've ever seen anywhere I have been. If we each get two rooms then we should be ready to open the doors and let the folks in. From the looks of the parking lot, I'd say we're going to have a packed church tonight," Kyle said. "I would like for y'all to sit on the deacon's bench behind me, since you made all this possible from the beginning to the end."

"I'm not even dressed for church, much less to sit up there for everyone to see," Betsy said.

"I don't think God looks at what a child of His is wearing. God is interested in your heart, and believe me He is very pleased with what He sees there tonight. Please humor me," he said.

"Might as well. Whole town knows we're both living out at Lottie's place." Declan shrugged.

"Five minutes. Let's light up the Sunday school rooms, then you can take your places on the deacon's bench and I'll open the doors. I can't thank you enough for this and for a decent parsonage and office. My mind is boggled at what all you have accomplished."

The oak deacons' bench with high arms was small enough that two people were squished pretty tight together on it. Suddenly, Betsy jumped up, removed the band holding her ponytail up, and shook her red curls free. She tucked her shirt into the band of her jeans and brushed away the dust that had settled on her jeans.

"Thank goodness I didn't spill any of that delicious tortilla soup Kyle served us for dinner and supper on my shirt," she mumbled.

"If you had, you would still be beautiful." He reached into his pocket and brought out a brass button and put it in her hand. "April of your freshman year in high school. I was a junior. We had to hide the Easter eggs for the little kids at church that year. This fell off your sweater."

"How..." She plopped down.

"I have more than twenty years' worth of little things in a box. It pains me to share them, darlin', but you need to know this is not an instant thing that started with a poker game," he said.

The doors swung open, and people swarmed inside the church, their eyes aglitter and gasps bouncing around. They looked and sounded like little kids on Christmas morning.

"I told you all..." Mavis sucked in a lungful of air as if she were about to deliver a lecture right there in the church.

"Hush and sit down, Mama," Russell said curtly.

"You are all..." Naomi pointed at several members of her family.

Henry pushed her hand down. "That's enough, Mama."

Both women puffed up like bullfrogs and sat down in their pews, each sending glares across the church at the other. Christmas music began to play softly in the background, and Kyle took his place behind the podium.

He held up his palms and leaned toward the microphone. "If I could have your attention, please." He waited until quiet settled over the amazed crowd like a soft layer of pure-white snow and then waved his hands toward all the decorations. "It's lovely, isn't it?"

A dozen amens and a church full of bobbing heads answered him.

"It was made possible by only two people in our congregation. They wanted the people of this church to have a program this year, and they asked to remain anonymous. Not only does the church look like this but my office doors are open. After I finish, take a look at the new rug and furniture in there and the most beautiful credenza I've ever seen. It will hold several of my wedding pictures, I'm sure. And the parsonage has new area rugs on the cold hardwoods, new living room furniture, a stove that has all four burners and an oven that works, a refrigerator with all the shelves, and a really nice bedroom suite. I'm totally amazed that this was all done in less than a month."

"Did those two up there on the bench do this?" Mavis yelled.

"The two that did it made me swear an oath of confidentiality, but the two on the bench, Betsy Gallagher and Declan Brennan, gave a whole day today to the church, making this possible for you to see tonight. We will have a Christmas program on Friday evening instead of the regular services. The Gallaghers will be in charge of the nativity; costumes are in the choir room. The Brennans will be in charge of the actual program, as in readings and music. Quaid, you will take care of that, yes?"

Quaid nodded without even looking at his grandmother.

"And, Angela and Jody, you will be Mary and Joseph with baby Christian having the role of the newborn Savior in the nativity?" Kyle asked.

"Yes." Angela stood up. "This is the miracle I prayed for, and we'll be so honored to have that part in the program. And I want everyone here to know that all this had to be by donation from different folks because I gave that angel on the tree to the cause. My granny hand crocheted it when I was a little girl."

Lottie popped up from her seat. "And that arrangement on the altar is my collection that Leland gave me through the years for Christmas. The lace cloth it's sitting on was hand made by my sweet sister."

Verdie was next. "The Christmas tree and skirt came from our ranch. The skirt was my great aunt's. Y'all will remember Ina. She was the pianist back before Polly started playing."

Honey Gallagher stood slowly. "I gave that silk floral arrangement on the piano. And I recognize some of those ornaments on the tree."

After several more testimonies, Kyle removed the microphone and carried it with him to the center of the stage. "This is what happens when folks begin to think of something other than themselves and put this ridiculous feud aside. There are decorations from the Gallaghers and the Brennans on the tree, all mixed up together. I understand a Gallagher donated the stable for the nativity and the costume Angela will wear in the program. But a Brennan gave the manger. The Sunday school rooms are all decorated too, as well as the fellowship hall where Christmas refreshments are laid out this evening. Take time to look at everything. Now, I'm going to ask a question, and I'm a patient man. I'll wait to let you think about it. I'd like for anyone in this sanctuary who would like to see this crazy feud end to stand up."

Russell Brennan was the first one. Mavis hissed something at him, and he shook his head, folded his arms over his chest, and winked at his son. Henry Gallagher was the first one on that side of the church, but he didn't beat Lottie, Verdie, Gladys, and Polly by much. One by one, others stood until finally Mavis and Naomi were the only two people still sitting.

Declan had to consciously keep his jaw from dropping as he looked out over a church full of people all voicing their opinions simply by standing to their feet. Evidently, Betsy felt the same way because her hand slid over his and squeezed.

"We did it," she whispered.

"You may sit down now. Mavis, do you have anything to say?"

"My people have spoken, and I will honor their wishes. I can't say that I'm not disappointed or that I'm ever going to like Naomi Gallagher, but the feud is over."

"Naomi?" Kyle asked.

She stood up and turned to face Mavis. "I'll do what my family wants, but I don't have to like it or you. The hatchet might be buried as far as the feud goes, but it will always be between us."

"This might take baby steps, but what has happened here tonight is a miracle. Now I want every one of you to stand up and mingle for a few minutes. Shake hands and sit somewhere totally different. Gallaghers will sit in the center section and on what was formerly known as the Brennan side. The Brennans will do the same," Kyle said.

Russell crossed the church in front of the altar, stuck out his hand toward Henry, and said, "Merry Christmas."

"Same to you," Henry said.

"Magic," Declan whispered.

The whole church had a different atmosphere when the folks sat back down. Mavis and Naomi hadn't budged an inch from their original pews, but there were Gallaghers around Mavis and Brennans around Naomi when it was finished.

"One more thing," Declan said.

"Don't ask me to hug Quaid Brennan. I'm not ready for that," Tanner said loudly.

Laughter filled the church.

Kyle nodded. "Baby steps. No, this other thing. I want a show of hands from everyone in the church who has ever read or saw *Romeo and Juliet*."

Several hands went up.

"Well, we have our own Romeo and Juliet right here with us tonight," Kyle said.

"Mama, he's not going to make us listen to Shakespeare, is he?" a little boy in the back of the church whispered loudly.

"No, son, I'm not, but I am going to tell you a story. Romeo and Juliet were in love, but they couldn't be together because of their families. It's a shame that something like a feud or a person's last name could stand in the way of real, lasting love, isn't it?"

Russell's head was bobbing up and down even though Mavis looked like she'd been sucking on green persimmons. Declan could feel what was coming, and he was ready for it. He'd thought about what Betsy had said all day, and he couldn't wait to spit out those three words that he'd never been able to spit out before.

"We have Romeo behind me and Juliet sitting right

beside him, and mainly what has kept them apart is the feud. Since it's over, I want your promise that no one will stand in their way," Kyle said.

"You got mine," Henry said.

"Amen." Russell nodded.

Declan eased up to his full height, pulling Betsy up with him. "Could I borrow that microphone for a minute?"

Kyle handed it to him and sat down in the bench behind them.

"This is for Betsy, but if the whole lot of you want to listen in that's fine because I'm not ashamed of any of it," Declan said as he dropped on one knee. "Betsy Gallagher, I love you. I have since we were in elementary school. Never thought I could tell you, but there. I've said it. I don't deserve you, but I want to spend the rest of my life showing you how much I love you." He looked up into her eyes. "Betsy Gallagher, will you marry me?"

"I love you too, Declan. Not since we were kids but just as fierce and just as strong. So my answer is yes," she said.

The applause could have been heard all the way to heaven.

Chapter 26

"Be still. You've always fidgeted when I'm trying to do your hair," Willa fussed at Betsy.

"I wanted to go to the courthouse, so don't gripe at me."

"And you are my only child, my only daughter, and you are going to have a wedding." Willa settled the crown of baby roses and white ribbons on a bed of red curls on top of Betsy's head. "And you are still fidgeting. I can't believe I'm going to stand up there as your matron of honor and watch you marry a Brennan."

"I'll *be* a Brennan in half an hour. We've asked Kyle to make it a quick ceremony."

Willa grabbed a tissue and dabbed her eyes. "My God, you are beautiful. My dress looks better on you than it did on me thirty-two years ago. We've done it. We've gotten a wedding that should have taken a year to plan ready in less than a week."

"Merry Christmas. Miracles do happen at this time of year. Declan and I are living proof. I wish Lottie were here," Betsy said as she turned toward the floor-length mirror on back of the door in the senior citizens Sunday school room. A hand went over her mouth, and her eyes misted. "Oh, Mama."

"My tomboy has turned into a princess," Willa whispered.

What had been pure-white satin had aged like fine

pearls to an ivory luster. Fitted sleeves ended in points on top of Betsy's hands and fastened with a dozen tiny buttons that matched the forty-two buttons up the back of the dress. The sweetheart neckline hugged her figure as if the dress had been tailor-made just for her. Willa fussed with the long train so Betsy could see what it would look like stretched out down the aisle as she went to the front of the church to meet Declan.

"I'm glad you didn't wear a veil. The roses in your pretty red hair are just the right touch," Willa said.

"Got any last-minute advice for me? I know this is still hard on the family even if the hatchet is buried," Betsy said.

"Marriage is a partnership. All relationships take hard work, but loving Declan the way you do, most of the time you won't even realize that it's work," Willa said. "And the family will learn. Baby steps, as Kyle said. Oh, a little something extra for today. A gift from your new father-in-law. These are the pearls that his great-grandmother wore the day she married into the Brennan family, and he would like you to have them." Willa put them around Betsy's neck and fastened the tiny, diamond-encrusted clasp.

"Mavis will lie down right in front of the altar and die."

"Probably not. She wouldn't give Naomi the satisfaction. Now, your bouquet." She put a dozen red roses tied with pretty green ribbons in Betsy's hands. In the middle of it all was a slightly faded green ribbon with a brass button attached to the end.

"I still don't know what that's all about," Willa said.

"It's my something old." Betsy smiled. "Let's go get

this done so I can eat wedding cake, and...you didn't forget the Twinkies did you?"

"I did not. There's a big basket of them on the table between the groom's cake and yours. I don't understand that either."

Betsy hugged her mother. "Someday I'll tell you all about it."

Declan's hands were clammy as he and his father waited in the front of the church. Family from both sides as well as more of the town of Burnt Boot were packed into the church that Christmas evening. New beginnings were everywhere, and so much at once was more than a little intimidating, even to a big, tall cowboy.

He'd teased Betsy when she wanted to get married on Christmas Day, but she said she did not want a long engagement and, besides, he would never forget their anniversary.

Music came from the speakers, and Declan looked at his father and Kyle.

"Don't look at me. Your fiancée took care of the songs she wanted played," Kyle whispered.

"The Time of My Life" played loud and clear.

Several of the old folks looked around in astonishment while Betsy wiggled her shoulders all the way down the aisle as the lyrics said that with her body and soul she wanted him more than he'd ever know. Declan smiled and nodded when the words said that she was the one thing he couldn't get enough of and this could be love because he'd never felt this way before.

When Betsy reached the front of the church, she

handed her bouquet off to Willa, threw her arms around Declan, and kissed him firmly on the lips.

"I love you, Declan Brennan," she said loudly enough for the whole church to hear.

The music changed. The Judds sang "Love Can Build a Bridge," and every single word fit the day, the end of the feud, and the love that Declan and Betsy shared. Betsy took the bouquet from her mother, removed one rose, and she and Declan moved away from the podium to the front pew. She gave a rose to Naomi, kissed her on the cheek, and moved all the way to the other end where Mavis was sitting, pulled another rose out of her bouquet, and handed it to Mavis, along with a kiss on the cheek.

As she and Declan made their way to the bottom of the steps leading up to the stage, the lyrics of the song said love and only love can join the hearts of men and that the first step was to know that it all began with them.

Declan led her up the steps to stand in front of Kyle again, and together they waited for the music to end. They looked into each other's eyes and sang with the recording, saying that when they stood together, they could do anything and that love could build a bridge between their hearts.

At the end of the song, Kyle cleared his throat and said, "I don't know if I can preach this wedding with the lump that's in my throat. I've never heard stranger song selections at a wedding or ones that were more fitting. So with that said and because Declan and Betsy have asked for a short ceremony, who gives this bride to this man to be married?"

"Her mother and I do. And remember, Declan, if you

don't treat her right, the whole Gallagher family will come down on you," Henry said.

"Yes, sir. She's owned my heart for years, and I promise I will love her forever," Declan said.

Henry kissed Betsy on the cheek and said, "And you treat him right. I know all about your temper, so he's got his job cut out for him."

"I promise, Daddy, to do my best." Betsy smiled.

Declan led Betsy onto the stage and Kyle went on, "Dearly beloved, we are gathered here..."

"You are stunningly beautiful," Declan whispered softly.

Betsy mouthed, *And you are sexy as hell.*

"I heard and saw that. Some things never change," Kyle chuckled.

Vows were exchanged. Rings were exchanged and then Kyle told Declan that he could kiss the bride.

He bent her backward for a true Hollywood kiss and then scooped her up in his arms, train trailing behind them as he carried her down the aisle toward the back of the church while Blake Shelton sang "God Gave Me You."

He set her down in the reception hall and drew her into his arms. "I never thought I'd see this day happen," he whispered as he started two-stepping with her to the music still playing. "I love you so much, Betsy Brennan. Want to rename our ranch the Double B?"

"No, the Double L is fine. It can stand for a double dose of love. And this, darlin', is nothing short of a Christmas miracle. Let's get this reception done so we can go home to our ranch and I'll show you how much I love you."

"Imagine Lottie selling it to both of us because she said the contest was a tie." He kissed her again.

"I think that's what she had in mind the whole time. Let's go to the reception. We've got Twinkies," she said.

"You will never cease to amaze me." He grinned.

"I hope not." She rolled up on her toes and brought his lips to hers among the whoops and hollers of everyone crowding into the room for wedding cake.

Read on for an excerpt from
Carolyn Brown's next book

Luck of the Draw

Coming soon from Sourcebooks Casablanca

The gleam in the old cowboy's blue eyes and the way he rubbed his chin was Adele's first clue that he definitely had something up the sleeve of his faded, old work shirt. He glanced first at her and then over at Remington Luckadeau.

She bit back a groan. The good old boys' club was about to raise its head. They'd argue that ranching took brawn and muscle and that a woman couldn't run the Double Deuce all alone—that women were respected in the ranching business these days, but when it came right down to the wire, he would feel better selling to a man.

No, sir!

She did not hold out any hope that the old toot would sell the ranch to her.

"Well, now." Walter Jones gave his freshly shaven chin one more rub. "I expect we've got us one of them dilemma things, don't we?"

That sly smile on Remington's face said that he already knew she would be going home empty-handed. With that mop of blond hair that kissed his shirt collar, those steely blue eyes, chiseled face, and wide shoulders—lord have mercy—any woman would roll over and play dead to give him what he wanted.

But not Adele.

She wanted the Double Deuce, and she'd do whatever it took to get it so she could have a place to raise her daughters. Remington Luckadeau could spit on his knuckles and get ready for a fierce battle.

The Double Deuce Ranch was absolutely perfect in every aspect. The two-storied, four-bedroom house couldn't be better laid out for Adele and her two daughters, Jett and Bella. The acreage was big enough to make a living but small enough that she could manage it on her own for the most part. And it was close to her family, the O'Donnells over around Ringgold, Texas.

"You both want the ranch, but I can only sell to one of you. I talked to my lady friend, Vivien, about it. I talked to God about it before I went to sleep, and I talked to my old cow dog, Boss, about it this mornin' before y'all got here."

"And?" Adele asked.

"And not a one of them was a bit of help. I don't know which one of you to sell to any more than I did yesterday after you'd both come and looked over the place and left me to think about it."

Adele had known there was another person interested in the ranch. Walter had been up front about that, saying he'd talked with Remington Luckadeau that morning and he was ready to meet Walter's asking price.

"We can't both buy it, so I guess you'll have to make a decision," Adele said.

Remington nodded. "Looks like it's up to you, Walter."

~

Remington, known as Remy to his friends, slid down in the kitchen chair and studied the red-haired woman sitting in front of him. The hard Texas sunlight flowing through the kitchen window brought out every cute little freckle sprinkled across Adele's nose. Faded jeans, a chambray shirt worn open over a bright-yellow tank top, and cowboy boots worn at the heels said that she was a no-nonsense rancher.

Those two feisty girls out on the porch were dressed pretty much the same way as their mother. Any other time, he might have tipped his hat and given her the option to buy the Double Deuce, but not today. The ranch was the perfect size for what he had in his bank account. It wasn't far from his Luckadeau relatives in Ringgold and St. Jo, Texas. And the house would be just right for him and his two nephews, Leo and Nick, the boys he'd inherited when his brother and sister-in-law were killed in a freak car accident. Six months ago, Remy had been the resident bad boy of the Texas Panhandle. He'd spent his weekends in local bars, dancing and sweet talking the pretty girls into his bed. His whole life had turned around when his two nephews were tossed into his life.

So today, Adele O'Donnell was going to have to walk away disappointed. Too bad, because he'd always been attracted to redheads, and he'd have loved to see how she felt in his arms on the dance floor of the nearest honky-tonk.

"So." Walter cleared his throat. "I've come to a decision."

Remy straightened up in his chair.

"The Luckadeaus are my friends, but so are the O'Donnells. So I can't sell this to you, Adele, or to you,

Remy, on the basis of friendship. Vivien and I have planned a monthlong cruise, and we are leaving in one week. We fly out of Dallas on the last day of May and get back home on the last day of June."

"I'll raise your asking price," Remy said quickly.

"It's not got to do with money. Here's what I am willin' to do, though. You both move in here together on the morning that me and Vivien leave. Y'all take care of this ranch for me for a month. When I get back, whichever one of you is still here can have it. If you both still want it, we'll draw straws or play poker for it. If you decide that you can't work together or that the ranch ain't what you want, you can call Chet to come take over for you. I've made arrangements with him so he'll be ready if you both leave. Only rule I've got is that you'd best take good care of Boss. Boss has been a good cow dog, and he likes leftovers from the table, so cook a little extra at each meal. He's not real picky. He'll eat most anything a human will, but he doesn't like pizza. And you have to take real good care of Jerry Lee too."

"Who is Jerry Lee?" Adele asked.

"He's my rooster. Pretty little thing, but he never has learned to crow in the morning. He's a late riser, so he crows either in the middle of the day or about dinner time in the evening. I named him Jerry Lee because he's got swagger and he sings real pretty, like Jerry Lee Lewis."

"I'll take good care of your dog and your rooster," Adele said, shooting a defiant look right at Remy.

"So will I." Remy nodded, coolly.

"Then it might come down to the luck of the draw." Walter chuckled. "So you've got a week to decide."

"What about the one who doesn't win the luck of the draw?" Remy asked.

"Then that one gets a decent paycheck," Walter said.

"I don't need to think about it. I'm in," Adele said quickly.

Remy nodded. "I don't have to think about it either."

Walter pushed back his chair and stood up. "Good, then I'll look for you both to be here a week from today. You've seen the place. There's four bedrooms upstairs, and the couch makes out into a bed in the living room. There'll be hay to cut and haul, fields to plow, and planting to do, as well as the everyday chores with feeding and taking care of the cattle. I've made a list of what I want done before I get back, and I'll leave it stuck to the refrigerator door."

"I'm not afraid of hard work," Adele said. "One question, though. How does Boss feel about cats?"

"Strange as it seems, he loves them. My wife, God rest her soul"—Walter rolled his eyes toward the ceiling—"used to have an old barn cat that had kittens real often. Boss thought he was their grandpa."

"Then you don't mind if we bring our cat?" she asked.

"Not a bit. You got a problem with that, Remy?" Walter asked.

Remy shook his head.

"Thank you," Adele said softly.

Crap! Remy didn't hate cats, and thank God the boys weren't allergic to them, but that soft, sweet, southern voice could easily distract him from his mission. Remy would have to keep on his toes every day for the entire month of June.

Walter started toward the door. The meeting was over. "Just bring your personal things. When I sell this place, it goes lock, stock, and barrel. Furniture, equipment, everything but my own keepsakes," he said. "Vivien and I are leaving at nine o'clock. If one of y'all ain't here, then the other one will automatically get to buy the ranch."

Adele pushed back her chair and, in one fluid motion, was on her feet. Remy had figured she was tall when he sat across from her and his long legs almost touched hers under the table. But when she stood, he got the full effect of the way her hips curved out from her small waist, and for a split second, he could feel her in his arms.

Remy shook the image from his head. He had a long, hot month ahead of him, and he needed to think of Adele as an adversary, not a potential date.

"Do we move?" Nick asked when he stepped outside onto the porch.

"Starting next week, we are moving onto the ranch to take care of it for Mr. Jones for a month," Remy told his fourteen-year-old nephew. "If we do a good job, he might sell to us in time for the Fourth of July party we're planning."

"Mama?" The smaller of the two girls Adele had brought along with her looked at her questioningly.

"Same deal for us, girls. We'll move here in a week to live for a month, then Mr. Jones will decide which of us gets to buy the ranch," Adele answered.

"You"—the girl pointed at Leo and wiggled her head like a bobble doll—"are going down. You don't know jack squat about a ranch, so you might as well give up before you even start."

"Jett!" Adele chided.

"Well, it's the truth. He don't even want to live on a ranch. He's a city boy who don't even know who Billy Currington is. He'd hate living on this ranch," Jett said.

"Just because you lived on a ranch don't mean you are that smart. Uncle Remy can teach me everything about ranching in one afternoon. I'm a fast learner," Nick smarted off.

"Me too." Leo combed his carrot-red hair with his fingertips and tipped up his chin three notches.

"Okay, boys. It's one thing to say something; it's another to do it. Let's get on home and get our things in order so we'll be ready to move. There's only four bedrooms, so you'll have to share."

Leo had already left the porch, and he kicked at the dirt.

"Uncle Remy, Nick gripes if I even leave a wrinkle in the bed. He's so neat that he shoulda been a girl," Leo complained.

"No!" Nick raised his voice. "He never picks up anything and—"

"Enough," Remy said. "Into the truck. We've got a lot to do and a short time to get it done."

Leo crawled into the big, black, dual-cab truck. Just before he slammed the door, he caught Jett's eye and stuck out his tongue.

"Young man, you're going to have to live in the same house and work with those girls," Remy said sternly.

Leo rolled his eyes upward. "They are so bossy. Living in the country isn't going to be easy, but living around those two prissy girls..." He sighed. "Do we really have to do this, Uncle Remy?"

"We'll come out stronger men," Remy assured him.

A picture of Adele's full, kissable lips flashed through his mind. "Prissy" wasn't a word he'd use to describe any of the O'Donnell women.

Nick groaned. "If we live through it."

"We are Luckadeau men. We'll take the bull by the horns, look him right in the eye, and dare him to charge at us." Even as the words came out, Remy wondered if he was talking to his nephews or himself.

"I'd rather fight a bull," Leo grumbled. "And they ain't bulls. They're girls, and we're Luckadeaus."

"Daddy used to tell us that when a Luckadeau sets their mind, it's set forever," Nick said.

"Your daddy was right." Remy nodded.

Moving the boys from their house in the middle of Denton, Texas, to a ranch would be tough on them, but Remy could not live in town. He'd been fortunate enough to sell his brother's house for enough to pay off the existing mortgage and put a little into savings for the boys' college fund.

Remy had worked on a ranch out in the Texas Panhandle for the past fifteen years. He'd started as a hired hand and worked his way up to foreman. Today, he had enough money in his bank account to buy the Double Deuce, and it was the perfect place for the boys to have a brand-new start. It damn sure wouldn't be easy to live in the same house with a woman like Adele and not flirt, but with the ranch as a prize at the end of the road, it was doable.

"So you boys going to help me make those women see that they don't really want our ranch? Or are we going to let them win?" Remy asked.

"Ain't no way I'm going to back down from them two," Nick declared.

"Me either," Leo chimed in.

"Let's look at another ranch. I don't want to live in the same house with those two obnoxious boys," Bella said as they drove away.

Adele smiled. "You must really not like those boys to be pulling out your four-dollar words."

"That tells you how much, Mama," Bella said.

"We don't have time to train them," Jett chimed in.

Adele didn't think they'd have to do much training. Not with a cowboy like Remy Luckadeau for an uncle. That man was comfortable in his skin, and there wasn't a doubt in her mind that he'd know the business every bit as well as she did. In any other circumstance, there could be chemistry between them. He was exactly what she'd always been attracted to—blond hair, blue eyes, and cowboy swagger—but he was also what she'd been running away from when she'd married Isaac Levy.

You see how that turned out, said that smart-ass voice in her head.

Yes, she did see how it turned out. Isaac was the only son of a family who had dealt in diamonds right in the middle of Dallas, Texas, for more than fifty years. When they'd married, he'd moved Adele into his penthouse apartment, and she'd lived the life she thought she wanted.

Right up until Bella was born, two years after the wedding. She'd started to yearn for her country roots.

A child needed fresh air and sunshine, not parties and nannies. Isaac loved her enough to buy a small, two-hundred-acre ranch between McKinney and Blue Ridge. The commute wasn't bad since he had a driver, but after Jett was born, he spent more and more of the weeknights at the penthouse.

"Why do we have to move from *our* ranch, anyway?" Jett folded her small arms over her chest.

"The same reason we had to change our last name to O'Donnell," Bella answered. "Father has a new wife and a son, and we don't matter anymore."

Her daughter's tone created a lump in Adele's throat that she couldn't swallow down. Tears welled in her eyes, but she kept them at bay. Bella had put it into the simplest language possible, but the story was far more complex than that.

"Your father will come to his senses some day," she said softly.

"But it might be too late," Bella declared. "He's mean, making us move off the ranch."

It wasn't the time or the place to tell the girls that part of the marriage problems had been her fault. Isaac thought he was getting a socialite who loved the fast lane, and he never would have asked her to marry him if he'd realized that she wasn't ready to break all ties to her country roots.

"We are going to love this new ranch so much that we'll never look back at the old one. Even though they don't have any ranchin' experience, I wonder if you two are big and mean enough to show those two boys that nobody can outwork three tough O'Donnell women."

Jett unfolded her arms, leaned up from the backseat

of the bright-red dual-cab truck, and patted her mother on the shoulder. "They ain't got a chance in hell."

"Jett!" Bella scolded.

"Well, Uncle Cash says that, and nobody fusses at him. Besides, I believe it. We're tough and mean, and we can out-ranch any old boy in the state of Texas," Jett said.

"We've got a week to pack all our things, put them in storage, and load up the truck with what we need for a month," Adele said as she turned east toward Gainesville.

Adele's cell phone rang, and she fished it out of her purse to find a picture of her sister, Cassie, smiling at her. She answered it on the fourth ring and hit the Speaker button so they could all hear.

"We have not bought the ranch yet," she said and went on to tell her sister the deal that Walter had come up with.

Cassie giggled the whole way through the story.

"What's so funny about that?" Adele asked.

"Those boys don't stand a chance—not any one of them: the grown one or the two kids," Cassie said. "I'll put my money on my sister and my nieces any day of the week."

"Yes!" Bella and Jett squealed at the same time.

"Thank you, Aunt Cassie. We won't let you down," Jett said.

"What are you doing today?" Adele asked her sister.

"Haulin' hay, but I'd rather be doing something else in the hayloft," Cassie said.

"Cassandra Grace O'Donnell!" Adele raised her voice.

"Don't you double-name me. Only Mama gets to do

that, and I was talking about kissing my boyfriend. He's really good at kissing." Cassie laughed.

"I miss y'all," Adele said wistfully. "If I buy this ranch, I'm having a big Fourth of July party to celebrate. Y'all had better be there."

"Wild horses couldn't keep me away. Is this new cowboy sexy? Maybe I'll visit for a weekend between now and then," Cassie said.

"No!" The girls' loud voices bounced around in the truck cab.

"Why? Don't you want to see me?" Cassie asked.

"We love you," Bella said, "but we don't want Remy Luckadeau in the family at all, and if he sees you, then he'll fall in love with you. Besides, we like Clinton just fine. Go kiss him in the hayloft, and stay away until the ranch belongs to us."

"If you promise to work hard and show that Mr. Jones that you are the right people to sell his ranch to, then I'll stay away until you've run those old boys off your land. But, girls, Clinton and I broke up last week. The new man in my life is Dusty Dillard," Cassie said seriously.

"Is he as pretty as Clinton?" Bella asked.

"No, but he's a lot nicer," Cassie said.

"I thought Clinton was nice, and I like his name better than Dusty," Jett said.

"Wait until you meet him. Are you taking Blanche?" Cassie asked.

"Of course," Jett answered quickly. "We wouldn't leave her behind. Mama, please tell me that man didn't say we couldn't bring Blanche."

"Mr. Jones said that we could bring our personal belongings, and since Blanche is our personal cat, then

I expect we'll take her with us. Besides, I asked about bringing a cat, and he said it was fine," Adele said.

"The old hussy would die if you left her." Cassie laughed again. "Isn't she about ready to pop out another litter in the next couple of weeks?"

"Yes, she is," Bella said. "And I hope both of them boys hate cats."

"And you, Sister Adele? How do you feel about living with a cowboy?"

"I'm not living with him. I'm sharing a house with him for only one month. And don't call me Sister Adele. I'm not a nun," Adele said curtly.

"These past two years you have been." Cassie giggled. "Promise you'll call me often," she said. "Got to go. The hay wagon is here, and it's time to stack bales."

The window on the phone went dark, and Adele hit the End button. She caught a movement in her peripheral vision and glanced to the right to see two little boys glaring at her from the windows of a black truck. A whole month with those two smart-ass kids just might make her move all the way to Wyoming or Montana.

She looked in the rearview mirror, and there was her daughter, Jett, giving the boys the old stink eye. The truck sped on by her, and she lost sight of it. No doubt about it—this was going to be a long month.

Acknowledgments

My eyes misted when I finished writing this last book in the Burnt Boot series. I've come to love these characters with their feuding and their passion so much. But like one of my readers reminded me recently, the stories never really end because they can be reread over and over again. With that in mind, I hope you've enjoyed this series and that it is one of those that will go on your shelf for you to reread occasionally.

I would like to thank Sourcebooks for buying this series, especially Dominique for buying my first cowboy book eight years ago; Deb Werksman for being my editor through many, many books; Susie Benton for all her amazing help; and all those folks behind the scenes who create amazing covers and do promotion work. And a huge thank-you to my fantastic agent, Erin Niumata, who has been with me for seventeen years. That's longer than a lot of Hollywood marriages last, folks!

To my readers: keep your boots on. There are more cowboys on the way, and a Luckadeau and an O'Donnell are about to vie for a particular ranch down in north central Texas. Also, thank you from the depths of my heart for supporting me. Y'all are truly awesome!

Merry Christmas to you all!

About the Author

New York Times and *USA Today* bestselling author and RITA finalist Carolyn Brown has published more than seventy books. Her bestselling cowboy romance series include the Lucky trilogy, the Honky Tonk series, the Spikes & Spurs series, the Cowboys & Brides series, and the Burnt Boot, Texas series. She has also launched into women's fiction with a Texas twang. She and her husband, a retired English teacher, make their home in southern Oklahoma. They have three grown children and enough grandchildren to keep them young. When she's not writing, she likes to spend time in her backyard with her two cats, Boots Randolph Terminator Outlaw and Chester Fat Boy, and watch them protect the yard from vicious critters like field mice, crickets, and spiders.

True-Blue Cowboy Christmas

Big Sky Cowboys

by Nicole Helm

Big Sky Christmas

Thack Lane has his hands full. For the past seven years, he's been struggling to move on from his wife's tragic death and raise a daughter all by his lonesome. He doesn't have time for himself, much less a cheerful new neighbor with a smile that can light up the ranch.

Christmas spirit? Bah, humbug.

With Christmas right around the corner, Summer Shaw is searching for somewhere to belong. When her neighbor's young daughter takes a shine to her, she is thrilled. But Thack is something else altogether. He's got walls around his heart that no amount of holiday cheer can scale. Yet as joy comes creeping back to the lonely homestead, Summer and Thack may just find their happily ever after before the last of the Christmas miracles are through...

Praise for *Rebel Cowboy*:

"A beautifully crafted romance."
—*USA Today Happy Ever After*

"A true page-turner." —*Publishers Weekly*

For more Nicole Helm, visit:

www.sourcebooks.com

Reckless in Texas

Texas Rodeo

by Kari Lynn Dell

Texas Homecoming

Violet Jacobs is fearless. At least, that's what the cowboys trusting her to snatch them from under the hooves of bucking bulls think. Outside the ring, she's got plenty of worries rattling her bones: her young son, her mess of a love life, and lately, her family's struggling rodeo. When she takes business into her own hands and hires on a hotshot bullfighter, she expects to start a ruckus, but she never expected Joe Cassidy. Rough-and-tumble, cocky and charming, Joe's everything a superstar should be—and it doesn't take a genius to figure out he's way out of Violet's league.

Joe came to Texas to escape a life spiraling out of control. He never planned on sticking around, and he certainly never expected to call this dry and dusty backwater *home*. But Violet is everything he never realized he was missing, and the deeper he's pulled into her beautiful mess of a family, the more he realizes this fierce rodeo girl may be offering him the one thing he could never find on his own...

Praise for Kari Lynn Dell:

"An extraordinarily gifted writer." —Karen Templeton, three-time RITA award-winning author

For more Kari Lynn Dell, visit:

www.sourcebooks.com